Shards of a Broken Crown

Raymond E. Feist was born and raised in Southern California. He was educated at the University of California, San Diego, where he graduated with honours in Communication Arts. He is the author of the bestselling and critically acclaimed *Riftwar Saga* (*Magician*, *Silverthorn* and *A Darkness at Sethanon*), *Prince of the Blood*, *Faerie Tale* and *The King's Buccaneer* and is co-author (with Janny Wurts) of *Daughter of the Empire*, *Servant of the Empire* and *Mistress of the Empire*. Feist lives with his wife, novelist Kathlyn Starbuck, and two children, in Rancho Santa Fe, California.

D1077915

Voyager

RAYMOND E. FEIST

Shards of a Broken Crown

HarperCollins*Publishers*

Voyager
An Imprint of HarperCollins*Publishers*
77–85 Fulham Palace Road,
Hammersmith, London W6 8JB

Special overseas edition 1998
This paperback edition 1999
1 3 5 7 9 8 6 4 2

First published in Great Britain by
Voyager 1998

Copyright © Raymond E. Feist 1998

A catalogue record for this book
is available from the British Library

ISBN 0-00-648348-8

Set in Galliard

Printed and bound in Great Britain by
Caledonian International Book Manufacturing Ltd, Glasgow

To Jon and Anita Everson,
who were with me from the start.

Acknowledgments

As is always the case, I am indebted to many people for the creation of this book:

The original creators of Midkemia, Steve Abrams, Jon Everson, and the rest of the Thursday/Friday Night bunch. Without their creativity, Midkemia would be far less than it is today.

My publishers for their belief and hard work. The enthusiasm and support is "above and beyond," especially my editor, Jennifer Brehl, who is both good at her job and a friend.

My good friend and agent, Jonathan Matson, for always being there.

My wife, Kathlyn S. Starbuck, for more reasons than I can list, and for being the best first reader anyone can ask for.

And for all of those out there who send me letters of praise or complaint, who let me know someone out there is reading the work. Time does not permit me to answer most of them, but they all get read.

And to Sean Tate, who thought up the character of Malar.

NORTHLANDS

The Great Northern Mountains

Stone Mountain

the Lake of the Sky

The Te

THE HIGH

Elvandar

Tyr-Sog

Yabon

Crydee

LaMut

Loriel

THE FAR COAST

THE GREEN HEART

The Grey Towers

Walinor

Hush

Zūn

Hawk's Hollow

THE KINGDOM

Carse

Ionri

Natal

Ylith

Queg's View

Calastius Mountains

DIMWO

Tulan

Bordon

Sethanon

THE GREAT VELT

THE ENDLESS SEA

THE FREE CITIES

Margrave's Port

Port Natal

Que

Deadmoor

Krondor

Lee

Palanque

Sarth

SORCERER'S ISLE

the STRAITS OF DARKNESS

THE KINGDOM OF QUEG

D'Orgin

D

LiMeth

Land's End

Landreth

SEA OF DREAMS

THE BITTER SEA

Durbin

Shamata

the Ghol

SCARLAK

Elarial

Ranom

VALE OF DREAMS
(DISPUTED BORDER)

Th

Caralyan

Trollhome Mountains

JAL-PUR DESERT

The Pillars of the Stars

THE EMPIR

MIDKEMIA

Character List

ACAILA—leader of the eldar, in the Elf Queen's court

ADELIN—elf in Elvandar

AGLARANNA—Elf Queen in Elvandar, wife of Tomas, mother of Calin and Calis

AKEE—Hidati hillman

AKIER—Lieutenant on *Royal Bulldog*

ALETA—young disciple in Temple of Acrh-Indar

ASHAM IBIN AL-TUK—Keshian General

AVERY, RUPERT "ROO"—merchant of Krondor

AVERY, KARLI—wife of Roo

BOYSE—Captain of Duko's forces

BRIAN—Duke of Silden

CALHERN, THOMAS—acting Lieutenant of Palace Guard

CALIN—elf heir to the throne of Elvandar, half-brother to Calis, son of Aglaranna and King Aidan

CALIS—"The Eagle of Krondor," special agent of the Prince of Krondor, Duke of the Court, son of Aglaranna and Tomas, half brother to Calin

CHALMES—ruling magician at Stardock

CHAPAC—twin brother of Tilac, son of Ellia

D'LYES, ROBERT—magician from Stardock

DE SAVON, LUIS—former soldier, assistant to Roo
DELWIN—constable in Krondor
DESGARDEN—swordsman in Krondor
DOKINS, KIRBY—snitch in Krondor
DOMINIC—Abbot of Ishapian Abbey at Sarth
DUGA—mercenary captain from Novindus
DUKO—General in the Emerald Queen's Army
DUVAL, MARCEL—squire from Bas-Tyra

ELLIA—elf in Elvandar, mother of Chapac and Tilac
ENARES, MALAR—servant discovered in wilderness
ERLAND—brother to the King and uncle to Prince Patrick

FADAWAH—former general commanding the Emerald
    Queen's Army, self-styled "King of the Bitter Sea"
FRANCINE "FRANCIE"—daughter of the Duke of Silden

GREYLOCK, OWEN—Knight-Marshal of the Prince's Army

HAMMOND—Lieutenant in King's Army
HERBERT OF RUTHERWOOD—scribe in Port Vykor

JACOBY, HELEN—widow of Randolph Jacoby, mother of
    Natally and Willem
JALLOM—Captain of Duko's army
JAMESON, JAMES "JIMMY"—elder son of Arutha, grandson
    of James
JAMESON, DASHEL "DASH"—younger son of Arutha,
    grandson of James

KAHIL—Fadawah's intelligence chief
KALEID—ruling magician at Stardock

LELAND—son of Richard of Mukerlic
LIVIA—daughter of Lord Vasarius

MACKEY—Sergeant of Palace Guard
MATAK—old soldier in Duko's command
MILO—owner of the Inn of the Pintail in Ravensburg, fa-
    ther of Rosalyn
MIRANDA—magician and ally of Calis and Pug

NAKOR THE ISALANI—gambler, magic-user, friend of Pug

NARDINI—Captain of captured Quegan ship

NORDAN—General in Fadawah's army

PAHAMAN—Ranger of Natal in Elvandar

PATRICK—Prince of Krondor, son of Prince Erland, nephew to the King and Prince Nicholas

PICKNEY—clerk at Krondor

PUG—magician, Duke of Stardock, cousin to the King, grandfather to Arutha, great-grandfather to Jimmy and Dash

REESE—thief in Krondor

RICHARD—Earl of Mukerlic

RIGGERS, LYSLE—the Upright Man, leader of the Mockers

ROSALYN—Milo's daughter, wife of Rudolph, mother of Gerd

RUDOLPH—baker in Ravensburg, husband of Rosalyn, stepfather to Gerd

RUNCOR—Captain of Duko's army

RYANA—dragon shape-changer, friend of Tomas and Pug

SHATI, JADOW—Lieutenant in Erik's company

SHO PI—former companion of Erik and Roo, student of Nakor

SONGTI—Captain of Duko's army

STYLES—Captain of *Royal Bulldog*

SUBAI—captain of the Royal Krondorian Pathfinders

TALWIN—spy for Arutha

TILAC—twin brother of Chapac, son of Ellia

TINKER, GUSTAF—prisoner with Dash, later Constable

TOMAS—Warleader of Elvandar, husband of Aglaranna, father of Calis, inheritor of the powers of Ashen-Shugar

TRINA—female thief, Daymaster of the Mockers

TUPPIN, JOHN—thief with lumpy face, leader of Krondor's "bashers"

VASARIUS—Quegan noble and merchant

VON DARKMOOR, MATHILDA—Baroness of Darkmoor, grandmother to Gerd

VON DARKMOOR, GERD—Baron of Darkmoor, son of Rosalyn and Stefan von Darkmoor, nephew to Erik
VON DARKMOOR, ERIK—Captain of the Crimson Eagles

WENDELL—Captain in Krondor
WIGGINS—Patrick's Master of Ceremony
WILKES—soldier in Erik's army

ZALTAIS—?

BOOK IV

The Brothers' Tale

Duty cannot exist without faith.

—Benjamin Disraeli
Earl of Beaconsfield
TANCRED, BK. II, CH. 1

Prologue

THE GENERAL KNOCKED.

"Enter," said the self-styled King of the Bitter Sea as he looked up from a hastily scribbled note just handed him by his Captain of Intelligence, Kahil.

General Nordan entered and shook off the snow from his cloak. "You found us a cold land to rule, Majesty," he said with a smile. He gave Kahil the briefest nod of greeting.

Fadawah, former Commanding General of the Army of the Emerald Queen, now ruler of the City of Ylith and the surrounding countryside, said, "At least it's a cold land with food and firewood." He waved in a vague fashion to the south. "We're still getting stragglers in from as far away as Darkmoor who paint a bleak picture about conditions throughout the Western Realm."

Nordan motioned to a chair and Fadawah nodded. While old companions, they observed the formalities, as Fadawah prepared to launch his spring campaign. The General still wore the ritual scars on his cheeks, marks given him when swearing loyalty to the Pantathians. He had considered attempting to find a witch or healing priest who could remove them, for when he had finally realized that the Pantathians were as much dupes as he was, he had killed their remaining high priest. As far as Fadawah was concerned, he was no longer bound to anyone. He was his own man, and he was in a rich land with an army. But Kahil had reminded him the scars were intimidating and kept the men in awe of him. Kahil had served the Emerald Queen before she had been destroyed by the demon, but he had proven a valuable and trusted advisor since the change in leadership of the invading army.

By last count over thirty thousand men had found their way into the south end of the province of Yabon. He had organized them, stationed them, and now controlled all the lands from Ylith south past Quester's View, north to the outskirts of Zun, west to the city of Natal, which was now occupied by more of his own men than their own pitiful defenses. He had also captured Hawk's Hollow, a small town, but one giving him control of a vital pass through the mountains to the east.

"Some of the men don't like the idea of staying," said Nordan. The stocky soldier rubbed his bearded chin, and cleared his throat. "They're talking of finding a ship and going back across the sea."

"To what?" asked Fadawah. "To a land burned out and overrun by barbarians from the grasslands? Besides the dwarven stronghold in the Ratn'gari Mountains and some surviving Jehsandi in the North, what is there left of civilization? Did we leave a city standing? Is there anything there to support us?" Fadawah scratched his head. He wore a single long fall of hair and shaved the rest of his head, another sign of his devotion to the Emerald Queen's dark powers. "Tell any of the men who are talking this way that come spring, if they can find a ship and take it, they're free to leave." He looked off into space, as if seeing something in the air. "I want no one here who isn't ready to serve me. We're going to have a serious fight on our hands."

"The Kingdom?"

Fadawah said, "You don't think they're going to sit idly by and not attempt to regain their lands, do you?"

"No, but they were terribly mauled at Krondor and Darkmoor. The prisoners tell us they don't have much of an army left to put in the field."

Fadawah said, "If they don't bring their Army of the

East over from Darkmoor, true. But if they do, we need to be ready."

"Well," said Nordan, "we won't know until spring."

"That's only another three months," said Fadawah. "We need to be prepared."

"You have a plan?"

"Always," said the wily old general. "I don't want a two-front war if I can help it. If I was stupid, I could find myself in a four-front war." He indicated a map on the wall of the room. They were currently occupying the estate house of the Earl of Ylith, dead by all reports along with the Duke of Yabon and the Earl of LaMut. "If our information is right, we face a boy up in LaMut." He rubbed his chin. "We need to take LaMut as soon as the spring thaw begins, and I want Yabon in our grasp by midsummer." He smiled. "Send a message to the leader in Natal . . ." He turned to Kahil. "What's his title?"

"The First Councilor," supplied his Captain of Intelligence.

"Send the First Councilor our thanks for his hospitality in providing billets for our men this winter, and send him some gold. A thousand pieces should do."

"A thousand?" asked Nordan.

"We have it. And we'll get more. Then withdraw our men and bring them here." He looked at his old friend. "That will at least keep the First Councilor on our good side until we return to Natal, take and keep it."

He pointed to the map. "I want Duko and his men down in Krondor by then."

Nordan raised an eyebrow in curiosity.

Fadawah said, "Duko makes me uneasy. He's an ambitious man." He frowned. "It was only chance that put you and me first and second on the Pantathian's roles, else we could be taking orders from Duko."

Nordan nodded. "But he's a good leader, and he's always obeyed without question."

"That he is, which is why I want him at the front. I want you down behind him, in Sarth."

"But why Krondor?" Nordan shook his head. "There's nothing there."

"But there will be," said Fadawah. "That's their West-

ern Capital, their Prince's City, and they will move back
there as quickly as they can.'' He nodded to himself. ''If
Duko can keep them busy until we seize all of Yabon, then
we can turn our sights on the Free Cities, this Far Coast
region.'' He pointed to the western coast of the Kingdom.
''We'll reoccupy Krondor and move back toward the old
battle line. What's that place?''

''Nightmare Ridge.''

''Well named.'' Fadawah sighed. ''I'm not a greedy
man. Being King of the Bitter Sea is enough. We'll let the
Kingdom of the Isles keep their Darkmoor and the lands to
the east.'' Then he smiled. ''For now.''

''But first we must retake Krondor.''

Fadawah said, ''No, first we must make them think we
want to retake Krondor. These Kingdom nobles are not stupid, they are not self-consumed like those of our homeland.'' He remembered how shocked the Priest-King of
Lananda had been when Fadawah and his army had refused
to heed his order to leave his city. ''These are smart men,
duty-bound men; they will come at us, and they will come
hard. We must expect that.

''No, let them think Krondor is the prize, and when they
realize we are firm in Yabon, perhaps they will negotiate,
or perhaps not, but either way, once we have control of
Yabon, we are here for good. Let Duko get punished lest
he become ambitious.''

Nordan stood. ''If you permit, I'll tell the men those who
wish to leave in the spring may.''

Fadawah waved his permission.

''Majesty,'' said Nordan, leaving Fadawah alone with
Kahil.

To Kahil, Fadawah said, ''Wait, then follow Nordan and
see who he speaks with. Mark the men who are the leaders
of these dissidents. They will have accidents before the
thaw, and then we can put to rest this nonsense about returning to Novindus.''

''Of course, Majesty,'' said the Captain of Intelligence.
''And I applaud your design in putting Nordan down in
Sarth.''

Fadawah said, ''Design?''

Kahil leaned over, putting his arm around Fadawah's

shoulder, and he whispered, "Put all your disloyal commanders to the south, to insure that when the enemy exacts their price for our conquest, those we can most afford to lose pay it."

Fadawah's eyes became unfocused, as if he was listening to something in the distance. "Yes, that is wise."

Kahil said, "You need to surround yourself with those who can be trusted, those who are loyal beyond a doubt. You need to return the Immortals to a place of prominence."

"No!" said Fadawah. "Those madmen served dark powers—"

Kahil interrupted. "Not dark powers, Majesty, but vast powers. Powers that can insure your rule not only in Yabon, but in Krondor, too."

"Krondor?" asked Fadawah.

Kahil clapped his hands twice, and the door swung open. Two warriors, each with ritual scars on his cheeks that matched Fadawah's, entered, and Kahil said, "Guard the King with your lives."

Fadawah repeated, "Krondor."

Kahil rose and departed, closing the door behind him. A faint smile passed across his face before he turned and left upon his next task, following Nordan and marking those men for death who displayed even the smallest hint of disloyalty.

Fadawah looked at the two soldiers and motioned for them to stand away from him. The scars on their faces reminded him of the dark and distant time he was caught up in the magic of the Emerald Queen and the lost months when the demon had ruled her army. He hated feeling used and would kill anyone who again attempted to use him as the Emerald Queen had.

He moved to the map on the wall and began to plan his spring campaign.

One

Winter

THE WIND HAD died.

Dash waited. The frigid bite of the air still brought tears to his eyes as he scanned the road below. The reconstruction of Darkmoor had been tedious, slowed by continuous snows and rain, as the winter proved a fickle one. If slippery ice wasn't making footing treacherous for those workmen attempting to rebuild the walls around the western portion of the city, then knee-deep mud stalled wagons carrying needed supplies.

Now it was icy again, but at least Dash was thankful there was currently no snow. The sky was clear, the late afternoon sun hinting at warmth that wasn't really there. Dash knew it was his mood as much as the weather, but this particular winter seemed to have lasted longer than any in his young life.

The sounds of the city carried through the still, icy air as the day wound down. With luck the new gate would be finished before sunset, and an extra modicum of security would be added to the sum of things that needed to be done yesterday.

Dash was tired, fatigued beyond anything he could remember in his twenty years of life. Part of it was from the seemingly endless list of things that needed attention, and the rest was from worry; his brother Jimmy was overdue.

Jimmy was acting the part of exploring officer, a scout behind enemy lines. Prince Patrick of Krondor had decided to move hard and fast against a threat of Keshian expansion into the southern flank of the Kingdom in the spring. That meant that the retaking of lands lost during the invasion the previous summer would be left to Owen Greylock, Knight-Marshal of Krondor, and Erik von Darkmoor, Knight-Captain of the Crimson Eagles, an elite mobile force of handpicked men.

Which had meant the Prince needed information on what the invaders were doing between Darkmoor and Krondor. And Jimmy had volunteered to go see what was going on.

He was now three days overdue.

Dash had come to the edge of the patrolled area, a series of burned-out walls that marked the western edge of the foulbourgh of Darkmoor. The Prince's army in the city insured that there was little danger within a day's ride of the city, but these partial walls and piles of tumbled masonry provided ample cover for ambush and had been refuge to more than one band of scavengers or outlaws.

Dash scanned the horizon, watching for his brother. The sounds of the winter woodlands below were few and infrequent. An occasional rustle as snow fell from tree branches, or the crack of ice some miles away as the thaw began. A bird call or the rustle of some animal in the brush. Sound carried for miles in the winter cold.

Then Dash heard something. A faint sound, coming from far away. It wasn't the sound of hooves striking hard dirt and rock Dash had hoped to hear. Rather it was the rolling crunch of ice underfoot. And whoever made the sound was coming toward him with a methodical step, even and unhurried.

Dash flexed his gloved fingers and slowly pulled his sword from his scabbard. If the previous conflict had taught him nothing else, it was to always be ready. There were no safe positions outside the fortress that was the city of Darkmoor.

In the distance he detected motion, and he focused on it. A single figure trudged along the road. He was moving at a plodding walk, and as Dash watched, he hurried to a slow trot. Dash knew he was walking one hundred paces, then trotting one hundred paces, a practice drilled into Dash and his brother by their arms teachers as boys. For a man without a mount it could cover almost as much distance as a horse could in a day, more over the course of weeks.

Dash watched. The figure resolved itself into a man wrapped in a heavy grey cloak; clothing designed to make it difficult to see the wearer from any distance in the gloom of winter. Only on the bright days when the sky was clear would the wearer be easy to spot.

As the man on foot came closer, Dash saw he was without a hat, but had his head covered in a thick cloth, a scarf or torn remnant of another piece of clothing. He carried a sword at his side, and his hands were clad in mismatching gloves. His boots were filthy with mud and ice.

The crunching of snow under his tread became louder by the moment, until he stood before Dash. He stopped and looked up, and at last he said, "You're in my way."

Dash moved his mount aside and swung the horse's head around toward Darkmoor. He put his sword away, urged the animal forward and walked beside the man on foot. "Lose your horse?" he asked.

Jimmy, Dash's brother, hiked his thumb over his shoulder. "Back there."

"That was pretty careless," said the younger brother. "That was an expensive horse."

Jimmy said, "I know. But I didn't feel like carrying him. He was dead."

"Pity. That was a *really* good horse."

"You don't miss him nearly as much as I do," said Jimmy.

"Would you like a ride?" asked Dash.

Jimmy stopped, turned, and regarded his brother. Neither son of Lord Arutha, Duke of Krondor, resembled the other. James looked like his grandmother, slight, blond, and possessing features that could only be called finely drawn, with sapphire eyes. Dash looked like his grandfather, with tight curls of light brown hair, dark eyes, and a mocking expression. In nature, they were as alike as twins. "About time you offered," said Jimmy, reaching up to take Dash's hand.

He swung up behind his brother and they rode slowly toward the city. "How bad was it?" asked Dash.

"Worse," said Jimmy.

"Worse than we thought?"

"Worse than anything we could have imagined."

Dash said nothing more, knowing his brother would report directly to the Prince, and that Dash would hear every detail.

Jimmy took the hot cup of coffee, sweetened with honey and made rich with cream, and nodded his thanks. The servant quickly departed, closing the door behind him. Jimmy sat in the Prince's private chamber, while the Prince, the Knight-Marshal Owen Greylock, Duke Arutha of Krondor, and Erik von Darkmoor patiently waited for his report.

Patrick, Prince of Krondor and ruler of the Western Realm of the Kingdom of the Isles, said, "Very well. What did you find?"

Jimmy finished his first sip of the hot drink, and said, "It's far worse than we feared."

Patrick had detailed five men to ride into the West, toward Krondor, his capital city, and only three of them had returned so far. The picture he was having painted for him could be called nothing but bleak. "Go on."

Jimmy put his cup down on the table and started removing his heavy cloak as he said, "I got to Krondor. It took some doing, but most of the remaining soldiers between here and there are nothing more than bandits. After a couple of months of snow, rain, and sleet, they are dug in, hugging their fires and trying hard to stay alive."

"What of Krondor?" Patrick asked.

Jimmy said, "It's almost deserted. There were a few people around, but no one wanted to talk to me, and frankly, I wasn't anxious to strike up many conversations myself. Most of those I caught a glimpse of were soldiers, foraging for what they could find in the rubble."

Jimmy stretched, as if tired. He took another sip of coffee. "Though what they could possibly find is beyond me." He looked at Patrick. "Highness, Krondor looks like nothing I've seen before or could dream of in my worst nightmare. Every stone blackened, and almost no board unburned. The smell of char still lingers in the air and it's been months since the fires. Rain and snow have yet to cleanse the city.

"The palace—"

"What of the palace?" asked Patrick, his voice anxious.

"Gone. The outer walls stand in place, but great breaches exist. The inner palace is little more than a huge pile of blackened rubble—the fire was so hot the timbers burned through and some inner walls collapsed. Only the ancient keep still stands, if you use the term 'stands' generously. It's a blackened shell of stones. I climbed the stone steps inside, for no wood remains untouched, and reached the roof. From there I could see the entire city and some distance to the north and west.

"The harbor is a sea of sunken ships, their masts blackened and rotting. The docks are gone. Most of the first street after the docks has been leveled. All the buildings in the western third of the city have been gutted or reduced to rubble, as if the fires burned the hottest there."

Arutha, Duke of Krondor, nodded. His father, Lord James, who had preceded him in his office, had fired the city to trap the invaders inside the flames, and had died, along with his mother, in doing so. Arutha knew the placement of Quegan fire oil in the sewers below the city would have concentrated the damage where his father would have judged it most appropriate, at the docks, near the ships unloading troops, then throughout the maze that had been the poor quarter of the city, then the merchant quarter.

"The central third of the city is seriously damaged, but there may be a building or two that can be salvaged on every street. The rest will have to be razed before any construction can begin. The easternmost third is also heavily damaged, but many of the buildings there can be restored."

"What of the outlying estates?" asked Erik, thinking of his friend Rupert's large house, a day's ride to the east of Krondor.

"Many burned to the ground; others were sacked and left empty. A few of them were being used as headquarters for what I took to be companies of the invaders, so I didn't get too close," answered Jimmy. He sipped at his coffee. "I was about to leave when things turned interesting."

Patrick and Arutha looked at Jimmy expectantly. Jimmy took another sip of coffee, then continued. "A command of at least a hundred men rode past where I was camped—" He glanced at his brother. "That little inn up the street from Weavers' Road, where you got into that fight?" Dash nodded. Looking back at the Prince, Jimmy continued, "It's atop a little rise, and had an intact roof, which was welcome, and best yet, provided an unobstructed view of High Street and Palace Road, as well as several other byways from the north gate."

"The men?" prompted Owen Greylock.

"If I understand the markings used by the mercenary companies, General Duko is now on his way to Krondor or is already there."

Erik swore. Then he glanced at Patrick and said, "Sorry, Highness."

Patrick said, "I understand. All the reports I've read tell me Duko is a worthy foe."

Erik said, "He's more than a handful. He kept constant pressure on our northern flank along Nightmare Ridge, without wasting soldiers. He's the closest thing the invaders have to a Kingdom general in his knowledge of tactics and deployment."

Owen nodded. "If he's in Krondor, and ordered to hold it, our job just became a great deal more difficult."

Patrick looked worried but stayed silent a moment. Then he said, "Why would they move into Krondor in strength? There's nothing left, they don't need it to protect their southern flank. Could they know of our new base down at Port Vykor?"

"Perhaps," said Owen. "Or they simply wish to keep us from using Krondor as a forward base."

Patrick suddenly looked tired, and worried, thought Jimmy. After another long silence, the Prince said, "We need more information than we have."

The brothers exchanged glances, each acknowledging what the other knew: they were among those most likely to be sent ahead to get that information.

Patrick asked James, "How long did you stay?"

"Long enough to see them start to secure the area, so I made for the eastern gate to get free before they spotted me. I got out of the city, but ran right into a patrol between Krondor and Ravensburg. I managed to get loose from them in the woods, but they killed my horse.''

Patrick said, ''Patrol? That far east?''

Owen nodded and said, ''Erik?''

Erik's expression showed he was as perplexed as anyone else in the room. ''We've gotten reports from refugees that General Fadawah might be pushing south again, or at least is making his presence known. If Duko's in Krondor, those rumors are true. But to have patrols already that far east means they're quickly deploying to welcome us should we march home.''

Patrick said, ''It's icy hell out there. What's he up to?''

''If we knew that,'' said Dash dryly, ''we wouldn't have to go slogging about in that icy hell.''

Owen smiled. Duke Arutha tried to hide his own amusement, but failed.

Patrick said, ''True,'' ignoring the breach of protocol. The winter shared in close quarters had turned this group into a fairly informal band of friends when court wasn't in session.

The invaders had been defeated at the Battle of Nightmare Ridge, but the destruction done to the Western Realm of the Kingdom of the Isles was unimaginable. As spring approached, and with it the ability to move his forces, Patrick was desperately trying to imagine what had happened to his principality.

Patrick turned to Greylock. ''How soon can you move?''

''Highness?'' asked Owen.

''How soon before you can move to retake the city?''

Owen said, ''I can marshal the men and have them ready to march in under a week. We've got some of the garrison scattered along the ridge and down toward the Vale of Dreams, but most are near enough to muster, though from what I've seen, we'll need better information than we have to know what strength we'll face.''

Patrick sat back. ''I was hoping for better intelligence.''

Jimmy glanced at his father, who shook his head slightly, warning him from making any comment. Dash allowed his brother the confirmation that what the Prince had just said was thoughtless by raising his eyebrows ever so slightly.

Patrick said, "We've got a massive front to the south, and all the major units of the Army of the East are ready to answer any invasion from Kesh, but we have limited resources to reclaim the Western Realm."

Jimmy said nothing.

Finally the Prince noticed Jimmy, nodded and waved his hand. "Dismissed. Get some clean clothing and bathe. We'll discuss this again at length after the evening meal."

Jimmy left, finding his father and brother following him out of the room. They paused just outside the door. Arutha said, "I've got to get back inside, but I just wanted to see if you were all right."

"I'm fine," said Jimmy, with a faint smile of appreciation for his father's concern. With the death of their grandparents, Arutha's features had taken on a drawn, haggard edge, from too much worry and too little sleep. "Just some cold toes."

Arutha nodded, squeezed his son's shoulder a moment. "Get some food and rest. This isn't half over, and while Patrick may be ready to storm the enemy, we need a great deal more information." He opened the door and returned inside to the Prince's council. Dash said, "I'll go with you to the kitchen."

Jimmy said, "Fine."

The two brothers walked down the long hall.

Erik entered the kitchen. He waved across the large stone room to Milo. The innkeeper from his hometown of Ravensburg had been put to work in the castle's kitchen, along with his wife, so they could be close to their daughter, Rosalyn, mother of the next Baron of Darkmoor. She and her husband Rudolph the baker lived in the castle where they took care of the baby baron.

Erik's own mother now lived in one of the buildings close by the castle—the long history of animosity between her and the Dowager Baroness made it prudent to keep the two women separated. The Baroness had been humiliated publicly for years by Erik's mother Frieda over Erik being the illegitimate son of the late Baron Otto. Erik's stepfather, Nathan, was furiously working in the Barony's smithy, readying weapons and other iron goods for the coming spring campaign. It was a socially awkward situation at times, but Erik enjoyed having his family close by.

Erik sat. "You all right?" he asked Jimmy.

"Just tired. Came close to not making it once, but it's not much of a story. I had just lost my horse and had to hide from a patrol for a while, and damn near froze hiding under a log. The snow was falling so they didn't track me after I had crossed some rocks, but I could barely move when they finally left."

"Frostbite?" asked Erik.

"Don't know," said Jimmy. "I haven't taken my boots off. My fingers are fine." He wiggled them.

"We have a healing priest here. The Temple of Dala, at Rillanon, sent one to provide advice to the Prince."

Dash grinned. "You mean the King bullied them into having one close by in case Patrick was wounded."

"Something like that," admitted Erik as he returned the smile. "Have him look at your feet. It wouldn't do to have you going toeless."

Jimmy chewed, then swallowed. "Why am I suspicious you're motivated more by my fitness for duty, Captain, than out of any concern for my well-being?"

Erik shrugged theatrically. "Because you have a reasonable comprehension of how things work in court?"

Jimmy suddenly looked very tired, as if letting down his mask. "How soon?" he asked.

Erik looked sympathetic. "The end of this week. Three, four more days."

Jimmy nodded. He stood and said, "I'd better find that priest."

"Down the hall from the Prince's quarters, next to my own. His name is Herbert. Tell him who you are; you look like a rag-picker."

Dash watched his brother leave and said, "As his feet thawed he could barely walk. I think that priest is going to earn his keep."

Erik took a cup of coffee from Milo, said thanks, then turned to Dash. "He already has. I've got a score of men fit for duty who would still be laid up if it wasn't for that priest. And Nakor."

"Where is that scrawny lunatic?" asked Dash. "I haven't seen him in a week."

"He's out in the city, gathering converts for his new faith."

"How goes the summoning of the Blessed to spread the word of Good?"

Erik laughed. "Recruiting those willing to work on behalf of good in the midst of winter, after a war has reduced the population to near starvation, is nearly beyond even Nakor's conniving ways."

"Any takers?"

"A couple. One or two are earnest, the others looking for a meal."

Dash nodded. "Is this next mission something I could do? Jimmy could use a rest."

"We all could," said Erik. Then he shook his head. "But you're not being spared, my friend, for we're all going."

"Where?" asked Dash.

"Krondor. Patrick can't sit here forever. And if what your brother has reported jibes with the other reports we're getting, the longer we wait, the stronger Fadawah's forces are going to get in Krondor. We may have to hit them with everything we have sooner than we'd like.

"With Kesh threatening our southern border, Patrick's been reluctant to return the Armies of the East. Well, the King has ordered some elements back. Seems some of the Kingdom's eastern neighbors are getting fractious now there isn't a large standing army or huge fleet there to keep them in line. So Patrick's in a hurry to retake Krondor before King Borric orders more soldiers home to the East."

Dash said, "So how many of us are going to Krondor?"

"The Eagles," said Erik, naming the special command of soldiers that had been gathered and trained by Dash and Jimmy's grandfather Lord James, the late Duke of Krondor. "We'll have some auxiliaries, Duga's crew"—he named a large force of former mercenaries who had come over to the Kingdom's side during the invasion—"and we'll be working with Captain Subai's Pathfinders."

"That's all?" asked Dash.

"That's all to start," said Erik. "We're not trying to conquer all of the Principality in the first week." He sipped at his coffee. "We were going to find a likely place to hold so we can stage, then we ride in and secure Krondor."

"Sounds easy," said Dash in a sarcastic tone. "If there wasn't another army already there." He studied Erik's face. "There's something else going on. Why is Patrick in such a hurry to secure the city? I can think of a half-dozen better places from which to stage a retaking of the West if I didn't care about Krondor; we could cut it off and starve out whoever's there, staging from a camp to the east."

"I know," said Erik, "but part of it is pride. It's Patrick's city, the capital of his realm. He was Prince of Krondor for only a short while before it was lost. And he followed a legend in that office."

Dash nodded. "Growing up in Rillanon, Jimmy and I met Prince Arutha only a few times; when I was old enough to appreciate him, he was getting on in years. But what my father and others said about him made him impressive, even then." He looked at Erik a moment, then said, "You think Patrick's of the notion that Arutha would somehow have held the city?"

"Something like that," said Erik. "The Prince doesn't confide in me. But there's more to it than just wounded pride. The other part of it is logistics. That harbor is going to be useless for years. If we had the manpower and equipment we had before the war in Krondor, all the workers, dredges, and a few cooperative magicians, even, it would still take a year to clear the harbor, maybe more. As it is now, I have no idea if Krondor will ever become the shipping center it once was.

"But we have a new port south of there, in Shandon Bay, Port Vykor, and for it to be any use to us, we have to insure we have a clear trade route between there and the rest of the West, which means Krondor needs to be secured. We don't need it, but we certainly can't have Fadawah's generals using it as a base to attack us." He lowered his voice, as if not wishing for a perverse fate to overhear. "If we get cut off from Port Vykor, we may never reunite the Eastern and Western Realms."

Dash nodded. "That makes sense."

Erik put down his now empty mug and said, "That's about all that does."

Dash nodded in agreement as Erik stood. Looking up at the tall, powerfully built captain, he said, "I haven't seen my sometime employer about lately. How fares your friend Rupert?"

Erik smiled. "Roo is hauling some ridiculous amount of goods through mud and ice to be first into Darkmoor with what we need." Then Erik laughed. "He told me he's the richest man in the world, according to his accounts, but has almost no gold left, so his only hope for recovery is to insure the Kingdom survives long enough to pay him back."

"An odd kind of patriotism, wouldn't you say?"

Erik smiled as he nodded. "If you knew Roo as well as I, you'd judge it entirely in keeping with his nature." Pausing for a moment as if considering a second cup of coffee, Erik looked with a faint show of regret at the empty mug. After a moment of silence, he said, "I'd best get back to see what Owen wants done."

He departed. Dash pondered what had been said there, amidst the bustle of the kitchen, then rose to find Jimmy and see how he fared.

The priest was just departing Jimmy's quarters when Dash arrived.

Sitting on the bed next to his brother, who lay under a heavy wool blanket, Dash said, "That was quick."

"He gave me something to drink, washed my feet in an unguent, then told me to get some sleep."

"How bad are they?"

"I was going to lose toes, at least," said Jimmy, "if he hadn't been here." With a nod of his head he indicated the departed priest.

"You paint a pretty bleak picture of what's out there."

Jimmy sighed. "I saw places where men had stripped the bark off of trees to make soup."

Dash sat back. "Patrick's not going to be happy."

"What's happened here while I was gone?" asked Jimmy, stifling a yawn.

Dash said, "We've got reports that things are stable up north, though no one has seen sign of that bastard Duko lately."

Jimmy said, "If Fadawah is sending Duko south, Krondor could be very difficult to seize."

"Yes," agreed Dash. "Kesh is not happy about what went on down in Stardock, and we've got elements of the garrison of Ran and half of the King's Own down near Landreth, just waiting for an excuse to move south. Kesh has pulled away from Shamata, but they're a lot closer than Patrick likes, and the vale is once again a no-man's-land. Negotiations are underway, even as we speak."

"The East?" asked Jimmy, this time unable to stop the yawn.

"We won't know until the spring, but some of the smaller kingdoms may get playful. Patrick and the King have exchanged messages, and I get the impression Borric wants some of his Army of the East back as soon as the thaw starts."

"What's Father say?"

"To me?" asked Dash. Jimmy nodded. "Not much," said Dash with a smile that reminded his brother of their grandfather in his more playful moods. "He's pretty close-mouthed about things."

"Mother?" asked Jimmy.

Dash nodded again. "I get the feeling it may be a long time before Mother visits us. She seems to find court life in Roldem preferable to living in a tent in the burned-out remains of Krondor, irrespective of the rank of Duchess."

Jimmy closed his eyes. "She and Aunt Polina are most likely shopping right now, or having gowns fitted for a banquet or dance."

"Most likely," agreed Dash. "But it's hard on Father. You've been away for most of the winter, and the few times you've been here you've seen him when he's busy."

"Grandfather and Grandmother?" asked Jimmy.

"Yes," said Dash. "When he's alone and thinks I don't notice, he broods. He knows there was nothing he could do, but he silently rages about it. I hope once spring comes and we start the campaign he'll snap out of it, but he's drinking more than he used to and seems withdrawn most of the time."

When Jimmy said nothing, Dash glanced at his brother and saw his chin on his chest, his eyes half-closed as he fought to remain awake. Dash quietly stood up and moved to the door. He took a long look at his brother, and for a moment saw an echo of their dead grandmother in his features, the pale skin and nearly white blond hair. Finding a tear coming unbidden to his eyes, Dash quickly left, silently closing the door behind, while he said a silent prayer of thanks to Ruthia, the Goddess of Luck, for the safe return of his brother.

"Erik!"

Dash turned to see Rosalyn hurrying down the corridor, and stood aside to let the young woman pass. Dash knew the girl felt overwhelmed at times by being the mother of the next Baron—she was Gerd's mother because of her rape at the hands of Erik's half-brother—and Erik was her closest friend. They had been like brother and sister as children, and he was the first person she turned to when in distress. Dash watched as she came to the Captain's door and started knocking.

Erik opened the door and said, "What?"

Dash hesitated a moment, then continued to walk past as Rosalyn said, "It's the Baroness. She's refusing to let me bathe my own son! It's just one more thing she's taken from me! Do something!"

Dash stopped and said, "Excuse me."

Both Erik and Rosalyn turned to the young man. "Yes?" asked Erik.

"I hesitate to intrude on the basis of overhearing a conversation I'm not party to, but to avoid any embarrassment, may I make an observation?"

"What?" said Rosalyn.

"Given her somewhat . . . forceful nature, the Dowager Baroness has actually been rather leisurely in acquainting your son with his new office."

Rosalyn shook her head. She had been a pretty girl growing up in Ravensburg with Erik, but the birth of two children, hard work in her husband's bakery, and the travail of the recent war had put premature grey in her hair and robbed her face of the softness Erik had known in his youth. Her eyes were now hard, and she was leery of hearing anything from Dash that would further remove her from her son.

"Gerd is now Baron von Darkmoor," said Dash, trying to be patient and instructive without sounding patronizing. Rosalyn might be an untutored common woman, but she wasn't stupid. "For the rest of his life, many of the things you did for him will be done by servants. Had you been Baroness, you would never have bathed him, nor changed his diapers, nor perhaps even nursed him.

"It's time for you to begin his education as Baron." Dash waved around, indicating the castle. "This is now the frontier of the Kingdom, until the West is retaken, and may continue to be a critical stronghold for years, far into Gerd's adulthood. Gerd is almost five years old, and soon will spend most of his day with tutors and instructors. He needs to learn to read, to write, the history of his people, riding, weapons, court protocol . . ."

Erik nodded, putting his hand on Rosalyn's shoulder. "Dash is right." The young woman looked defiant and Erik felt her shoulder tense under his hand. He smiled. "But there's no reason you can't stand nearby and watch as the servants care for him."

Rosalyn said nothing for a moment, then nodded and turned off to retrace her steps to where her son was housed in the Baron's quarters of the castle. Erik watched her retreating back, then turned to Dash. "Thanks for pointing things out."

"I hesitated to insert myself into your conversation, but it's only the truth."

Erik glanced down the hall to the corner where Rosalyn had turned out of sight and let his eyes fix on the distant space. "So many changes. We all have so much to adjust to."

Dash said, "Again, I don't mean to presume, Captain, but if you require any assistance . . ."

Erik smiled. "I suspect I will. And I will count on you and your brother. If you haven't heard yet, you're both being assigned to my command."

"Oh?" said Dash.

"It's your father's idea. He's going to take a hand personally in this coming campaign."

Dash nodded. "He's his father's son."

Erik said, "I didn't know your grandfather well, I must say, but well enough to know that's a compliment."

Dash grinned. "If you had known him better, you might not think so. Ask my mother if she ever decides to return to the West."

"Anyway," continued Erik, "the King has his hands full in the East, with most of his army absent and his navy sunk, in keeping the Eastern Kingdoms from starting trouble. The Prince has Kesh in the South, so that leaves it to our merry little band to rcclaim the West."

"Why does that not fill me with joy?" asked Dash rhetorically.

"I believe you would be in need of a healing priest if it did. You would obviously be bereft of your senses."

"When does this campaign begin?" asked Dash.

"When you hear the first sound of ice breaking in the West, start packing."

Dash said, "I heard ice break this morning."

"Well, get packing," said Erik. "We leave for Krondor within the week."

Dash nodded. "Very good, Captain."

As Dash turned away, Erik said, "One other thing."

"What, sir?" asked Dash.

"Your office as Court Baron does you no good in the army, so you and James are both being given the rank of Knight-Lieutenants."

"Thank you, I think," said Dash.

"Tomorrow head down to the quartermaster and draw uniforms for yourself and James."

"Sir," said Dash with a weak salute, then he turned and walked toward his own quarters. Muttering to himself, he said, "Damn. I'm in the army."

Jimmy tugged at his ill-fitting black tunic. "Damn. I'm in the army."

Dash laughed. He gently elbowed his brother, indicating the Prince was about to speak.

"My lords, gentlemen," he began, addressing the gathering in his audience hall, formerly the Baron von Darkmoor's. "The King requires the presence of most of the

Army of the East along the Keshian border and to the east. That leaves it to what is left of the Armies of the West to drive the remaining invaders from our shores.''

Dash whispered to his brother, ''Perhaps we shouldn't have sunk all their ships. It makes the trip home so much more difficult.''

Arutha, Duke of Krondor, threw his younger son a dark look, and Dash fell silent, while Jimmy attempted not to laugh aloud. One thing James admired about his younger brother was an ability to find something funny in almost any situation, no matter how bleak.

Prince Patrick said, ''Of course it does,'' looking directly at Dash.

Dash had the good grace to blush before his Prince.

''But we can arrange to transport them home at a later time. First they must surrender.''

Dash tried to wish himself invisible.

Patrick continued. ''Intelligence confirms that this General Fadawah is seizing the opportunity created by the Emerald Queen's defeat to fashion a little Empire for himself.''

He walked to a map and took a pointer and indicated the area between Krondor and Ylith. ''From Sarth to Ylith, Fadawah's forces are in complete control.'' The pointer swept to the east. ''They control the forests up to the mountains, and most of the passes to Nightmare Ridge. We have a stable front along the ridge.

''To the north''—the pointer moved north of Ylith— ''he's run into some stern opposition at LaMut. Earl Takari's holding the city, but barely. Only the harsh winter kept Fadawah from taking the city.'' Looking at Arutha, he said, ''Tell me of Duke Carl.''

Arutha said, ''The Duke is a boy. He's barely seventeen. Earl Takari is only three years older.''

The men in the room knew the fathers of the two nobles mentioned had died in the invasion. Arutha continued, ''But Takari is Tsurani stock, and has been studying under his Swordmaster since he could walk. He'll hold LaMut until the last man if needs be.

''Carl may be a boy, but he's surrounded by a strong, if small, army.'' Arutha nodded to a man standing behind Erik von Darkmoor, a tall, dark-haired man wearing a kilt and sporting a longsword hung over his back. Dash and Jimmy knew him to be the leader of a company of Hadati hillmen from Yabon, by name of Akee.

Akee said, "Most of my people are serving in Yabon. Fadawah will not take Yabon."

Almost to himself Patrick said, "But come spring he'll be inside the walls of LaMut, and all the Tsurani honor in that city won't keep him from doing it." Patrick was silent a moment, then said, "Can Duke Carl's forces save LaMut?"

"Yes," said Owen. "If we can assume we'll have no trouble from the Brotherhood of the Dark Path"—he used the common term for the moredhel, the dark elves who lived to the north—"and count on the elves and dwarves, and the Free Cities keeping the western front stable, then Carl can strip his garrison, leaving what he must along his eastern flank, and move the bulk of his men south to LaMut. He should be able to hold Fadawah under those circumstancs."

"If he does, can he then retake Ylith?" asked Patrick.

Akee glanced at Erik and Arutha, both of whom nodded to him. Akee looked at Patrick and said, "No, he cannot. He would need three times the number of swords he has at his call to stand a chance of retaking Ylith. He can hold where he is, unless this General Fadawah turns his entire force northward—which he won't do if he's moving soldiers south to hold Krondor—but Duke Carl cannot retake Ylith."

"My lords and gentlemen," said the Prince, "LaMut is, by necessity, the anvil." He looked at Owen Greylock and said, "My Lord Marshal, your army must by needs be the hammer."

Owen said, "It's a small hammer, Patrick."

The Prince said, "Indeed, but Kesh is arrayed in force along our southern border, what's left of our fleet is keeping Queg and the Durbin pirates at bay, and some of the eastern kings are getting ambitious. You'll have to make do with your current force."

Owen said, "That's barely twenty thousand men, against how many? A hundred thousand?"

Patrick said, "We can't just let them keep what they've

taken until we resolve these other issues, can we?''

His question was greeted by silence.

Patrick looked from face to face in the room. ''I'm not ignorant of the flaws of my own ancestors. We took every inch of land from somebody else to make the Western Realm. Only Yabon joined the Kingdom willingly, and that because we saved them from the Brotherhood of the Dark Path, else they would have fallen.

''But the only reason there's a Baron von Darkmoor in the first place is the bandit ancestor of your own Captain Erik was too tough a nut to crack, and it was easier to make him a Kingdom noble and let him keep the land he had already taken than it was to kill him and put some king's idiot nephew here in his place.'' Patrick's voice began to rise. ''And several other accommodations have been made over the years, allowing former enemies to become valued vassals.'' Now his voice was raised to the point of yelling. ''But I'll be damned to the Seventh Hell if I let some murdering bastard set himself up as 'King of the Bitter Sea' and rule over *my* Principality. If Fadawah does, it will be with one foot on my dead body!''

Dash and James exchanged glances. They didn't need to say anything. The message was clear. Owen Greylock and Erik von Darkmoor, and what remained of the Armies of the West, would have to retake the Principality without any outside assistance.

Owen cleared his throat. Patrick glanced at his Knight-Marshal of Krondor and said, ''Yes?''

''Is there anything else, Highness?''

Patrick was silent a long moment, then said, ''No.'' To the men in the room he said, ''My lords and gentlemen, you are all under Marshal Greylock's command from this moment on. Treat his orders as if they are my own.''

He lowered his voice. ''And may the gods smile on us,'' he said. And left.

The nobles in the room began muttering comments to one another, then Owen said, ''My lords!''

Silence returned to the hall.

Greylock said, ''We move in the morning. I expect to have advanced units in Ravensburg by nightfall, and scouts to the walls of Krondor by the end of the week.'' He glanced from face to face, then said, "You know what to do."

The men began to file out of the room, and Erik came to stand before Dash and James. "You're with me," he said, turning and walking toward a small door off to one side.

The brothers found their father waiting in the room already, and in a moment Greylock entered, closing the door behind. "I just wanted to let you two know," said Owen, addressing the brothers, "that you're going to be given the dirtiest, most thankless job we've got."

Dash smiled. "Smashing!"

Jimmy threw his brother a dark look, and said, "What is it?"

"Jimmy, you're in charge of our special advance unit."

"Special advance unit?" asked Jimmy.

Arutha nodded. "Him," he said, pointing to Dash.

Dash rolled his eyes heavenward but said nothing. He had long ago accustomed himself to being under his older brother's direction whenever they were working together.

Arutha said, "Owen said he needed a couple of sneaky bastards to operate behind enemy lines." He smiled at his sons. "I told him your parentage wasn't in doubt, but that you were sneaky enough for the job."

"When do we leave?" said Jimmy.

"Now," said Erik. "There are a pair of horses waiting for you by the postern gate, with supplies for a week."

James said, "A week? That means you'll want us inside of Krondor when your scouts reach the walls?"

Owen nodded. "Or close by. Leave those uniforms here and dress like a couple of free swords. If you get caught, tell them you're Valemen looking to enlist."

Dash grinned, but his tone was mocking. "Oh, joy. We're playing at spies again."

Jimmy again looked at his brother as if he were crazy, and said, "You do find the oddest things entertaining."

Arutha looked at his two sons and said, "We just got confirming intelligence that Duko has come south."

"That's the stick in the anthill, isn't it?" said Dash.

Arutha nodded. "Indeed. If Duko gets established in Krondor before we do, he threatens Port Vykor. Cut off

Vykor and we have no communications with the fleet; cut off the fleet, and we have no chance to resupply from the Sunset Islands and the Far Coast."

Owen said, "It might be a feint, with Sarth being his real objective. But there's a report that a second force moves south along the road from Hawk's Hallow under the command of Nordan, Fadawah's second."

"That's a lot of soldiers slogging through the ice and mud," said Jimmy.

Arutha said, "Krondor's harbor is useless; Fadawah knows this. We don't know if he knows of Vykor's harbor down in Shandon Bay, but if he does, then this isn't a feint."

Jimmy glanced at his brother, then said to his father, "So you want us to find out which?"

"If possible," said Arutha. "If he's just trying to slow down our march, so he can reinforce Sarth, we have to know."

Dash looked around the room, then asked, "Anything else?"

Arutha said, "Stay alive?"

Jimmy smiled. "We always plan on that, Father."

Arutha came and embraced his sons, Dash first, then Jimmy.

Dash said, "Come on, we have some riding to do this night."

Jimmy resumed looking dubious as they left the room.

Two

Wilderness

Dash SIGNALED.

Jimmy took out his sword and ducked behind the boulder. Dash left his own position on the south side of the King's Highway and dropped into a ditch that ran parallel to the road for several hundred feet.

The brothers had been riding for two days. The thaw had begun and there was actually some warmth in the sunlight when it came out from behind the seemingly constant cloud cover. But the temperature didn't fall below freezing anymore, and the rain helped melt the snow. As Dash lay in the cold mud he wished for the ice again. The ooze slowed travel and he didn't seem able to get dry, even when staying close to a fire at night.

They had heard voices in the woods ahead a few minutes ago, had dismounted, tied their horses, and advanced on foot. As the sound of approaching feet grew louder, Dash chanced a glance over the edge of the berm, and saw a ragged band of travelers looking about in a fearful manner as they moved eastward along the King's Highway. There was a man and woman, and children, three of them, though one—Dash couldn't tell if it was a girl or boy under the heavy hood—seemed almost of adult height.

Dash stood as Jimmy came from behind the boulder. The

man in the van of the small party of refugees pulled a wicked-looking hand scythe from under his ragged cloak and held it in menacing fashion as the others turned as if to flee.

"Hold!" Jimmy shouted. "We'll not harm you."

The man looked dubious, the others fearful, but they halted their movement. Jimmy and Dash both put away weapons and slowly approached.

The man didn't lower his scythe. "Who be you?" he said, his words heavily accented.

Jimmy and Dash exchanged glances, for the man spoke with the accent of one who had come from Novindus. This man at one time had been a soldier with the invading army of the Emerald Queen.

Dash held up his hands to show he was not holding any weapon, and Jimmy stopped moving. Jimmy said, "We're travelers. Who are you?"

The woman ventured to step from behind the man's protection. She was gaunt and looked weak. Jimmy glanced to the others and saw that the children were equally underfed. The tallest of the three was a girl, perhaps fifteen years of age, though appearing older for the deep dark circles under her eyes. Jimmy returned his attention to the woman, who looked at him and said, "We were farmers." She pointed to the east. "We're trying to reach Darkmoor. We hear there's food there."

Jimmy nodded. "Some. Where are you from?"

"Tannerus," said the woman.

Dash pointed at the man. "He's not from Tannerus."

The man nodded. He motioned at himself with his free hand and said, "Markin. From City of the Serpent River." He glanced around. "Long way from here."

"You were a soldier of the Emerald Queen?" asked Jimmy.

The man spat on the ground and it looked as if the gesture was taking most of his strength. "I spit on her!" He started to wobble and the woman put her arms around him.

"He's a farmer," she said. "He told us his story when he came to us."

Jimmy looked at Dash, then motioned with his head back toward the horses. Dash didn't need to be told what was on his brother's mind. He turned and walked back while Jimmy said, "Why don't you tell us his story."

"My man went to fight for the King," said the woman. "Two years ago." She glanced back at the three children and said, "My girls are fit to work; Hildi's almost grown. We did all right for the first year. Then the soldiers came and took the town. Our farm was far enough away we weren't troubled for a while."

Dash returned leading the horses. He handed the reins to Jimmy, then went back and opened a saddlebag. He returned a moment later, unwrapping a bundle. Once opened, he revealed some heavy travel bread, thick with honey and nuts and dried fruit, and some jerked beef. Without hesitation the children passed their mother and grabbed what they could.

Dash glanced at Jimmy and nodded slightly. He gave the rest of the bundle to the man, who passed it along to the woman and said, "Thank you."

"How did an enemy soldier come to be guiding your family to Darkmoor?" asked Dash.

The woman and man both nearly wept in gratitude as they chewed on the heavy bread. After swallowing, the woman said, "When the soldiers came, we hid in the woods, and they took everything. We had only what we had carried away. Then out of spite they burned the roof off our house and broke down the door. Sticks and thatch was all it was, but it was the only home the girls had known."

She glanced about, afraid other threats might appear suddenly from the surrounding woods. "Markin found us when we were trying to rebuild our house. It was never what you'd call fine, but my man had spent years adding to it, making it more than just a hut. But the soldiers had burned it down and the girls and me had no tools."

"I find them," said Markin. "They needed help."

"He came and he fought for us. Other men came, many with swords and bows, but he kept them from taking me or the girls." She glanced at him with obvious affection in her eyes. "He's my man now, and he's a fair da' to the girls."

Jimmy sighed. To Dash he said, "We'll hear stories like

this one a hundred times before we're through.''

"Why Darkmoor?" asked Jimmy.

"We hear the King's there and there's food for the ask-ing.''

Jimmy smiled. "No, the King's not there, though he was last year. But there's food for work.''

"I work good," said the foreign-born soldier.

"Can we go?" asked the woman.

"Yes," said Dash, motioning for them to pass.

Markin said, "You soldiers?''

Jimmy grinned. "Not if we can help it.''

"But you noble man. Markin can tell.''

Dash said dryly, "I've known him all my life and can tell you he's far from noble most of the time.''

The old soldier studied the two, then said, "If you try to look like common men, you don't.'' He pointed down to Jimmy's feet. "Dirty, but nobleman's boots.''

He motioned for the woman and girls to follow him and moved carefully on, not taking his eyes off the brothers until his small band was past. Then he turned and hurried along, taking his position in the van, against any other un-expected encounters.

"First time I regretted having comfortable boots," said Dash.

Jimmy looked down and said, "Well, we may be muddy, but he's right.'' Glancing around, he added, "This is a place of little food and even less comfort.''

Dash remounted his horse. "I suspect by the time we get to Krondor we won't look quite so prosperous.''

Jimmy also mounted, and said, "Maybe we should get off this highway.''

Dash said, "The north road?" He referred to an old road his one-time employer, Rupert Avery, used regularly to move goods, avoiding the tolls charged on the King's High-way.

Jimmy shook his head. "No, that's almost as busy as this one, and those woods are going to be full of deserters and bandits.''

"The south?''

"Slower going, but there are enough trails along the lakes if we don't head too far into the southern hills.''

Dash said, "Since Kesh pulled south to the old border, everything from here to their nearest garrison is going to be wilderness."

Jimmy laughed. "What's the difference if we run into fifty deserters from the Emerald Queen's army, or fifty bandits, or fifty Keshian mercenaries . . ." He shrugged.

Dash made a show of shivering under his heavy cloak. "Let's hope whoever's down there is hugging their fires. As any sane man would do."

Dash urged his horse forward and soon the two brothers were riding south at a steady walk. "Why do we do these things?" he asked.

Jimmy said, "Because our King commands and we obey."

Dash let out a theatrical sigh. "I thought it was something like that."

Softly, Jimmy began to sing a very old song:

> *"To Kesh's heartland or Queg's harsh shore,*
> *Our blood, our hearts, our lives and more,*
> *For honor's sake do we obey,*
> *And go over the hills and far away . . ."*

The sound of cracking ice rang through the cold morning air and both brothers pulled up just before entering a clearing. Using hand signals, Jimmy motioned for Dash to move south along the edge of the clearing while he circled north.

Dash nodded, dismounted, and tied his horse to the branch of a small birch tree. Jimmy did likewise and moved silently away.

Dash moved through the thinning trees, bordering a burned-out farm, he judged from the appearance of tree stumps nearby. The sound resolved itself into a repeated hammering at ice.

Dash saw a man in the distance.

A slender figure, he crouched over the frozen ice on a large pond, perhaps a hundred yards away from where Dash watched, hammering at the ice with a rock. Up and down the rock moved, and Dash couldn't help but be fascinated with the sight.

Dash couldn't get a good look at the man, but his clothing seemed a hodgepodge of rags and ill-matched garments. He might have worn boots, but all Dash could see was a collection of rags tied around each foot for warmth.

Dash saw movement in the woods beyond the pond and judged Jimmy was in place. He waited.

Jimmy walked slowly out of the woods and the man leaped to his feet with astonishing speed. He turned away as Jimmy shouted, "Wait! I won't hurt you!"

Dash slowly took out his sword as the tatters-clad man hurried toward him, trying to keep his movement from alerting the ragged man. As the man reached the first line of trees, Dash stepped out, extending his foot, and tripped him.

The man went down in a tangle of clothes and turned over, scuttling backward as he shouted, "Don't kill me!"

Dash moved quickly to put the point of his sword before the man's face, as Jimmy caught up, out of breath.

Dash said, "We're not going to hurt you." To demonstrate his good intentions, he quickly sheathed his sword. "Get up."

The man got up slowly as Jimmy leaned over, hands on knees, and said, "He's fast."

Dash grinned. "You'd have caught him had you had another mile or so to overtake him. You've always had endurance, if not speed." Turning his attention to the figure on the ground, he said, "Who are you and what were you doing?"

The man slowly rose, as if ready to bolt at the slightest threat, and said, "I am called Malar Enares, young masters." He was a slender man, with a hawk nose sticking out over a large rag wrapped around his face. His eyes were dark, and they shifted back and forth between the brothers. "I was fishing."

Jimmy and Dash exchanged glances, and Dash said, "With a rock?"

"To break the ice, young sir. Then when the fish comes up to sun himself, I would strip bark and make a noose."

Jimmy said, "You were going to snare a fish?"

"It is easy if you but have patience and a steady hand, young sir."

Dash said, "I hear Kesh in your speech."

"Oh, no, mercy, young sir. I am but a humble servant of a great trader of Shamata, Kiran Hessen."

Jimmy and Dash had both heard the name. A trader with Keshian connections who did a great deal of business with the late Jacob Esterbrook. Since the destruction of Krondor, the boys' father, Lord Arutha, had pieced together several accounts that had clearly indicated two facts, that Esterbrook had been a long-standing agent of Great Kesh, and that he and his daughter were both dead. Jimmy could see what Dash was thinking: if Esterbrook had been a Keshian agent, so then could Kiran Hessen.

"Where is your master now?" asked James.

"Oh, dead I fear," said the thin man with a display of regret. "Fourteen years was I his servant, and he a generous master. Now I am alone in this cold place."

James said, "Well, why don't you tell us this story."

"And show us how you planned on catching those fish," said Dash.

"If I might have some hair from your horses' manes," said the ragged man. "Then it would be so much easier."

"Horses?" asked Dash.

"Two young noblemen such as yourselves didn't walk into this forsaken wilderness, I am certain," supplied Malar. "And I heard one of them snorting a moment again." He pointed. "That way."

Jimmy nodded. "That's fair."

"What do you need hair from their manes for?" asked Dash.

"Let me show you."

He walked toward the place where Dash's horse had been tied, and said, "The ice was almost broken when you startled me, young sir. If you would but use the hilt of your sword to break it open, that would be a great service."

Jimmy nodded and started back toward the icy pond.

Dash asked, "Now, about how you came to be lost in this forsaken wilderness."

"As you are no doubt aware," began Malar, "there was much trouble between Kesh and the Kingdom lately, with Shamata for a time being deeded to the Empire."

"So we had heard," said Dash.

"My master, being of Kingdom allegiance, decided it

wise to visit his holdings in the North, first in Landreth, then Krondor.

"We were traveling to Krondor when we encountered the invaders. We were overtaken and my master and most of his other servants were put to the sword. I and a few others managed to flee into the hills, south of here." He pointed southward with his chin, as he reached Dash's horse. Malar reached up and gripped a few hairs from the horse's mane, yanking expertly, and came away with several long strands of hair. The horse moved at the unexpected pressure, snorting displeasure. Dash reached out and took the reins from the tree branch where they were tied, and Malar yanked out some more hairs. He repeated the procedure twice more. "That is sufficient," he observed.

"So you've been in these hills how long?"

"More than three months, young sir," said Malar, as he started deftly weaving the hair into a braid. "It has been a bitter time. Some of my companions died from hunger and cold, and two were captured by a band of men—outlaws or invaders, I do not know which. I have been alone for all of three weeks or so, I judge." He sounded apologetic as he said, "It is difficult to keep track of time."

"You've survived in these woods for three weeks with nothing but your bare hands?" asked Dash.

Malar started walking toward the pond, continuing to weave the horse hair. "Yes, and a terrible thing it has been, sir."

"How?" asked Dash.

"As a boy I was raised in the hills above Landreth, to the north of the Vale of Dreams. Not as hostile a land as this, but still a place where the unwary can perish easily. My father was a woodsman, who put food on your table with bow and snare, as well as gold in his pouch from guiding men through the hills."

Dash laughed. "He guided smugglers."

"Perhaps," said Malar with a broad shrug. "In any event, while the winters in the hills near my home are nowhere near as inhospitable as here, still a man must have skills to survive."

Malar moved slowly as he approached the hole. He glanced skyward to see the angle of the sun, then moved to face it. "Do not let your shadow cross the hole," he instructed.

Dash and Jimmy followed behind. The man from the Vale of Dreams slowly knelt and said, "Fish, I have been taught, see movement, so we must move ever so slowly."

Dash said, "This I must see."

Jimmy nodded.

Malar said, "The sun shines through the hole in the ice, and the fish swims up to feel the warmth."

Jimmy looked over the man's shoulder and saw a large brook trout lazily circling the hole. Moving slowly, Malar inserted the noose of horsehair into the water, behind the fish. The trout ceased moving for a moment, but Malar resisted the urge to move quickly, instead inching the snare toward the fish's tail.

After another long minute, the fish darted away, and Malar said, "Another will come. They see the light and think insects may land upon the surface."

After a silent five minutes, a trout appeared near the edge of the hole. Dash couldn't tell if it was the same fish or a different one. Malar again started moving the noose slowly and got it around the fish's tail. With a jerk, he snared the trout and yanked it out of the hole, landing it on the ice, where it flopped.

Dash couldn't see the man's face behind the rags that covered it, but the crinkles around his eyes showed Malar was smiling. "If one of you young gentlemen would be so kind as to light a fire, I will catch some more."

Jimmy and Dash exchanged glances, then Jimmy shrugged. Dash said, "I'll get some wood. You find a campsite."

They hurried off while the strange man from the Vale of Dreams sought out another fish for supper.

For three days they moved slowly toward Krondor. Several times they had heard distant voices and the sound of men moving through the woodlands, but they had avoided contact with anyone.

Jimmy and Dash both found Malar an enigma. He had surprising skills for wilderness survival, odd for one claiming to be the servant of a rich trader. On the other hand,

Jimmy had confided to his brother, the servant of a rich smuggler might prove in need of such skills. Still, they were pleased to have him along, for he had found several shortcuts through the undergrowth, had identified edible plants that supplemented their stores, and had proven a reliable night sentry. As they were walking their horses, leading them more than half the time, his keeping up had proven to be no difficulty. Jimmy judged they were less than a week's travel from Krondor.

At midday they heard horses in the distance, from the north. Jimmy spoke at a low conversational level. "Duko's men moving along the highway?"

Dash nodded. "Probably. If we can hear them from here, we've headed back toward the highway." He turned to Malar. "Do you know of any southern route to Krondor?"

"Only the highway that loops around from Land's End, young sir. But if we are nearing the King's Highway, within a few days we should start encountering farms."

Jimmy was silent for a long moment, then said, "They'll almost certainly be burned out."

"But," suggested Dash, "if they are, no one is likely to be living in them, and we might slip into the city unnoticed."

"No farmers, you mean," corrected Jimmy. "But they'd be decent shelter for some very unpleasant men with a fondness for weapons, I bet."

Dash's brow furrowed, as if thinking he should have thought of that, but a moment later, his grin returned and he said, "Well, then, we will just blend in. You've told me often enough how unpleasant I can be, and I am certainly fond of my weapons."

Jimmy nodded. "Two more hired swords will scarcely be noticed. And if we can get close to the city, we'll find a way inside. There are enough holes in the walls, that's for certain."

Malar said, "You've been to Krondor, then, young sir? Since the war, I mean."

Jimmy ignored the question, saying, "We've heard of the damage."

Dash agreed. "More than a few people left Krondor and came east."

"This I know," said Malar, falling silent.

They moved on through the woods for the rest of the day and made a cold camp that night. Huddled under their blankets, Jimmy and Dash stayed close together while Malar took the first watch. They slept fitfully, coming awake many times.

In the morning, they resumed their journey.

The woods were filled with the sounds of the thaw. In the distance the cracking of ice rang through the suddenly warm air as ponds and lakes began to lose their frozen skins. Large mounds of snow fell from trees in sudden, wet attacks on the travelers, while everywhere water dripped from branches. The footing beneath their feet alternated between crusty patches of ice and thick mud which gripped at boots and horses' hooves. The constant noise was a backdrop against which the occasional sounds of spring could be heard. The distant call of a bird that had returned from the south early, seeking others of its kind. The faint rustle in the distance of small creatures coming out of their winter's burrows stilled as they passed, only to resume after a while.

When they paused to rest, Jimmy tied his horse to a low tree branch and motioned for Dash to do likewise. Dash did as he was bid, and said, "Keep an eye out. We're going to relieve ourselves." He moved to where Jimmy stood, making a show of urinating into the snow.

Dash did likewise, whispering, "What is it?"

"Have you formed an opinion of our chance companion?" asked the older brother.

Dash shook his head slightly, saying, "Not really. I'm certain he's more than he claims, but I have no idea what."

"There's not a lot of fat on him," said Jimmy, "but he doesn't move like a man weak from hunger."

Dash said, "Do you have a theory?"

Jimmy said, "No. But if he's not the servant of a rich trader, what's he doing up here?"

"Smuggler?"

"Maybe," answered Jimmy, doing up the front of his trousers. "Could be anything we could imagine."

Remembering what their grandfather had cautioned them

over the years about leaping to conclusions, Dash said, "Then we'd best not imagine anything."

"Wait and see," agreed Jimmy.

They returned to the horses, and Malar hurried off to relieve himself away from the trail. When he was out of hearing range, they continued. Jimmy asked, "Remember that abandoned farm a day's walk this side of where we met Malar?"

"The one with half a thatch roof and the fallen-down cow shed?"

"That's the one. If we bolt, and get separated, meet there."

Dash nodded. Neither chose to discuss what to do should the other never appear.

Malar returned and they started off. The servant from the Vale of Dreams had been as closemouthed as the brothers. Part of the reason was the environment. The nights were still and even in the day noise carried. They knew they were approaching an area likely to be patrolled by the invaders; they were leading their horses rather than riding them, as, even in the woodlands, a rider presented a much higher profile in the distance than a man on foot or a horse. Periodically they stopped to listen.

Rains came later that afternoon and they sought out what shelter they could, finding a hut of some sort, burned out, but with just enough thatch to give slight respite.

Sitting atop their saddles, hastily removed to get them out of the weather, they took stock.

"We've got another day's grain, then we're done," said Dash, knowing his brother was just as aware of supplies as he.

Malar said, "Shouldn't there be winter grass under the snow, sirs?"

Jimmy nodded. "Not much in it, but the horses will eat it."

Dash said, "If there are horsemen in Krondor, they'll have fodder."

Jimmy said, "The difficulty will be in persuading them to share, brother."

Dash grinned. "What's life without a challenge or two?"

The rain stopped and they resumed their trek.

Later that afternoon, Malar said, "Young sirs, I believe I hear something."

All conversation ceased and the three stopped walking as they listened. The frigid days of winter had given way to a promise of spring, but it was still cold enough they could see their breath in the late afternoon air. After a moment of silence, Dash was about to speak when a voice echoed from ahead. It spoke a language neither brother recognized, but they knew it was the Yabonese-like tongue of the invaders.

Glancing around for a place to hide, Jimmy pointed and mouthed the word, *There*.

He indicated a large stand of brush that surrounded an outcropping of rocks. Dash wasn't sure they could secret the horses behind it, but it was the only thing nearby that offered shelter from whoever came their way.

Malar hurried around the upthrust rocks and pulled aside a low branch, allowing Jimmy and Dash to lead their horses around to a relatively sheltered hiding place. In the distance horses could be heard.

Dash's horse's nostrils flared and her head came up. Jimmy said, "What?"

"This witchy mare is in heat," whispered Dash as he tugged hard on her bridle. "Pay attention to *me*!" he demanded.

Malar said, "You ride a mare?"

"She's a good horse," insisted Dash.

"Most of the time!" agreed Jimmy, hissing his words. "But not now!"

Dash tugged on the horse's bridle, trying to focus her attention on himself. An experienced rider, Dash knew that if he could keep her attention, she might not call out to the horses that were approaching.

Jimmy's gelding seemed relatively indifferent to the proceedings, though he did look on with some interest as the mare's excited state built. Dash held tight to the mare's bridle, rubbing her nose and speaking close to her ear in a reassuring fashion.

The riders came close and Dash judged there must be at least a dozen of them from the clatter. Voices cut through the air and a man laughed. These were men who patrolled a familiar area and expected nothing out of the ordinary.

Dash held tight to the bridle and continued to speak softly to his mare as the horses came to the point of closest approach on the trail. Suddenly Dash's horse pulled backwards and her head came up.

For an instant there was a tiny hope she might come back to him, but then she called out her greeting, a loud whinny.

Suddenly shouts filled the air and other horses answered the mare's call. Jimmy didn't hesitate. "That way!"

Malar shoved through underbrush and ignored scratches from branches as he went where Jimmy had directed. Jimmy came next, leading his gelding, eyes wide and nostrils flaring from excitement. The mare balked and resisted as she screamed her welcome to the other horses. A stallion's herd cry answered, and Dash knew the only way he could control his mare was from her back. Letting her head come around toward the stallion, he quickly swung up onto her back, exposing himself to view.

He didn't hesitate, and slammed heels into her flanks. Urging her into a gallop, he seemed to burst from the underbrush toward those riders arrayed on the trail. Then he was past them, moving away from his brother and Malar, and the chase was on.

From a vantage point a short distance off, Jimmy turned and saw the riders wheel and charge after Dash. Malar, almost out of breath, puffed as he said, "Sir, will they catch him?"

Jimmy swore. "Probably. But if they don't, he should try to get back to that farmhouse. That's what we planned."

"Shall we turn around?" asked the servant.

Jimmy was silent. After a moment he said, "No. Dash will either be captured, in which case we can't help him escape, or he'll win free. If he gets back to that farmhouse we found the day we met you, he'll wait one or two days, then return to Darkmoor. If we go now, we'll have no more information than he will."

"We go to Krondor?"

"We go to Krondor," said Jimmy. He glanced around, seeking any sign of other riders in the area. As the sound of Dash and his pursuers faded into the distance, he pointed and said, "That way."

As quietly as they could, the pair set off.

* * *

Dash rode as hard as he could, despite the balky mare, who wanted to turn and greet the stallions behind. Every hint of hesitation from her brought a hard kick to her sides as he used every skill he had to keep her heading down a windy woodland trail made dangerous by mud and ice, overhanging branches, and sudden turns.

Dash knew that if his old riding instructor, the King's own horsemaster, could see what he was doing, he'd be shouting at the top of his lungs, telling Dash to slow down. Dash knew his race across treacherous footing was unbelievably dangerous and foolhardy.

He couldn't spare a glance back to see how close his pursuers might be, but the noise behind him told him all he needed to know: they were close. It would take a stroke of luck for him to lose them. He knew that to them he was a dimly-seen figure on a horse moving through the long shadows of the woodlands, but as long as he stayed on the trail, they would be able to stay close and not lose him.

He had a rough idea where he was. There were a dozen or more woodland trails to the east of Krondor that led to farms throughout the area. He knew that eventually—if he outran his pursuers—he'd hit the King's Highway. A horse's scream and a panic-stricken rider's cry told Dash that one of his pursuers' mounts had lost footing and was down, probably breaking a leg.

Dash glanced to the left and saw the trees thinning as he reached a clutch of farms, open fields that were dotted with burned-out buildings. He hesitated for a moment, but to try to ride across muddy fields would be far worse than staying on the trail. Here the mud was a nuisance, slippery muck over hardpan compacted by years of wagons, riders, and foot traffic. The mud in the fields was deep enough for an adult horse to sink up to the point where it would be unable to move.

The horse labored as Dash pushed her along the trail; lack of grain and fodder had shortened her endurance and she was blowing hard as she struggled to obey his commands. Then he saw a stone path, and a glimmer of hope appeared.

He almost caused her to fall, so abruptly did he pull the

mare around, but once she got her feet back under her, she sped off in the desired direction. Dash said a silent prayer to Ruthia, Goddess of Luck, and gathered his horse under him for a jump. The fence along the road was mostly broken down, but he needed to land on a relatively narrow pathway that was blocked by one of the few remaining intact sections and a closed gate.

The horse was tired, but athletic enough to easily clear the fence, landing on the wet stones. The reassuring clatter of hooves on stone told Dash that Ruthia at least didn't say "no."

He stole a glance to his left and saw several of the riders attempt to cut him off by veering into the muddy field. He smiled to himself.

Making sure the horse was heading exactly where he wanted, he chanced another look back and saw that the horses in the field were now half buried, attempting to pull their hooves out of the deep, thick muck.

Dash gained precious seconds as the riders who followed on the road chose to double back and work their way around the intact fence. He now had a chance.

The sun was now out of sight behind the trees ahead, as the long shadows of late afternoon crept across the fields. He rode past a burned-out farmhouse and saw the stone path he was on passed the door and continued on toward the foundation of a burned-out barn. He continued to ride, but slowed as he reached the terminus of the path.

Dash could only spare a moment to let the horse rest, as curses from behind told him those trying to reach him were now also mired in the mud. Dash judged the way to his right was more substantial footing than elsewhere—at least he hoped that was the case, and set off, letting his horse move at a trot until she slowed down due to the mud.

The sound of the mare's hooves hitting tightly compacted sand caused Dash to feel a surge of hope. It was quickly extinguished when he heard riders coming hard behind on the stone path.

The trees were close enough to give the illusion of safety, but Dash knew that if he couldn't get into them at least a minute ahead of the riders behind him, he wouldn't be able to shake them.

He urged his mare on to a loping canter and glanced back. The riders were just now reaching the edge of the farmhouse, and again hope rose up within Dash. Their horses were lathered and their nostrils were flaring wide. They were almost as exhausted as his own. They must have been at the end of their patrol, or they weren't getting enough to eat, but for whatever reason, they didn't look as if they had enough left to overtake him—as long as he could keep his own exhausted mare moving.

He reached the treeline and ducked under a low-hanging branch. As quickly as he could, he picked his way among the trees, varying his course and trying to keep clear of those behind. He hoped there were no trackers behind, but then, considering the terrain, realized a blind man could follow his trail.

Glancing around he saw a small outcropping of rock that rose up a slight incline and appeared to be flat on top. He turned the horse and walked her up the rise, and found the rock ran off along what appeared to be a smaller trail. He jumped off and led her down the trail.

Exhaustion was curbing her desire to call to the stallion, as she could barely catch enough breath to walk after Dash. He pulled her reins and she reluctantly set out at a fast walk behind him.

Shadows deepened as the sun lowered in the west, and Dash moved deeper into the woods. If Jimmy and Malar had stayed clear of pursuit, they would be approaching the city several miles to the south. Dash wondered if he should attempt to cut back behind his pursuers and try to find his brother and the stranger from the Vale of Dreams.

Dash considered the best that would bring him would be to get him haplessly lost. There couldn't be so many people in Krondor that if both brothers reached there safely, they couldn't find one another. At least Dash hoped that was true. Hearing the riders coming closer to the point where he had left the trail below, Dash hurried deeper into the woods.

Jimmy gripped Malar's arm and said, "We join there." He indicated a point in the road where a fairly steady stream of travelers had been coming past the woodlands, at the edge of what had once been the foulbourgh outside the walls of Krondor. "I'm a mercenary from Landreth and you're my servant."

"Dog robber," said Malar.

"What?"

"The term is 'dog robber.' To feed his master, a mercenary's servant will steal scraps from a dog if necessary." The slender man smiled. "I have served as such. You, though, will be obviously false to any Valeman who might happen to be here."

"You think that likely?"

"It would be better should you be a young man from the East of the Kingdom, who lately served in the Vale. Claim no company. Say you worked for my departed master. I do not know what you expected to find in Krondor, young sir, but in the backwashes of war many things happen. We are seeing that ahead."

Jimmy was forced to admit that was true. Where he had seen nothing but frost-covered stones and a few fires just weeks before, now he saw dozens of huts and tents, a veritable community springing up almost overnight. As they walked down the road, Malar leading Jimmy's horse, Jimmy drank in the sights and sounds.

Evening was upon them and fires dotted the landscape. Hawkers shouted from ahead, offering food, drink, the company of a woman. Hard-looking men lounged near fires, watching guardedly as Jimmy and Malar moved past.

A man hurried over holding a steaming pot, and said, "Hot food! Fresh rabbit stew! I have carrots and turnips mixed in!"

From the expressions on the faces of those nearby, Jimmy surmised two things: the "rabbit" was probably a less wholesome dinner item than advertised, and most of the people nearby were hungry.

But some sort of order had been imposed, and armed men who seemed near to the point of killing for food merely watched with fixed expressions as the man passed holding out the meal. "How much?" asked Jimmy, not pausing.

"What have you?" asked the peddler.

Malar elbowed Jimmy to one side. "Begone, O stewer

of cats! My master has no use for such foul-smelling garbage,'' he shouted.

Instantly the two men were almost nose to nose, screaming insults at one another, and almost equally abruptly a
deal had been struck. Malar gave the man a copper coin, a
ball of yarn he had been carrying in his pocket, and a very
old rusty dagger.

The man gave over the pot and hurried back to his campfire where a woman offered him another crock of the hot
stew. He set out to find another customer. Malar motioned
for Jimmy to move to the side of the road and squatted,
holding the crockery. He held it out and spoke softly, ''Eat
first and give me what's left.''

Jimmy squatted, not wishing to sit in the mud, and ate
the stew. If it was rabbit, it had been a rabbit of diminutive
stature, and even the carrots and turnips had a strange taste.
Jimmy decided it best not to consider how long they had
sat in some abandoned root cellar before that enterprising
peddler had found them.

He ate half the contents of the bowl and gave the rest
over to Malar. While his newfound servant ate, Jimmy
looked around. He had seen enough military camps to recognize he had blundered into one. Warriors, camp followers, peddlers and thieves, all resting until they had a reason
to move on.

Jimmy wondered about the reason for the gathering, and
the reason that would make them move on. Many of the
warriors were from the invading army that had ravaged the
Western Realm the year before, but he saw enough Keshians and a few Quegans mixed in to decide that these were
deserters, opportunists, weapons runners, and the dregs
washed up in any backwater of a war.

Putting aside the bowl, Malar looked at Jimmy. ''Young
sir?''

''Let's head into the city,'' said Jimmy.

''And do what?'' inquired the Valeman.

''Look for my brother.''

''I thought he was to go back east,'' said Malar.

''That's what he should do, but he won't.''

''Why?''

''Because he's . . . Dash.''

They moved through the tent village and headed toward
the city gate.

Three

Confrontations

P UG FROWNED.

The Keshian Ambassador's smile was forced, almost painful, as he finished his latest message from his government.

"My Lord Gadesh," said the Kingdom's representative, Baron Marcel d'Greu, his own smile just as false. "That's impossible."

Pug glanced at Nakor, who sat to his right. The latest round of negotiations between the Kingdom and the Empire of Great Kesh was proving to be a simple restatement of the last round.

Nakor shook his head and said, "Why don't we take a small recess, my lords, and give ourselves time to ponder these requests?"

Kalari, a Tsurani Black Robe who was representing his government, the Empire of Tsuranuanni, as a neutral observer, said, "Excellent idea, my friend."

The two ambassadors retired to the quarters that had been provided to them, and Pug led Nakor and Kalari to another room, where Miranda waited next to Kalied, the leader of the most powerful of the three factions of magicians in Stardock.

Kalied appeared to be older than Pug, despite the fact

Pug was nearly twenty years his senior. Pug appeared to be a man in his mid-twenties, his rejuvenation courtesy of the freed life energies that had been trapped in the Life-stone.

Miranda, looking like a woman in her mid-twenties, smiled at her husband. "Any joy?"

"None," said Pug, taking a mug of ale offered by a student who was acting as servant to those representing the interests of Stardock in the negotiations between the King-dom and the Empire of Great Kesh.

"I must confess," observed Kalari, "these negotiations seem far more ritualistic than I anticipated." He sipped at a hot cup of coffee and nodded in appreciation at the flavor of the brew. He was a bald-headed man of middle age, still slender and fit and possessing a penetrating pair of blue eyes. "Is it my unfamiliarity with the nuances of the King's Tongue, or some lack of insight into the Keshian culture, or is this simply a restating of previous claims and de-mands?"

"No," said Nakor, "there is nothing wrong with your appreciation of this situation."

"Then what is the point?" asked Kalari. "My own Empire's traditions include negotiations, but usually it's be-tween Tsurani Lords. I'm afraid your notion of diplomacy is a little foreign to me."

Kalari had been sent by the Assembly of Magicians on Kelewan, to insure that whatever interests Tsuranuanni had in Stardock were represented. Trading between the former enemies, the Kingdom of the Isles and the Empire of Tsur-anuanni, had been cyclical over the years. For nearly fifty years a major upheaval in Tsurani society had resulted from the rise to prominence of House Acoma and their innova-tive leader, the Lady Mara, the Servant of the Empire. Her son, Justin, had ruled the Empire despite several political plots to return the Empire to the older traditions Mara had set aside. Turmoil had resulted from many of the changes, at various times limiting trade between the two worlds to a trickle, but currently a stable period had endured almost ten years, and the Empire wished to see nothing disrupt their commerce with Midkemia.

Pug said, "Well, if you consider us to be Thuril, but

with more swords, you might consider the needs we face.''

Kalari nodded. Thuril had been the only nation to resist his empire on the homeworld, and had forced the Empire to a guarded peace. ''Well, since the Servant of the Empire overturned so many of the Assembly's prerogatives, we've had to constantly relearn things. I think endless babble around a table to no point, though, may be a difficult process to master.''

Nakor laughed. ''Actually, it's really easy. That's why diplomats do it so much.''

Kalari regarded the strange fellow. Nakor had been given his seat at the negotiations by Pug. Known as Milamber on the Tsurani homeworld, Pug was a figure of legend, almost as awe-inspiring as the Lady Mara. That fact alone had blunted some of the Tsurani Great One's astonishment at Nakor being included in these sessions. To all outward appearances, the self-styled ''High Priest'' of some unknown order was nothing more than a ragged vagabond, perhaps a confidence trickster who played the fool. Yet there was something about the odd little man that made Kalari cautious of judging him too quickly. Behind his constant irreverent humor an intellect of great scope was at work, and every fiber of Kalari's being told him a man of great magical ability also wore the guise of a common gambler recently turned man of religion. He might claim powers that came from the Gods, or merely ''tricks'' as he often commented, but Kalari sensed this was a being of power second only to Pug's at the table.

Kalari put aside his nagging suspicions about Nakor. Whatever else, he did find the man from the nation of Isalan in Great Kesh amusing and amiable. ''Well, then,'' said the magician, ''you'll have to brief me on how best to proceed with this pointless wrangling.''

Nakor said, ''Find someone else. I think them just as tedious as you do.'' Nakor took a sip of ale. ''Besides, the matter of how things end up has already been decided.''

''Really?'' said Pug. ''Care to share with us your reasoning?''

Nakor grinned, as he always did when about to share the gift of his perceptions and insights with the others. ''It's easy.'' He pointed around the room. ''You could figure this out, too, if you tried." Miranda exchanged wry smiles with her husband. Nakor continued, "The Kingdom was hurt, but not fatally. Kesh knows this. They have spies. They know that while the King wants troops back in the East, it's not because there's any real trouble there. If Kesh makes trouble, the King orders the Prince to keep the soldiers. And if Kesh waits until the Armies of the East leave, that gives Patrick more time to dig in, get ready, and deal with any Keshian adventures."

Nakor shook his head. "No, Kesh knows that they lost what the Kingdom gave them when they tried to press their advantage. They know the best they can do is maybe some trade concession or another, but they'll never get back what they were granted for protecting the Kingdom's southern flank." He glanced from face to face. "They're trying to figure out how to admit publicly they were stupid without admitting they were stupid."

Kalari laughed. Even the usually taciturn Kalied was forced to smile. Pug said, "So it's a matter of honor?"

Nakor shrugged. "More a matter of avoiding punishment back home. Generals Rufi ibn Salamon and Behan Solan have much explaining to do to their Emperor when they return to the City of Kesh. They've got to be given a really good story to explain how they lost by getting greedy what they had gained by the Emperor being generous. You know they had no authority from Kesh to try to grab all of the vale, don't you?"

Pug fixed Nakor with a narrow gaze. "And how do you know that?" asked Pug.

Nakor said, "I move around. I listen to things. Generals may keep their mouths shut, but soldiers talk. Soldiers serve in the General's tent, then they talk to traders and camp girls, and the traders and camp girls talk to wagon drivers, and pretty soon everyone knows what the General's doing.

"Kesh doesn't want a war, even if the Kingdom is weak. They've never fully pacified the southern nations below the Girdle of Kesh. The Keshian Confederacy would rise up again at any excuse, and your King knows this. So, the Empire doesn't want war, and the Kingdom doesn't want another war—they're busy with the one they have now—and we all sit around while the outcome is already known."

"Save one thing," said Pug.

Nakor said, "Stardock."

Kalied said, "That matter is settled."

Pug shrugged. "I know it is. I told Nakor to make whatever deal necessary to get you to help save the Kingdom; the threat of you acting against Kesh if they turned aggressor tipped the balance in our favor. But there's still the matter of explaining to the King how I managed to give away one of his duchies."

Kalied said, "I am dining with the members of the council. As Robert de Lyes has decided to continue serving in Darkmoor with the Prince, we need to replace him on the council." He rose and said, "But keep in mind, Pug, despite your legendary power and our abiding respect for what you founded here, Stardock is no longer your personal fiefdom. We have Nakor's pledge that you would honor the arrangements he made to gain the Kingdom our aid. The council now governs, not on your behalf while you're off somewhere, but on behalf of all those who reside here. You are entitled to no more or less a voice than any other member of the Academy."

Pug was silent for a moment, then said, "Very well. I will honor that pledge and insure the Kingdom acknowledges your autonomy."

"Autonomy?" said Kalied. "That's an interesting choice of words. We prefer to think of it as independence."

Nakor waved away the remark. "Don't be stupid. Pug can convince the King to let you govern yourself, but don't expect him to make the King accept the proposition of an independent entity located entirely within the boundaries of the Kingdom. Besides, while you protect the Kingdom from Kesh, the Kingdom also protects you from Kesh. Do you think for a moment the Emperor would be as generous?"

Kalied said nothing for a long moment, then said, "Very well. I will present this to the council, and I am sure they will choose not to be 'stupid' in this matter." With a dark look directed at Nakor, he bowed to the others in the room and departed.

Kalari turned to Nakor and said, "I assume your earlier comments on diplomacy are more in the theoretical area rather than from practice?"

Miranda laughed. Pug joined in. "Well, I still have a lot to explain to the Prince, and I think there's no putting that off. I suspect that Patrick will be even less enchanted with the idea of an autonomous Stardock within his borders than Kalied."

Miranda said, "We go to Darkmoor?"

Pug nodded. "Nakor?"

Nakor nodded. "I'm done here. The Blue Riders are again ensconced among the students, to make sure magicians who train here don't get too stuffy. Besides, I need to spend some time with Dominic and some of the other Ishapians who have ended up next to the Prince. Let me fetch Sho Pi, and we'll all go together."

He left, and Kalari said, "Pug, a question."

Pug turned to regard the Tsurani Great One.

"Since coming to Stardock on behalf of the Emperor, I've pieced together a view of how things stood here. I'm curious as to why you, yourself, didn't come to the Assembly and seek our aid in dealing with the threats from this Emerald Queen." He lowered his voice. "I'm not sure what fully transpired here, but I get the strong impression that a great deal more was at stake than most people understand."

Miranda and Pug exchanged glances, and Pug said, "Yes, but I am not free to share details.

"As for why we didn't seek Tsurani aid, our relationships with the Empire have never been the same since Makala."

Kalari said, "Ah," and nodded in understanding. A Tsurani Great One, Makala had come to the Prince of Krondor's court years before, ostensibly to act as a liaison between the Assembly on Kelewan and the Prince, but in fact had come as a self-appointed spy determined to discover the secret of what truly happened at Sethanon at the end of the Riftwar.

He had been motivated by loyalty to the Empire and the fear of some Kingdom plot or weapon of great power, and had actually discovered the secret of the Lifestone. Through agents who chanced upon one another near Sethanon, he had become a party to a conspiracy involving the Brotherhood of the Dark Path. Only the intervention of a renegade moredhel chieftain had prevented a major catastrophe.

Makala and four of his allies from the Tsurani homeworld had ensorceled the great dragon oracle that lived below the city of Sethanon, and were on the verge of
unlocking the Lifestone when Pug and his companions had
arrived. That secret had died with Makala and his four companions, deep in the chamber below the city. His betrayal
of the trust given him had strained relationships between
the Kingdom and Empire for a decade. Only members of
the Assembly on Kelewan and a few trusted advisors to the
Prince of Krondor knew of the incident; it served as a cau-
tionary tale on both sides of the rift. Since then, all business
between the Empire of Tsuranuanni and the Kingdom of
the Isles had been conducted in the most formal, cautious
of fashions. More than once it had been suggested that the
rift between the worlds be permanently closed, yet trading
between them continued. But it was now limited to the one
rift located on Stardock, hence the Empire's presence at
these negotiations. They were anxious that this one passage
between the worlds be kept open.

"Yet," said Kalari, "it seemed prudent to you to request
our help in that display of might we arranged for the Keshians?"

Pug shook his head and shrugged. "Nakor."

Kalari returned the smile. "He is the *most* unusual fellow."

Pug agreed.

Miranda said, "What will you tell Patrick?"

Pug let out a long, tired sigh. "Many things; none of
which he will enjoy hearing."

Prince Patrick appeared on the verge of rage. His normally light complexion reddened and his voice rose. "Autonomous? What is that supposed to mean?" he shouted.

Pug sighed. Unlike his predecessor, Prince Arutha, Patrick lacked vision. Pug reminded himself that in most ways
the Prince was a young man, and unlike Prince Arutha, who
had leadership thrust upon him, a young man untempered
in the cauldron of war. While his city had been destroyed,
Patrick had been safe in the East, at the King's insistence.
Pug suspected much of Patrick's ill humor came from frus-

tration and his inability to do other than his father's bidding.

With even tones, Pug said, "The magicians at Stardock require—"

"Require!" shouted Patrick. "They *require*?" He stood up from his throne, formerly the state chair of the Baron of Darkmoor, and took a step down to stand directly before Pug. "Let me tell you what their King requires. He requires their unswerving loyalty and *obedience*!"

Pug looked at his grandson, the Duke Arutha, who gave his head a slight shake, indicating there was little use in talking to the Prince when he was in a rage. Pug didn't care. He was three times the Prince's age and had seen more than most men did in a dozen lifetimes and he was tired. "Patrick," he said evenly. "Sometimes you lose."

"These are our citizens! They live within the borders of the Kingdom."

Nakor, who had been silently standing to one side with his student, Sho Pi, said, "Only if the old borders are still there, Highness."

Patrick's head came around and he said, "Who gave you leave to talk, Keshian?"

Nakor returned an insolent grin. "Your King, many years ago, if you remember? And I am Isalani."

Wearying of the scene, Pug said, "Patrick, what's done is done. It's an unhappy solution, but at least it's a solution. You can't deal with the invaders to the west, Kesh to the south, and the magicians at Stardock. You must start somewhere; Stardock is the easiest. With the community there guaranteed their autonomy, Kesh will have to remove itself back to the old border. That's two problems solved. Then you can reclaim the West."

Patrick said nothing, forcing himself to calm down. "I do not like it."

Nakor said, "The King won't like it much either, but he'll understand. Prince Erland spent time in Kesh. He saved the Emperor and knows the Empress well. Very well," he added with a grin. "Erland will go down and visit again and soon things will be back to normal along this border."

"Except I'll have lost Stardock."

Pug said, "You'll lose a great deal more unless you agree." He looked the young prince squarely in the eyes. "Sometimes ruling is hard choices, between bad and worse. Agree that Stardock can rule itself, and you defeat Kesh."

Pug's wording made the young Prince pause. After a moment he spoke. "Very well. Prepare documents, my lord duke," he said, using Pug's formal rank as Duke of Stardock. "It is your duchy we're losing. I'm sure Father will have another office or something for you. After all, he did explain you were some sort of royal cousin and need to be treated as such."

Pug glanced at his wife. She returned a slight shrug. He was young, she seemed to say in agreement with his own thoughts. Pug started to turn away, but Patrick continued to speak. "I think, though, that you'd best explain directly to the King what is at hand here."

Pug turned back to face Patrick. "You wish me to prepare a report for the King."

Patrick's expression showed his temper was still getting the better of him. "No, I wish you to use whatever magic arts you have to take yourself to Rillanon. In fact, I command you to do so, *my lord duke*! Perhaps being wiser than I, the King can discern how this isn't some sort of treason." He glanced at Miranda. "If your *wife* isn't an agent of the Empire, I'll be astounded."

Pug's eyes narrowed and he remained silent.

"You'll need to demonstrate that loyalty I currently find lacking, magician, if you're to regain this court's favor."

"Demonstrate?" said Pug softly. "I have labored to my utmost to prevent the destruction of all we hold dear."

Patrick said, "I've read the reports. I've heard the tales. Demons and spawn of the lower hells. Yes, magic to warp the world to darkness, and all the rest of it."

Arutha looked from one man to the other, saying, "Highness! Grandfather, please! We have much to do and contention in our ranks does us no good."

Pug looked at his grandson, and slowly he said, "I am not attempting to contend, Arutha. My only purpose has been, from the first, to serve."

He stepped forward and his voice was filled with menace. "If you command, my prince, I will obey. I will take the time to visit with the King. If you are not satisfied with my performance in recent months, perhaps he will be persuaded that the price I paid demonstrates my commitment.''

''Perhaps!'' said Patrick. He spat hot words. ''You gave away a duchy that by all reports you have neglected, and I have a city lying in ruins, as well as my entire Principality to the west in thrall to hostile forces. Who between us has lost the most?''

Pug's throat burned as color rose in his cheeks. In a hoarse whisper he said, ''Lost? You *dare* speak to me of loss?'' Stepping up so that he was mere inches from the Prince, Pug looked up at the taller, younger man. ''I lost nearly *everything*, you child! I lost a son and a daughter, and the man she loved who was as another son to me. William, Gamina, and James gave their lives for Krondor and the Kingdom. You sit this throne for a few years, Patrick. When you've lived as long as I have, should you be that fortunate, remember what you said here.''

Patrick appeared embarrassed as he realized he had overlooked the death of Pug's family in the war. Still, his temper got the best of him, and as Pug turned to walk away, Patrick's voice thundered, ''I will not be addressed in that manner, magician! Duke or not, royal cousin or not, you will come back here and beg my pardon!''

Pug spun. Before he could speak, Arutha turned and stood directly before his Prince. ''Highness!'' He put a restraining hand on Patrick's shoulder. In a whisper he said, ''This brings nothing good! Calm yourself and we'll revisit this tomorrow.'' Whispering, he added, ''Patrick, your father will not be pleased at this.''

Before the Prince could speak, Arutha turned and said, ''Grandfather. If you and your lady would dine with me tonight, we can discuss exactly what sort of communication with the crown shall be undertaken.'' To the remaining courtiers in the hall, he said, ''That will be all today. This court is adjourned.''

He hustled Patrick through a door to the apartment set aside for him during his stay in Darkmoor, not allowing the Prince to further inflame the situation. Pug turned to Miranda, who said, ''That boy needs some training.''

Pug said nothing, merely offering his arm to his wife and

leading her to the rooms put aside for them. He knew his grandson would come to see them as soon as the Prince had been placated.

Arutha looked like a man aged years in a few hours. His eyes, normally bright and alert, were now deeply sunk with dark circles under them. He sighed and nodded thanks as Miranda handed him a goblet of wine.

"The Prince?" asked Pug.

Arutha shrugged. "It's difficult. During the war he seemed content to follow Father and Uncle William's lead. The preparations for the city were underway by the time he arrived in Krondor, and he simply agreed to whatever Father wanted.

"Now, he's out of his element. He is being asked to make decisions that would have taxed the wits of the best generals in this Kingdom's history." He sipped his wine. "Partly it's my fault."

Pug shook his head. "No, Patrick is responsible for his own actions."

"But Father would have—"

Pug interrupted. "You are not your father." He let out a slow sigh. "No one is James. James was unique. As was Prince Arutha. The Western Realm may never again see men as able as them gathered together at one time." Pug grew reflective. "It all began with Lord Borric. I have never known a man his equal. Arutha was his equal in many ways, perhaps his superior in some, but on the whole, Borric raised two sons the Kingdom needed.

"But from there we are seeing a diminution of the line. King Borric was seasoned in his travels to Kesh, but nothing like his father the Prince." Pug looked out a window at the distant torchlight along the palisades of the castle. "Perhaps it's just the years passing, the ability to think back with history's perspective, but at the time of the Rift-war there was a sense in the West that eventually we should prevail. Now I realize that came from Prince Arutha, your father at his brashest and most reckless, others who led and those who followed."

Looking at his grandson, Pug said, "You must step forward, Arutha. You will never be the man for whom you were named, and you will never be your father, but nature didn't intend for you to be either of those men, no matter how worthy they were. You must become the best man you are capable of. I know the war took as much a toll on you as it did me. You alone of all those here know what I feel. Men like Owen Greylock and Erik von Darkmoor must rise to meet the needs of the nation.'' He smiled as he added, ''You are more capable than you think. You will be a fine Duke of Krondor.''

Arutha nodded. His mother, Gamina, was Pug's daughter by adoption, but he had loved and treasured her as much as he had his son, William. To lose them both within days of one another had been terrible. ''I know that it was worse for you, Grandfather. I mourn my parents. You mourn your children.''

Pug said nothing, swallowing hard and gripping Miranda's hand. Since the end of the war he had been revisited time and again by a wave of profound sorrow and pain, and as much as he hoped for the sense of loss to pass, it didn't. It grew muted at times, even forgotten for hours at a stretch, but in any quiet, reflective moment, it returned.

Even his marriage to Miranda had been hastily conducted, as if any delay might steal moments away from them. Pug and his new wife had spent as much time together as possible, dealing with the revelations of their past lives and the need to discuss their future. Yet every moment together, no matter how joyous, was overshadowed by the sense of loss, the sense of work yet undone, and the sense that nothing could ever return to them that which was lost.

Pug nodded at his grandson's words. He sighed. ''Arutha, you and I have never had the opportunity to be close. After my first wife's death I distanced myself from your mother. Watching her grow old was a fate I tried to avoid.'' He looked deep into his grandson's eyes. ''There is much of both your parents in you. I know your father trained you from birth to serve, and your life was never your own, but I also know he would have found a less demanding role for you had he found you lacking; you would not be allowed to follow after him had you been less a man than what you are. So, again I say, you must step forward. Patrick may prove a worthy ruler someday, but that day is not here yet. And it has often been our history that one in the role of advisor limited the choices placed before the rulers.'' Remembering the rule of mad King Roderic, Pug said, ''Perhaps we could have used more of such men in the past.''

Arutha said, ''I'll try, Grandfather.''

Miranda said, ''I don't presume to advise, as I've never done well with obeying rulers in my day, but you'll have to do more than try before we're done.''

Arutha looked as if he was ready to wilt. ''I know.''

A servant announced supper was ready, and they adjourned to the next room. As Pug preceded his grandson, he knew one of the reasons Arutha was so fatigued: from worry over the whereabouts of his own sons.

Jimmy looked around. A series of patrols had been coming through the area for the last two days. They had tried to enter the city and discovered that no one was being allowed through the established checkpoints. Whoever was in charge inside Krondor, General Duko or someone else, had decided that Kingdom infiltration was a serious threat and had sealed the city.

Those mercenaries and traders who had gathered outside the city walls were not troubled, as long as they didn't cause trouble. A brawl had erupted the night before at a large bonfire some distance away, over a gambling debt, woman, or insult, Jimmy didn't know, but it had quickly been quelled by a detachment of warriors from the city who rode out and scattered everyone in sight. There had been nothing gentle or orderly about it, a simple raid to disperse, conducted with speed and efficiency. A half dozen men lay dead, while others were moaning and nursing injuries as the strike force returned to the city, but order had been restored. Most of the men outside the walls had come for booty, the opportunity to loot, or to gain steady pay, not to storm a well-fortified city.

Jimmy had judged the city fairly easy to retake should Patrick and his army be sitting outside the walls, but they weren't. They were in Darkmoor or en route, and by the time they reached Krondor, the fortifications would be reaching daunting proportions. Workers—freemen or prisoners, Jimmy didn't know which—were up each day at dawn, repairing the damage from the final assault on the city the previous summer.

He had chanced a leisurely ride past the main eastern gates, and saw that they had been successfully replaced. While not as grand as the originals, the new gates looked stout and well crafted. Accomplished carpenters were among those working for the invaders, as most every man of fighting age on the distant continent of Novindus had been pressed into the army.

It was nearly sundown on their second day when Malar asked, "Young sir, are we to find a safe place to sleep?"

Jimmy shook his head. "I think I've seen enough outside. It's time to go inside the city."

"Forgive my ignorance, but if each gate and breach is manned in the fashion we have observed so far, how do you propose to do this thing?"

Jimmy said, "There are more ways in and out of Krondor than are apparent. My grandfather knew them all, and he made sure Dash and I knew of every one of them before we left."

"Is your brother likely to find a similar entrance?"

He motioned for his "servant" to follow him, and they walked slowly past a group of sullen-looking fighting men, getting ready to settle in for another cold night around a campfire with little food or prospects. "Knowing Dash, he's already in the city."

Dash sat with his back against the dirty stone wall. The other prisoners did likewise. Men crowded together on both sides, but he didn't object; the weather was still cold and his captors spared no fuel to keep the slave pen heated. He wore only his undershirt and trousers. His boots, jacket, cloak, and all the other possessions he had carried were taken from him.

He had managed to evade the patrol that had followed him and had ridden to the edge of Krondor. There he had found a thriving community of traders, thieves, camp followers, and others assembled outside the gates of the city. The invaders had closed the city to anyone not among their own forces and an odd truce existed along the eastern wall.

With many breaches in the walls, the peace was kept by
patrols riding among those gathered outside the walls: a
mix of Kingdom deserters, displaced farmers, workers, and
mercenaries looking for employment. Among the invaders
and Kingdom soldiers no small number of Keshians, Quegans, and fighters from the Free Cities of Natal were in
evidence.

Dash had made the mistake of attempting to sneak into
Krondor. If a man could enjoy freedom outside the walls,
inside the walls only those who had served in General
Duko's army were freemen. He had managed to stay out
of sight for a day, but had run into a patrol and while being
chased had ducked into a seemingly empty building which
in reality had housed a half-dozen armed soldiers who were
off-watch. They held him until the patrol caught up and,
without even asking his reasons for being in the city, had
beaten, robbed, then incarcerated him.

That had been three days before. Dash was letting his
bruised and aching body recover; he had no doubt that
given half a chance he could escape, and this time he
wouldn't make the mistake of thinking the city was deserted. It wasn't. In fact, it was turning into something far
more lively than he would have thought from Jimmy's report.

He had spent two days working on restoring a fortification on the north wall. He had tried to overhear the guards'
gossip, but the fact was he could barely understand them.
His brother had the gift for language. Dash could speak
passable Keshian and Roldem, after having both languages
drilled into him as a boy in the King's court in Rillanon.

But he had barely been exposed to the Quegan, Natalese,
and Yabonese dialects which, although descended from
Keshian, were almost other languages to his ear. And this
common tongue of Novindus was even more removed from
Kesh than those.

Still, he was able to judge that something odd was happening or about to happen. The soldiers on patrol and those
inside the city seemed as concerned about what was taking
place to the north as they were concerned about what might
be coming from the east.

"Time to go," said a voice next to Dash.

Dash nodded to the man as he stood. The man was named Gustaf Tinker, though his last name suggested a grandfather's trade, for he had been a mercenary soldier from the Vale of Dreams. Dash had found out the first night that most of the prisoners were hapless locals, townspeople, fishermen, and farmers from nearby. Gustaf was something of an oddity, as the Kingdom soldiers had been segregated from the other prisoners. They didn't get worked, but they weren't executed either. Dash had no idea what General Duko thought he might do with them; use them for hostages, perhaps. But as a result of the segregation, Gustaf and perhaps one or two others among the fifty or so men herded nightly into a room designed for a half dozen might prove useful allies when Dash made his break for freedom.

Another of the men, Talwin, was almost certainly a thief, but Dash had avoided too much conversation with him. Once into the sewers of the city, a local thief might prove a useful guide, but as long as they shared a cell together, Talwin would just as likely turn Dash in to the guards as a Kingdom spy as not for an extra ration.

The door opened and the men gratefully left the cramped room and shuffled out into the hallway. They were housed in a half-burned tannery in the North Quarter of the city. Most of the rank-smelling businesses—slaughterhouses, dyers, fish mongers, among others—were clustered here, so the area provided two benefits to invaders: large relatively undamaged buildings, and a close proximity to an area of the wall which badly needed repair. In the East Quarter, Dash suspected the workers were being housed in abandoned stables and sheds.

The guard motioned and the first man in line moved out of the hall, into the cold morning light. As Dash came out into the light, he blinked, and was startled to discover the almost ever-present cloud cover had moved inland. The day promised to be warm, which was a mixed blessing. During the day he barely felt the cold, given the amount of work he was required to do, but at least the next night might be more forgiving.

He followed along and waited until the boy who took care of food and water appeared, and as anxious as his companions, he grabbed the single slab of bread offered. It was a coarse and unappetizing meal; the grain was so ill-ground that men had been known to break teeth on husks or small pieces of gravel. The water ration had been cut with a small amount of wine. Some men had come down with the belly flux a day or two before Dash's capture, and the invaders were certain a little wine kept it from spreading.

All too quickly the morning meal was over, and they were off to work. Dash joined four other men attempting to move a large wall stone that had fallen during the battle of Krondor. They were to get it over to a makeshift crane, built by an invading engineer more adept at engines of war than civil engineering. Yet Dash had seen the wooden contraption lift larger stones several times in the last two days and he was certain that it would continue to serve for a while.

Why was there so much urgency in the rebuilding of Krondor? For Duko to deny the city to Patrick made sense. For Duko to attempt to hold it for any length of time made little sense. Dash smelled a mystery, and as much as he wanted to escape, he also wanted to discover what exactly was taking place around here before doing so.

A man grunted and the stone was lifted; quickly a net was pulled under. Dash used the moment gained while the other men tied off the net to the crane to turn to Gustaf and ask, "You anxious to stick around?"

The soldier, a quiet man of middle build, showed the slight smile which was his most dramatic expression, and said, "Of course. There's such an opportunity for advancement."

Dash said, "Yes. Another dozen deaths and you'll be first in line for bread and water in the morning."

"What do you have in mind?" whispered Gustaf.

Noticing they were being watched by Talwin, Dash said, "I'll tell you later."

Gustaf nodded and made no comment as the crew moved over to repeat their labors with another large stone.

Four

Underground

Dash FLINCHED.

The wind had turned cold again after the previous day's springlike warmth and he was still sporting many bruises, which seemed to sting more when the cold hit them. Still, the exercise seemed to be keeping him from getting stiff. He hadn't had the opportunity to talk to Gustaf again since he had mentioned the possibility of escape. Talwin had taken to staying close by, a turn of events which worried Dash. He could only guess at the man's motives; either he was also looking for escape and judged Dash and Gustaf likely allies in such a break, or he was an informer. Dash decided he could spend another day or two trying to discover which.

The guards shouted for the midday break, and the boys with the bread and watered wine hurried through the ranks, distributing their welcome fare. Dash sat down right where he worked, on the next large rock to be returned to the wall, while Gustaf sat with his back to the wall they were repairing. Dash took a bite and said, "Either I'm getting used to this or they've found a better baker."

Gustaf said, "You're getting used to it. Remember the old saying, 'Hunger is the best sauce.' "

Dash studied the warrior from the Vale of Dreams. At

first it had seemed his entire conversational repertoire consisted of head nods, grunts, and the occasional "yes" or "no." But since last night he had opened up a little to Dash.

"How'd you get caught here?"

"I wasn't," said Gustaf, finishing his meager meal. He sipped his watery wine and said, "I was a guard on a caravan . . ." He glanced around. "It's a long story. The short of it is we were intercepted and captured by Duko's men and those of us who lived through the fight ended up here."

"How long has it been?"

"Too damn long." He frowned. "Must be a couple of months now. The days blur. It was snowing when I got here."

Dash nodded. "Caravan?"

Gustaf shrugged. "My employer wasn't the only merchant to think he could steal a profit by being the first one bringing goods into the city. From what I've seen around here, this general isn't interested in trading much. He seems willing to let folks fend for themselves on the other side of the wall, but in here it's a military camp."

The order to resume work was passed down the line and Dash said, "I get that impression."

Gustaf smiled. "You're not as dumb as you look."

"Back to work!" shouted a guard, and the four men nearest Dash and Gustaf began moving the rock back into place in the wall.

Jimmy motioned with a slight tilt of his head. Malar nodded that he understood and signaled for the boy to come over. The urchin was filthy, covered from head to toe in soot and grime. He smelled as if he had been swimming in a cesspool, and Jimmy thought him a likely source of information.

Malar spoke with the boy for a few minutes, then gave him a coin, telling him to run off. He returned to where Jimmy leaned against the wall in a pose of indifference and said, "Young sir, the boy was, indeed, working in the sewers. They pay him to crawl into the smaller culverts and pipes, ridding them of burned wood, mud, and the like."

Jimmy shook his head slightly in irritation. "Damn. What are they doing down there?"

In a low voice, Malar said, "Apparently repairing the sewer, much as they seem to be repairing everything aboveground on the other side of the wall from all reports."

"But why?" asked Jimmy rhetorically. "The sewers are sufficient for his army. With a little work, he can keep them flowing enough so his men don't fall ill." Jimmy scratched an imaginary itch on the side of his face. "But from what we've heard, he's trying to put them back to the state they were in before—" He had been about to say before "Grandfather blew up the city," but changed it to "the city was taken."

"Perhaps this General Duko likes things orderly."

Jimmy shook his head in baffled silence. He had read every report that had reached Darkmoor on the enemy before and after the Battle of Nightmare Ridge.

Duko was probably their best field general, and third in importance after Fadawah and Nordan. Jimmy couldn't begin to guess what he was up to. Had he been fortifying the city for an attack from the east or south, that might have made some sense, though the defenses would still be less than ideal when Patrick's army arrived.

Had he continued to rip Krondor apart, adding to the destruction—to deny it to the Kingdom—would have made sense. But repairing the damage done, as if he was going to occupy the city for a long time, that made no sense.

"Unless . . ." said Jimmy softy.

"Young sir?" asked Malar.

"Never mind." He looked around. "It's going to be dark in the next hour. Come with me."

He led Malar through the busy streets in the tent city and toward an alley, really just a passage between freestanding walls, all that was left of two businesses. He ducked into the alley without waiting to see if he was being watched, and heard Malar follow.

It would be easy to become lost in Krondor, Jimmy knew from his last visit. With all the destruction, landmarks didn't exist. Yet the patterns were the same, and if one constantly remembered where one was relative to one of the few intact recognizable features in the city, it should be possible to find one's way. At least Jimmy hoped this was so.

He heard movement before he saw it, and ducked back, almost knocking Malar over. Someone walked along the abandoned street, coming closer. Jimmy and Malar hunkered down, fading into the darkness between the walls.

Shortly, a pair of armed men hurried by, upon what errand Jimmy could only guess. Jimmy waited, to see if they returned or if others followed. When no one else appeared after a few minutes, he moved across the road to a burned-out inn.

Hunkering down behind a section of still-standing wall, Jimmy whispered, "This inn has a way into the sewers. If it's not blocked, and if the sewers are still intact, we can get inside the city. Most of the sewer is cut off from out there to in there," he said pointing toward the city, "but there is an old collapsed wall of a cistern that we can wiggle through."

"Is that a good idea, young sir?" asked Malar. "From what we've heard it seems difficult to remain inside without being pressed into a work gang. At least that seems the general opinion."

"I don't plan on being seen," said Jimmy. "You're free to make your own way from here on, if you choose."

"Living by my wits is an old habit of mine, young sir, but I suspect you and your brother are my best opportunity to find something beyond that." He studied Jimmy for a moment, as if weighing risks against possible rewards, then said, "You and your brother are two men of some position, I suspect. If so, and if I serve you to a good ending, then perhaps I may salvage something from what has so far been a horrible turn of fate." He fell silent for a moment again, then said, "If you will have me in your service, I will go with you."

Jimmy half shrugged. "I guess that makes you my servant in fact, then. Tell you what you must do. Should anything happen to me, return as best you may to the East. Long before you reach the Kingdom Army you will almost certainly be apprehended by Kingdom advanced scouts. Probably Hadati hillmen or Krondorian Pathfinders. If it's Hadatis, see if there's a man named Akee with them. If

Pathfinders, ask for Captain Subati. Have either of those men take you to Owen Greylock or Eric von Darkmoor and tell them everything you've seen so far. Without a name, you'll be taken for a Keshian deserter or looter or something, and it might be a long time before anyone heard your story. And they must know what we've seen.''

"But what have we seen?" said Malar, genuinely perplexed.

"I'm not sure, which is why we must get inside the city. But whatever it is, it's not something we anticipated.''

"That's bad.''

Jimmy grinned. "Why do you say that?''

"Because the unanticipated is always bad.''

Jimmy's grin broadened. "Always?''

"Always. There is no such thing as a pleasant surprise.''

"I remember this girl once—''

"Did she end up breaking your heart?''

Jimmy nodded with a smile now rueful. "That she did.''

"You see. If you can anticipate, you can stay beyond harm's reach.''

"You sound like a man of experience," suggested Jimmy.

Malar's eyes narrowed. "More than most men know, young sir.''

Jimmy looked around. The shadows had deepened as the sun had lingered in the west, and now the sky above was turning a stunning shade of violet as night approached. "It's dark enough we won't be noticed, I'm thinking.'' He led Malar into the rear of the old inn, having to carefully pick his way across a section of timbers, what was left from a collapsed doorway and wall section, as well as part of the ceiling above. The roof was gone, and blackened timbers above showed starkly against the darkening sky. They moved cautiously, then Jimmy said, "It's around here somewhere.''

He knelt and looked around. He moved some smaller debris covered in thick soot, raising a stench of wet charcoal. "Some of the wood is rotting.''

Malar said, "There is a ring of iron there, young sir.''

"Give me a hand," said Jimmy as he cleared the top of the trapdoor.

As the two men pulled, Jimmy said, "This used to be the back room at an inn controlled by the Mockers."

"Mockers?"

"Thieves," said Jimmy. "I thought their fame reached into the vale."

"The only thieves with whom I had contact were those who used quill and parchment, not dagger and guile. Businessmen."

Jimmy laughed. "My brother would agree; he used to work for the worst of the lot, Rupert Avery."

"That's a name I have heard, young sir. My late master had cause to curse him more than once."

They got the trap moved and swung it back, letting it fall. The opening yawned at them like a black pit. Jimmy said, "I wish we had some light."

"You expect to travel in such gloom?" said Malar, a note of incredulity in his voice.

"There is no light on the brightest day down there." He found what he was looking for, the ladder down, and as he swung himself down onto the topmost rung, he said, "There are lights down there if one but knows where to look."

"If you know where to look," Malar muttered under his breath.

They carefully descended into the darkness.

Dash winced, but not from the cold; rather he flinched at the sound of a lash striking a man down below. He, Gustaf, Talwin, and a few other men he had come to know were laboring atop the wall just to the north of Krondor's main gate. Dash glanced over at Gustaf, who nodded, indicating everything was all right. Suddenly they both turned. A man screamed a few yards off as he lost his footing; in that brief instant, the man knew with dread certainty he was going to fall and no amount of will or prayer would keep him alive. His anguish and terror filled the afternoon air as he toppled sideways and fell to his death on the cobbles below. Gustaf flinched at the sound of the body striking the unyielding rock. They were repairing the battlements and the footing was treacherous, made doubly so by loose stones and constant fog in the mornings and evenings.

"Keep your wits about you," said Dash.

"You don't have to tell me that twice," said Gustaf.

Dash chanced a look over the wall and saw the usual confusion of the foulbourgh, soldiers milling around, street vendors, and the other human flotsam drawn into this eddy of the previous year's war. Somewhere out there, he fervently wished, his brother Jimmy was getting the information needed to alert Owen Greylock that something strange was taking place in Krondor.

Given the lack of resources, General Duko was doing an admirable job of restoring the city to its earlier status, at least from a military point of view. The merchants and other residents of Krondor would see years pass before the city came close to returning to its former prosperity. Too much damage had occurred for that to be anything but a distant dream. But from a soldier's point of view, Krondor would be close to its previous level of defensibility in less than a year's time, perhaps as quickly as nine or ten months.

Dash wished mightily he could get loose of this work gang, scout around, and find out what was going on, but the reality of the situation was that any man who wasn't an invader was a slave. Whatever Dash's father had been thinking, it would have made more sense to have sent along one of the men who had traveled to Novindus with Erik von Darkmoor, someone who spoke the language and had a fair chance of passing for one of the men from the continent across the sea.

Even if he got free, Dash knew his only hope was to get beyond the wall, blend into the populace there, and find his way to the East, where he was certain his father had other agents waiting for sight of either brother.

Dash was certain his father had sent other agents into the city, and throughout the surrounding countryside. It would be unlike him not to. Besides, thought Dash as he helped hoist a large rock up to the battlements, the ghost of Duke Arutha's father, Lord James, would haunt him if he didn't. As Dash bruised knuckles on the harsh stone and began putting mortar into place, he thought that his grandfather's ghost would be welcome about now. Certainly, if anyone could puzzle out what was happening in Krondor it would be the legendary Lord James.

Jimmy cursed in the darkness as he bruised his shins against an unexpected stone. "Is the young gentleman certain he hasn't lost his way?" came Malar's voice out of the blackness.

Jimmy said, "Keep quiet. It's certain we're not the only ones down here. And yes I know where we are," he said. "We turn right and another dozen paces on the right should be the place we're looking for." As if to prove the point, he turned to the right and moved into a small passage. Malar kept both hands on the right wall as he awkwardly followed.

After a few minutes they moved slowly through the gloom, then suddenly Jimmy said, "We're here."

"Where is here, sir?" asked Malar.

"One of the many hiding places for . . ." A sound of rustling, as if something was being moved, came from where Jimmy stood. Then Malar shielded his eyes as a small spark was struck, blindingly bright after the long time spent in the dark.

The torch was dry and caught at once, and Jimmy said, "Let's see what we have here." He rummaged through the contents of the hiding place, a false stone in the wall at waist height.

"How did you know where to look?" asked Malar.

"My grandfather had reason to spend some time in the sewers." He glanced at Malar. "He was a city employee."

"A sewer worker?"

"At times," said Jimmy. "Anyway, he told me that from whatever thieves' entrance into the city, you move to the first intersection, then to the right, and about twelve paces to the right, a cache would be found. Seems the Mockers wanted to make sure that if they got chased down into the darkness, they could find light and some tools." He waved at the cache. "Observe." He patted each item as he named it. "A good length of rope. A large breaker bar. A water skin. A dagger, torches, or a lantern."

"A lantern with a shutter would prove safer," said Malar.

"True," agreed Jimmy, "but as we don't have one, we must settle for what is at hand. There may be other caches still intact, and perhaps we can find a lantern there."

He glanced around in the murk and said, "Gods!"

Malar said, "What?" concern obvious in his tone.

"Look at this mess."

"Sir, it's a sewer," replied Malar, irritation in his voice.

"I know that. But look at the walls and the water."

Malar saw then what Jimmy meant. While expecting moss-covered stones and brackish water, he didn't expect to see every surface covered in soot. He glanced at his own hands and said, "Sir, I think we must bathe once we get above, else we shall surely be noticed."

Jimmy glanced at his servant and said, "If I've scratched my chin as much as you, it is certain I look like a chimney sweep."

Malar said, "You're filthy, sir."

Jimmy said, "Well, no one said this would be easy."

As he set off, he heard Malar mutter, "No one said it would be impossible, either."

Dash nodded and Gustaf jumped. He landed behind the big stone they were attempting to move, and ducked out of sight of the guards. He held a piece of broken crockery he had secreted in his shirt two days before and quickly sawed at a key rope in the net used to haul the stones.

The rope net was a clever device that could be placed around the stone, fitted under the corners as men used levers to raise them. Once hoisted aloft, a quick pass of two ropes beneath the stone put on a second lifting net, and once above the intended destination, the two ropes were removed, and the stone lowered a few inches as the webbing loosened, dropping the stone. Dash knew a practiced crew of stone masons could do this with a tolerance of a mere fraction of an inch. With Dash's crew, they were happy to get the stone within an inch of ideal tolerance. The only masons in Krondor were Duko's engineers, and there was a severe language problem with most of the workers.

Gustaf stepped around from behind the stone, nodding to Dash. "Haul away," he shouted.

Dash stepped back as two men readied the ropes to be passed under the stone, and watched. The stone lifted two feet in the air, then suddenly tilted as a loud snap sounded. The strand Gustaf had cut had parted, and now the stone hung a few feet off the ground, spinning slowly. The two men with the support ropes backed away.

"Get it down!" shouted a voice from below, and suddenly the rock was dropped.

"No!" said the foreman, too late, as men who should have slowly lowered the stone released the rope. Instead of settling quietly to the ledge, the rock bounced a bit then teetered, as Dash had hoped, then slowly started to fall.

"Look out!" cried a man near Dash as men started scrambling out of the way.

"Come on," Dash said to Gustaf as confusion erupted.

They hurried past a guard standing still in fascination as the rock slid outward, overhanging the parapet, slowly moving to balance a moment in the air, then start its dramatic fall to the cobbles below.

Dash, Gustaf, and some other men hurried down a flight of stone steps, as if intent on helping those below. But at the base of the wall, Dash moved quickly to his right, into what appeared to be a slight gap in the stones. The others ducked into the gap after him.

The ancient wall of Krondor was hollow in places, storage sheds used to house grain, water, and weapons against siege. Many of the old storage rooms had been used during the last war, but several had been left empty, like these along the easternmost wall.

Dash had waited a week to find this one, an ideal exit from captivity if he had judged correctly. Either there was a sewer entrance here, or a passage to another abandoned storage area that had one. The only danger would be if they were caught ducking into this room, or if the passage to the next room was blocked by fallen masonry. They would be missed at the head count done each meal break and that was only an hour off.

In the gloom, it was difficult to find the entrance, but Dash managed. Below a heavy layer of ash and dust lay a wooden pallet, used to keep grain off the damp stones. Below that was a man-sized hole, covered with a simple iron grate. Dash whispered, "Give me a hand," and two other men stooped next to him.

In the faint light coming in through the broken wall, Dash could make out the profiles of Gustaf and Talwin. Gustaf was what he appeared to be, but Talwin had Dash concerned. Yet here he was risking broken fingers to get the grating up, without any hint of betrayal.

The grate came up and was moved out of the way. Dash started to lower himself down, and said, "It's going to be difficult, dropping into the dark, but you should hit water about seven, eight feet below you, so expect that. Face the same way I am and move to your right. You won't see a thing, but I know my way around down there."

He let go, which was among the most courageous acts of his life, as every fiber of his being screamed to hang onto the stone and not fall into darkness. For a brief instant it felt as if he had made some terrible misjudgment, for it seemed as if he fell through blackness for a long time, yet only a moment after letting go his feet struck water. He bent his knees and hit the stones under the water and lost his balance. He fell forward, his head going completely under the foul water, and he came up, blowing hard to keep anything in that sewer out of his nose and mouth. His grandfather had warned him about that, claiming that many thieves had fallen in the sewer only to later sicken and die from it.

He quickly stepped to his right, and a moment later another man fell through the hole into the darkness. "Here," said Dash, and the man moved toward him in the blackness.

Then two other men came through, and Dash said, "Who's here?"

"Gustaf," said the second man down.

"Talwin," said the next voice.

"Reese," said the third, and Dash remembered the tall quiet man with whom Talwin spoke from time to time. "I saw you three move and took the moment. No sense standing around like sheep."

Dash doubted that; he was certain Talwin had alerted Reese something was afoot, but he didn't care to debate that now. "Good," he said aloud. "We can use all the help we can getting out of here."

"Now what?" said Gustaf. "We're in the darkest pit I've seen and the foulest smelling, and what are we to do next?"

Dash said, "This is part of the old sewer under the wall. If we keep moving back toward the city center, we'll find a way out of Krondor."

"Why not just move away from the city if we're under the wall?" asked Reese.

"Because this"—Dash's hand struck the stone next to which he stood—"is the outer limit of the sewer. To get on the other side of the wall you better be able to chew rock."

"Damn," said Gustaf. "I thought we'd slip out under the wall or something when you told me of the sewers."

"They never connected the sewer in the foulbourgh with the inner city. It would make it too easy for an invader to slip in." Dash muttered, "As it is, a good crew of sappers could still get in within weeks if they knew this was here. There's one breach to the other side of this wall, but we must go into the city to eventually get there."

"Well, which way do we go?" asked Talwin.

Glancing up at the faint light of the hole above, Dash oriented himself. "Get over here."

The men gathered near him. "Gustaf, put your right hand on my right shoulder." He felt the mercenary's strong hand take a grip of his tunic. "Talwin, do the same to Gustaf, and Reese bring up the rear. Listen for my instructions." Dash put his right hand on the wall and said, "Let's go, slowly. And if you lose your grip, sing out."

They moved off into the gloom.

Jimmy turned suddenly and put his hand over Malar's mouth as he let the torch fall to the stone walkway next to the sewer. As he hoped, the torch began to fail and flicker, allowing Jimmy to step on it, putting out the light. Malar had the presence of mind not to be too shocked by the move, and he endured standing there with Jimmy's hand over his mouth.

When Jimmy removed it, Malar heard what Jimmy had,

men moving cautiously down another tunnel, nearby. Whispering as quietly as possible, Jimmy said, "Someone's coming."

Malar nodded.

They stood motionless, listening to the faint sound of men moving slowly. Then one spoke. His voice was muffled and distant and nothing of what was said came through, but Jimmy would have bet a purse of gold they were invaders on patrol. Something about the quality of the speech hinted at an accent. They waited until the sound died out, as the strangers moved away.

Jimmy knelt and felt around in the dark until he located the torch. It was still hot to the touch. He struck a spark with flint and got the flame going again and said, "We may have to lose this if we run into another patrol."

"You mean walk around down here blind!" said Malar, obviously upset at the thought.

"I know my way around here pretty well," said Jimmy, expressing a confidence he didn't feel. "Besides, if we're apprehended by the invaders, we're either dead men or prisoners, and I'd rather take my chances retracing our route back to the other side of the wall than those two choices."

"Agreed, yet your words fill me with little confidence, young sir."

Jimmy said nothing, but glanced around the corner, making sure that no one had quietly snuck up on them. "This way," he said, leading Malar toward a large yawning tunnel entrance that opencd up across from where they stood. This required them to step down into the filthy water. They slogged through the slowly moving mass of floating char, and less savory debris, and entered the blackness.

Dash felt fingers dig into his shoulder as the sound of men echoed from a distance. In the blackness they couldn't tell from which quarter the sound originated. Nerves were frayed and Dash was concerned one of the three men would panic. Gustaf seemed solid, if nervous, Talwin was quiet, but Reese was given to blurting out pointless things, either questioning how much farther they'd have to move in the gloom, or expressing his apprehensions.

There were places along the way where light came down

from above, faint cracks in the street above, or a broken culvert admitting some illumination. Dash was always surprised how bright these areas looked after complete darkness, but knew it was an illusion. He could only see a dozen yards or so on either side of a source of light, and once past, they fell back into a gloom darker than any night he had endured.

The first place he had hoped to find some torches or a lantern according to his grandfather's description had provided no secret cache of useful items. If there had been a secret stone in the corner he couldn't find it. Not the least bit immodest, Dash knew it wasn't there, for if it had been, he would have found it.

The second location was already empty. Someone had emptied it. Dash didn't know if it had been stripped of its contents during the fall of the city or days, even hours before he reached it.

He was leading the men northward as much as he could, knowing his best chance for escape was around the area formerly known as Fishtown. It was one of the few places in Krondor you could enter the bay and with a little swimming find yourself outside the walls of the city. Dash didn't know if the other men could swim, and for the most part he didn't care. While he wanted to see these three men to safety if possible, he'd willingly sell them out to get his information back to the Prince.

Keeping one hand on the wall, he led them deeper into the darkness.

Jimmy motioned toward the faint light. Malar nodded, whispering, "A way out, young sir?"

"Perhaps. Boost me up on your shoulders so I can take a look."

Malar knelt, and when Jimmy put his left boot on the servant's shoulders, Malar stood, grabbing Jimmy's ankles to support him as he was lifted to a point just below the light. Jimmy fought for balance a moment, but Malar kept his motion steady, and Jimmy kept his position as he grabbed a support in the floor above him to keep from falling.

"Great!" said Jimmy. "It's a cellar door, off its hinges."

Jimmy got his fingers in the crack and pushed. "I can't get any leverage." He said, "Let go," and as Malar complied, Jimmy jumped down to stand before his servant. "No way to get it open."

"Are there no stairs in this accursed dungeon?"

Jimmy chuckled. "Hardly a dungeon; a maze, no doubt. But you're right and I'm an idiot." He sighed theatrically. "There are several places with stone steps up to basements." He looked around in the gloom, barely illuminated by the faint flickering of his torch. "If I'm not mistaken, one isn't too far from here. Pray to whatever gods you worship that the top of the steps is unblocked."

Malar muttered an almost silent benediction and followed behind Jimmy.

Dash heard something ahead of him in the dark and whispered, "Don't move!"

The men behind him stopped their forward motion as sounds around them echoed. "What is—" began Talwin.

He never finished as Reese struck him from behind, knocking him from his feet. "Here!" he shouted.

Suddenly men were swarming in the dark and lanterns uncovered, blinding Dash momentarily. He blinked trying to see beyond the brilliant lights, but could only see dark shapes hurrying toward him. Thinking of nothing else to do, he leaped forward, trying to dodge between two of the shapes. One man lunged at him, missing, while the other was slow in turning, with Dash past him before he could be intercepted.

Dash slogged as quickly through the knee-deep water as he could, and behind a pair of lanterns he saw movement. Dodging to his right, he rushed to another potential exit as arms grabbed him from behind, dragging him down into the water.

Dash turned, kicking hard, and felt his foot strike the man's leg. Dash scuttled backwards in the water, and another man seized him. A voice in the gloom said, "They're making too much noise! Shut them up!"

Dash felt pain for a brief moment as someone struck him hard behind the ear with a billy club, then he sank into unconsciousness.

*   *   *

Jimmy pushed the trap up and with relief he found that
it moved. He glanced around under the slight opening he
created, and seeing no movement, he heaved. The large
wooden trap swung over, to crash noisily against the floor
behind him. He hurried up into the dark room as a cloud
of soot exploded into the air from the trap.

Malar sneezed as he came up. The room was the back
storage area of a tannery near the river to the north of the
city, and it had taken Jimmy most of the day and into the
evening to discover it.

The roof of the building was gone, probably accounting
for its being abandoned, as the nights would still be cold.
Jimmy looked around and saw lights in a few buildings
nearby, but nothing close by. Malar could be seen in the
faint light inside the building. "If I'm as dirty as you, we'd
better stay out of sight."

"Good advice, young sir," agreed the servant. "You are
dirtier than a coal seller. One glance at us, and any fool
could tell we had been somewhere we should not be."

A sound caused Jimmy to hold up his hand. "What—"

At once he pulled his sword, as men came swarming into
the room, over the burned-out wall and through the single
door. Only a fool would fight, as more than a dozen swords
were leveled in their direction. Jimmy made a clear gesture
of letting the sword fall from his hand as he stepped back.

Hands roughly grabbed him and tied his arms behind,
while two men did the same to Malar. They all wore rough
fighting garb, leather, and gambesons, but no metal armor,
which would make noise and warn away someone coming
up through the trapdoor.

With a heavy accent, a man came to stand before the two
and said, "Watch a rat hole long enough, and a rat peers
out, eh?" Glancing at Malar, he said, "Or two." To the
men he said, "Bring them along," and Jimmy and Malar
were hustled out the door and down the street.

Dash waited in silence. He had recovered his wits as he
was taken to what he presumed had once been an underground storage shed. There was no light. He had explored

his environment by touch and on a couple of occasions wished he hadn't.

It was a roughly twelve-by-twelve-foot room, with a single door barred from the other side. He felt up and down both edges, but all hinges and locks were on the other side. He was inside until someone released him. From the stench, several rodents had recently died in the room. Had he eaten in the last two days, he probably would have added to the mess, but his captors would have to be satisfied with subjecting him to a fit of the dry heaves.

After several painful minutes of gagging, he had managed to overcome the impulse. Now, about two hours later, he judged, he barely noticed the odor unless he thought about it.

Mostly he was attempting to chart his best possible course. That he was in this dark room rather than being hauled before one of General Duko's officers suggested to Dash that he was a prisoner of someone besides the invaders. The first possibility to occur to him was that he had been captured by Kingdom soldiers hiding from the invaders. If so, he could quickly identify himself and recruit them.

More likely, he was in the clutches of outlaws, and in that case, he would have to bargain. His companions were missing, probably locked away in a similar room somewhere nearby.

Suddenly light shone around the edges of the door and he could hear footfalls approaching. As bright as the light seemed through the cracks, when the door was opened, it blinded him. A voice from without said, "You awake?"

"Yes," said Dash, finding his voice was harsh from dryness. "Any chance of water?"

"Let's see if we let you live, first," came the gruff answer.

A pair of hands reached in and yanked Dash to his feet, and he was pulled into a larger room. Shielding his eyes from the glare of the lantern, he glanced around the room. It was indeed the basement of a burned-out inn or hotel, and he had been locked in a storage closet. There were ample signs of life in the building, for crates and bales of goods were stacked around the room.

A half dozen men surrounded him, none with weapons evident. It was obvious they felt confident enough that they could keep him from escaping. As he blinked against the light from the lantern, he noticed that one man did hold a large billy, and he was sure he would use it if Dash made any sign of attempting to flee.

"What now?" said Dash.

"Come along," said the man with a lumpy visage.

Dash said nothing and followed, walking behind two men, with two more guarding the rear. The last man stayed in the storage room, for what reason Dash could only imagine.

Dash was led down a long dark tunnel, one with a lantern at each end, featureless and damp. He listened, but only heard the sound of boot leather and nails on stone. If they were close to the city streets above, those streets were deserted.

The man in front pushed open a door, allowing the others to enter a very large room. It had a dozen torches guttering in sconces. A wooden table, not too badly charred, had been hauled down from the destroyed tavern aboveground and now served as the site of what Dash took to be some sort of court or tribunal.

At the head of the long table sat an old man. He looked deformed, or crippled, as he hunched over with left shoulder lower than the right, his left arm in a sling. Around his head he wore a scarf, covering his left eye. Below it, Dash saw the man's face was scarred, badly burned. A young woman stood to his right. Dash looked at her closely. Under other circumstances she would have warranted a second glance, as she was tall, slender, and under the soot and mud, still attractive, with dark hair and eyes. But in these circumstances, what commanded Dash's attention was her fashion—dressed like a man and armed to the teeth; he saw a sword, daggers in belt and boots, and he was certain she had more weapons secreted on her, such being the practice of thieves. She wore a dirty white shirt, now almost charcoal color, a leather vest, men's riding breeches, and a red scarf tied around her head. Dark hair fell from under the scarf, and down her back.

With a surprisingly deep voice, she said, "You stand accused."

Dash summoned as much confidence as he could manage in such circumstances and said, "No doubt."

The lumpy-faced man said, "Before you're convicted, have you anything to say in your defense?"

Dash shrugged. "Would it do any good?"

The old man chuckled and the man who had first apprehended Dash glanced his way. "Probably not," he said, "but it won't hurt."

"May I first inquire of what crime I'm being accused?"

The lumpy-faced man again glanced at the old man, who waved a curt gesture of permission. "You stand accused of trespass. You were found someplace you were not given permission to pass."

Dash blew out a long breath. "So that's it, then. Mockers."

The young woman glanced at the old man, who motioned with his good hand for her to come close. He whispered in her ear, and she said, "Why do you think us thieves, Puppy?"

"Because smugglers would have cut my throat and been on their way, and Duko's guards would have had me under questioning up there." He pointed upward. "You've separated me from my companions, which means you're trying to find conflicts in our stories, and one of my companions brought you down on us; Reese seems more likely to be a thief than anything else I can imagine." Glancing around the room, he said, "So this is what's left of Mother's?"

The old man said something, and the woman said, "What do you know of Mother's? You're not one of us."

"My grandfather," said Dash, knowing that at this point he had nothing to lose and everything to gain with the truth.

"What about him? Who is your grandfather?"

"Was," said Dash. "My grandfather was Jimmy the Hand."

Several people spoke at once, and the old man signaled for silence. The young woman leaned over and then repeated his words. "Your name?"

"Dashel Jamison. My father is Arutha, Duke of Krondor."

Without waiting, the girl said, "So you've come spying for the King."

Dash attempted a grin. "Well, the Prince, actually. But yes, I'm here to scout out Duko's defenses, so that Patrick can retake Krondor."

The old man waved a badly burned hand and spoke to the woman, who said, "Come closer, Puppy."

Dash did as he was told and came to stand before the old man and the young woman. The old man's one good eye studied Dash's face for a long moment as the woman held a lantern close to it, so every detail could be seen.

Finally, the old man spoke loud enough for all to hear. "Leave us." His voice sounded close to ruined, dry gravel being scraped, a strangled sound.

Everyone but the woman did, instantly and without hesitation, and the old man said, "Well, then. It is a small world, boy."

Dash leaned over to study the burned features before him and he said, "Do I know you, sir?"

"No," said the old man slowly, as if every word hurt. "But I know you by name and lineage, Dashel, son of Arutha."

"Am I to know your name, sir?"

The woman glanced at the old man, but his one good eye stayed fastened upon Dash. "I'm your great-uncle, boy, that's who I am. I'm the Upright Man."

Five

Confrontations

ARUTHA FROWNED.

Pug stood at the door studying the Duke of Krondor a moment, before he said softly, "May I speak with you a moment?"

Arutha glanced upward and waved him in. "Grandfather. Please."

"You appear distracted," said Pug, sitting in a chair across a large oak table Arutha used for work.

"I was."

"Jimmy and Dash?"

Arutha nodded as he looked out a window at the warm spring afternoon. His eyes narrowed. They were deep sunk and had dark bags underneath, revealing the lack of sleep that had plagued him since sending his sons into harm's way. There was grey in Arutha's hair; Pug hadn't seen so much just a month before.

Arutha looked at Pug and said, "You needed to see me?"

"We have a problem."

Arutha nodded. "We have many. Which particular one are we discussing?"

"Patrick."

Arutha stood and moved around the table to the door and

glanced through. A pair of clerks outside were hunched over documents, reviewing reports and requests for supplies, lost in their work.

Arutha closed the door. He returned to his seat and said, "What do you propose?"

"I propose you send a message to the King."

"And?" Arutha looked directly into the magician's eyes.

"I think we need another commander in the West."

Arutha sighed, and in that moment Pug could hear the fatigue, stress, worry, and doubt in the man, expressed in as eloquent a fashion as if an orator had spoken for an hour. Pug instantly knew the outcome of this discussion before Arutha said another word. Yet he allowed the Duke to continue. "History teaches us that we often do not get the best men for a particular job. It also teaches us that if the rest of us do ours, we'll somehow manage."

Pug leaned forward and said, "We are this close"—he held forefinger and thumb apart a scant portion of an inch— "to war with Great Kesh. Don't you think it proper to finish the one we have before we start another?"

"What I think is immaterial," said Arutha. "I counsel the Prince, but it's his realm. I'm only allowed to manage it for him."

Pug remained silent and stared at Arutha a long moment.

Suddenly Arutha allowed his temper to get the better of him, slamming his hand down on the table. "I am *not* my father, damn it!"

Pug remained silent for another moment, then said, "I never said you were . . . or that you should be."

"No, but you were thinking, 'How would James have dealt with this?' "

Pug said, "It was your mother that read minds, Arutha, not I."

Arutha leaned forward. "You're my grandfather, yet I hardly know you." He glanced upward toward the ceiling, as if collecting his thoughts, then said, "And that means you hardly know me."

"You were raised on the other side of the Kingdom, Arutha. We saw each other from time to time . . ."

Arutha said, "It's difficult growing up surrounded on all sides by legends. Did you know that?"

Pug shrugged. "I am not sure."

Arutha said, "My father was 'Jimmy the Hand,' the thief who became the most powerful noble in the Kingdom. I was named for the man who is almost unarguably the most brilliant ruler the Western Realm has known.

"The King and I have discussed what it's like to be the sons of such men, on several occasions." He pointed his finger at the magician and said, "And you . . . you look like my son. You look younger now than you did when I was a child. You're turning into a figure of mystery and fear, Grandfather. 'Pug, the Eternal Sorcerer!' The man who saved us during the Riftwar."

Arutha stopped, weighed his words, and said, "Borric, before he became King, once told me that our roles would be far different than our fathers'. Arutha had been thrust into command in Crydee, a situation demanding action without hesitation, without doubt.

"Father was the brash boy who saved Arutha, then became his most trusted adviser and friend. Between the two of them there was always an answer."

Pug laughed, and it wasn't a mocking laugh. "I'm sure they would argue they had their share of doubts and mistakes, Arutha."

"Perhaps, but the results were there. As a child I grew up hearing the stories in Rillanon, tales told to entertain the eastern nobles who had never seen Krondor, let alone the Far Coast. How Prince Arutha had saved Crydee from the Tsurani host, and had journeyed to Krondor where he found Princess Anita. How father had helped smuggle them both from the city, then later helped get Earl Kasumi to see the King."

Arutha became more reflective. "I heard the story of the renegade moredhel, and the rogue magician from Kelewan, and I was told of the attack on the Tear of the Gods. I heard of the Crawler and his attempt to take over the Mockers, and the other stories of Father's more reckless youth." He looked at Pug. "I wasn't a noble reading dry reports, but a boy hearing tales from his father."

Pug said, "What are you telling me? That you don't feel equal to the task?"

"No man can be equal to the task of putting the Kingdom right, Grandfather." He narrowed his gaze. "Not even you."

Pug took a deep breath, then relaxed. "So Patrick won't give up Stardock?"

"He wants it all back, Grandfather. He wants this city rebuilt in his lifetime to a glory beyond what it was before. He wants Kesh completely out of the vale. He wants the Bitter Sea cleared of Quegan raiders and Keshian pirates, and when Borric finally dies, Patrick wants to go to Rillanon to take the Crown, to be known as the greatest Prince in the history of the West."

Softly Pug said, "Save us from monarchs with vanity."

"Not vanity, Pug. Fear."

Pug nodded. "Young men often fear failure."

"I understand his fear," said Arutha. "Maybe if I had been given a different name, George or Harry, Jack or Robert, but no; I was named for the man Father admired above all others."

"Prince Arutha was a very admirable man. Of all the men I've known, he was among the most gifted."

"A fact of which I'm painfully aware." Arutha sat back, as if seeking some comfort. "If Arutha were still Prince, and Father still Duke, perhaps Patrick's dreams of returned glory would prove possible. As it is today . . ."

Pug said, "What?"

"We are lesser men."

Pug's expression turned dark. "You are tired. You are tired and you are worried about the boys." He stood. "And about Patrick and the Kingdom and everything there is in this life to be worried and tired about." He leaned over the desk and said, "But know this: you are able. And as long as you're my grandson, I will not let you forget that. The boys are my great-grandsons. Gamina may not have been the daughter of my body, but she was the daughter of my heart, and I love all her children and grandchildren none the less for this." He reached across the table and put his hand on Arutha's shoulder. "Especially you."

Moisture came unbidden to Arutha's eyes. "Me?"

Softly Pug said, "You may not be as much like your father as you would wish, but you are more like your mother than you'll ever know." He removed his hand and turned to go. "I'll leave you. Rest, and dine with me to-night when you've had a chance to refresh yourself." He reached the door and said, "Try not to worry too much about the boys. I am sure they are safe."

He opened the door and left, closing it behind him. Arutha, Duke of Krondor, sat silently and thought about what his grandfather had just said to him. At last he allowed himself the luxury of a long sigh, then turned to the work still before him. Perhaps he would take the opportunity to rest a bit before supper that evening. And as he regarded the report on top of the pile, he thought, The boys are able. Grandfather is most likely right, and the boys are safe.

Jimmy's head snapped backward as the soldier stepped through the blow. Jimmy's eyes watered from the pain and his vision turned red for a moment. His knees wobbled and he felt himself start to go, but the other two guards who held him kept him upright.

"All right," said the interrogator, speaking the King's Tongue with a very heavy accent. "Again." He paused. "Let's start again. Why were you sneaking into Krondor?"

Malar was held by another two soldiers. His nose bled and his right eye was puffy, as he had stood his turn at interrogation. Jimmy was now very pleased that he and Dash had told him nothing.

Jimmy shook his head to clear it, and said, "I told you. I'm a mercenary from the East, and this is my dog robber. I'm looking for work."

"Wrong answer," said the man, and he struck Jimmy again. Jimmy collapsed, unable to make his legs obey, and was held entirely by the two soldiers.

Jimmy spat blood, and through rapidly swelling lips said, "What do you want me to say?"

"Every mercenary outside the walls has been told to stay out of Krondor. If you were a freebooter you would know this." He nodded and the two men moved to the wall, and let Jimmy slump to the floor. The man knelt, putting his own face down near Jimmy's.

The soldier was a brutish-looking fellow, with a beetle brow and thick black hair that hung down over his shoulders. He sported a short black beard, and at this close quarter, Jimmy could see he bore an assortment of scars on his neck and shoulders. The man grabbed Jimmy's hair and said, "Either you're a fool or you're a spy. Which is it?"

Jimmy paused for dramatic effect, then slowly he said, "I came looking for my brother."

The soldier stood and motioned and the two other soldiers picked Jimmy up and moved him to a chair. They were gathered in a large bedroom of an inn, converted to a cell of sorts.

Jimmy and Malar had been dragged there the night before and the interrogation had started at once. For an hour they had been routinely questioned and beaten, then left alone. Just as they were able to relax, the door would open and the questioning would begin again. Jimmy knew the oddly timed schedule was deliberate, designed to unnerve them. Despite the overt brutality of the man questioning them, the entire process was very well thought out and subtle. It was designed to disorient him without rendering him incoherent. It was a methodical approach looking to ferret out mistakes and inconsistencies. Jimmy had fought to concentrate to the limit of his ability to prevent any such lapse; he was attempting to turn the situation to his advantage.

One fear of his was that they already had Dash in custody. If so, the admission he was searching for his brother might dovetail into Dash's arrest if he was already here. In a way, it was the truth, and being the truth, it would prove far more convincing than the most artfully concocted lie.

"Your brother?" said the man, holding a fist cocked to deliver another blow. "What brother?"

"My younger brother." Jimmy leaned back in the chair, letting his left arm hang over the chair back, keeping him upright. "We were jumped a few miles from the city by bandits and rode toward Krondor." He paused for a long moment, then as the interrogator started to menace him with his fist, he blurted, "We got separated. The bandits chased him, so we doubled back and followed after. We dodged the bandits, as they came back our way, so we know they didn't have him—couldn't see any leading his horse, and it was a good horse so they'd have kept it." He swallowed. "Can I have some water?" he croaked.

The man in charge nodded and one of the guards stepped

out of the room and returned a moment later with water.
Jimmy drank eagerly, then nodded toward Malar. The man
who had been questioning Jimmy nodded and the servant
was given a cup of water to drink.

"Go on," instructed the interrogator.

"We checked all the camps outside. No one had seen
him."

"Maybe someone already cut his throat."

"Not my brother," said Jimmy.

"How do you know?" asked the interrogator.

"Because I'd know. And because whoever cut his throat
would be wearing his boots if he was."

The interrogator looked down at Jimmy's feet and nodded. "Good boots." He motioned to one of the men in the
room, who ducked out and returned a moment later holding
a sack. He opened the sack and dumped the contents on
the floor. The interrogator said, "Are these your
brother's?"

Jimmy looked at the boots. He didn't need to pick them
up. They were identical to Dash's: the same bootmaker in
Rillanon had made them for the brothers. Jimmy said, "In
the left one you'll see the mark of the bootmaker, a small
bull's head."

The man nodded. "I've seen it."

"Is my brother alive?"

The man nodded. "At least he was until two days ago.
That's when he escaped."

Jimmy couldn't help but smile. "Escaped?"

"With three others." The man studied Jimmy a moment,
then said, "Bring them." He turned and walked out of the
room; Jimmy and Malar were hurried after him, a guard on
each side.

They were taken to what had been the common room of
the inn, and Jimmy finally recognized where he was. He
was in what was left of a very palatial inn called the Seven
Gems, not too far from the heart of the Merchants' Quarters. He was a few blocks from Barret's Coffee House,
where most of the major financial business of the Western
Realm had been conducted. Glancing around the room,
Jimmy decided the inn had survived relatively intact. There
was ample smoke damage and all of the tapestries that had

decorated the place were gone, but the furniture was intact, and the rooms still able to be locked. He had been questioned in one of the back storage rooms, near the kitchen, and was now being led into the far corner of the commons, where a curtain separated a large booth from the rest of the room.

Sitting in the booth was a trio of men, all clearly military from their dress and manner. The man in the center was looking over a parchment, a report of some sort, Jimmy guessed. The interrogator moved to the front of the table and leaned over, speaking in a soft voice. He glanced up at Jimmy, nodded to the interrogator, who departed, leaving Jimmy standing alone with the three men. They seemed intent upon the paperwork before them, and left Jimmy standing for a long time before the centermost man's attention returned to him.

"Your name?" asked the man in the center.

"I'm called Jimmy," he answered.

"Jimmy," repeated the man, as if testing the sound of the name. He studied Jimmy's face, and Jimmy studied his.

He was a middle-aged man, probably in his late forties or early fifties. He still looked fit, though what once had been hard muscle had been thinned by hardships on campaign and a cold, hungry winter. He had the look of a fighter, from his greying dark hair tied back to keep it from his brown eyes, to the hard set of a jaw kept clean-shaven. Something about him looked familiar to Jimmy, and suddenly it struck him: in manner and voice the man resembled what he remembered of Prince Arutha from Jimmy's childhood. There was a no-nonsense hardness to him, a calculating intelligence that would be fatal to underestimate.

The man said, "You are a spy, of that I am almost certain." He spoke the King's Tongue, but his accent was slight.

Jimmy said nothing.

"But the issue here is are you a bad spy or a terribly clever one." He sighed, as if thinking on this. "Your brother, if that is really who he is, was a far better spy than I had thought. I had him under observation, yet he managed to escape. We knew of the sewers under the walls, yet didn't know of that particular entrance. Once he was in there, he was gone." The soldier looked at Jimmy, as if measuring him, then said, "I won't make that mistake again." He reached for a mug nearby and drank what appeared to be water. Jimmy was impressed by the man's speech, for even with almost no accent, it was clear he had studied the language, for he spoke with the practiced precision of someone not born to the tongue.

He then said, "I have determined that those boots which you claim belong to your brother are made by a particularly well-regarded cobbler in Rillanon, your nation's capital. Is this correct?"

Jimmy nodded. "It is."

"Would it be unreasonable to assume that common mercenaries are not likely to acquire a matching set of such boots unless they are not, in fact, common mercenaries?"

"Not unreasonable at all," said Jimmy. The man speaking to him motioned to one of his two companions, who left the booth, fetched over a chair, and allowed Jimmy to sit. Jimmy nodded his thanks, then said, "Would it be immodest to claim we are uncommon mercenaries?"

"Not in the least," said the man. "Though it would smack of insincerity."

Jimmy said, "I am at your mercy. If I'm a spy or not is of little matter. You can kill me at your whim."

"True, but murder holds little appeal for me. I've seen far too much of it over the last twenty years." He motioned to the remaining man who sat at his side, and the man rose from his seat and offered Jimmy a mug of water. "I'm sorry we don't have anything more flavorful, but at least it's clean. One of the major wells to the north has been cleared and is running fresh again. Your Duke James left nothing behind that provides much comfort."

Jimmy feigned indifference to hearing his grandfather's name. This invader was very well informed about things in Krondor and the Kingdom to know about Duke James and Rillanon's better bootmaker.

"But we manage," said the man. "Feeding the workers is difficult, but the fishing has been good and there are those willing to sell to us for the little booty we've found in Krondor."

Jimmy was intrigued. He was also wary. This man was

apparently unconcerned by what he said, and appeared to
be someone of some importance among the invaders.

The man stood and said, "Can you walk?"

Jimmy rose and nodded. "I'll manage."

"Good. Then come with me."

Jimmy followed the man out of the door of the inn. Outside the afternoon sun was brilliant and Jimmy squinted.
"We must walk, I'm sorry to say. Horses are a staple of
our current diet." He glanced at Jimmy. "Though a few
are maintained to carry messages."

They walked along a busy street. While almost every
man was armed and obviously a warrior, a few were workers and a few women were seen here and there. Everyone
seemed occupied with some task, and none of the usual
idle habitues of the city were in evidence: the drunks, pros-
titutes, confidence men, and beggars. Also noticeable by
their absence, the street urchins who flocked in rowdy
gangs through the poor and workers' quarters of the city.

"If I may ask," said Jimmy, "where's my dog
robber?"

"He's comfortable," said the man. "Don't worry about
him."

The man who was walking beside him said, "Jimmy, if
you are a spy, you're most likely wondering what it is
we're doing here in Krondor."

Jimmy said, "It is a question that has crossed my mind.
I may not be a spy, but it's obvious there's more going on
here than a simple staging for a spring offensive. You've
got soldiers on the outside of the walls anxious to enlist
and you're not enlisting them. You have a great deal of
work underway, but some of it"—he pointed to a nearby
building where two soldiers were hanging a new door—
"clearly not military in nature. It's as if you've come to
Krondor to stay."

The man smiled, and again Jimmy was reminded of the
old Prince, for this man had the same cryptic half-smile
Arutha had evidenced when amused. "Good observation.
Yes, we're not planning on leaving anytime soon."

Jimmy nodded, his head still ringing from the beating he
had taken. He said, "But you're turning away swords who

will help you hang on to this place when the Prince's army returns.''

"How many spies are among that band outside?" asked the man.

"I couldn't begin to guess." Jimmy shrugged. "Not many, I wager."

"Why?"

"Because no man of the Kingdom can pass himself off as one of your own. We don't speak your language."

"Ah," said the officer, "but you have. Some of your countrymen have been among us for years. We first became of aware of a group calling itself 'Calis's Crimson Eagles' before the fall of Maharta. We now know they were Kingdom agents. We know they were with us from time to time." They reached the walls and the man motioned for Jimmy to climb with him up a flight of stairs to the ramparts.

As they climbed, the man continued. "We who were commanding never had a clear picture of this campaign. To understand what we became, you need to know what we were before." They reached the ramparts, and the man motioned for Jimmy to follow. They reached a section of the wall freshly refurbished, the stones set firmly in place with new mortar. The man motioned beyond the wall, toward the east. "Out there is a nation, your Kingdom." He turned to regard Jimmy. "In my homeland we have no such nations. There were city-states, ruled by men who were petty or noble, who were acquisitive or generous, wise or foolish. But no ruler's power existed beyond a week's ride by his soldiers." He motioned toward Jimmy. "You people have this thing in your mind. This idea of a nation. It is an idea I am most intrigued by, even captivated by. The notion that men who live more than a month's travel from a ruler swear to that ruler, are willing to die for that ruler—" He stopped himself. "No, not the ruler, this nation. Now this is an amazing idea.

"I have spent much time this winter speaking with those among our prisoners who could teach me, men and women of some education or experience, who would help me understand this concept of this Kingdom." He shook his head. "It is a grand thing, this nation of yours."

Jimmy shrugged. "We tend to take it for granted."

"I understand, for you have never known otherwise." The man looked out over the wall. Below was a sea of tents and makeshift shelters, campfires and the sounds of humanity, laughter, shouts of anger, the voices of peddlers, a child crying. "But to me the notion of something larger than what I can take and hold—for my employer or for myself—that is a wondrous notion."

The wind blew and the afternoon smelled of salt and charcoal. The man said, "Tell me, why is this city built here?" He glanced westward. "If there is a worse harbor in the world, I've not seen it."

Jimmy shrugged. "The story says the first Prince of Krondor liked the view of the sunset from the hill upon which the palace was built."

"Princes," said the man, shaking his head. He sighed loudly. "We are dredging that terrible harbor. We have found those who call themselves 'Wreckers' and they are using their magic to raise hulks for us. We manage one every three days, and will have the harbor cleared before next winter."

Jimmy said nothing.

"We know you marshal what's left of your fleet down in Shandon Bay, in the village you call Port Vykor. We have no fleet, but we will have ships, and we will hold the city."

Jimmy shrugged. "May I ask why?"

"Because we have nowhere else to go."

Jimmy looked at the man and said, "If there was a way back to your home . . . ?"

"There is nothing there." He glanced toward the east. "There is my future, one way or another." Then he looked toward the west. "Out there is a land ravaged by over twenty years of war. No city of size remains. Those few that do are small backwaters, barely more prosperous in their glory than Krondor is now in her ashes. They are city-states of tiny men with no sense of the future. One day is much like the next."

He turned toward Jimmy and studied him a long time. "I'm fifty-two years old next Midsummer's Day, lad. I've been a soldier since I was sixteen years of age. For thirty-six years I've been fighting.'' He glanced at the city as the sun began to lower in the west. ''That's a damn long time to be dealing in blood and slaughter.'' He leaned on the parapet as if tired. ''For the last twenty I've served demons or black gods, I don't know which, but I know that the Army of the Emerald Queen was made up of men beguiled by dark forces, lured by promises of wealth, power, and immortality.'' His voice lowered. ''Or propelled by fear.'' He looked down, as if reluctant to look Jimmy in the eyes. ''I was ambitious when I was young. I was anxious to make a name for myself. I formed my own company when I was eighteen. I was commanding a thousand men by twenty.

''At first I was glad to serve the Emerald Queen. Her army was the greatest my land had known. With conquest came booty, gold, women, more recruits.'' He closed his eyes as if remembering. ''But after a while the years slip by and you find the string of women hold no interest, and there's only so much gold you can carry with you. Besides, there's nothing to do with it but hire more men.''

He looked at Jimmy and pointed with his thumb over his shoulder, to the north. ''My old friend Noradan is up there, at my back. If I know Fadawah, I am to be left here to be ground to a fine dust by the returning army of the Prince of Krondor. I am to slow him down and bleed him, while Noradan builds up a barrier across the highway to the north of here, to stand at Sarth.'' He glanced over his shoulder, as if somehow able to see to that distant town. ''That's a hell of a defensive position, that abandoned abbey. Once he's dug in, it will take your Prince all year to dig him out.''

Looking again at Jimmy, he said, ''Meanwhile, Fadawah is going to take your city of LaMut. He won't go on to Yabon this year, being content to throw up a position south of that city and starve it for a year. He has the means to keep reinforcements and supplies from reaching the city while he repulses your forces from the south.''

Jimmy said, ''Why are you telling me this?''

''Spy or not, I want you to carry a message for me to the Prince. I believe he's still in Darkmoor, but have no doubt he has forces no more than a day's ride to the east. I'll arrange an escort to a likely point and turn you loose.''

"Why not just send a message?"

"Because I think you are a spy and I think you're likely to be believed. If I send one of my own men, or a captive who wasn't known to the Prince or his men, I think it might take too long to convince him of my intent. And time is a commodity neither of us has."

Jimmy said, "You're General Duko."

The man nodded. "And I've been sent out by one of my oldest comrades to die. Fadawah and I have served in various campaigns together since we were hardly old enough to shave. But he fears me, and that's my death warrant."

"What do you want me to say to Prince Patrick?"

"I have an offer for him."

"What's the offer?"

"I wish to negotiate a settlement of our differences."

"You're willing to surrender?"

"Nothing that simple, I'm afraid." The General smiled a half-smile that Jimmy found both reassuring and unsettling. "Patrick would likely throw me and my men into a camp and get around to shipping us back to Novindus when he found the means, and that could be years down the road."

"You're turning coat?"

"Not quite. Surrender or take his gold for service, either way I end up a man looking for a boat back to a land that has no place for me. No, Jimmy, I need a different solution. I need a future, for me and my men."

"What do you wish me to tell the Prince's men?"

"Tell them that I have handpicked the men with me here in Krondor. Tell them those I had reservations about were left behind with Noradan. I can vouch for my men." He looked into Jimmy's eyes a moment. "Tell your Prince of Krondor I will swear fealty to the crown, in exchange for land and titles. Grant me estates and income, and I will lead the army north to visit with my old friends Noradan and Fadawah."

Jimmy was silent for a moment. He was both astonished at the suggestion and amazed at the logic behind it. He shook his head. "I don't know what he will say."

"If we knew what he would say, we wouldn't have to send you, now, would we?"

Jimmy shook his head.

"Come, get something to eat, and leave at first light." He led Jimmy down the stairs.

Jimmy watched the man's back and considered what he wanted. In a single breath he had set a price: forgive the assault on the Western Realm, and more, grant the man a patent of nobility, name him Earl or Baron of some lands in the West, and give him the power to rule over those lands. Jimmy shook his head. Would Patrick do it, or would his temper doom men on both sides of the wall to more useless bloodshed?

Dash sipped at the watery soup and said, "So then what?"

"We stayed in that basement a week or more. Hard to judge being in the gloom all that time." The old man motioned to put aside his bowl, held in a badly deformed hand, and the young woman moved to take it before it fell to the floor. "Thank you, Trina," he said.

His voice was as scarred as his face, but after getting used to the sound of it, Dash understood him well enough.

The three men who had come with Dash were still missing, and only Dash, the old man, and the woman thief sat around the simple wooden table.

"What should I call you?" asked Dash.

"Your grandfather insisted on calling me Lysle. It was a name I hadn't used in more score of years than I can count, but it serves. I've had so many in my life I barely know which one is truly mine."

"Lysle, you were telling me about Grandfather and Grandmother."

"James set fire to the oil he rigged in the sewers. We knew it would be a close thing and it was. I was in the escape tunnel ahead of them, and when the explosion came I shot from the mouth of the tunnel like a cork from a bottle of sparkling wine. I was badly burned, as you see, and had half my bones broken, but I'm a tough nut."

The woman named Trina spoke. "And we found a healing priest who worked on him."

"Damn near killed the man, making him do his healings over me, my merry band of cutthroats did. But they saved me before the poor brother of Killian passed out from exhaustion. He squeezed a few years more of life for me, while I set matters in Krondor right.''

"Grandfather and Grandmother?"

The old man shook his head. "James and Gamina were last in the tunnel, behind me. They never had a chance, boy.''

Dash had known his grandfather and grandmother were dead; his great-grandfather Pug had said so, but upon finding the Upright Man alive, a faint hope had been rekindled in Dash. Now it was extinguished again, and the pain was again felt.

Lysle said, "If it is any comfort, I know they died quickly, and together."

Dash nodded. "Grandmother would never have wanted to live without Grandfather."

"I never knew my brother well, Dash. We had met once as young men, and then again a few years ago." The old man laughed, a dry chuckle. "He put me out of business, actually, and damn near got me killed by some of the more ambitious men in the Mockers.

"But those few days I spent with him and your grandmother, they were my chance to hear the stories. I'm sure you heard most of them. Prince Arutha and the journey to Moraline, the fall of Armengar, where he got the idea for that nasty fire trap that got himself killed. I heard how he had journeyed to Kesh, during that matter with the Crawler, and when Lord Nirome had tried to depose the Empress. He told me of his rise in power and the time he spent ruling in Rillanon.

"I had thought myself something of a man of some accomplishments. When my father had died, one of his most trusted lieutenants had seized control of the Mockers, naming himself the Virtuous Man. I in turn deposed him and called myself the Sagacious Man. And I returned to the name Upright Man to signal an agreement I had with your grandfather and create the false impression I had deposed myself with the members of the Mockers.

"But my accomplishments pale next to those of Jimmy the Hand. The thief who ruled in turn the two mightiest cities in the Kingdom. He who was the most powerful noble in the nation. What a man he was.''

Dash nodded. ''When you put it that way, I see what you mean. To me he was Grandfather, and he had lots of wonderful stories. I sometimes forgot they were true.''

The Upright Man said, ''Now, the question is, what to do with you?''

''Me?''

''You're here spying for your father. That's not a problem, in and of itself, but the fact is you've seen me, talked to me, and letting you go is a problem.''

''Would it make a difference if I swore to say nothing about you to anyone?''

The old man laughed his dry chuckle again. ''Hardly. You're who you are, boy, and things might remain on the square between us for a while, but eventually, when things return to something like before around here, the day will come when some Mocker will create a problem that will call a little too much attention to us. It happens from time to time. And then you'll find yourself wondering just where your loyalties lie, to your Prince or your old Uncle Lysle. Considering our deep family bond, I have no doubt you'd turn me in the first chance you get.''

Dash stood up. ''Grandfather taught me better.'' He glanced at the girl, and then at his great-uncle. ''Besides, the Mockers I've seen don't exactly look a menace to the sovereignty of the nation at the moment, and then there's the small matter that we don't presently control Krondor.''

''That's a matter of some weight, true. And it gives me pause about ordering your death. You don't presently pose a threat. What do you think you can manage for us if we help you get free and back to your father?''

Dash said, ''I can't promise anything. I don't have the authority. But I suspect with a little conversation, I can get Father to authorize a general pardon for any of your people who help us retake the city.''

''A little fighting for an amnesty?''

''Something like that. Having a few of you inside the walls at key locations at the right time could save a lot of lives under the walls.''

''Well, let me think on this, and then I'll tell you what

I'll do tomorrow. Get some rest and don't try to escape.''

"What of my friends?''

"They're being cared for. I don't know how important they are to you, but I'm counting on them having a little call on your loyalties, so I can keep you in line.''

Dash nodded and the old man hobbled to the door. "Trina will keep you company for the night.'' Dash tried to look pleased, but the woman's dark glare made it clear amusing byplay would be lost on her.

After the door closed, Dash sat down on a pile of straw in the corner, obviously his bed for the night. A long moment of silence passed as Trina sat on the chair by the table watching him. Looking at his guard, he said, "Well, then. Do we tell one another our life stories?''

Taking out her dagger, the woman began to clean her fingernails with the point. She put her feet up on the table and said, "No, Puppy. We do not.''

Sighing, Dash lay down and closed his eyes.

Six

Choices

Nakor frowned.

He scanned the room of the warehouse in Darkmoor he was currently using as a base of operations, and said, "This will not do."

Sho Pi, his first disciple, said, "What, master?"

Since becoming self-appointed head of the Church of Arch-Indar, Nakor had ceased objecting to being referred to as "master" by the young former monk of Dala. Nakor pointed to the wagon that was being unloaded outside his new "church," and said, "We ordered twice that."

"I know," shouted the driver of the second wagon as it pulled up. "Hello, Nakor."

"Hello, Roo!" shouted the former gambler turned high priest. "Where is the rest of our grain?"

"This is all there is, my friend," said Rupert Avery, once the richest man in the history of the Western Realm, now the proud owner of three wagons, three teams of horses, and an amazing debt owed him by a near-bankrupt Kingdom. "Most of what I can buy goes to the Prince, to feed the soldiers."

"But I have gold," said Nakor.

"For which I am eternally grateful, for without your patronage, I would be unable to buy even the meanest grain out there. My credit is overextended in the East, I am forced to sell my holdings there to pay off my debts, and the money that's owed me is coming from a presently nonexistent Western Realm.''

"You seem unusually happy for a man in such dire straits," observed Nakor.

"Karli is going to have another baby."

Nakor laughed. "I thought you were put off by children."

Roo smiled, his narrow face showing an almost boyish aspect as he nodded. "Once I was, but when we fled Krondor and reached Darkmoor, well, that time cooped up with them almost every day, I came to learn a great deal about my children." His smile faded and he said, "About myself, as well."

"Learning about one's self is always a good thing," observed Nakor. "After you unload, come inside and I'll make us some tea."

"You have tea?" asked Roo. "Where did you get it?"

"A gift from a woman who had hidden it from before the war. It is not very fresh, I'm afraid, but it is tea."

"Good, I'll join you when I'm done here."

Nakor went inside the building, where another disciple was overseeing a class of students, five this time, listening to the introductory lesson on the role of good in the universe. Nakor realized that most, if not all, were there for the meager food his church provided after the lecture, but he was always hopeful someone would answer the call. So far he had recruited five new students, for a total of six counting Sho Pi. Given he had unilaterally decided to create a church for one of the four greatest Gods in the Midkemian universe, it was a very modest beginning.

"Any questions?" asked the disciple, who had himself heard the lecture for the first time only a few weeks before.

Four of the students looked back with expressions showing limited comprehension, but one tentatively raised her hand.

"Yes?" asked the disciple.

"Why are you doing this?"

"Why am I doing what?" said the disciple.

Nakor stopped and listened.

"Not you, all of you. Why are you preaching this message of good?"

The disciple looked at Nakor with near panic on his face. He had never been asked anything so basic, and the simplicity of the question was confounding him.

Nakor grinned. "I'll answer, but first I must know, why do you ask?"

The girl shrugged. "Most who preach are servants of one of the common gods, looking for something. You seem to be asking for nothing, and I wish to know what is the catch?"

Nakor grinned. "Ah, a cynic! How wonderful. You, come with me. The rest of you, wait here and you'll eat."

The girl rose and followed.

Nakor turned as he led her into what had once been a shipping office and now served as his personal quarters. A half-dozen sleeping mats were strewn across the floor, and a small brazier heated a pot of water. "What is your name, girl?"

"Aleta," answered the young woman. "Why?"

"Because you interest me."

The girl looked Nakor up and down frankly, and said, "Well, priest, you don't interest me if you're looking for a companion."

Nakor laughed. "That's funny. No, you interest me because you're curious." He poured tea and handed her a small cup. "It's not very good, but it's hot."

She sipped at it and said, "I agree. It is not very good."

"Now, about your question. I will answer you if you tell me what brought you here."

"I worked at an inn to the west of here before the war. It is now ashes. I almost starved during the winter. I have managed to stay alive without having to spread my legs or kill anyone, but I'm hungry, and your monk said there's to be food."

"A frank answer. Good. There will be food," said Nakor. "As to why we do this, let me ask you a question. What is the nature of good and evil?"

The girl blinked, and Nakor studied her as she framed her reply. She appeared to be in her middle twenties. She had a plain face, with wide-set eyes that made her appear to be as curious as her questions showed her to be, and her nose was straight. Her mouth was full, and her chin was strong, and the entire effect was more attractive than not, Nakor decided. She wore a heavy cloak over her dress, but Nakor had glimpsed enough of her as she had crossed the former warehouse to judge her slender, perhaps even wiry.

At last she said, "Good and evil *are* natures. They have no nature. They are what they are."

"Absolute?"

"What do you mean?"

"I mean do good and evil exist in some absolute sense?"

"I suppose so," said the girl. "I mean, I think men do what they do and sometimes it's good and sometimes it's evil, and sometimes I'm not sure, but out there, somewhere, good and evil exist, I guess."

"Good guess," said Nakor, smiling. "How would you like to stay with us?"

"That depends," she said, skepticism clearly evident. "For what purpose?"

"I need smart men and women. I need people who realize that what we're doing is important, without taking themselves too importantly."

Suddenly the girl laughed. "I've never taken myself very seriously."

"Good, neither have I."

"What is it you're doing?"

Nakor's manner and voice turned serious. "Out there are forces beyond your understanding. Beyond mine, too." He grinned, then returned to a serious demeanor. "Many of those qualities many people think of as being 'abstractions' are truly objective entities. Do you understand me?"

The girl shook her head. "I have no idea what you just said."

Nakor laughed. "Very good. You are honest. Let me put it another way. The Good Goddess is sleeping. She is in a trance caused by evil forces. To awaken her we must do good in her name. If enough of us work on her behalf, she will return to us and evil will be driven back into the shadows where it belongs."

"I understand that," said Aleta.

"You don't believe it."

The former barmaid said, "I don't know. I've never been much of one for gods and goddesses. But if it will fill my stomach, I'm willing to believe for a while."

"Fair enough." Nakor rose as Roo came into the office. "We'll feed you for as long as you wish to stay here, and you'll learn to do good in the Lady's name."

The girl departed and Roo said, "Another convert?"

"Perhaps," said Nakor. "Potentially. She's brighter than most."

Roo said, "Attractive, too, in a funny way. Not pretty, but attractive."

Nakor grinned. "I know."

Roo sat and Nakor offered him a cup of tea. "Sorry the order is short, but everyone is being shorted right now. I just finished a shouting match with Prince Patrick's quartermaster. The army is ready to march, but they lack stores and I can't promise as much as I've already brought from the East, let alone what they want." He sipped at the hot liquid and said, "Not good, but it'll do." Putting the cup down, he continued, "I can't even find wagons. I could bring more if I could get wagons, but most of the cartwrights in Salador are building for the army. If Patrick would convince the King to let me have his wagons, I could deliver them stocked with goods, but they're bringing more equipment—arms, saddles, blankets, and the like."

Nakor nodded. "You need to get your businesses here back up and running."

Roo laughed. "If only I could."

"What about building wagons here?"

"No cartwrights. I know a little about keeping them—I was raised a teamster, after all—but not about building one. I know a little carpentry, but I don't know the metal work, and turning a wheel is a special skill."

Nakor said, "If I can find you some cartwrights, would you do something for me?"

"What?"

"A favor."

Roo smiled. His narrow face showed his own wry sense of humor coming to the surface. "You're setting me up, aren't you?"

Nakor laughed. "Never trick a trickster."

"What is it?"

"If I can get you six cartwrights, I want you to commission a statue to be made for me."

"A statue? What for?"

"I'll tell you after I get the men. Will you do it?"

A calculating look crossed Roo's face, and he said, "Make it six cartwrights, a master smith, and three lumbermen, and I'll commission two statues."

"Done," said Nakor, slapping the table with his hand. "I'll have them for you tomorrow. Where should I send them?"

"I converted a warehouse outside the city to an office here in Darkmoor. I'll use it as a base until I can return to Krondor. Go out the eastern gate, and at the first road, turn left. It's the large green warehouse on the right. You can't miss it."

Nakor said, "I'll find it."

"There's something about that girl," said Roo, indicating where Aleta had gone. "I can't quite put my finger on what it is."

"She's someone important I think."

Roo laughed. "As long as I've known you I've never pretended to understand you."

"That's as it should be," replied Nakor. "For I have never understood myself."

"Can I ask you something, as a friend?"

"Of course."

"Over the years you've claimed you only know tricks, yet you manage the damnedest things that I can only call magic. Now you're starting a religion. Now, my question is, what are you really up to?"

Nakor grinned. "I'm starting something important. I'm not sure how it will turn out, and I doubt if I'll be around to see it at the end, but I'm doing something that may be the most important thing I've done in my life."

"And may I ask what that is?"

Nakor used his hand to indicate the poor building in which they sat. "I'm building a church."

Roo shook his head. "If you say so. Tell me, Nakor, has anyone ever called you mad?"

Nakor laughed. "Often, and most of the time they're serious."

Roo rose. "Thanks for the tea. I'll see what I can do about the grain, and if you get me those workers, I'll have those statues commissioned for you."

"I'll see you tomorrow."

Sho Pi entered and said, "Master, those who came to hear the lesson are ready for food."

"Then let us feed them," said Nakor.

The odd gambler turned religious leader halted at the office door and watched the five who were there a moment. Four of them would be gone after their bellies were full, but the girl, Aleta, would remain. And without knowing why, Nakor knew that a major part of his future path had turned a particular way because she was now here. He didn't know how he knew, but he was certain that from this time forward, she was the most important person in his newly founded church, and her life must be protected above everyone else, including himself. Keeping his thoughts to himself, he entered the warehouse and helped his disciples feed the hungry.

Erik pointed and said, "What do you see there?"

"Something's coming along the road," said Akee, the Hatadi hillman. "A single man, on horseback."

Erik squinted against the setting sun. Sure enough, what had been a faint movement, a speck of darkness against the bright sky, resolved itself into the figure of a man on horseback, trotting along the King's Highway.

Erik von Darkmoor, Captain of the Crimson Eagles, and a mixed detachment consisting of members of his own company, Hadati hillmen, and members of the Royal Krondorian Pathfinders were spread out on either side of the highway. "One of ours?" asked Erik.

Akee said, "I think so. I think it's Jimmy Jamison."

"How can you tell?"

The Hadati smiled. "You learn to recognize a friend by the way he sits his mount."

Erik turned to see if the man was joking and saw that he wasn't. During the winter Erik had spent enough time with the Hadati hillman and his company to come to respect him and even like him as much as one could the somewhat standoffish hill fighters. Akee was a leader in his village and considered an important voice in the council of the Hadati people up in Yabon, that much Erik had come to understand.

He had also discovered the man was the grandson of a companion of the former Prince of Krondor's, one Baru, called the Serpentslayer, and as a result, Akee was considered very sympathetic to the Kingdom, a quality not universal among the independent and tough-minded hill people of Yabon. Of all the people living within the boundaries of the Kingdom, the Hadati were among those most aloof. The fact that any had answered the Duke of Yabon's call for scouts was directly related to Akee's having been among them.

Jimmy rode closer and Erik and Akee left the shelter of the woods and rode toward him. Jimmy reined in until he recognized the two familiar figures, then he raised his hand in greeting.

As they stopped before him, Erik nodded, and Akee said, "You look as if you've been through something unpleasant."

"It could have been worse," said Jimmy.

Erik asked, "Dash?"

Jimmy shook his head. "He was captured for a while, but he got away. I don't know if he's somewhere in the city, or if he got loose. If he's loose, he's on his way back here. If he's in the city and is caught, I've got assurances he won't be harmed."

"Assurances?" said Erik.

"It's a long story. One I need to tell Prince Patrick, or at the least Owen Greylock."

"You're in luck," said Erik. "I'm heading back toward Ravensburg, where Owen has his forward command. The Prince is still in Darkmoor, but the roads are ours between here and there, almost as peaceful as before the war. You can reach the Prince in less than a week."

Jimmy said, "Good. I have grown very tired of the road and would love nothing more than a hot meal, a bath, and a soft bed."

Erik nodded and said to Akee, "Have your scouts move west for another day and report back."

Jimmy said, "There's no need. General Duko is recalling all his patrols. The only thing you need fear are bandits and some bored mercenaries camped under the walls. You can move your entire command to the outlying estates and build your camps there, less than a day's ride from the city."

Erik looked curious, but he only said, "I think I had better ride back with you, Jimmy."

"Where's your camp?"

"A few miles ahead." Erik waved good-bye to Akee, and turned his horse around as Jimmy urged his back to a walk. Erik moved his hand in a half-circle and said, "We have control of all the woods for miles on each side of the highway."

"You haven't had a lot of problems in the last few weeks, have you?"

"No, actually. A few bandits, some deserters, and a couple of run-ins with some mercenaries from our neighbors to the south, but we've seen little of Fadawah's forces for a while."

"Duko's looking to cut a deal with Patrick."

"He's willing to turn coat?" asked Erik. Erik had served two tours across the sea and was familiar with the Novindus mercenaries' tradition of serving the highest bidder. The dependence on such forces was one of the reasons, Erik was convinced, that no one had successfully built an empire down there, until the Emerald Queen had started her conquests.

"Not exactly," said Jimmy, filling in Erik on Duko's proposal.

Erik whistled. "I don't think Patrick is going to be pleased with this one. From what Greylock's told me and what I saw before I left Darkmoor, the Prince is spoiling for a fight, Kesh, invaders, he doesn't care who."

Jimmy said, "I'll leave it to my father and Owen to convince him. It's too good a turn of the cards for him to not agree. He saves thousands of lives and accelerates the retaking of the Western Realm by a year if he agrees."

Erik said nothing, but considering what he had seen of

the hot-tempered young Prince, he was not convinced Patrick would see it that way.

Dash regarded the boots, trousers, and jacket that had been secured for him by the Mockers. They were serviceable, but nothing remotely as good as the ones taken from him by his captors.

Lysle Riggers, the Upright Man, looked at him as he rose to leave. "Not yet, boy." The old man waved away Trina and the others of his company in the room, leaving Dash alone with his great-uncle. When the door was shut behind Trina, the old man said, "You must understand something. I don't think you're going to get your amnesty for us, so this conversation may have no meaning. If you do not, shortly I will die. Healing priests can only do so much, and I am an old man, anyway. Another will come forward to take the office I hold. Who he will be I cannot know, though I have a couple of guesses. John Tuppin might take the office—he's strong and shrewd and many are afraid of him. Trina might, if she's smart and silent, which she is, and can keep behind the scenes. But whoever it is, the agreements you and I reach will not be binding upon him. As I said, if you can't get the Prince to agree to giving us pardon for past crimes, it doesn't matter.

"But if you return with promises, they had best be kept, for if you are forsworn to the Mockers, no matter how high you rise, where you live, or what great office comes to you, eventually one of our brotherhood will find you in the night and your life will end. Do you understand?"

Dash said, "I understand."

"Know this as well, Dashel Jamison: once you step through that door you have taken blood oath not, by word or deed, to betray what you have seen here, nor may you bear witness against any who you've met. It is an oath made by silence, for you may not live to leave Mother's without such oath."

Dash didn't like being threatened, but he had heard enough stories about the Mockers from his grandfather to have no doubt that what Lysle was saying was not an idle threat. Dash said, "I know the rules as well as anyone born here."

"No doubt you do. My younger brother struck me as being a man with little modesty. I suspect you know as much about the workings of the Mockers as my own men." The Upright Man waved a bony scarred hand at Dash. "Before he came to my little shop, years ago, to tell me how the land lay and how I would be required to conduct the business of the Mockers, I would have wagered our ways and secrets were inviolate. In moments I learned that Jimmy the Hand had been watching us as we had been watching him, more, he had others watch us while he was not about. In the end, he was a far better Duke than I was leader of the Mockers."

Dash shrugged. "If Patrick does as I request, it all ends, anyway."

The old man laughed. "Think you that a pardon will take this ragged brotherhood of ours and set our feet upon the straight and narrow path? Within minutes of such pardon some of our more reckless youth will be cutting purses in the market square or breaking into warehouse cellars, young Dash. The dodgy path is as much a part of who we are as it is a choice in life.

"Some, like your grandfather, find an escape, a way to better themselves, but most are confined to Mother's and the sewers of the city, the rooftops—the Thieves' Highway—and a short life ending with a hangman's rope. It is as much a prison as the one in the basement of the palace, this life, for there is little chance of escape."

Dash shrugged. "At least everyone, you, Trina, the rest, will have a choice. Most men can't ask more than that."

The old man laughed his dry laugh. "You're wise beyond your years, Dash, if you really understand that and are not merely mouthing words heard at the knee of another. Now go."

Outside Dash found his three companions from the work gang waiting. Gustaf and Talwin were together, while Reese stood next to some Mockers. "You coming with me?" asked Dash.

Reese shook his head. "Not me. I was a Mocker before they caught me, and these are my people. This is my home."

Dash nodded. Looking at the other two, he said, "You?"

Gustaf said, "I'm a swordsman without a sword. I need a job. You hiring?"

Dash smiled. "Yes, I'll hire you."

Talwin said, "I just want to get out of the city."

"Then it's the three of us."

Trina came and stood before Dash. "Well, Puppy, I'll show you back to the safest way out. Wait until nightfall, then get out of the outer camps. Rumors are starting to circulate that the Prince's army is getting close and men are sleeping close to their swords. There aren't many friends to be found in a place like that."

Dash nodded and asked, "Weapons?"

"We have some for you," said the heavyset man who had been his first captor, the man Dash knew as John Tuppin. "We'll give them to you just before you leave."

Dash nodded. "Then let's be off."

He glanced over his shoulder at the closed door, behind which sat the old man who claimed one of the most mysterious names in the history of Krondor, the Upright Man. Dash wondered if he'd ever see the old man again.

They set off in the gloom.

Pug sat quietly considering the choices that were rapidly approaching. Miranda watched him.

After a few moments, he turned his attention from whatever image hung in the air outside his window and said, "What?"

She laughed. "You were millions of miles away, weren't you?"

He smiled at her. "Not really. Just a few hundred. But I was years away."

"What were you thinking of?"

"My past, and my future."

"Our future, you mean."

He shook his head. "There are still some choices left to me alone."

She rose up from her seat next to the fireplace. A small fire, more for comfort than warmth, which had been allowed to burn down to coals, smoked there. She glanced at it, and came to stand before her husband. She settled easily into his lap and said, "Tell me."

"Gathis's choice. The Gods' choice, really."

"Have you decided what you must do?"

He nodded. "I think for me there is only one choice."

After a moment of silence, she said, "Care to share it with me?"

He laughed, kissing her on the neck. She squealed appreciatively, then playfully pushed herself away. "You'll not divert me that easily. What are you thinking?"

Pug smiled. "When I lay in Death's Hall, I was given the choice to become your father's heir."

At mention of Macros the Black, Miranda frowned. She had never had a close relationship with her father, and the primary reason for that had been his association with great powers. His role as human surrogate for Sarig, the lost God of Magic, had reduced his role in her life to a scant decade out of nearly two hundred years she had lived so far.

Pug continued. "I can't be Sarig's agent on Midkemia. That's not my role."

"From what you told me, your other choices weren't that appealing."

Pug looked worried. "I didn't die, so that narrows my choice down to one: I must live and watch destruction and death and lose that which is most dear to me."

She returned to his lap, and said, "That has already been fulfilled. Your daughter and son were taken from you, weren't they?"

Pug nodded, and she could see the echoes of pain still not dulled within his eyes. "But I fear there is more to lose."

She settled into his arms, resting her head on his shoulder. "There is always the potential for loss, my love. Until we are at last dead, we can lose. That is the irony of life. Nothing is forever."

Pug said, "I am almost a hundred years old, yet I feel like such a child."

Miranda laughed and held him close. "We are children, my love, and I'm twice your age. Compared to the Gods we are infants, just learning our first steps."

"But infants have teachers."

"You had teachers," she said. "So did I."

"I could use one now, I think."

Miranda said, "I shall teach you."

Pug looked at her. "You will?"

She kissed him. "And you shall teach me. And we shall teach your students on my father's island, and they shall teach us. We have books yet to be read and understood, and we have the Hall of Worlds, through which we can reach out to wisdom undreamed of on this tiny orb. And we have ages to do it."

Pug sighed. "You make me feel as if there's hope."

Miranda said, "There is always hope."

There came a knock at the door and Miranda stood, allowing Pug to rise to answer the door. Outside stood a royal page, and he said, "My lord, the Prince requests your presence at once."

Pug glanced at Miranda, who shrugged in curiosity but said nothing. He nodded to her, and followed the page.

He wended his way through Castle Darkmoor, until he came to the old Baron's quarters, being used presently by Prince Patrick. The page opened the door and stepped aside, allowing Pug to enter.

Patrick looked up from old Baron Otto's desk and said, "Magician, we have a problem I hope you can deal with."

"What may that be, Your Highness?"

Patrick held up a rolled-up parchment. "A report in from the North. The Saaur have decided to put in an appearance."

"From the North?" Pug looked puzzled. When he had persuaded the Saaur to quit the field in the final battle for Darkmoor, their leader, the Sha-shahan, had vowed a blood price would be extracted for the wrongs done the Saaur. But to the North lay the armies of Fadawah, the most likely object of that vengeance. How could the Saaur have returned to their old allies after withdrawing? Pug said, "Where in the North, Highness?"

"The northeast! They've wintered north of us, between the mountains and the woodlands of the Dimwood. They've occupied the southern end of the Thunderhell Steppes, and now they've struck southward."

"Southward!" Pug echoed, alarm in his voice. "They've attacked us?"

Patrick threw down the parchment. "Read about it. They

overran a detachment held in reserve in the foothills, to reinforce whichever gap Fadawah might attempt to breach along Nightmare Ridge. They slaughtered every man in the company.''

''Are they continuing to move?''

''No,'' said Patrick. ''That's the good news in this. They seem content to butcher three hundred of my soldiers, then withdraw. They left us a warning, though.''

''What is that?''

''They left three hundred stakes in the ground. Atop each was a man's head. It's a clear challenge.''

''No, Highness,'' corrected Pug. ''It's not a challenge. It's a warning.''

''A warning to whom?'' Patrick said, his anger barely held in check.

''To anyone. To us, to Fadawah, to the Brotherhood of the Dark Path, any creature of intelligence who is near enough to see the skulls. Jatuk is telling us that the Saaur are claiming the Thunderhell Steppes for themselves and for us to stay out.''

Patrick considered it and said, ''Save nomads, weapons runners, and outlaws, no one lives there I would care to name Citizen of the Kingdom, but it's still our Realm. I will be damned to the lower hells before I allow an army of aliens to overrun my troops and declare themselves an independent nation within our borders.''

''What would you have of me, Highness?''

''In the morning I'm sending a detachment of soldiers northward. I would appreciate it if you'd accompany them. You were the one to get the Saaur out of the war. If this Jatuk wants to turn his anger against Fadawah, I'll withdraw my soldiers along the northern ridge and even give him supplies to go assault Fadawah in Yabon. But I can't have this bloody business go unchallenged.''

''What would you have me tell them?''

''Tell them they must cease this hostility against us, and withdraw from our lands.''

''To where, Highness?''

Patrick said, ''I don't care where. They can have safe conduct to the coast, and they can swim home for all I care, but I won't have them telling me to stay out of any part of my own Principality! There's been too damn much of that lately!'' Patrick's voice was rising and Pug could tell anger was getting the best of him.

"I will be pleased to go, Highness."

"Good," said Patrick, his tone leveling off. "I've sent word to Captain Subai, who's in charge of the northern elements of our forces along the ridge, that someone would be coming. I want you to have him accompany you and I want this matter resolved. I've got enough to worry about with this business down in Stardock, Kesh acting foolish, and Fadawah living in my Principality to have the Saaur act up.

"If they'll listen to reason, I'll listen to reason. Have them tell me what we must do to get them out of our Kingdom and I will do it. But if they refuse, there's only one thing you can do."

"What is that, Highness?"

Patrick looked at Pug as if he were missing the obvious. He said, "Why, you must destroy them, magician. You must obliterate them from the face of the world."

Seven

Opportunity

JIMMY GRIMACED.

Ho had one good night's sleep, in Owen Greylock's camp, then had spent the next five days in the saddle, tiring out a string of relay horses. He and the Knight-Marshal of Krondor rode as quickly as possible to Darkmoor, where Prince Patrick's court was established.

Now he stood outside Patrick's quarters, having ridden in just before dawn. He waited along with other courtiers, while the Prince was dressing for the day's court, and thanked all the gods he could think of that at least here an ample supply of Keshian coffee was still to be found. Tsurani chocha was a reasonable substitute, but nothing kept him going like a hot mug of coffee, cut with a tiny bit of honey.

"James!" said a familiar feminine voice from behind, and Jimmy was suddenly wide awake. He turned to see a young woman approaching.

"Francie?" he asked in astonishment.

In a serious breach of court protocol, the girl threw her arms around Jimmy's neck, and said, "It's been years!"

Jimmy hugged the girl back. He then stepped back and regarded her. "You're all grown up," he said, admiring that fact. She was a tall girl, slender yet muscular in his embrace, as if she had spent a great deal of time outdoors in vigorous physical activity. Her face was lacking the usual cosmetics of the women of court; sun freckles lightly brushed her cheeks and nose. Her hair, usually a light brown, was lavishly streaked with blond highlights. She wore a very mannish vest and trousers, white shirt, and riding boots.

"I was just coming back from an early morning ride with Father and saw you standing here. Let me go change and put on something more appropriate. Where can I find you?"

As the Prince's door opened, Jimmy said, "Wherever His Highness puts me, but most likely in the officers' mess."

She nodded. "I'll find you." Kissing him lightly on the cheek, she dashed off, and Jimmy was forced to admire the way she moved.

Owen, who had stood silently next to Jimmy throughout the exchange, said, "And that would be . . . ?"

"The Duke of Silden's daughter, Francine. She used to play with Dash and me when we lived in Rillanon and business would bring Lord Brian to court. She's Dash's age, and last time I saw her she was just a skinny kid. She had a terrible crush on me for the longest time."

"Ah," was all Owen said, as the Prince's page appeared.

The page saw Greylock, and said, "Marshal Greylock, His Highness will see you first."

Owen motioned for Jimmy to follow him, and they entered Patrick's quarters.

The Prince remained seated behind his desk, cluttered with papers and a small silver tray with hot rolls and a pot of coffee. Duke Arutha sat quietly at the left end of the desk. He looked at his son and smiled. "I can't tell you how pleased I am to see you. Dash?"

Jimmy shook his head. "He's out there somewhere." Arutha's smile faded.

Patrick finished a mouthful of roll and said, "What news of Krondor?"

Owen said, "Jimmy brings a message from General Duko."

Patrick asked, "From General Duko?"

Jimmy said, "The invaders are having a falling-out, it seems." He outlined what Duko had told him of his suspicions regarding Fadawah and Nordan, and finished up with, "So the General has a proposal to keep himself and his men from being sacrificed and return Krondor to Your Highness without bloodshed."

Patrick's face was an unreadable mask. Jimmy could see the Prince already could sense where this was going. "Go on," said the Prince of Krondor.

"Duko sees no point in returning to Novindus. The continent is a waste after ten years of warfare, and . . ." Jimmy paused.

"Go on," repeated Patrick.

"He sees something special in our idea of a nation, Highness. He wishes to belong to something larger than himself. He proposes to return Krondor to Your Highness, and to swear fealty to the crown. He will turn his army northward, and march against Nordan up in Sarth."

Patrick's color started to rise. "Swear fealty!" He leaned forward. "And perhaps he wishes to be named Duke of Krondor in place of your father, as well?"

Jimmy attempted to keep it light. "Nothing so grand, Highness. A Barony, perhaps."

"Barony!" Patrick exploded, slamming his hand on the table, upsetting the coffeepot and spilling the hot liquid over the rolls and across a dozen parchments. The page standing nearby sprang to clean up the mess while the Prince stood up. "The murdering dog has the effrontery to seize my city then hold me up for a Barony to give it back! The thief has no lack of gall." He looked at Owen and Arutha. "Is there any reason I shouldn't order the army into the field and simply hang the bastard after we retake Krondor?"

Arutha said, "There are several reasons, Highness."

Patrick looked at him. "They are?"

"By making a bargain with Duko, we take the enemy's forces and reduce them by a third. We increase our forces by that much. We save the lives of countless men. We then have an advance unit to throw at Sarth, and we free up men needed to reinforce the southern marches, holding Kesh at bay." Arutha seemed reluctant to continue, but finished by saying, "If Duko is being forthright and this isn't some sort of elaborate ruse, it's too good an opportunity to pass up."

"Invade my realm, steal my city, destroy my citizens' lives and property, then turn around and extort a patent of office from my father, and it's 'too good an opportunity to pass up'?" Patrick looked at Arutha, and shouted, "Are you bereft of all reason, my lord?"

Jimmy stiffened in anger at his father being addressed in such a way, but said nothing. Arutha, showing the patience of a parent faced with a child throwing a tantrum, said, "I am reasoning very well, Highness." Then, in the tone a schoolmaster used with a student, he calmly said, "Sit down, Patrick."

Prince of the Western Realm or not, Arutha had been one of Patrick's tutors, and old habits were hard to break. He sat behind his desk, looking daggers at Arutha, but remaining silent.

"You must think like a Prince. No matter what else you do with the invaders, you must also deal with Kesh. They are only restraining themselves because the magicians at Stardock are as likely to destroy their forces as they are ours should either side not abide by the present truce. The *only* way you can deal with Great Kesh is from a position of strength.

"You must reclaim Yabon. To do that you must clear the Western Realm west of the Calastius Mountains, and to do that you have to take Sarth. If you are forced to fight for Krondor, you will not be able to launch a campaign against Sarth until the middle of summer, *at the soonest*!" Arutha's temper was also rising, but he did a masterful job of keeping his tone under control. "If you have any sort of protracted campaign against Sarth, that means a winter campaign against Ylith or holding off until the following year. By then LaMut will have fallen. If you give Fadawah another winter to consolidate his holdings, we may never regain the North!" He lowered his voice. "Fadawah has already bribed key officials in the Free Cities. They're trading with him from all reports. In three months, his army will be better provisioned than our own. He's also making overtures to the Quegans, who are likely to listen, given how badly they were treated during the invasion." He glanced at Owen.

Greylock said, "Taking Ylith is going to require naval support, Highness. If Fadawah is as clever as he seems, he'll have Quegan ships anchored in the harbor by the time we get there, and that would mean another war with Queg."

Patrick looked as if he was frustrated to the point of tears. But he kept his voice and anger under control as he said, "So you're telling me unless I make a bargain with this murderous scum I may be fighting a three-front war I can't win?"

Arutha sighed loudly. "That's exactly what we're telling you, Highness."

Patrick's fury was barely held in check. He was intelligent enough to know that Arutha was right, but angry enough to be unwilling to admit it. "There must be another way."

"Yes," said Owen. "You can march to the walls of Krondor, through the assembled mercenaries camped outside, swarm the city and fight house to house for a week, then spend another month licking your wounds and getting ready to march north."

Patrick seemed to lose his anger. "Damn," was all he said. For a long moment, he was silent, then one more time he said, "Damn."

Arutha said, "Patrick, you can't reject this offer. An invading general is seeking to make a separate peace with us, and only the King can reject that offer. Do you want to guess that your father will say no? He'll ratify any deal you and I strike with Duko, that much I know. All we need are some assurances that this isn't a trick of Fadawah's."

Jimmy said, "Highness, I only spent a few days with the man, but I think him sincere. There's a . . ." He paused, searching for the right words to describe what he saw in Duko.

"Say on," prompted Patrick.

"There's something in the man, a hope. He's tired of the killing, the endless conquest. He told me of the time when he discovered the evil that possessed the Emerald Queen, when she created her Immortals, her Death Guard, the men who surrounded her and who willingly died for her, one each night, so that she might keep intact her death magic. By then any man who showed the slightest hesitation was destroyed, common soldier or general, it didn't matter. That was demonstrated early in the campaign when some captains tried a revolt, and all were impaled, with the bulk of her army forced to march by the men while they still twitched as they died. After the fall of Maharta, General Gapi was staked out over an anthill for letting Captain Calis and his men escape. That showed no one, no matter what rank, was safe from her wrath. Companies were instructed to watch other companies, so no one knew who could be trusted not to report if even a hint of defiance was suspected.

"Duko spent the winter talking to Kingdom prisoners, soldiers and commoners, some officers from the garrisons down at Land's End and up at Sarth. He's fascinated by our way of living, our government, our Great Freedom, and he thinks it a wondrous thing, our idea of nation. He was trapped, a prisoner, and jailer of every other prisoner in the army." Jimmy took a deep breath, and said, "I think he wants to be part of something bigger, something that will live on after his death and something about which he can feel giving his life might be worthwhile."

Arutha said, "And he's been betrayed by his own commander. He may be exactly what he says he is."

"I want reassurances," said Patrick sharply. "I want whatever guarantees you can dream up to convince me I should bring this murdering butcher into our nobility."

Owen laughed.

"Is there something funny in this, Lord Greylock?" asked the Prince.

"Only that I imagine an ancestor of yours may have said exactly the same thing about the first Baron to live in this castle," said Greylock, smiling.

Patrick paused, then sighed. After a moment, he chuckled. "One of my teachers told me the King of Rillanon had drunk himself into near insensibility over the need to accept Bas-Tyra into his service, rather than hang him from the walls of his city."

"Many of our most noble lords had ancestors who were

nothing more than enemies we chose not to hang, Highness," said Arutha.

"Well," said Patrick, "we have no shortage of openings for nobles in the West. Where shall we place 'Lord' Duko?"

Arutha said, "There are several Earldoms, a score of Baronies, and one Duchy in need of new nobles."

Owen said, "We need a Duke of the Southern Marches."

Patrick looked at James. "What do you think of throwing that rabble in Krondor at the Keshians?"

Jimmy said, "Highness, I hesitate to advise . . ."

Patrick looked sharply at Jimmy. "Don't get modest on me at this late date, James. You'd be the first in your family in three generations and I wouldn't believe it anyway."

James smiled. "If you move Duko and his men down into the Sutherlands, between Shandon Bay and Land's End, you could move those soldiers up into Krondor and still keep a presence along the border to the southwest. We can assume there are Keshian agents all over who are keeping the Emperor's generals up on our dispositions by the minute. You could then turn at Krondor and move straight up to take Sarth, before Nordan gets dug in."

Patrick looked at Owen. "Greylock, you're Knight-Marshal of Krondor. What do you think of young James's thesis?"

Owen knew exactly what he thought of it; he had been discussing this plan with Jimmy the entire journey from his headquarters camp to Darkmoor. "It's risky, Highness, but far less risky than trapping Duko between our army and Nordan's and making his men fight for their lives. And if we move them down to face Kesh, we don't have to worry about Duko's men facing their former comrades, or any spies Fadawah might have in their ranks. Besides, half the men living in the Vale of Dreams are mercenaries, fighting for us or against us at whim; Duko may be exactly the man to rule such as those." He paused, as if thinking about his next statement, which had been rehearsed in his mind many times already. "If we continue to dredge the harbor, and get the city back into a semblance of order in the next month, we can drive on to Sarth in six weeks. That would put us six weeks ahead of schedule. We could be at the gates of Ylith before the fall rains come.''

Patrick said, ''I'll prepare messages for my father. If I can't give the murderous bastard to the hangman, I'll give him to the Keshians. We'll need to send a message to welcome our newest Duke into the 'family,' and let him know to prepare for a mobilization of his men.''

James rose, and said, ''If Your Highness will excuse me?''

Patrick waved him away, and Arutha rose. ''If I may be excused for a few minutes to speak with my son?''

Patrick nodded and turned to his page. ''Have a scribe come here at once.''

Arutha led his son out to the waiting room and moved away from the others gathered to await the Prince's pleasure. Softly, so as not to be overhead, he said, ''What of Dash?''

''We were separated. Malar and I—''

''Who's Malar?'' interrupted Arutha.

''A servant from the Vale of Dreams we encountered. His caravan was attacked and he survived in the wilderness for a month or more.''

''Malar,'' said Arutha. ''That name's familiar.''

''Malar Enares,'' Jimmy supplied. ''That's his full name.''

''Yes, it's familiar, but I can't place it.''

''I don't know why you'd know it, Father. His master was an important merchant, perhaps that's where you know it from.''

Arutha said, ''Most of my records are still in boxes from when we evacuated Krondor. Normally, I'd have my clerk look for that name. If I still had a clerk.''

Jimmy said, ''Well, if you recognize the name, he's more than he seems to be. I'll keep an eye on him if he's still around when I get back to Krondor.''

Arutha put his hand on Jimmy's shoulder. ''Do that. Rest now and be ready to leave in a day or two. Patrick should have something to send to Duko in two days at the outside. We'll need some sort of ceremony and pomp, a formal surrender and an investiture of office. I wish old Jerome was still alive.''

Jimmy grinned. "Grandfather never got along with him."

"No, but he was as good a Master of Ceremony as I've ever known. If you needed the proper welcoming ceremony for a creature from the lower hells, he could find it for you and have it ready on short notice."

Jimmy said, "I think a meal and a nap will do for me right now."

"By the way," said Arutha, "Lord Silden is here. He brought Francine with him."

"I saw her, just before I went in to see you and the Prince. She was coming in from a morning ride. She's grown up."

"I remember you used to think her a pest when you were children in Rillanon. Does she still want to marry you?"

Jimmy laughed. "Only if I'm lucky. I'm having the mid-day meal with her if I can stay awake."

Arutha smiled. "You'll manage." Then his manner turned somber. "I just wish we had some word about your brother."

Jimmy nodded. "Me too."

Arutha squeezed his elder son's shoulder briefly, then returned to the Prince's office. Jimmy thought about lunch with Francie and decided he wasn't as tired as he had been before. He decided he might wander down to the guard captain's office to see if any reports from the West had come in since the night before. He might be lucky and hear something of Dash.

Pug moved through the door of the "temple," finding it empty. From behind the converted warehouse he could hear the sounds of shouts and children laughing. He hurried through the empty building, past a makeshift altar, through a kitchen area, and into the work yard attached to the old warehouse.

Nakor squatted near a child who was blowing bubbles with soapy water. Other children chased and grabbed at the bubbles, but the former gambler stared intently at a bubble being formed on the end of the little boy's pipe. It expanded, as Nakor said, "Slowly, slowly."

Then, as it reached the size of a melon, the little boy

gave in to the impulse to blow hard, and it popped as a stream of tiny bubbles surged from the tip of the pipe. The other children in the yard erupted in laughter, shrieking with delight as the bubbles sailed away on the afternoon breeze.

Pug laughed and Nakor turned. At seeing the magician, Nakor's face split into a wide grin. "Pug, what wondrous timing!"

Pug approached and they shook hands. "Why?"

"The bubble. A thought came to me while watching these children and I needed to ask you something."

"What?"

"That story you told me, of when you, Tomas, and Macros went back to the dawn of time, remember?"

"I could hardly forget that," replied Pug.

"You said there was this gigantic explosion that launched the universe outward, didn't you?"

"I don't know if I put it exactly like that, but yes, that's basically what happened."

Nakor laughed and did a tiny dance for a minute. "I have it!"

"Have what?"

"I have been wrestling with a thought since you told me that story, years ago. Now I think I understand something. Watch the boy as he blows a bubble." He turned to the boy. "Charles, again, please."

The boy obliged by blowing a single large bubble. "Watch it expand!" insisted Nakor. "See how it grows larger!"

"Yes," said Pug. "What is the point?"

"It's a drop of soapy water, but you force air inside, and it grows! It gets bigger, but the content of the water droplet is the same. Don't you see?"

"What?" asked Pug, genuinely perplexed at Nakor's latest revelation.

"The universe! It's a bubble!"

Pug said, "Oh . . ." He paused. "I don't see."

Using his hand, Nakor made a curving motion, as if describing a sphere in the air. "The stuff of the universe, it was blown outward, like the soap bubble! Everything in the universe, *is on the surface of the bubble!*"

Pug stopped a moment, considered what he heard, then said, "That's amazing."

"Everything is moving away from everything else at the same speed! That's the only way it's possible."

Pug was genuinely impressed with the insight. "Now, what does it mean?"

"What it means is we now have a clue as to how things in the universe work. And that might give us a better understanding of what it is we do in the middle of this universe."

"On the surface, you mean."

"On the surface," conceded Nakor.

"Then what is in the middle?" asked Pug.

Nakor grinned. "The void. That grey stuff you talk about."

Pug paused. "That would . . . make sense."

"And when you create a rift, you bend the surface of the bubble!"

Pug shook his head. "You just lost me."

"I'll explain it all to you some other time. Now, if I could just figure out how the Hall of Worlds figures into all this. . . ."

Pug said, "You'll think of something, I am certain."

Nakor said, "You had a reason to visit with me?"

"Yes, I need your help."

Nakor said, "Children, continue playing."

"Who are these children?" asked Pug as Nakor led him back into the temple.

"The sons and daughters of people who live nearby, people who are attempting to rebuild their ruined homes and businesses, but who have no place for their children while they do. We give them a safe place to leave the children rather than let them run the streets."

"And when the businesses are rebuilt, the children will return to help their parents."

"Correct," said Nakor. "In the meantime, we build some nice credits with people who will be inclined to help us out along the way. Skilled tradesmen, for the most part."

"You're really committed to this Temple of Arch-Indar, aren't you?"

"I'm committed to getting it built," said Nakor.

"After that?"

Nakor shrugged. "I don't know. I'll leave this to someone better able to run it than myself. It's not really my calling. If it were the Temple of the Lost God of Knowledge, maybe, though I think I've had enough of Wodar-Hospur's handiwork for a lifetime." He referred to the magic codex which he had possessed for many years, an artifact which had given him incredible knowledge and power, but which had also threatened his sanity.

"What then?"

"I don't know. I think I'll move on."

They reached Nakor's office and Pug closed the door behind them. "Are you thinking of leaving Sho Pi in charge?"

"I don't think so. He's . . . heading for a different path, though I'm not sure what that might be."

"Someone else?" asked Pug as he sat.

Nakor nodded. "I'm not sure, but I think I may know who."

"Care to enlighten me?"

"No," said Nakor with a grin as he sat down. "I might be wrong, then I would look foolish."

"Heaven forfend," Pug said dryly.

"Now what sort of help do you need from me?"

Pug explained the situation with the Saaur to the north, then finished by saying, "Patrick wants me to deliver an ultimatum, and if they refuse to depart from the Kingdom, he's ordered me to destroy them."

Nakor frowned. "Tales of your powers have been circulating for some years, my friend. I thought it but a matter of time before someone in authority attempted to bend you to their cause."

"I've served the Kingdom without orders before."

"True, but you've never been under the authority of an impetuous boy before."

Pug sat back in his chair, and said, "I've never considered myself under anyone's authority since coming to my power. As a Great One of the Tsurani Empire, I was outside the law, subject to no authority save my own conscience and a mandate to do what was best for the Empire.

"Since returning to Midkemia, the crown was content to

leave me alone, to let me conduct my business down in Stardock as I saw fit. King Borric, and King Lyam before him, were satisfied knowing I would do nothing to cause harm to their realms. Now, about this 'go destroy our enemies' order of Patrick's, I'm not sure what's best to do.''

Nakor pointed at Pug. ''You've lived on another world, Pug. That boy up in the castle has barely spent more than a couple of years of his life off the island of Rillanon. You've been a slave and a man beyond the law of the land, you've labored in a kitchen and you are afforded the rank of Duke. You've traveled in time.'' Nakor smiled. ''You've seen a lot of things.'' He lost the smile. ''Patrick's a scared boy, but he's a scared boy with a bad temper and an army who will obey him. That's a dangerous combination.''

''Maybe I should go to the King.''

Nakor said, ''Perhaps, but I'd save that option until you've talked to the Saaur and seen if you can convince them to leave.''

''Would you consider coming with me? You have a wonderful knack for knowing what to do in unusual situations.''

Nakor was silent a moment, then said, ''Preventing the death of many would be a good act. Yes, I'll come with you. But you could do me a favor, first.''

''What?''

''Come with me.''

Pug stood and followed Nakor out of the office. In the far corner of the large hall Sho Pi and a pair of acolytes were in discussion. Nakor shouted, ''Sho Pi, you keep an eye on the children. I'll be back.''

He took Pug through the streets toward the castle, but short of where they would normally turn to approach the main drawbridge of the castle, they turned and followed another street down toward a burned-out section of the city. Reaching a checkpoint, they were halted by a pair of guardsmen, wearing tabards of the Baron of Darkmoor. ''Halt,'' said one in a bored tone of voice.

Nakor said, ''This is Pug, Duke of Stardock, on a mission for the Prince of Krondor.''

''Sir!'' said the guard, coming to attention. He might not have seen the magician before, but every soldier in the

West knew of him by reputation and he looked the part.

"We need to commandeer a score of prisoners for a work detail," said Nakor.

"I'll fetch some guards to accompany you," said the sentry.

"No need," said Nakor, holding up his hand. "We can take care of ourselves."

He motioned for Pug to follow and hurried by before the guard could object. Pug said, "We'll be fine."

They entered an area of a half-dozen city blocks, razed by fire and catapults, where the prisoners of war were being kept. Nakor found a large boulder and climbed atop it. He shouted in the language of Novindus, "I need some workers."

A few men nearby looked over and one or two continued to pay attention, but no one came near. Nakor waited a moment, then climbed down. "This isn't working. Come along."

He hurried deeper into the milling camp of men. On all sides dirty and hungry-looking mercenaries sat in idle conversation. As he moved deeper into the press of men, he said, "I need some carpenters, cartwrights, wheelwrights, wagon makers!"

One man said, "I used to be a carpenter, before I was forced to fight."

"Can you turn a wheel?"

The man nodded. "I can shave spokes, too."

"Come with me!"

"Why should I?" said the man. He was in his fifties, grey-haired, and looked filthy and miserable.

"Because you've got nothing better to do, have you? And you'll get better food and you'll get paid."

At that the man said, "Paid? I'm a prisoner."

"Not anymore, if you want work. I'll make you a priest of Arch-Indar."

"Who?" asked the man in confusion.

"The Good Lady," said Nakor impatiently. "Now, just come along and say nothing."

The exchange was repeated a half-dozen more times, until Nakor had selected seven men with the required experience. Several others had come forth, but lacked the requisite skills. When they had returned to the pair of guards manning the exit, Pug said, "I'm taking these men with me. They have skills I need for a project."

"Begging your pardon, my lord," said the senior guard, "but this is highly irregular. We have no orders."

"I'll take full responsibility," said Pug. "I'm on a mission for the Prince."

The senior soldier exchanged glances with the junior, who shrugged. The first soldier said, "Well, then, I guess it's all right."

They led the prisoners back to the temple, and Nakor shouted as they entered, "Sho Pi!"

The first of his disciples hurried over. "Yes, master?"

"Get these men some food and some clean clothing." He glanced back, and added, "After they take baths."

Sho Pi nodded. "I will, master."

"Then send a message to Rupert Avery and tell him his workers are waiting for him."

Pug said, "Workers?"

Nakor nodded. "Roo's going to start up a little wagon-building enterprise as soon as we return to the camp in the morning and get him some lumbermen."

"Lumbermen?" asked Pug.

Nakor grinned. "I'll explain it all as we travel."

Pug returned the smile.

Nakor said, "One favor more."

"What is that?"

Nakor lowered his voice. "I strongly urge you to require the Lady Miranda stay behind."

Pug said, "Miranda can take care of herself."

"I fear not for her competence, but rather that well-demonstrated temper of hers. You are going in harm's way, even if the risks are minimal. She might not react well to a threat."

Pug said, "I doubt she'd cause another war, but I see what you mean." He was thoughtful for a moment, then said, "I think I'd like her to visit Tomas and see how things are to the north, anyway. We're getting almost nothing from Crydee or Elvandar, and if we're going to be moving quickly to retake Ylith, knowing how the struggle for Yabon goes is vital."

"She has the means to travel there?"

"There are some 'tricks' my wife is capable of that you and I need to learn. She can transport herself without patterns or devices."

"That would be *very* useful."

Pug said, "You and I, I'm sorry to say, will be traveling by horse. I can fly, but not if I'm carrying you along."

Nakor said, "It's better than walking."

Pug laughed. "You have a wonderful capacity to see the good in most situations."

Nakor said, "It helps at times."

"I'll send word when I'm ready to leave. Two more days, I think."

"I'll be ready," said Nakor as Pug left.

Eight

Preparations

Dash SIGNALED.

The guards at the sentry post waved him and his companions forward.

Dash, Gustaf, and Talwin had trudged along the road for three days, not catching sight of anyone, save for what they took to be a roving bunch of bandits late the second afternoon. Duko had pulled back his forces to just outside of Krondor, so the patrols that had caused the brothers so much difficulty just a few weeks earlier were now nonexistent.

The nearest soldier said, "Who goes there?"

Dash answered, "I'm Dashel Jamison, Baron of the King's Court."

Gustaf and Talwin exchanged surprised glances at that, but said nothing. They knew something odd had gone on while they were prisoners of the Mockers, and that Dash had spent time alone with their leader, but beyond that they only knew the young man was leading them away from captivity and toward what they hoped would be a warm meal, clean bedding, and employment.

"Gar!" shouted the first soldier to the second. "Go get the sergeant!"

The second soldier started up the road at a trot, toward

the distant lights of the Kingdom's forward encampment. Dash and the others halted before the first soldier. The man stood in awkward silence a long minute, then said, "If I might ask, m'lord . . ."

"What?" said Dash.

It was obvious the soldier was curious how a noble of the Prince's court could end up in such disreputable attire with questionable company late in the day on the wrong side of enemy lines, but he restricted himself to asking, "Would you like some water?"

"Yes, thank you," answered Dash.

The soldier passed over a water skin and Dash drank, handing it to Gustaf, who then gave it to Talwin. Dash said, "I think I'll sit," and he moved over to the side of the road and sat.

His companions joined him. They sat in silence, ignoring the curious sentry.

A short time later a group of riders approached from the Kingdom camp, leading three horses. A sergeant jumped down from the first horse, handing the reins to the sentry, and said, "Baron Dashel?"

Dash stood up and said, "That's me."

"Captain von Darkmoor is at the forward location and is waiting for you and your companions, sir."

The three men rode with the escort a scant mile up the road to Erik's camp. He was waiting outside his headquarters tent and said, "Dash! Your father will be pleased to hear you got back in one piece."

"What of my brother?" asked Dash as he dismounted.

"He arrived about a week ago; he and Owen hurried off to see the Prince and your father. Come inside."

Erik gave instructions to a soldier to find a place for Gustaf and Talwin to spend the night, and once inside his command tent said, "Hot food is on the way."

"Good," said Dash, sitting heavily in a camp chair next to a large map table. He glanced at the map and said, "Getting ready to assault Krondor?"

Erik shook his head. "We may not have to, if your brother's message from Duko is not some sort of lie."

"Message?"

"Jimmy got himself captured and was turned loose by Duko, bringing an offer to Patrick."

"What sort of offer?" asked Dash.

"Duko wants to change sides."

"You could have fooled me," said Dash. "I was stuck on a work detail for a few days and he's rebuilding Krondor as fast as he can."

An orderly arrived with two wooden bowls filled with hot stew, simple by any standard, but the smell of which set Dash's mouth to watering. Behind him came two other soldiers, one bearing cheese and bread and the other two large mugs of wine.

Dash set to, and after the soldiers left, Erik said, "You'd better fill me in on what you saw."

After a few chews and a swallow, Dash said, "I got caught by Duko's men and put to work in a gang."

Erik said, "Interesting. They caught Jimmy coming into the city and took him for questioning."

Dash said, "I was already in the city and looking like a rat catcher, so they must have assumed I had just avoided capture for a while. I don't know, but that would make sense. For all that Duko's doing there, it's still pretty confusing in places."

Erik nodded. "So you were in a work gang."

Dash took a sip of wine. "Yes, until I got out with three other men. We slipped into one of the sewer culverts under the outer wall and headed into the city. That's when we got grabbed by the Mockers."

"So the thieves still control the sewers of Krondor?"

"I wouldn't exactly call it 'control' as much as that there are some places Duko and his men haven't found yet, and they have a couple of safe ways in and out of the city."

Erik took a drink of wine and said, "That would have been a blessing if we were going to assault the city."

"You think he's sincere about wanting to change sides?"

"I don't know," answered Erik. "Your brother seemed to think so, and he convinced Greylock, and if I know your father, they'll all convince the Prince."

Dash shook his head. "That creates a problem for the Mockers."

"What?"

"I promised them some sort of amnesty or pardon if they helped get us into the city during the coming attack."

Erik rubbed his chin. "With Krondor in ruins it does seem a little trivial being worried over a man's past before the war. I mean, should we hang someone for cutting purses two years ago while we pardon a man who burned down parts of the city last year?"

"Politics," said Dash. "Fortunately for you and me, we don't have to make that decision."

Erik's gaze narrowed. "Don't discount your own counsel too much, Dash. I'm sure your father and the Prince will want your opinion on the matter."

Dash sat back, swallowed another mouthful, and said, "I have one idea. Just pardon everyone inside the walls and get on with it." He motioned with a fork over his shoulder. "I have no illusions about those mother-killers back there, and even fewer about the Mockers, despite my grandfather's wonderful stories. Most of those invaders would be rioting within weeks if they were forced to play garrison soldiers, and the thieves will be cutting purses or throats within a day of being pardoned." Speaking around a mouthful of food, Dash shook his head. "No, the only difference between having the Mockers help us to get into the city or having Duko open the gates is me keeping a promise."

Erik raised an eyebrow. "Is that a problem?"

"Only if the Mockers decide I forswore my promise and put a death mark on me."

Erik nodded. "Let me know if I can help."

Dash said, "I will. Though I suspect Father and Jimmy have persuaded Patrick to do whatever it is that Patrick is going to do."

"Well, do you want to wait here and see if they're heading our way? I could send word you're alive. Or do you want to ride on to Darkmoor?"

Dash yawned. "Right now I just want to sleep on something softer than a pile of straw on a stone floor."

Erik gave him a rueful look. "Then you might do well to ride on tonight. We don't have a lot of down-stuffed mattresses in camp."

"I know," said Dash, pushing himself back from the

table. "I was just expressing a desire. I'll take a soldier's pallet if that's what fate provides. I've slept on the ground with this tattered cloak wrapped around me for the last three nights."

"Well, we'll get you some better clothing," said Erik. "We have spares, though you'll be back in uniform."

Dash shrugged. "As long as they're free of lice and fleas, I won't complain about fashion."

Erik laughed. "You can always hang your rags over the campfire."

"A dog soldier's washing," said Dash. "Yes, I've heard of that approach; then your clothing stinks of woodsmoke for days. I'll settle for a uniform and you can burn these."

Erik laughed. "You can have the extra bedroll over there and bunk in with me tonight. I'll try not to wake you when I turn in later." He moved toward the tent flap. "I have to check on some things before . . ." He turned and saw that Dash was already on the pallet and asleep. Moving outside, Erik turned his mind to the tasks at hand, though for a brief moment he considered how odd the situation before him was becoming.

Well, he decided, he'd leave it to the Prince and Duke to decide if Duko was being straightforward or not, and then, as always was the case, he would follow his orders the best way he knew how.

Pug reined in and the leader of his escort shouted the order to halt. The patrol heading toward them was decked out in the black of Krondor's Crimson Eagles, the special unit founded by Calis, Erik von Darkmoor's predecessor, and at their head was a familiar face from the last winter at Darkmoor.

"Nakor! Magician!" shouted Jadow Shati, Lieutenant of the company. "What brings you this way?" He signaled behind him and his patrol also halted.

"We're up to see Captain Subai and then on to see if we can sort out this mess with the Saaur," said Pug.

Jadow's brilliant smile suddenly fled. "Man, ask Nakor. We've faced them Saaur, down across the sea. Tough and fast. Takes three of us for each one of them unless we're heavily armored. What do you think the chances are of the

Prince sending the Royal Lancers this way, magician?''

"I'm hoping that I can convince the Saaur that fighting us is a waste on both sides.''

"Well, that would be novel. From what I've seen of them, peaceful isn't the first word that springs to mind when thinking of them.'' He glanced over his shoulder, then said, "Ride on another hour and you'll hit our main camp. I'm out for a couple of days, so perhaps I'll see you on your way back.'' He looked at Nakor. "How's your new religion going?''

Nakor sighed theatrically. "Being good is difficult, Jadow.''

The good-natured former Sergeant laughed. "You state the obvious, my little friend.'' He waved his patrol after him. "Let's ride.'' As he passed the leader of the patrol from Krondor, he accepted their sergeant's salute with a wave and nod.

Pug said, "Let's go see the Captain.''

Nakor said, "Let's go eat. I'm hungry.''

Pug laughed. "You're always hungry, my friend.''

"You know,'' said Nakor as they rode along, "I had this odd notion—''

"Really,'' said Pug, interrupting. "You'll have to tell me of it some other time.''

Nakor laughed. "No, I mean *really* odd.''

"Definitely some other time,'' said Pug.

"Very well,'' Nakor responded.

They rode in silence as they approached Captain Subai's camp. It was set up in a clearing near the base of some foothills rising steeply to the west. Pug could see the road rose sharply beyond the camp, and judged this to be the northern boundary of the area considered secured from invaders. To further reinforce that impression, he could see a heavy breastwork had been constructed across the road on the northern side of the camp. Glancing around, Pug could see why this location had been picked for the headquarters camp. There was ample room to the south for the area to be quickly reinforced, but to the north the terrain rose sharply on the west; to the east of the road, the bank was almost a cliff face, and below it any soldiers coming down along the base of the hills would be trapped in a narrowing defile. A pair of archers could hold off anyone coming along that way.

Soldiers hurried along to take Pug and Nakor's horses. The men were dressed in both the garb of the Royal Pathfinders and the Crimson Eagles. Pug and Nakor dismounted, and Pug asked one of the soldiers where Captain Subai's tent was located. The soldier indicated a large tent in the very center of the camp, and Pug gave his thanks.

Pug turned to the Sergeant leading his escort, and said, "Thank you, Sergeant. Rest tonight, then lead your men back in the morning. We'll be fine here."

The Sergeant saluted. He turned and gave the order to dismount, and asked the second soldier where his men could care for their mounts. As the soldier directed the Sergeant, Pug and Nakor walked toward the command tent.

There was a single soldier sitting in a camp chair outside the tent. As they drew near, Pug saw that it wasn't a lazy sentry, but rather the Pathfinder Commander himself. He was hard at work oiling up a leather harness. Pug had heard that Pathfinders tended their own equipment and didn't relegate anything to the army's usual cadre of blacksmiths, tanners, and armorers. Erik had once commented to Pug that they took very good care of their horses, an area in which Erik was an expert. He glanced up and recognized the magician.

"Duke Pug," he said slowly as he stood and saluted. "To what do I owe the pleasure of this visit?"

Pug said, "To Prince Patrick's instructions, I'm afraid."

The Captain, a gaunt man with prematurely grey hair and a face and hands the color of tanned leather, stood. "What orders?"

"I'm to venture down to the flatland to the east of here, then strike up into the Thunderhell Steppes, find the Saaur, and convince them not to attack our forces again."

The Captain raised an eyebrow in his most expressive reaction since Pug had first encountered him in Krondor. "Good luck to you, m'lord." He put down the harness and said, "Will you be needing anything from me or my men?"

Pug said, "I regret to say I must impose on you for an escort. The Prince thought it necessary."

The Captain smiled. "From what I've heard of you, I

find that difficult to believe. Still, if the Prince commands, we obey. I'll have a patrol ready to accompany you at first light. Until then you'll have to make do with a rough camp. I'll have a couple of my men double up in a tent, so you and your friend here can share one."

"Thanks," said Pug. He glanced at Nakor. "You'll sleep alone tonight, my friend, as I plan on staying another night with my wife."

"Going to flit back down to Darkmoor?"

"No, Miranda's at Sorcerer's Isle, and I want to see her again."

Nakor grinned. "I remember what it was like to be in love." He sighed. "That was a while back, though."

Pug took out a Tsurani transportation orb and said, "This is the last one. I'm going to have Miranda teach me the trick of getting around without one of these things." He started looking around the landscape. To attempt to use the orb to go to a destination not well known to the user's mind was almost certain death. "Let me take a few minutes and get the location of this camp fixed in my mind so I can find my way back here in the morning."

"By all means," said Nakor. "But don't break it," he added with a laugh. "It's going to take her a while to teach you, and somehow I don't imagine you're going to start learning tonight!" Pug ignored Nakor and wandered off, looking intently at the surrounding landmarks. Nakor turned to Subai. "Things quiet around here, Captain?"

Subai nodded. "The invaders hold the other side of the northern passes, but they're not trying to cross the ridge of the mountains. Our patrols can get within a few hundred yards of their positions before they come swarming out, but they only chase us a little way. They seem content to stay where they are."

"Undoubtedly," said Nakor. "They're fortifying defenses before every avenue of attack."

Subai nodded.

"I suppose you've found a few ways over the mountains they haven't found out yet."

"A few. Mostly goat trails and footpaths. There are a couple of places we might infiltrate a squad or two, potentially put men at their back as we drive north, but no place

we could stage on the other side for a major offensive.''
The Captain glanced westward, as if seeing through the
mountains to where the enemy was on the other side.
''Over there, just a week's ride if it were a straight path,
lies Sarth. If we could somehow get inside there, seize the
old abbey above the town, and stage there, we could launch
a flank attack in support of any forces coming from the
south and clear out the invaders in a few days, rather than
the weeks it's going to take.''

Nakor said, ''Maybe there's a way.''

''What are you suggesting?'' asked the Captain.

''I'm trying to remember a story Duke James told me a
long time ago.'' He was silent a while, then said, ''I need
to send a message to Duke Arutha. Do you have something
I can write with?''

''In my tent,'' said Subai.

''Good,'' said Nakor, heading inside.

Subai looked up to see where Pug was now, and saw
that the magician had vanished.

Miranda looked up and saw Pug standing there. She
jumped up, hurried to him, and threw her arms around him.
''I missed you.''

Pug echoed the sentiment. They hadn't been apart since
the end of fighting almost six months earlier, and it had
taken him almost a week to reach Subai's camp in the
mountains.

''How are things around here?'' Pug asked after their
embrace.

Miranda said, ''Much as we left it. Gathis conducts the
daily business of the island in an exemplary fashion and it
seems Robert d'Lyes has become something of an organizer
around here. He's taken to reestablishing the class schedule
that lapsed with your last departure.''

Pug smiled. ''Good. I'll have to speak to him before I
leave in the morning.''

She kissed him. ''But not until after dinner. I want you
to myself for the next few hours.''

He smiled and said, ''Not until then.''

They spent the next two hours alone, then sent word to
have supper brought to their quarters. After dining, Gathis

appeared outside the door as servants were removing the dinner trays.

"Master Pug," he said in greeting. The tall goblinlike creature was always formal when addressing anyone, from Pug to the most menial of servants. Though, even the most menial of servants on this island was a student of magic, from one end of Midkemia to the other, and from distant worlds.

"Gathis," Pug acknowledged. "How is everything?"

"That is why I wished to speak to you. I fear something is amiss."

"What is that?"

"It would be better if you and Mistress Miranda were to accompany me."

Pug and Miranda exchanged glances, but said nothing, nodding to Gathis, who turned and led them out the door and along the long hallway which separated Pug's personal quarters from the rest of the large central house that dominated Villa Beata—the Beautiful House as it was known in the ancient language of Queg.

He led them outside and across a meadow, and instantly Pug knew where he was leading them. As before, when he reached a grassy hillside, Gathis waved his hand and a cave materialized. They entered and again Pug saw the small altar upon which rested the statue of Sarig, the lost God of Magic. Miranda gasped. The first time they had seen the statue, the features upon it resembled those of her father, Macros the Black. "The face is blank!"

"Yes, mistress," said Gathis. "I came here a few days ago and saw what you see now."

"What does it mean?" asked Miranda.

Pug said, "The gods are waiting."

"For what?" she asked, touching the statue.

Pug's voice was soft. "For Sarig's new avatar, his new human agent on this world."

Miranda said, "Does this mean you?"

"No," said Pug. "When I lay near death in the healing glade of Elvandar, when Lims-Kragma spoke to me, I was given three choices. Death was the first." He looked at Miranda. "I could not leave you."

She smiled.

"The second choice was eternal life, but the price was becoming Sarig's next avatar. I would have replaced your father."

"I don't think I would have cared much for that." Then she looked at Pug. "What was the third choice?"

Pug said, "Nothing I care to talk about."

Anger flared up in Miranda's voice as she said, "Tell me!"

"I will die someday."

She moved around to stand directly before him, between Pug and the statue. "You're not telling me something. What?"

"Only that at the end of my life I will know . . . hardship."

Miranda's eyes widened. "What have we known already?"

"That was how I looked at it. If we can get through what we've already survived, what more should I worry about."

Coolly, she said, "Are you telling me everything?"

Pug shrugged. "I'm probably forgetting something." With a light tone he said, "Remember, I was almost dead at the time I had this conversation."

Gathis said, "The future is not fixed, though it can be difficult to change if events gain enough momentum."

Pug nodded, and Miranda said, "I have no idea what that means. What are you hiding?"

Pug said, "Only that in exchange for a very long life and a great deal of power I will have to eventually pay a high price."

Miranda said, "There's no 'only' about that."

Gathis said, "We all have prices to pay."

Pug changed the subject. "You've been the keeper of this shrine for ages, Gathis. What do you think this means?"

"I think a time of change is upon us, Master Pug, and soon someone will present himself to fill the void left by Macros's death."

Pug said, "I think you are right. Perhaps it's one of the students." Pug remained silent a moment, then said, "Someone will find this shrine."

Gathis said, "I have evolved a very subtle but powerful spell to disguise it, Master Pug."

"I know. I lived on this island for decades and never suspected it was here, but whoever is fated to become Sarig's next tool will somehow find this place."

Gathis pondered that observation, and said, "I think that is a likely possibility."

"We will await that day. In the meantime," he said to Miranda, "let's return to the house. I want to see a little of how things are running here, then I want to rest before returning to Subai's camp in the morning."

They returned to the house, and as they crossed the center courtyard, they encountered a group of students sitting around the fountain, enjoying the quiet spring evening. As Pug approached, they all respectfully rose, save for a Brunangee Fire Singer whose snakelike lower body made it impossible for her to do more than raise her roughly humanoid upper torso in an approximation of a slight bow. Pug waved them all back to where they had sat.

Robert d'Lyes said, "Pug, it is good to see you again."

"How have you found life on our tidy little island?" asked Pug. He had brought the young magician along with Miranda to the island during the winter. Robert had resigned as a member of the council at Stardock and had nowhere else to go. Patrick seemed indifferent to the idea of a court magician, so Pug decided to employ him at the island.

"It's a wonderful place," said Robert. "I've learned more about my arts in the last month than I did in the previous two years at Stardock."

Miranda and Pug glanced at one another. "That's impressive," said Pug, motioning for Gathis and Miranda to sit on a nearby bench. "You were the youngest member of the council and rose faster in the learning of your craft than any student we had at Stardock. And you're learning even faster here?"

Robert smiled. He had chosen to affect a beard in imitation of Pug, a flattery Pug didn't find appealing, but which he chose not to comment upon. "It's astonishing. What I find even more wonderful is that with practitioners of magic from other worlds I'm learning things Chalmers and Kalied never would have dreamt of.''

Pug was now genuinely intrigued. "Oh, really? Care to give me an example?''

Robert nodded, his youthful enthusiasm clearly evident. He turned to the Fire Singer and said, "Takkek showed me something a few days ago that I've been practicing.'' He moved away from the group and started to sing. It was a faint sound, as if half-whispered, but clearly singing. The words were impossible to understand, as if the mind refused to grasp them and they were forgotten as soon as they were heard. Yet there was a pattern to them, a mildly hypnotic rhythm that caused Pug to glance around at the other students. They were sitting and watching with rapt expressions as Robert continued his song.

A flame appeared in the air, a foot or so before Robert's face. It was the size of a baby's finger, but clearly it was a flame. It flickered and danced in the wind, then suddenly went out. Robert looked tired, but elated, as he said, "I'm just now starting to understand a little of what Takkek has shown me, but give me time.''

"I am impressed,'' said Pug. "Under the old labels used by the Tsurani Assembly, that's Lesser Path magic, and should be close to impossible for you to perform.''

Robert laughed. "I'm convinced Nakor was right: there is no magic, just tricks, and if we open our minds, we can learn anything.''

Rising, Pug said, "Well, enjoy the evening and don't set fire to the house. Miranda and I are off. Oh, Robert,'' said Pug, turning to face the student.

"Yes, sir?''

"Gathis says you've been doing a good job in my absence. Continue to help out, if you would, please.''

"It's my pleasure,'' said the student.

Pug and Miranda returned to their quarters. As they reached the door, Pug said, "That really was quite remarkable.''

Miranda laughed and pushed him through the door. Playfully she said, "I'll show you something remarkable.''

She shut the door.

*   *   *

Nakor glanced up as Pug popped into view. A soldier carrying a bundle of wood dropped it when suddenly there was a black-robed man standing where there had only been empty air the moment before. "Hello!" Nakor called happily.

Captain Subai was close by, talking to a young officer wearing the black tabard of Krondor's Crimson Eagles. A few Pathfinders could be seen around camp, but their numbers were few. Pug knew that the majority of them were high in the mountains to the west, scouting the enemy and ready to return with reports on any movement of Fadawah's forces. Their reputation for tracking, scouting, and stealth in the woodlands was legendary, rivaling that of Kesh's Imperial Guides and the Rangers of the Free Cities of Natal. Only the elves were said to be better.

Subai said, "Lieutenant Gunderson will lead the patrol accompanying you."

Pug saw that the Captain was providing an escort of a dozen men. One, a trailbreaker Pug judged, was a Pathfinder, and he started riding ahead, while the others waited for Nakor and Pug to mount their horses.

Subai pointed at Nakor. "I'm pleased to see that one go. I don't know what's more irritating: his constant preaching on the subject of 'good,' or his luck at cards."

Pug laughed. "I have a hunch which was more irritating."

Subai said, "We've packed provisions for two weeks."

"I'll find them in less time than that," said Pug as he hiked up his black robe and climbed into the saddle.

"Just make sure you find them before they find you. By all reports they come out of the grasslands like a wind and are over you before you even hear them coming."

Nakor said, "I've seen them. You can hear them coming."

Subai smiled, and Pug said, "Any other advice?"

"Don't get killed," said the Captain without a smile.

Pug nodded. "I have other plans." He nodded to the Lieutenant and the order was given to ride off.

Nakor said, "I was talking to the Captain about some trails over the mountain. As soon as we get back from this nonsense, we have to get back to Darkmoor and find Greylock and Erik. I think I have a plan that could shorten the war.''

Pug turned and said, "Tell me about it."

Nakor outlined what he had thought of as they rode down a small trail leading into the woodlands below.

For five days they rode, and except for one sighting of a band of riders who veered off at the patrol's approach, the journey was uneventful. They had left the foothills the day before and were riding across grasslands, heading toward the southern entrance to the Thunderhell Steppes, a broad break in two ranges of hills, less than five miles across.

They reached a point near signs of a large old campsite, and the Lieutenant ordered a halt. "This was our reserve camp. There were wooden walls, a dirt outer barrier, a drop gate. They overran it and killed everyone." He motioned with his hand. "They staked the heads in an arch starting here."

Pug said, "Then this is where we will part company, Lieutenant."

The young officer said, "I though we were to accompany you until we found the Saaur."

"A reasonable assumption but incorrect," said Pug.

Nakor said, "Honestly, Lieutenant, we can take care of ourselves and having you along might cause us some extra trouble, trying to keep you all alive."

The Lieutenant said, "Then may I ask why we're here at all, sir?"

"Because I didn't feel like arguing with your Captain, if you must know," said Pug.

"Do you mind if we wait, sir?"

"Don't bother," said Pug. "If I don't get killed, I'll be traveling back to Darkmoor a lot faster than you can get there."

The magician's reputation was widely spread throughout the army, and he was also a Duke, so whatever reservations the young officer might have felt were kept inside. He merely saluted and said, "Very well, m'lord. Have a safe journey."

"You, as well," replied Pug.

Nakor said, "Well, then, let's get there."

Pug nodded and urged his horse forward.

They had traveled less than a mile when Nakor said, "Do you hear it?"

Pug said, "Yes."

In the distance, like the sound of distant drums, the thunder of the hooves pounding across the plains carried to them. Pug knew and Nakor had seen those horses, twice the size of the sturdy cavalry mounts they rode. Astride each would be a Saaur, twelve feet tall, reptilian warriors.

Soon dust could be seen in the distance.

Pug turned to make sure the Kingdom patrol was retreating and was pleased to see it was almost out of sight.

"Let's wait here," said Nakor.

Pug nodded. "They'll be here soon enough."

They waited, and in the distance they could see riders on the horizon. The Saaur were coming.

Nine

![rule]

Negotiations

JIMMY WAVED.

Dash returned his brother's wave as he rode into the courtyard of Castle Darkmoor. After spending the night in Erik's company, he had taken a horse and ridden to the Prince's court. He had exchanged mounts like a relay rider, anxious to get to court.

Dash dismounted and turned the reins of his horse over to a groom and embraced his brother. "I was concerned I might not see you again for a while," he said.

Jimmy smiled. "I feared the same, too. Yet again, though, the Brothers Jamison survive."

"Barely," said Dash. "I got away from a work gang, only to be trapped by the Mockers."

"Come along, tell me all about it while you bathe. Father's in court with the Prince and will be anxious to see you when you're presentable. It appears we won't need any details on defenses, as we seem to be reaching an accommodation with General Duko."

"So Erik von Darkmoor tells me." He glanced around. "Where are the troops ready to march, the brave banners and loud trumpets?"

"Ah," said Jimmy, a dark cloud crossing over his face. "The departure is delayed."

"Delayed?" Dash looked confused. "I would have thought Patrick would have hurt himself to get into Krondor as quickly as possible. The earlier the city is secured, the faster we can turn north toward Sarth and start retaking the Bitter Sea coast and Yabon."

"There are other issues." Jimmy pulled on his brother's arm. "Come along. Get a bath and we'll talk."

Dash sighed. He trudged along after his brother.

Dash sputtered as Jimmy poured another bucket of hot water over him. "So then he turned you loose?"

"Yes," said Dash, "but I don't think there was a lot of family devotion in there. What I saw looked like a pretty pathetic bunch, and I suspect he knew that killing me would protect very little, while turning me loose might actually gain him something."

"Well, if Duko doesn't turn out to be the grandfather of liars, we won't need the Mockers' help getting into the city."

"I'm for that," said Dash. "I've seen enough bloodshed to last me the rest of my life."

Jimmy put down the bucket and handed Dash a towel as he climbed out of the bathtub. A servant had laid out clothing on the bed and left the brothers alone. Dash toweled dry, and said, "Does it bother you?"

"The killing?" asked Jimmy.

Dash nodded.

Jimmy sat back on the windowseat. "Sometimes. When Grandfather used to talk about the things he and Prince Arutha did, killing was . . . something you did to the enemy. The stink of the dead wasn't part of Grandfather's stories."

"Except that one about the living dead in the brothel," said Dash with a laugh. "To this day I don't know whether to believe it or not. Having to burn the building down to the ground to get rid of them."

Jimmy shared the humor. Then his smile faded. "Given what we've seen in the last two years, I'm disinclined to put false to anything Grandfather told us."

Dash nodded. "Do you ever ask yourself why we do these things?"

"Almost every day," said Jimmy.

Dash pulled on his shirt. "Good, what's the answer?"

"Because we go where duty calls us."

Dash stepped into his trousers. "Duty?" He reached for his boots and sat on the bed to pull them on. "These aren't as good as the ones I lost in Krondor."

"They were the second best pair you brought with you from Rillanon; I checked your wardrobe."

Dash nodded. "Anyway, Grandfather always talked of duty, but I saw where he grew up, firsthand, and I have no idea why he felt that way."

"What way?" asked Jimmy. "I'm not sure I'm understanding you."

"I mean he felt so deeply his duty to the Kingdom. Those Mockers I talked to looked at it as you or I might look at taking vows to serve Sung."

"Celibacy was never high on my list of virtues," admitted Jimmy.

"That's what I mean. Grandfather had Father as deep into the idea of King and Nation before we were born as if he was teaching a religion. I'm just at a loss to wonder how Grandfather got that way."

Jimmy looked at his brother as he finished dressing. "Interesting question. Perhaps Father can give you an insight. I suspect that if all those stories we heard were true, and if life with the Mockers was as unappealing as I suspect it was, Grandfather might have been moved by a very deep sense of gratitude."

Dash glanced in a looking-glass and judged his appearance acceptable for an interview with the Prince. "I don't think it's that. It's more than gratitude." He looked at Jimmy. "Is there anything you can imagine that would get you to break your vows to the crown?"

Jimmy stopped almost in midstride; the concept was too alien to imagine. "Turn traitor?" He stopped and said, "I can't imagine what it could be. Perhaps some sort of perfect love . . ." He shook his head. "No, because I can't imagine any woman who loved me turning against something I hold that dear."

"Speaking of women, did I see a page hurry by wearing the livery of Silden?"

"Yes, you did," said Jimmy with a grin.

"Is Francie here with her father?"

Jimmy nodded. "Yes."

"And does she still have that crush on you?"

Jimmy's grin widened. "I hope so." He laughed. "We had lunch the other day. She's turned out just as you might expect."

Dash opened the door and said, "If memory serves she was obnoxious and beat you up with some regularity."

"No," said Jimmy, stepping through the door. "It was you she beat up. I was too big. Beside, she fancied herself in love with me."

"Well, then, back to the point, is there something there?"

Jimmy walked down the hall with his brother. "Seriously, I don't know. I suspect, however, I may have nothing to say in the matter, nor will Francie."

"Patrick?"

"That's the delay I spoke of. Suddenly Dukes are winging their way like birds in migration toward Darkmoor."

"All with eligible daughters?"

Rounding a corner, moving past guards standing at their posts, Jimmy said, "I think the King worries that with war coming, another heir might prove valuable."

They climbed the steps in the main hall that led to the Baronial great hall, where Patrick currently held court. "The curse of twins."

"Erland would never do anything against his brother, we know that, but there's more than one noble who might link his fate to one of Erland's sons should a rival claim be possible. If Patrick doesn't wed and beget a son . . ." He let the thought go unfinished as they reached the audience hall.

Nobles had been trickling into Darkmoor since the thaw, and now the modest Baronial hall was packed to the point of overcrowding. Dash said, "We'd better take Krondor back just so we can get into a hall big enough to hold this lot."

Jimmy said, "Shhh." He pointed to where their father stood next to the Prince. It was the most formal-looking court they had witnessed so far in Darkmoor, for Patrick wore his purple mantle, his ermine stole, and his circlet of gold. Arutha was likewise attired formally in a black tunic with golden trim, scarlet leggings, and his chain of office, with his Ducal seal hanging from it. At his side he wore the sword once borne by his namesake, carried by Erik von Darkmoor to Arutha.

The brothers waited at the rear of the hall as the Prince disposed of the day's business. Then a young page announced, "This day's court is at an end, my lords and ladies."

Patrick stood and everyone in the room bowed. As the Prince departed, Arutha saw his sons and motioned for them to join him.

They crossed the still-crowded court, and when they reached the dais upon which the throne was placed, Arutha hugged his younger son. "I can't tell you how pleased I am to see you."

"Of course you can," quipped Dash.

Arutha said, "Come, you must fill in the Prince on what you learned in Krondor."

Dash followed his father and brother into the Prince's private office.

Nakor said, "Do you think they'll get tired of this?"

Pug said, "Eventually, or they'll run out of arrows."

Pug had erected a mystical barrier around the two when the Saaur had first closed on Nakor and him, as it was clear they weren't coming to talk, but rather were charging with lances down. These appeared to be young Saaur warriors, eager to shed blood. Several of them had been seriously injured when their lances struck Pug's invisible barrier and shattered, throwing them from their saddles. For almost a half day since, the Saaur had been content to take up position a dozen yards from the two men and fire arrows at them.

The chaos which followed seem to amuse Nakor, though Pug was disturbed by the attempt to kill them without conversation. They appeared two relatively helpless men, unarmed and alone. Their own horses had panicked at the onslaught of the Saaur riders, the massive horses bearing down like a rolling tide.

Pug had allowed his and Nakor's mounts to flee before putting up his barrier, and now he regretted the decision. They were without the food and water in the saddlebags, with nothing for sustenance except for Nakor's seemingly inexhaustible supply of oranges.

He produced one, split the skin, and began to devour it. "Want one?"

"No, thank you; maybe later," said Pug. "This shield spell is more than adequate to keep them out, but I do have to spend a little energy keeping it intact."

"It's a good thing they don't have any spellcasters along, isn't it?"

"Things could get a little difficult," agreed Pug.

Nakor squinted and said, "Then things might get difficult soon." He pointed to the distant horizon beyond the milling, angry riders who were still firing arrows at them.

In the distance another band of riders was approaching at speed, and from the banners being carried by heralds at the front, Pug assumed someone of importance was coming to investigate this problem. He said, "Well, if I tell you to run, don't hesitate."

Nakor said, "I run very well when I need to."

As the new band of riders pulled up, those already surrounding the protective sphere moved back, allowing a group of a dozen riders to come close and inspect the two humans. Pug recognized the leader, Jatuk, the Sha-shahan of all the remaining Saaur.

The young warriors fell silent as their leader reined in his mount. The leader jumped down from his horse and walked to stand just inches the other side of the energy barrier. "Why have you humans come to trouble the Saaur?" he demanded.

Pug glanced at Nakor, who shrugged.

Pug looked at Jatuk and said, "Why do you war upon us, Sha-shahan of all the Saaur?"

"I make no war upon your kind, Black Robe."

"There are three hundred dead soldiers of my King back there who would argue that," Pug replied.

"If they could still argue," Nakor added.

"They refused to depart," said Jatuk. "They were told we claim these grasslands."

Pug said, "If I lower this barrier, may we talk?"

Jatuk waved his hand in agreement. "We camp here!" he shouted, and instantly the fifty or so riders surrounding the two humans dismounted and started to organize a camp. Several led horses away and drove stakes for pickets while others began building fire pits. Still others rode off toward a nearby river, to carry water back.

Pug let the barrier lapse, and Jatuk said, "I remember you, Black Robe. It was you who brought me Haman's dying words, of our betrayal at the hands of the Pantathians. I will speak with you in truce, and you may leave freely when we are done."

"Me too?" asked Nakor.

Jatuk didn't deign to answer, merely waving away the question as he turned his back on the pair. He walked to his horse, held by another Saaur warrior, and with a gesture indicated he wanted his travel pack. The warrior complied and handed down a bag that a human would have been hard-pressed to carry.

Pug was again staggered by the scale of the Saaur. The average warrior topped out at twelve feet tall, with a few slightly taller. Their horses were close to twenty-five hands compared to the seventeen or eighteen hands of a heavy Midkemian warhorse. Pug was also impressed at their efficiency in setting up camp. He reminded himself these were originally a nomadic people, who despite having constructed great cities on their homeworld of Shila, had remained nomads at heart. The majority of the Saaur roamed the great grassy plains of Shila, thousands of horsemen and their families and herds accompanying them on their endless trek.

A demon attack had ended that great civilization. Of the millions of Saaur who had dominated their homeworld at its height, less than ten thousand had survived on Midkemia. Pug assumed that the last few years of warfare had kept their numbers low, but knew they were a people facing a grim future if they couldn't find a respite from warfare.

A fire was built and Jatuk motioned for Pug and Nakor to join him. His reptilian face was surprisingly expressive, and the more Pug watched those giant warriors the easier it became to see individual differences. A warrior took the role of Jatuk's servant, providing him with a wooden bowl of water for him to refresh himself with. He washed face and hands, and at the end ran a damp towel across the back of his neck. That gesture was the most reassuring thing Pug had seen of the Saaur, for it was the most humanlike display he had seen that didn't involve bloodshed.

While traveling through the destroyed world of Shila with the spirit of the last Lore Master of the Saaur, Haman, Pug had come to learn a lot of the people of that world and their history. He doubted human and Saaur could ever be close friends on Midkemia, but he thought with some work, they could become respectful of one another, leaving each other alone for the most part, as humans and elves, and humans and dwarves, tended to. He knew humanity didn't need another enemy like the moredhel, goblins, or trolls, especially not an enemy as physically powerful and determined as the Saaur.

Jatuk said, "We placed the heads of those men who would not quit the grasslands on poles to stand as warning. Yet you ignored the warning to seek us out. We are tired of your kind, Black Robe. We have known nothing but death and loss since coming to this world." He motioned to the northeast, up the vast Thunderhell. "This is land we understand. There are rolling plains, water, the cattle we have taken thrive here."

Pug nodded. Then he said, "But it is not your land."

"This is not our world," said Jatuk bitterly. "So we must take what we can." He gazed to the south. "You have suffered, you humans of the Kingdom, and I now understand that it was through no fault of yours that we were brought here. But we have no means to return home, and even if we could, what would we find there, Black Robe?"

"A burned-out world populated by starving demons, hunting one another down for food until only one is left. In time, it will starve and wither. Finally, it will die."

"So there is nowhere to go."

Pug said, "Perhaps there is."

Jatuk looked at Pug and said, "Where?"

"I don't know yet, but Midkemia is a big world. Here the grasslands appear vast, but you know your own history. Once your forebears were as you are now, a small band abandoned upon Shila by the Valheru called Alma-Lodaka.''

Despite having learned the truth of their "goddess's" nature in the last year, old habits died hard, and the older Saaur bowed their heads in reverence at the Green Mother's name.

"But over the ages," Pug continued, "your nation grew until you had conquered the entire globe. You and your children may be content to wander the Thunderhell, to fight the nomadic tribes that already claim this land, but eventually you'll return to the villages and towns of my nation. You will either have to make war or change your ways.''

Jatuk was silent. "What can we do?"

Pug said, "Abide. Leave those of us to the south alone and we will leave you alone. When we have disposed of Fadawah and his men, and have restored peace to our land, we shall turn our minds and will to the problem of finding the Saaur a proper home."

Jatuk thought on this, and at last said, "Do not take too long in making things so, Black Robe, for my people are coming to like living here. Should too much time pass, we shall resist leaving."

"I understand," said Pug. To himself he added, Now if I can only get Patrick to understand. He pushed that thought aside as food was put before Nakor and him, and decided the opportunity to learn more about the Saaur was too good to ignore. He would worry about Patrick's reaction when he returned to Darkmoor in the morning.

Patrick said, "You did what?"

Pug said, "I gave them assurances we would aid them in relocating *out* of the Kingdom after we disposed of Fadawah."

"But they agreed to leave?"

"Yes, if we can find them a reasonable alternative."

"Find them an alternative!" Patrick shouted.

The full court was about to commence, and the Prince was holding an impromptu interview with Pug, Nakor, Arutha, and his sons. "Those monsters killed three hundred of my men!"

Arutha said, "A misunderstanding, Highness."

"A misunderstanding?" Patrick appeared unconvinced. Turning to Pug he said, "Why did you disobey me? I ordered you to destroy them if they wouldn't quit the Kingdom at once."

Pug was growing tired of the young Prince's manner. "Highness, I am not an executioner. I have fought for the Kingdom, but I will not use my powers to destroy an entire race because you are piqued."

"Piqued!" Patrick's temper exploded. "You dare to talk to me in such a fashion?"

Pug stood, looked at Arutha, then said, "Explain things to the boy, or I will go to his father and have this discussion with the King. And when I get finished, Borric may have to reconsider who is running this half of his Kingdom."

The Prince's eyes widened, and as Pug turned to leave, Patrick shouted, "I have not given you leave to depart!"

Pug ignored the Prince and walked out through the door. Nakor stood and said to Arutha, "I'd better go with him." To Patrick he said, "And you better listen to him, boy. For he is powerful enough to be your greatest ally, or your worst enemy."

Patrick's mouth fell open at the little man's added insult. He looked at Arutha, who only shook his head slightly and said, "We have court, Highness."

Dash and Jimmy exchanged glances but said nothing. Patrick stood motionless for a long minute, then composed himself. "You are right, my lord duke. We mustn't keep the court waiting."

As Jimmy and Dash ducked out of a side door, Jimmy said, "Duke Pug has a lot of confidence in his ability to persuade the King he's right to embarrass the Prince that way."

They walked toward the courtyard. Dash said, "From everything I've heard . . . well, it's probably a well-earned confidence." He glanced around. "Look, we both know that Patrick's got a temper. We had enough fights with him when we were children. And we know the King kept him off the throne of Krondor an extra year because he didn't think he was ready."

Jimmy's voice lowered. "Well, he wasn't."

"He's still not," said Dash.

Jimmy regarded his brother and very quietly said, "Ready or not, he is the Prince of Krondor. We are servants of the crown. We have no choice."

Dash said, "Father better keep him under control, or a lot of us are going to die because we have no choice." Dash's voice turned slightly angry. "Look, this isn't a play-yard argument over who gets to ride the pony first, or who is going to pick first for the ball game. This is war, and it's not going to be a pretty one."

Nakor came around the corner. "Ah, there you are. I've been looking for you."

Jimmy grinned. "For what?"

"I need to get some information from you, and if you have what I need, we need to go retake the Abbey of Sarth."

Dash and Jimmy's eyes opened wide at that last statement. "Retake the abbey?" asked Dash.

"If you remember, your grandfather once told me a story about the time he had to sneak into the Abbey of Sarth with that renegade moredhel chieftain."

Jimmy looked at Dash. "Do you remember any story like that?"

"No," said Dash. "I thought I'd heard every story Grandfather ever told."

From behind them a voice said, "No, you didn't."

They looked to see Duke Arutha standing there. "But I remember that story."

Nakor grinned. "Subai has a goat trail over the mountains that leads to a little valley down near the base of the mountain upon which the old Ishapian abbey sits."

Arutha paused for a minute, then said, "So while we're conducting the business of establishing a court in Krondor, sending armies around here and there, and while Fadawah's agents are closely watching, you want to sneak over the mountains, find that secret entrance into the basement of the abbey, capture and hold it until Greylock can drive up into the town, and secure the area?"

"Something like that, but leave out the 'you' business. Someone a little younger should run this raid." He glanced at the brothers, who looked at each other.

"No," they said simultaneously. "That's a task for the Eagles or Pathfinders!" added Dash.

Arutha said, "We'll talk about it. But Nakor's right. If I can remember what Father told me about that entrance, and if it's still there and usable, we could shorten this war by a year."

He walked away, heading for the Prince's morning court, and Jimmy turned to Nakor. "Is Pug all right?"

"He's just frustrated," said Nakor. "Patrick wants quick solutions and Pug knows the same itch, but he's old enough to know that the quickest solutions often are the ones with the highest price." He put his hands on the brothers' shoulders and moved along the hall with them. "He must weigh things in his mind, decide where his true loyalties lie."

Jimmy said, "Loyalties lie? He's a noble of the Kingdom; he was adopted into the royal family."

"But he has larger responsibilities," said Nakor. "Remember, he didn't just save the Kingdom from destruction; he saved the entire world of Midkemia, including all those men on the other side, the Saaur, any Pantathians who may be alive out there, the Brotherhood of the Dark Path, everyone."

Jimmy said, "But he can't just toss aside his loyalty to the Kingdom."

Dash said, "Don't be so sure."

"I don't think he's going to toss anything aside," said Nakor as they walked into the courtyard. "At least not lightly."

Pug popped into view on the bank of a river. "Hello!" he called.

A moment later a voice called back, "Welcome, magician."

"Have I leave to enter?"

"You are welcome in Elvandar," came the reply as a figure stepped out from behind a tree.

"Galain!" said Pug as he waded across the sandy ford he always preferred to use to enter the elven woods.

The young—by elvish standards—warrior stood with the tip of his longbow on the ground in a relaxed posture. "I came to watch when Miranda showed up two days ago. I thought you might come by shortly."

"I'm glad you did. What news of the court?"

"The court is in mourning. He who was your companion, and once was Duke of Crydee, has left us for the Blessed Isles."

Pug nodded. Martin Longbow had been approaching a hundred years of age and had lived his last here, with the people who had raised him as a child. "Marcus and Margaret?" asked Pug, referring to Martin's children.

"They came, with their mates and children, and they collected the body of their father. The returned him to Crydee, to bury in a vault as is their custom."

"How long ago?"

"Not long, a few weeks. Marcus and his party left the banks of the river less than two weeks ago."

Pug nodded. "That would explain why word had not reached us. It will take weeks more for Marcus to send word by ship to Port Vykor. The Prince will not have heard it." He looked at the elf. "Thank you for telling me. That one was a true friend, the last save Tomas, from my first years in Crydee."

"He was well loved by us all."

"How are the others?"

"Save that loss, all is well." He shouldered his bow and said, "The Queen is well, as is Tomas. Prince Calin and Redtree hunt together. Despite the war to the east of us, the invaders do not try to cross into Crydee, so they do not trouble our borders."

"How is Calis?"

Galain smiled. "He most of all is well. Since his birth I have not known him to be as happy as he is. I think the release of the Lifestone has freed him from a dreadful part of his heritage."

Pug said, "I am impatient to see my wife."

"I understand," said Galain, "from what I've seen. So far I have not had the fortune to meet she who will be my wife."

"You're young," said Pug dryly. "Barely past a century."

Galain smiled. "This is true." He held up his hand and

said, "I will see you back at the court in a few days."

"I can take you with me," said Pug.

"I have other duties. I must make a patrol along the river you humans call Crydee. I just came this way to greet you."

Considering the number of times he had visited the elves, Pug correctly interpreted the remark and said, "Thank you for making the effort."

"You are welcome."

Pug activated the device he carried and found himself floating above the treetops a half-mile from where he wanted to be. He barely got control of his powers in time to keep from falling to his death and landed gently. Feeling shaken, he examined the Tsurani sphere and saw a fading along a portion of it that told him it was no longer usable. He regretted the loss of the device. His ability to quickly move from place to place was now gone, until he learned the trick Miranada had of moving at will without aid.

He put it back inside his robe. Several other such devices were being studied back at his island by his students, and another might prove useful. He remembered the days of free trading with the Empire of Tsurannuani through the rift gates. Now there was only one, at Stardock, closely monitored on both sides. For a dark moment he wondered if there was anything mankind couldn't make a mess of; not for the last time in his life he cursed Makala, the Tsurani magician whose badly conceived treachery had caused the estrangement between the two worlds, all motivated by the highest ideals: to serve the Empire.

Well, he thought, dwelling on past failures once you'd learned all there was to learn was just heaping futility on failure. He put aside reminiscences and started walking.

A short time later he reached the large clearing that surrounded Elvandar, keeping it apart from the surrounding forest. As every time before, he found himself captivated by the sight of it. Even in the brightest daylight the colors of the trees were otherworldly. The magic of the place was powerful, but subtle, a sweet counterpoint to what nature had fashioned, a wonderful feeling of rightness.

High above large branches with flattened tops formed walkways between boles, and along the base of the trees cooking fires and tanning racks, pottery wheels, and other craft areas sat. Pug was greeted by several elves who recognized him, and those who did not nevertheless nodded in greeting.

He made his way along the climbing path of steps and branches until he was at the center of the great elven city. At the boundary to the Queen's court, he found Tathar, the Queen's seniormost advisor, waiting. "Magician!" Tathar said, extending his hand to shake in the human fashion. "It is good to see you again."

Pug said, "It is good to see you as well, old friend." He glanced around and said, "It is good to again be in Elvandar." He looked at Tathar. "My wife?"

"She is with the Queen and Tomas," answered the old advisor. "Come."

He led Pug into the heart of the Queen's court, where Queen Aglaranna, Tomas, and Miranda were sitting in conversation. Seeing his boyhood friend, Tomas rose, but it was Miranda who reached her husband first. "I didn't think you were coming!" she said, delighted to be wrong.

"I didn't think I was either," said Pug. "But I had a bit of an argument with Patrick—"

"The Prince of Krondor?" asked Tomas. He smiled down at his short friend.

Pug looked up at his boyhood foster brother; even in that tall, slightly alien figure, Pug glimpsed the image of the kitchenboy with whom he had lived as a child. "The very same. He wanted me to go obliterate the Saaur and I thought offering them a peaceful alternative might prove a wiser course."

Tomas nodded. "Crush your enemies without mercy." He shook his head. "I remember those impulses all too well, my friend."

Pug allowed Miranda to escort him to Aglaranna's throne, where he bowed and said, "Greetings, My Lady."

"Welcome, Pug."

"I am grieved to learn of a friend's departure," Pug said.

Aglaranna said, "He passed as happy as he could be, given his life. No one can ask more. He bade us good night and never awoke. He was at peace. For one of your race, he lived a very long time."

Pug nodded. "But I will miss him. As I miss all the other friends of my youth."

"I understand," said the Queen. "That is why you should visit more often. We eledhel abide far longer than you humans." Then considering Pug's and Miranda's age, she amended that to, "Most of you humans, that is."

Pug said, "This is true." Glancing around, he said, "Where is Calis?"

Miranda smiled. "He's not too far away. I suspect, anyway."

Tomas grinned. "There's a woman . . ." He shrugged and winked.

Pug said, "Calis?"

"One from across the ocean, whom Miranda brought to us. With two beautiful boys who need a father."

"Is it . . . serious?" asked Pug.

Tomas laughed. "My wife's people are very different from you and me, Pug. And from my son. He is but half-elf, unique in the world, and he has spent a great deal of time among humans." Tomas leaned over and whispered in a mock-conspiratorial tone, "I think he's taken, but he doesn't even know he's tasted the hook!"

Tathar laughed and said, "This is true. Among our people we have the recognition, the sudden knowledge that a mate is before you. Not all our people know this certainty, and to them falls the difficult task of slowly building a bond with another who has also not known the recognition. With Calis and Elien, it is the difficult way. But often it ends in a love as profound as the first."

Miranda smiled. "I think I sensed something in her when I first found her and the boys. I think it will all work out."

Aglaranna turned to an elf nearby and said, "Would you carry word to my son, please, and have him attend us for supper this evening. Have him bring Elien and her sons, too."

The elf bowed and hurried off.

"What brings you to us?" asked Tomas.

"I wished to see my wife," said Pug with a smile. "And I wished an evening among friends, where the air doesn't carry the memory of war, smoke, and blood. I wanted a quiet night before I start another quest."

"A quest?" asked the Queen. "For what do you seek this time, magician?"

"I need to find the Saaur a homeland," said Pug. "Else we may have yet another war upon us before we sort out the one already here."

Miranda said, "Well, then, we'll leave in the morning."

"I was going to go alone," said Pug, "but the Tsurani orb is no longer working—I almost broke my neck when it left me hanging in midair—and I don't know where I'm bound for."

"So you need me to show you how to get around?"

"Something like that."

Miranda smiled. "I don't know if I will."

"What? Why?" asked Pug.

Poking a finger into his chest, she said, "Because I *like* being able to do something better than you."

At that the rest of the Queen's court laughed, and they relaxed as pages brought wine and food; soon they were joined by Calis and the woman from across the sea, and her sons. And at least for this one night, they put thoughts of war and the threat of war away and enjoyed the company of good friends.

Ten

Investments

Jimmy FROWNED.

Prince Patrick had just leaned over to whisper something in Francie's ear and she blushed as she laughed. The Duke of Silden pointedly chose to ignore this breech of etiquette. The Dukes of Rodez, Euper, Sadara, and Timons glanced over and returned to their conversations. Their daughters, all resplendent in their finest gowns, allowed their gazes to linger a bit longer before returning their attentions to the various young courtiers at the table.

Dash had to turn away so as not to laugh at his brother's unhappiness.

The hall at Castle Darkmoor was now overtaxed in the opinion of the Prince's Master of Ceremony, a dour man named Wiggins. He had been a clerk in the court of Krondor, but had occasionally helped with state functions for the old Master, Jerome. Because of that small advantage, he had been named to the office on Patrick's resurrection of the court in Darkmoor. He resembled nothing as much as a very nervous bird as he fluttered about the room, from one noble to the next, attempting to insure everyone's needs were met, despite shortages of food, ale, and wine.

Mathilda, Dowager Baroness of Darkmoor, sat on the left of the Duke of Silden. While no longer young, she still possessed a court-bred ease and charm, learned while growing up among the powerful eastern nobles. The Duke, a widower, was an obvious target for a woman of her breeding. He appeared mildly interested.

Dash cast a glance back at his brother and saw that Jimmy was attempting to be interested in something said by the daughter of an eastern Earl; which one he couldn't remember. She was a pretty enough girl in a vapid way, and Dash's amusement at his brother's frustration turned to sympathy. Francie was clearly the most interesting young woman in court, if not the most beautiful, and the time Jimmy had spent with her over the last couple of weeks had awakened something; at the very least, a proprietary impulse if not something deeper.

Dash knew that neither he nor his brother would be free to follow their heart's call as long as they were in service to the crown. They were too highly born, being the sons and grandsons of Dukes. Jimmy would most likely advance to a similar high office, and Dash would probably end up an Earl if he continued in service.

Which meant neither son would have a great deal to say in the matter of whom they would wed. That detail would be up to their father to a lesser extent, and the King's pleasure to a greater extent. Factionism in the Kingdom was a way of life, and keeping the two realms closely allied an ongoing problem. The East had the population, the wealth, and the political strength. The West had the natural resources, the potential for growth, and all the problems of a frontier: enemies, disorder, and constant difficulty governing. Marrying off the eligible daughters of one realm to the sons of the other was a time-honored method of keeping the two realms close, and no more eligible son existed than the future King.

Francie glanced over at Jimmy and smiled at him, then returned her attention to Patrick. Dash leaned over and said, "We should ask Father."

"Ask him what?" Jimmy turned, looking confused.

"Who the King wants his son to marry. You don't think for a moment that hasn't already been decided, do you?"

Jimmy considered this, then smiled. "You're probably right. If Father doesn't know, then no one does."

Jimmy waited until Duke Arutha looked his way, then motioned with his head. Arutha nodded, then rose and came around to stand behind Baroness Mathilda. He whispered something to the Prince, who waved him away with a smile, and moved around to where his sons stood. They bowed toward the Prince, who wasn't looking at them, then walked from the table.

Once the three were outside of the hall, Dash observed, "We're going to have to start turning away nobles if they continue to show up."

Arutha said, "More are coming. The court here in Darkmoor is to be as visible and noisy as we can make it. We will find rooms for as many who arrive as possible, first here, then in the nearby city. The rest will be quartered outside the wall, in pavilions and campaign tents. There is to be a month of public celebration."

Jimmy's mouth opened in disbelief. "This can't be true?"

"It is," said Arutha.

Jimmy said, "But we have to finalize our deal with Duko—"

"That's been accomplished. We sent him terms and he replied this morning."

"What arrangement has been agreed to?" asked Dash.

Arutha motioned that they should walk. He headed out toward the central courtyard of the castle. The halls were thronged with pages, servants, and guards, attending the needs of a score of visiting nobles. "Within a month's time, our former enemy will become Duke of the Southern Marches."

"Lord Sutherland!" exclaimed Jimmy. "That's incredible."

"Patrick would rather not give him anything, and the King would prefer to name him Baron of Land's End or something equally . . . local. I persuaded them both otherwise."

"Why, Father?" asked Dash.

"Because Duko has, to all effects, a personal army of close to twenty-five thousand men. He may dream of something more noble than his previous calling as a sword-for-hire, but most of his soldiers have no allegiance to the

Kingdom. I convinced the King that he might be the only hope for us to keep those men under control and make them Kesh's problem rather than our own.''

Dash got a calculating expression. "If he's a Duke . . . This means he answers to the Prince, and not to you.''

"I have my hands full. And if Patrick has direct control over Duko, he may come to trust him.''

Jimmy smiled. "Yet you will be advising the Prince on all matters pertaining to the Southern Marches.''

Arutha nodded. "And it keeps other political issues in balance.''

Jimmy and Dash both knew that meant Duko would be permitted to appoint his own captains to key locations along the southern borders, probably gaining titles for them. There were presently more offices than nobles to fill them due to the high mortality rate of the recent war in the West. Eastern nobles would already be pestering the King for some of those titles—more to the point, the taxes their lands brought. None of those, however, would be willing to venture to the West to directly rule them. Absentee rulership was not an alien concept in the Kingdom, but it was frowned upon in the West. There were too many problems —Queg, Kesh, the Brotherhood of the Dark Path, among others—to leave the administration of a Barony, let alone an Earldom or Duchy, to a bailiff or seneschal. A few key offices would be given to western nobles' second or third sons, so that Duko wouldn't be able to build a structure beneath him of only personal retainers.

Jimmy said, "Let me change the subject.'' He indicated the young women dotting the room. "Is there anything we should know . . .''

"About what?'' queried Arutha.

Dash said, "Has Patrick made a decision on who is going to be the next Princess of Krondor?''

Arutha glanced around, seeing if anyone was listening. "Our two most recent queens were from Roldem. Borric, and Lyam before him, were anxious to fix alliances in the East.'' He put his hands on his son's shoulders. "You have the blood of Roldem in you. You know your mother's people. They are vain and proud of their heritage and think of themselves as a people apart. This is why we have seen so little of your mother.'' There was a bitter note in Arutha's voice neither son had heard before.

They both knew their parents' marriage had been arranged by their grandfather, Duke James, and had been as advantageous to the Kingdom as the two marriages of the last two kings to Roldem's royal daughters. Dash and Jimmy's parents had always been able to maintain a pose of wedded happiness in public, though the boys both knew the marriage was far from ideal. Only now were they learning just how strained the relationship between their parents truly was.

Dash said, ''So it must be a Kingdom bride?''

Arutha nodded. ''The King has said so, to me, in private. And it must be an eastern noble's daughter. Preferably one from a Duke with a great deal of influence in the Congress of Lords.''

''Brian Silden,'' said Jimmy.

''Borric has determined to let his son have the privilege of liking the woman who is to bear Isle's future King. So there are five likely candidates for the position of Princess.''

Jimmy said, ''Have you any inkling of who Patrick will ask to wed?''

Arutha regarded his son closely, and said, ''Francine will be our next queen. All that remains is the timing. Patrick and she have been friends since childhood. He genuinely enjoys her company. There have been far worse foundations for state marriages in our time.''

Jimmy looked stricken.

Dash said, ''Are you all right?''

Jimmy glanced from his father to his brother. ''I just didn't . . . realize.''

Arutha said, ''What? Are you in love with her?''

Jimmy looked at his father and said, ''I'll never know.'' Without another word he turned and walked away.

Arutha looked at Dash, who said, ''Let him have some time to himself.''

''I didn't realize,'' said Arutha.

''He didn't either,'' said Dash. ''That's the problem.''

''What is?''

''Taking things for granted.'' Looking at his father, he

said, "Did Grandfather ever ask you if you wanted to serve the crown, Father?"

Arutha looked as if this question was equally perplexing as what he had just witnessed. After a pause, he said, "No, of course not."

"Why 'of course not'?"

"Because I was just a boy. I began, much as you did, running errands for him, then I was given work with the Royal Pages, then the Squires."

"But when you became a man, did he ask if you might wish to do something else?"

Arutha looked at Dash and said, "No. He never did."

"Did you ever consider you might have had a happier life if he had?"

Arutha was silent a moment, then said, "That may be the oddest question I've ever heard, son."

Dash shrugged. "I'm full of very odd questions these days."

"Why did you ask that?"

"Because I'm not certain I wish to continue in service to the crown."

"What?" said Arutha. His tone was a mix of surprise and disbelief. "What would you do?"

Dash shrugged. "I don't know. Perhaps return to Mister Avery's employ. He is a very wealthy man."

Arutha laughed. "On paper. The King may make good on repaying him by the time his grandchildren are running Avery and Jacoby."

Dash smiled. "If I know Roo, he'll find a way to amass another fortune before that."

Arutha put his hand on Dash's shoulder and said, "If you wish to be released from service to the crown, I can manage that. But please wait until after we get Fadawah out of Ylith. We have few enough competent men to serve."

"I'll agree to that." Lowering his voice, Dash asked, "What comes next?"

"Publicly, a very large engagement party next week. During which Patrick secretly goes to Ravensburg, where he'll meet Duko, who will kneel before him and swear fealty. Then the newly appointed Duke of the Southern

Marches will return to the city and a hopefully quiet movement of soldiers will be underway. Those mercenaries who've been kept outside the walls will be allowed in. Many will be hired to man the garrison as others leave to find work along the Keshian border. By the time Patrick's wedding is over and he returns to Krondor, the city will be firmly in our hands, without having alerted Fadawah too far in advance that he's lost his southern command.''

Dash's expression turned suspicious. ''Where in all of this is the Duke of Krondor? Why aren't you leading Patrick into his palace in triumph?''

''I'm needed elsewhere a while longer. There are things to be done only I can see through to the end.''

Dash said, ''Forgive me if I say that sounds decidedly odd.''

''Odd or not, it's true. Now go find your brother and see if he really is in distress. If so, go get him drunk and find a tavern wench to take his mind off of Francine.''

Dash said, ''I'll try,'' and went off in search of his brother.

Arutha watched his younger son depart and stood lost in thought for a moment, then he turned and headed back to the banquet hall. There was still much that had to be arranged before any of the plans he had set in motion could continue on to fruition.

Erik von Darkmoor and Rupert Avery sat at a table in the Charging Boar, one of Darkmoor's better taverns, when Jimmy and Dash entered. Jimmy looked drunk already, and Erik stood and signaled across the crowded common room. ''Over here!''

Dash saw him and led a somewhat off-balance Jimmy over to the table. ''Join us!'' said Roo cheerfully.

A plump barmaid came by, and Erik indicated a round of ale for the four of them. Dash said, ''No, thanks. He's had enough.''

Erik looked surprised, but said nothing as he waved away the barmaid.

''What brings you out of the palace, young nobles?'' asked Roo.

"We needed a change of air," said Jimmy, his voice edged in bitterness.

Roo glanced at Erik, and Erik said, "Something sounds amiss."

Dash leaned over, and in conspiratorial tones said, "A woman."

Erik laughed, and when Jimmy's expression darkened, put up his hands in supplication. "I make no jest, young Jimmy. It's just . . . unexpected."

Roo nodded. "We would have wagered neither of you would ever be seeking solace in an ale jack because of a woman."

Jimmy said, "It's not that simple."

"It never is," agreed Roo.

Both brothers knew of Roo's involvement with Sylvia Esterbrook, the daughter of a Keshian agent who had played Roo like a flute, causing him to cheat on his wife, compromise his own business, and the welfare of the Kingdom. He had been, by all reports, a model husband since then, but they understood his lessons had been hard-learned.

"So who's the girl?" asked Erik.

"The Duke of Silden's daughter," replied Dash.

"Ah," said Erik, as if he understood. "She's not interested, or . . . otherwise engaged?"

Dash looked around the room, "The latter, but it's not widely known."

Erik apparently understood the context of the remark. He stood up. "I've got to return to the castle." He turned toward Roo and said, "Give my best to Karli. And the children."

"And my affections to Kitty," returned Roo.

After he had left, Roo said, "I should be getting along, too. I've got a lot to do in the morning. I've got a shipment of wagons bringing grain for Nakor's temple due in at first light."

Jimmy said, "I haven't seen Nakor since Pug stormed out of Patrick's court. Where is he?"

"He's smart enough to know when to get out of sight," answered Roo. "He's been down at his temple the last couple of days."

Roo nodded. "I have on more than one occasion felt like sleeping anywhere but at home. I understand. If you need, come by the house. We have room if you don't mind sleeping under a wagon." He laughed. "Well, young lords, good night."

The barmaid came by again and said, "Would you like something before we close for the night, young sirs?"

Dash said, "Thank you, but no. We'll be on our way."

Jimmy said, "I'm not going back to the palace."

"Fine," said Dash. "But at least let's walk some, so you can pass out in a more agreeable place."

Jimmy's expression brightened. "I know! Let's go see Nakor!"

For lack of any better suggestion, Dash agreed. The two brothers left the tavern, and Dash kept one hand on Jimmy's arm, half-guiding, half-supporting as he stumbled along.

Jimmy groaned. His head pounded and his eyes felt as if they were glued shut. His mouth tasted as if someone had tossed in table scraps a week earlier and left them to ripen.

"Would you like some water?"

Jimmy forced his eyes open and instantly wished he hadn't, as the pounding in his head increased in intensity. Hovering over him was a woman's face, and as his eyes focused, he saw the rest of her swim into shape. He lifted his head and got his right arm under himself and reached out with his left hand.

She placed a water cup in it and he drank. Suddenly he knew it was a bad idea: his heart began to thunder and his skin flushed, and perspiration began to bead on his brow. He knew he was experiencing the worst hangover of his life, and eventually the water would be necessary, so he forced himself to drain the cup. "Thanks," he said in a hoarse whisper, handing the cup back.

"Your brother's in there," she said, pointing to the office Nakor used as his personal quarters when staying at the temple.

"Do I know you?" croaked Jimmy.

"I don't think so," said the young woman, with a faint

smile. "I know you, however. You're the Duke—the old Duke's grandson, aren't you?"

Jimmy nodded. "James, son of Duke Arutha, and yes, Lord James was my grandfather. They call me Jimmy."

"You can call me Aleta." She studied his face. "A woman?"

He nodded. "I guess."

Glancing him over, she observed, "Well, you're not much to look at now, but I've seen you in a couple of the taverns I've worked, and when you're not drunk or hung over, you're not a bad-looking fellow. I don't expect you hear 'no' very often."

"It's not that," he said, rising slowly. "I just found out she's marrying someone else."

"Ah," said Aleta, as if she understood. "Does she know?"

"What?"

"That you're killing yourself with ale over her?"

"No. We were friends as children . . ." He squinted at her. "Why am I telling you this?"

She smiled. "Because you need to?"

He took another drink of water. "Thank you. I think I'll see what my brother is doing."

He walked on shaky legs through a warehouse bustling with activity. When he was almost to the door of Nakor's office, the large outer doors to the warehouse swung open and filled it with light. Jimmy turned to see a wagon being driven up to and then into the entrance, with other wagons behind it.

The door to the office opened behind Jimmy, and Nakor came rushing out. "Roo!" he shouted as he passed Jimmy. "You're here with the food!"

Dash followed and stopped next to his brother. "Are you alive?"

"Barely," croaked Jimmy. "What happened?"

"You attempted to drown yourself in ale. You failed."

"I know, but how did we get here?"

"Father sent me after you and told me to get you drunk and in the arms of a tavern wench."

"Seems you succeeded with half the order."

"Well, there were a couple of ladies willing to accommodate, but you seemed in no mood."

"I'm a mess," said Jimmy. "I don't really know how I feel about all this."

Dash shrugged. "Maybe that's the best. We've both known since childhood we were to have no say in who we wed. With Father being Duke of Krondor, it's too important we wed for the good of the state."

"I know, but I feel so . . ."

"What?"

Jimmy sighed. "I don't know."

"It isn't about Francie, you know," said Dash.

"No?"

"No," said Dash. "If she's the Queen there's nothing to keep the two of you apart; the Gods know the court is well practiced in looking the other way. No, it's something else. It's about you and what you really want."

"I don't understand."

"I don't think I do, really, but it's about you." He looked at the wagon. "I still half expect to see Jason on one of those wagons," Dash said reflectively.

Jason had been an employee of Rupert's Bitter Sea Company when Dash had served there, and had been feeding information to Rupert's rival, Jacob Esterbrook, because of his misguided love for Jacob's daughter. He had died in the war.

As the first wagon entered the warehouse, Jimmy said, "Tell me, who's that girl?"

"Which one?" Dash asked.

"That one over there, who gave me water. She said her name was Aleta."

"Then you know more of her than I," said Dash. "Why don't you ask Nakor."

"There's something odd about her. Nice, but odd."

Dash said, "There's Luis!" He hurried past Jimmy to the second wagon, where Luis de Savona sat next to a woman Dash didn't recognize. Luis jumped down, and Dash said, "Luis! It's good to see you again."

Luis shook hands with Dash and said, "It's good to see you again, young Mr. Jamison. I was grieved to learn of your grandparents' death." Luis had spent the winter in

Salador, overseeing Roo's holdings in the East while Roo had worked in Darkmoor.

Dash said, "I appreciate that." He then noticed the woman as she climbed down off the wagon. "Mrs. Avery?" he said in wonder.

Karli Avery had been a plain-looking, pale and plump woman. The woman who was stepping before him was slender, tanned, and while still not pretty, had an alive, expressive face that commanded attention. "Dash!" she said, taking his hands and kissing his cheek. "How are you?"

"I'm just fine, Mrs. Avery, but you . . . you look so different!"

She laughed. "There's been a great deal of work and not much food all winter. Loading and unloading wagons, learning to drive them, caring for the children. Spending days in the sun; it all changes a person."

"Quite so," observed Dash. Jimmy approached, and Dash said, "You remember my brother, don't you?"

Both said hello to Jimmy, and Dash said, "What of the children, and Mrs. Jacoby?"

"All back in Salador, under Helen's care," said Karli, "only it's no longer Mrs. Jacoby. She's Mrs. de Savona now."

Dash laughed and playfully struck Luis in the arm. "You got married!"

Roo walked over with Nakor at his side. "He most certainly did."

Nakor congratulated his old companion, and said, "I hope you're at last happy."

Luis smiled. "As happy as I'm likely to be, you odd little man."

"That will have to do," said Nakor. To Roo he said, "Did you get my grain and my statue maker?"

Roo said, "I haven't found the sculptor yet, but here's your grain."

"Did the wagon makers prove useful?" asked Nakor as he began inspecting the contents of the two wagons. Other wagons were arriving outside.

Roo said, "Very. I'm of a mind to be early into Krondor; there may be a very large number of skilled artisans and craftsmen among the invaders. If I can recruit them . . .''

Jimmy and Dash exchanged glances. Jimmy asked, ''How do you know they'll be free to work, considering there's a war going on?''

Roo laughed. ''I'm not without my sources, and I knew Patrick was going to cut a deal with Duko about an hour after you did.''

''Sources?''

''Your father,'' said Roo, laughing. ''He's not quite as evil-minded as your grandfather, but your father is no slouch when it comes to making sure he has all his resources ready. Besides, I'm the largest single debt-holder on the Royal Treasury, so he has to keep me apprised of what's going on.''

Jimmy said, ''Well, then, I expect you'll recover your losses before you're through.''

Nakor said, ''If he doesn't get himself killed first.''

Roo threw Nakor a dark look. ''I'm not volunteering for any more hare—brained missions, you can bet. From now on I'm a conservative family man, a businessman who will stay home and look after his holdings.''

From nearby another voice said, ''After we take care of a little job.''

All eyes turned to see Erik von Darkmoor standing nearby. ''I came looking for all of you; how convenient I find all of you together.'' To Dash and Jimmy, he said, ''Report to your father, now, gentlemen.''

The brothers didn't hesitate, and started for the door. As Jimmy passed the young woman who gave him water, he said, ''Thanks again.''

She nodded and smiled and said nothing.

Erik turned to Nakor. ''Can you reach Brother Dominic?''

Nakor nodded. ''He's due back from Rillanon, soon. He's supposed to be bringing me word as to the Temple of Ishap's willingness to support our efforts here. I suspect he is either in Salador or on the road from Salador to here.''

''I'll send a patrol eastward, looking for him. If he somehow gets here before they find him, please let Duke Arutha know.''

Nakor nodded. ''Why, if I may ask?''

"You can ask," said Erik. "I can't answer. You'll have to ask Duke Arutha."

Nakor said, "I might."

To Roo, Erik said, "I need to speak with you." He glanced at Luis and Karli, saying, "Excuse me, please."

He led Roo to a distant corner of the warehouse-turned-temple, and when they were alone, he said, "Who do you have still working for you in Sarth?"

Roo asked, "What makes you think I have anyone working for me in Sarth?"

Erik said, "Roo, it's me you're talking to. Now, who do you have still working for you in Sarth?"

Roo said, "John Vinci. He acts as an independent trader; he specializes in bringing in contraband from Queg. That's why it's not widely known he works for me."

"Good. We need to visit with him."

"What?" said Roo. "We? Visit?"

Erik said, "We need to see how things are in Sarth before we turn northward. We need to come back with a detailed report before Owen takes the army and moves to crush Nordan in Sarth. We've sent scouts around the area, and most of them have come back, but we can't tell how strong the deployment is inside the town. We need to get inside and look around."

Roo looked his boyhood friend in the eye, and said, "When you say 'we,' you're speaking of the Kingdom army, right?"

"No, I mean you and I need to get in there and scout."

Roo said, "No!"

"You must," said Erik. "You're the only man we know who has a plausible enough story that can get us into Sarth without getting our throats cut."

"What story?"

"You're a well-known Kingdom merchant who has openly traded with Queg and the Free Cities. You're reputed to put a profit above everything else. If you were to sneak into Sarth—especially with your friend Vinci ready to corroborate your story—even if we get apprehended, you'll be convincing in your role as the greedy merchant anxious to set up trade before his competition does."

"We?"

"I'm going, too," said Erik.

Roo still looked unconvinced. "So you'll be standing beside me on the gibbet again? Only this time there won't be any Bobby de Longville to haul us to our feet and explain we're being reprieved to serve the crown.

"No, thank you. I've done my service and been pardoned for my crimes."

"You want to see any of the money the crown owes you, ever again?"

"It's my most ardent hope."

"Then I'd consider this, Roo."

He glanced around. "This isn't the place to talk. Come to the castle tonight and seek me out in my quarters. I'll explain more then."

Roo said, "For the sake of our friendship, I will, but I'm not going on any more stone-headed missions, Erik."

The smuggler's boat sailed silently up the coast, hugging as close inshore as possible, without shoaling out on the reefs which dotted the shoreline between Krondor and Ylith.

Roo and Erik had ridden to within a half-day's walk of the coast, just beyond a checkpoint Duko had established, and escort riders had taken the horses back to Owen Greylock's forward position. An unofficial channel of communication was already in operation, and even though few outside of the Prince's immediate circle knew of the coming change in loyalties on Duke Duko's part, there were rumors of change in the wind.

Most of them planted by Duke Arutha's agents.

The current one being carefully fostered was that the Kingdom couldn't mount an offensive this year against the invaders in the North, due in the main to Kesh's threatening presence on their southern flank. Additionally, it was rumored, the Prince would be leaving soon for the East, to get married in the royal palace at Rillanon, leaving the command in the West to Owen Greylock, with express orders to hold where they were, defend where necessary, but to seek no offensive.

Roo had been astonished by the scope of the deception. He had been told by Erik that Arutha's agents were already in Krondor, quietly undertaking the transfer of power, with as little fanfare as possible. It was Erik's passionate hope that by the time the Armies of the West were ready to redeploy, not only would the enemy be taken by surprise, but they would have been lulled into a state of complacency.

A crewman whispered, "We're nearly there. Get ready."

Roo said, "Are you sure this is necessary?"

"Absolutely," said Erik.

The Captain ordered sail lowered and a small boat was put over the side. Neither Erik nor Roo were sailors, but Erik felt competent enough to row a boat into a quiet fishing village without calling too much attention to themselves.

The boat was lowered and Erik and Roo shimmied down ropes to get into the skiff, and by the time Erik had the oars in the oarlocks, the smuggler had his sails up and was putting out toward deeper water. The current here ran southeast, and Erik was forced to work to keep on course, trying to come in at a fishing village in a sandy cove just south of Sarth.

Roo said, "Are you all right?"

Erik pulled hard and the boat seem to jump forward. "Everything's fine."

The sound of breakers wasn't loud, as the surf was relatively calm, but it still picked the boat up as the combers ran up on the shore, turning into breakers. Erik pulled and the boat seemed to be climbing a hill, only to slide backward a bit as the wave broke just in front of them.

Suddenly the bow of the boat dipped and Roo glanced over his shoulder and realized he was looking at water. "Erik!" he shouted as the wave crashed down upon him, drenching him to the skin in moments.

The boat wallowed and turned sideways as Erik fought to keep it pointed at the beach. The boat tipped to the left, then suddenly it flipped, and Erik and Roo both were tossed into the water.

Roo sputtered as he came up, and to his irritation found he was only waist deep in water. He looked around and saw Erik standing a few yards away. The boat, upside down, was being pushed into the sand by the waves.

Wading over toward Erik, Roo was about to comment on Erik's boat-handling skills when a lantern a dozen yards away was unshuttered. Men stood at the edge of the water, visible in the lantern's light; torches were lit. Soon, Erik and Roo could see a score of armed men, many with bows or crossbows pointed in their direction, facing them from the dry sand. In the distance, behind them, the faint outlines of the fishing village could be seen.

Roo turned to Erik and said, "Everything's fine?"

Eleven

Disposition

Roo SNEEZED.

Erik sipped at a hot cup of Keshian coffee. They were sitting in a large hut near the beach, warming themselves before a fire while their clothing was drying on a line strung in front of the rude stone fireplace.

The leader of the smugglers who had met them on the beach said, "Sorry for the scare, Mr. Avery. John said to cover the cove and make sure you got ashore safely." He was a nondescript fellow, ideal for smuggling, one whom a soldier or guardsman was unlikely to look at twice. The only thing that differentiated this man and his companions from common workers was the assortment of weapons they carried.

Roo said, "I wish we'd have had enough time for him to answer the note. So I would have known we were to be met."

The smuggler's spokesman said, "As soon as your clothing is dried out, we'll leave." He glanced out the door of the hut. "Or maybe a little damp, because we have to be out of here before dawn."

"Patrols?"

"Not so's you'd notice," said the man. "But there is a checkpoint up the road we need to pass, and the guards that we've bribed are relieved at dawn. You'll go in place of two men who will stay here. We've got some goods stashed away from our last cargo and we'll have to hurry to be in the town before dawn. No one will suspect anything.''

Erik nodded.

Roo inspected the clothing and said, ''We'll change once we get to John's. He's sure to have some dry clothing.''

Erik sipped the coffee. ''This tastes fresh,'' he said.

''Should be. Got it off a packet boat from Durban yesterday. It's part of that cargo we'll be carrying in.''

''Keshian ships are putting in here?''

''And Quegan traders, too,'' said the leader. ''Kingdom ships are staying close to Port Vykor and escorting Far Coast traders to and from the Straits of Darkness.'' He made a wide sweeping gesture. ''Fadawah's got a few ships left from the invasion, and he's keeping them up near Ylith. So there's no one to keep ships away from these beaches, but it's tough getting anything into the town unless you have the checkpoint guards bribed.'' The leader moved toward the door. ''I've got things to do.'' He motioned to the other smugglers, who departed, leaving Roo and Erik alone.

Erik said, ''I told you Vinci would get your note.''

''You had more confidence in my agents than I,'' Roo answered. ''It seems your faith was justified.''

Erik said, ''There are a lot of things at risk, Roo, and we need your contacts as well as our own to pull off this counterstrike.''

''What's the Prince's plan for that old abbey? If Fadawah's got any brains, it's packed to the limit with enough men to strike down the mountain and ruin any attack up the coast.''

''Arutha's got plans for the abbey.''

Roo shook his head. ''Every time I hear any member of the royal court has plans, I'm reminded that most of the time we served involved running very hard from people who were trying equally hard to catch and kill us.''

Erik said, ''That's one way of putting things.''

They spoke little for the next hour, as their clothes dried enough to put on. An hour before dawn, the leader of the smugglers said, ''We must go.''

Roo and Erik quickly dressed, their clothes still slightly

damp. They went outside and gathered up bundles of goods, and climbed a steep path that cut straight up the side of a small cliff behind the village. Fishermen were moving down toward the beach where they would launch their boats and spend their day as their fathers and grandfathers had before them. They took no notice of the smugglers, and Roo assumed the inhabitants of the village were paid a handsome sum to pretend the smugglers were invisible.

They climbed the cliffs until they reached the plateau above, a large stretch of dirt and grass they quickly crossed to reach the road. They moved swiftly down the road until they came in sight of a barricade. It was a sturdy affair of dirt, reinforced with wood and stones, sporting an impressive array of steel-tipped wooden stakes to repulse riders. To pass it, the smugglers had to move to the side of the road, step down into a shallow gully, then circle around to the back of the barricade. A wagon or a man on foot could easily negotiate it, but attackers up the road would be forced down to the cliffs on the sea side, where another large barricade was erected, or into thick woods steeply rising up the side of a small mountain, impassable by any but the occasional goat or deer.

As they hurried past the guards, the leader of the smugglers stopped and handed over a pouch and nodded, without a word, to a soldier who was equally silent.

Then they were past the checkpoint and down the road into the town of Sarth.

The rear door to the storage room closed after the last smuggler departed. It was attached to the back of John Vinci's shop, the second floor of which was his home. A single lantern illuminated the room, which was stacked with small boxes and bundles of goods he would sell in his shop: cloth, needles, thread, iron goods—kettles, pots, and pans—rope, tools, and other necessities for those living in and around Sarth. Vinci turned and said, "Bad news, Roo."

"What?"

"Lord Vasarius has agents in town."

Rupert said, "Damn. Any who know me from my visits to Queg?"

"Almost certainly. You'll have to keep a very low profile," Vinci said. "You can stay out back in the smaller worker's shed. I have no one using it now. Vasarius's men are due to sail back to Queg by the end of the week. Once they're gone, you should be able to move about freely."

John Vinci was the son of an escaped Quegan galley slave who had made his way to the safety of the Kingdom. He spoke the language of the island nation like a native, and traded with smugglers and sea captains attempting to avoid Kingdom customs officers.

He had come to Roo's attention when he had gained possession of a valuable necklace, one which Roo had eventually used to ingratiate himself to Lord Vasarius. He had then achieved several profitable trades with the Quegan noble, leading up to planting a rumor of a treasure fleet which had caused the leading nobles of Queg to dispatch their warships to attack the fleet of the Emerald Queen as it exited the Straits of Darkness the previous Midsummer's Day. The most powerful lords of Queg had seen the vast bulk of their ships sent to the bottom, the single most devastating naval defeat in their history.

Most knew that Rupert Avery of Krondor somehow had a hand in this, for while there was no direct line proving he engineered the ruse, there were ample reports of rumors started by men who served on his ships, or who worked for his agents. Without being told, Roo knew he was a marked man in Queg and that to be discovered outside Kingdom protection meant his life would be measured in hours, if not minutes. Even in the Kingdom he would have to forevermore be vigilant against assassins hired by Quegan gold.

Roo looked at John. "I can hide out until we have to depart, if necessary. But Erik needs to look around. Can you provide believable cover?"

John looked dubious. "I don't know. There are so many strangers in Sarth, perhaps. If he could pass as a Quegan or Keshian mercenary, no doubt. But all Kingdom citizens who bear arms are known to the local soldiers."

Erik said, "I don't have to go armed. If I'm one of your workmen . . ."

Vinci shook his head. "I only employ casual labor, Erik. Things are a little slow now, given the occupation." He said, "Let me think about this. You two sleep and take it easy. I'll send one of my children out with some food in a while, then sleep. Maybe by tomorrow morning I'll have thought of some reason to be walking around town with someone as noticeable as Erik."

"Buy something," said Roo.

John's eyebrows went up. "What?"

"Buy something. A building, a business, a house. Something over on the other side of the town that will let you move back and forth. Make Erik . . . a builder. Someone you're going to pay to repair things."

Vinci said, "There are several businesses that are abandoned or for sale."

"Good, let it be known you're taking the opportunity to seize profit, and are willing to buy whatever anyone has to sell."

"How, by the way, am I paying for this?"

"If you actually have to buy something, John, you'll pay for it as you always do, with my gold."

Vinci grinned. "It usually comes back with a profit attached."

"True," said Roo, returning the grin. "That's why you're doing so well."

John opened the door to the front part of his store, and the stairs leading up to the living quarters above, and said, "Food will be here shortly. After you finish, head out that rear door to the shed on the other side of the yard and get some sleep."

Erik turned to Roo as the door closed. "A builder?"

"Just pick up some loose wood, look at it, toss it aside, and grunt. Take along some parchment or paper and scribble on it. Look around a lot. If any of the soldiers start talking like they know something about carpentry, nod in agreement."

Erik leaned his chair back, so that he balanced on two legs, resting his head against the wall. "Well, it's a better plan than I have. I hope things back in Darkmoor are working out smoother than they are here."

Jimmy shouted, "No!"

Arutha said, "There will be no argument!"

Dash stepped between his brother and father and said, "Calm down, both of you."

Arutha said, "My orders are not subject to your approval, James!"

Jimmy said, "But you, leading a raid . . . it's preposterous."

Nakor and Father Dominic stood nearby, watching the exchange. Arutha said, "I am the only one here who remembers Father's story about the secret entrance into the abbey at Sarth. I don't remember all of it, but I stand the best chance of having things come back to me as I walk around the base of that mountain."

Jimmy looked at Father Dominic. "Don't you know the way?"

Dominic said, "I know where the door is, in the subbasement of the abandoned library, that leads to the tunnel outside in the hills. I don't know if I could find the entrance from the outside. It's been twenty years since I've even been down to the base of the mountain."

Jimmy was about to speak when Dash said, "What do you want us to do?"

Arutha said, "I need someone in Krondor overseeing the rotation of troops. When Von Darkmoor and Avery get back from their scouting mission at Sarth, I want to be able to strike before Nordan sees the attack coming."

"Which is why Greylock is already up at the forward lines getting ready," said Jimmy.

"Yes," replied Arutha. "I'll give you details before you go, but by midday tomorrow I want you on the road west."

Jimmy said, "I don't like this one little bit."

Nakor grinned. "You make that obvious."

Dash said, "Come on. We have to get our kits together."

As the boys reached the door out of Arutha's office, Arutha said, "Jimmy, Dash."

They stopped at the door. "Yes?" asked Dash.

"I love you both very much."

Jimmy hesitated a moment, then returned to embrace his father. "Don't do anything stupid and heroic," he whispered to his father.

"Aren't I supposed to be saying that to you?" asked Arutha.

Dash hugged his father and said, "You know it wouldn't do any good."

"Stay alive, both of you," whispered Arutha.

"You, too," said Jimmy.

The brothers left the room. Arutha turned to Dominic and said, "What does the Ishapian Temple have to say to us, Brother?"

Dominic, a man nearly eighty years of age, but appearing barely twenty-five due to the healing magic of the Lifestone, said, "Many things, my lord duke. May I sit?"

Arutha indicated they both should, and Dominic said, "It took some persuasion, but I am living proof of my claims. Besides, I was seniormost in rank in the West and my words carried some weight."

"And your warning saved your library at Sarth."

"To be frank, that was not entirely providential."

"What do you mean?" asked Arutha.

"I don't think it a breach of trust to reveal it was your grandfather who warned us to be ready to move the library when certain things occurred."

"Really?" said Arutha.

Dominic got a perplexed expression on his face. "But what I find odd was when he arrived at Sarth to find me and take me to Seathanon, prior to our confrontation with the demon, he didn't seem to remember he sent us the warning."

"Maybe he didn't," said Nakor.

"Why?" asked Arutha.

"Because maybe he hasn't sent the warning, yet."

Dominic said, "Time travel?"

Nakor shrugged. "Possibly. He's done it before."

Arutha nodded. "That's possible. I get the feeling there's a great deal more to all this than Grandfather has told me, or than you've told me."

Nakor said, "True. But that's for your own good."

Arutha laughed. "You sound like me, talking to my children." To Dominic, "So, will the Ishapian Temple support Nakor's efforts?"

"Yes," said Dominic, "though they are somewhat dubious as to the net effect. Yet they understand the need."

"I'm dubious, too," said Nakor, "and I started the Temple of Arch-Indar."

Arutha said, "You are the most amazing man. What is the exact purpose of your order, again?"

"To bring about the restoration of the Goddess of Good, as I told you before."

"Yes, you are a wonder," said Arutha dryly.

Nakor said, "Yes, I am, aren't I? But I think my little temple will not be what it needs to be until we find the real head of the order."

"I thought you were the high priest of Arch-Indar," said Arutha.

"Only until the real one shows up. Then I'll return to doing what I do best, traveling and learning things."

"Well, until this person puts in an appearance, what are you going to do?"

Nakor said, "Do tricks, tell stories, provide food, get people to listen to the message of the Good Lady."

Dominic said, "First must come belief. When people begin to understand that good flows from Arch-Indar, then they will begin the long task of bringing her back to us."

"I don't pretend to understand everything involved with temple politics," said Arutha. "I have read notes left by my father and Prince Arutha, and I get the distinct impression they were privy to secrets that were not passed along to me."

Dominic said nothing.

"Very well," said Arutha. "I will trust that nothing in this poses a threat to the Kingdom, which is my charge and area of concern. Besides, it seems to me that spreading the doctrine of doing good can harm no one."

Nakor shook his head. "Would that it were true. Men have been put to death for preaching good."

Arutha said, "Well, at least not in the West while I'm Duke of Krondor." Looking at Dominic he said, "If I can find this entrance to the old abbey, can you get us inside?"

Dominic said, "I can. The entrance is locked from within. But there is a secret control that will open it from without. Your father found that control."

Arutha smiled. "He always claimed he was the best thief in the history of Krondor."

"Skill or luck, he recognized it, disarmed a trap, and activated the entrance. Almost gave one of our brothers a heart attack when he showed up inside our library."

Arutha said, "The question becomes how many men to bring with us."

Dominic said, "I know only a little of warcraft. You must bring a small enough company that we are not detected while moving through the mountains and large enough that once inside we stand a good chance of securing the abbey."

"Can you draw me plans of the abbey?"

"I lived there fifty years, Duke Arutha. I can show you every hallway and closet."

"Good. I will have a scribe visit with you in the morning. If you can have them finished by the end of the week, I would be appreciative. If we're going to be in position to get inside the abbey when Owen strikes up the coast at Sarth, we need be on the way up the eastern trail along Nightmare Ridge by then."

Dominic bowed and said, "I am at your disposal. If someone could show me to a room? It's been a long journey from Rillanon."

Arutha rang a small bell and a page opened the door to his office. "Show Brother Dominic to my quarters and bring him whatever he needs."

"Your quarters?" asked the Ishapian.

"I will not be needing them tonight, I'm afraid. I have many things to do before first light tomorrow. Perhaps a nap after the morning court."

Dominic nodded and bowed again, following the page out of the room.

Nakor said, "At least you've enough sense to put a bedroll behind your desk, if you need to catch a nap."

Arutha smiled. "You don't miss much, do you?"

"I'm a gambler, remember? If I missed things I'd be broke or dead."

"Are you coming with us?"

"No," said Nakor. "It sounds interesting, but I think I need to be here. Dominic brings a great gift from the Ishapians. They will share the power they gain from the Tear of the Gods with us. When we have found the true leader of our temple, we will send him to Rillanon and there he will be given this power.

"That power will turn my little warehouse into a true temple, where prayers will be answered, and miracles performed. Men will learn of good and then help recreate the Good Lady."

Arutha said, "A worthy undertaking." He rose. "If you'll excuse me, Nakor, I do have work. And if you need anything for your temple and I can help before I go, I will do my best."

"Thanks," said Nakor, as he walked to the door. "Come back alive, if you would. A new Duke might not be so willing to listen to me."

Arutha laughed as he opened the door to his office. "Well, as much as I'd hate to inconvenience you by getting killed, I think I would be even more inconvenienced."

"True. See, it's to both our benefit if you stay alive."

Arutha laughed again as he closed the door behind Nakor. Still chuckling, he sat back down behind his desk and considered the mountain of work before him. The smile faded as he picked up the first report he needed to review and, after scanning it, placed it in a pile to review with his clerk in the morning.

He picked up the next piece of paper.

"Jimmy!" called Francie as he started down the hallway.

Jimmy turned and saw her hurrying after him. "Hello," he said coolly.

She slipped her arm in his and said, "I haven't seen you for a while. Has your father had you out and about?"

Jimmy said, "No, I've been working here, but have little time of my own." Very gently and slowly, he disengaged his arm from hers.

"Jimmy, what's wrong?" she asked.

Jimmy felt his color rise, and suddenly he was choking on unexpected emotions. "What's wrong is it isn't appropriate for me to be overly familiar with the future Queen of Isles."

Her color rose in a blush and she looked down at the floor stones. "I should have known your father would tell you."

"Why didn't *you* tell me?" he asked.

She looked up at him, and her eyes were rimming with moisture. "I don't know. I didn't know . . . how you'd take it. Before I came to Darkmoor, I thought I knew how I felt about you . . . about us. Then when I saw you, and we dined together and those walks together . . . I don't know. Things just didn't seem the same as they did when we were children."

Jimmy said, "That's because they're not the same. We're not children."

She looked him in the eyes, then impulsively leaned forward and kissed him on the cheek. "You were always my best friend, Jimmy. I love you more than any boy I've known. I want you to be happy for me."

Jimmy flushed. "Happy because you're going to be Queen, or because you're going to marry that ass Patrick?"

"Don't be that way," she said softly. "Daddy says someone has to keep Patrick in line, and that's why he wants me to be a strong Queen. It's one of the reasons the King wants me to marry Patrick."

Jimmy said, "Look, I don't know what to say. I only know that whatever we want doesn't matter, and that you'll marry Patrick, and I'll marry whoever Father tells me to marry, and that will be the end of that. It's never been any other way."

She squeezed his hand. "Be my friend?"

He nodded. "I'll always be that, Francie."

A tear formed and started down her cheek. "I'll need friends like you when I'm Queen in Rillanon."

He found his own feelings rising and said, "It's just . . ."

"What?"

Softly he said, "We'll never know what we could have been, don't you see?"

She nodded. "I see. But there's never been a choice for either of us, has there? We can't let our feelings distract us from our duty." She looked into his eyes a moment, then added, "I will always love the boy who used to play with me in the palace at Rillanon, and who used to laugh when I beat up his little brother. I'll cherish the time we spent sneaking into all those places we weren't supposed to go. I never forgave you for being boys and getting to do boy things, while I had to learn to be a lady." She sighed. "But I will never be able to fall in love, my dearest Jimmy. And neither will you. Don't mourn for something that never was. Just be my friend."

Without another word she released his hand and hurried back down the corridor.

Jimmy stood quietly for a long minute, then slowly turned and resumed his walk down the corridor.

Dash signaled and Jimmy turned and waved. They were a hundred yards ahead of the first column heading into Krondor. A delegation of Duko's men were waiting a mile outside the city and Jimmy wanted the column to wait until an exchange of documents was completed.

Jimmy urged his horse forward and rode to a point just before the obvious leader of the group. Jimmy saluted and said, "I am Baron James of the Prince's court." He recognized the man as being one of Duko's captains. Then he remembered his name. "How are you, Captain Boyse?"

The Captain, a muscular man with a long beard and hair, nodded. "Well, Baron James."

Jimmy reached into a pouch sewn into his cloak and pulled a thread, unraveling the top seam. He reached into the pocket and pulled out a sheaf of documents. He handed them to Boyse. "This is the final communication between Prince Patrick and our newly named Lord Sutherland. This will confirm his appointment to office—the ceremony will be held when Patrick returns to the city. There are several orders and instructions, but they just reaffirm what the Duke already knows."

Captain Boyse stroked his chin. "You know, when Duko . . . I mean the Duke, first told me of this deal, I would have bet my life it would never take place." He shrugged. "What do I know?" He pointed to the southwest. "A troop of five hundred men, foot and horse alike, are already on the march toward Land's End. We will occupy that fortress by week's end." He smiled. "I understand we may have to dislodge a few Keshians who have wandered into that town from the desert?"

Jimmy nodded. "Bandits, mostly."

"You've brought the replacements?"

"Up the road," said Jimmy.

"Good." He handed the documents to one of his lieutenants, and said, "I will happily trade this garrison duty for some scrapping along the frontier. Some of my men are city men, who were carpenters or masons, fishermen and the like, back home, but I was always a soldier." He looked around as if trying to see beyond the limits of his vision. "Duko's a thinker; he talks about this nation of yours. He tells us this new pledge of loyalty is a good thing." He looked at Jimmy. "I do not know of such things. I am trained to fight and kill and die if needed. But I trust Duko. He has been my leader for more than half my life, and he was not much more than a boy when I pledged service to him. So, if Duko says we are now servants of your Prince, and that we fight for this nation we tried to take last year, then we shall serve your Prince and fight for this nation. I don't claim to understand it, but I will do as Duko orders, for he is my General."

Jimmy nodded. "I understand. And for that reason, he will continue to be your General." Then Jimmy smiled. "And perhaps someday he will have a son, who will grow up to also be your General."

Boyse laughed. "That would be something, wouldn't it, Baron James?" He turned his horse around and said, "Call your men. Let us ride into Krondor together."

Jimmy signaled and Dash rode forward, and the column behind him also moved up. When they were formed up with Boyse and his companions, they started forward, and for the first time in almost a year, the agents of the Prince of Krondor were reclaiming his city for the crown.

Dash hurried along the street, dodging workers and peddlers. Life was returning to Krondor, and there were endless tasks before them. Several hundred mercenaries from outside the walls had been given employment and sent to the borders to the south. Others were being recruited for caravan escort and garrison duty in the area between Darkmoor and Shamata, replacing soldiers who were being sent to this front.

Workers, shopkeepers, and some minor nobles had returned in the last two weeks. Two messengers from Fadawah had been intercepted, and reassuring reports returned by other messengers, soldiers loyal to Duko who could be trusted to report only what Duko wanted Fadawah and Nordan to know.

Dash judged it would be only a matter of two or three weeks more before it was obvious to Fadawah and Nordan that Duko had turned coat. The story that a big wedding in Rillanon would keep the Prince away from the West for a year, and that Keshian agitation along the border would keep the Kingdom from attempting to retake Krondor, had been widely circulated. Duko's latest message to Fadawah included a note that a Keshian agent had made preliminary contact with him inquiring about the possibility of formal treaty with the "King of the Bitter Sea," which Duko hoped would keep Fadawah overconfident for a while longer.

Dash turned a corner, heading into a burned-out portion of the city that was far down the list to be rebuilt. The note he had received had been short and to the point. No signature had been affixed, but he had no doubt who had sent it.

Dash worried about the presence of Keshian agents in the city. The transfer of soldiers was taking place slowly. The logistics of getting those patrols to pre-determined locations, having those men switch clothing with Kingdom regulars, and change places, was very complex. To any casual observer, it appeared that a half-dozen or so patrols rode out throughout the day and returned later. What wasn't apparent was that they were composed of different men. The one place Duko's men remained was at two checkpoints south of Nordan's position in Sarth. So far there had been no mistakes.

Dash reached the appropriate place and stepped inside the burned-out shell of a tavern. As soon as he was inside the fire-blackened walls, a voice in the shadows said, "You come alone, Puppy?"

Dash's expression let Trina know what he thought of being called "Puppy." "I'm alone."

She jerked her head to one side, indicating a door to a rear room. He moved toward it, and it opened. John Turpin stood in front of the doorway and said, "Sword."

Dash removed his sword from its scabbard and handed it to him. "Through there," he said, indicating another door.

Dash moved to that door, and when it didn't open, he tripped the latch. Inside he found the Upright Man sitting at a table, a half-drunk flagon of water next to him.

"Nephew," he said with dry humor. His voice was as raspy as Dash remembered.

"Uncle," said Dash with the same dry humor.

"Have you news for me?"

Dash sighed. He sat in the second chair at the table without being asked. "As you can see, we were not in need of your help in taking the city. Duko gave it willingly."

"At no small price, I hear," said Lysle Riggers with a chuckle. "Duke of the Southern Marches."

"There's to be a general amnesty."

The old man studied his great-nephew and said, "I don't hear the 'but,' though it is there."

"It's to be applied only to those who fought against the Kingdom, as they swear loyalty to the crown. It will also be extended to any man who volunteers for service now."

"But not petty thieves such as the Mockers."

"Only if you join the army," said Dash. "I tried. My father has no need to be busying himself or his judges with accusations of crimes before the war." Dash shrugged. "Fact is, anyone likely to bring complaint is no longer living here. When merchants return, who is to say what was taken before the war and what was looted or lost during the sacking of the city?"

Lysle chuckled. "True. All true. However, there are those among our brethren who have the death mark on them already, and who are known to your father's constables."

Dash let out a long sigh. "I know, but if they'll serve the crown, they'll be pardoned for their crimes."

"I'm a little old to serve, don't you think?" asked the Upright Man.

Dash said, "I don't think there's anyone besides myself, Jimmy, and Father who has an inkling of who you might be. And while I'm sure there is a very long list of crimes for which you might be hung, why bother?" He looked at his great-uncle and said, "If Grandfather didn't want you taken, why should we?"

"Your grandfather needed me alive to control the Mockers," said Lysle. "It may be some time before the Mockers are effective enough to be in need of controlling again." He let out a long, tired sigh. "I most certainly will not be here to see it. And I do not know if the next Upright Man, or whatever he calls himself, will care to make deals with the crown." He pointed a finger at Dash. "You and your father are clever enough, but once I'm gone, you'll not be able to make demands of the Mockers the way your grandfather made of me."

Dash said, "I know. If you have nothing more, I have a great deal to do."

The Upright Man waved him away. "We're done, Dashel Jamison. From now on, we are Mockers and you are the Prince's man. If you come back into the Poor Quarter after dark, you are as much at risk as any other man."

"I understand," said Dash. He returned to the door, then paused and said, "But if there's something I can do without compromising my oath to the Kingdom, send me a message, will you?"

The old man laughed. "I'll consider it. Now go."

Dash moved into the second room and found John Turpin gone. His sword hung over the butt end of a burned-out timber. He retrieved it and moved through the next door. As he expected, Trina wasn't in the outer part of the building either. He left the devastation of the inn and moved away. He paused a moment and tried to remember the name of that particular inn, then it came to him. It had been called the Rainbow Parrot, and it had once been owned by a friend of his grandfather's, a man named Lucas. Caught up for a moment in reflection on old stories of his grandfather, Dash almost didn't hear the footsteps behind him.

He spun and had his sword out before the man came within a half-dozen paces. The man coming at him was dressed like a rag picker and was thin and dirty. He came to a halt and, putting up his hands, backed away, then turned and ran.

Dash put up his sword and considered that it would be

a long time before Krondor was what it once had been. Then as he left to return to the palace, he considered the Poor Quarter was probably safer now than it had been before the war.

Dash reached the palace and was again astonished by the amount of work going on; there must have been a hundred masons at work, most of whom had been soldiers serving in Duko's army before the war. But they were making progress in getting the palace repaired. Other workers washed soot from walls, hauling away rubbish and debris, even hanging screens and other decorative touches in some of the larger rooms on the main floor. Entering the hallway, he saw Jimmy hurrying toward him. "There you are!" said Jimmy.

"What is it?"

"We've got troubles," said Jimmy, turning to walk beside Dash toward the Prince's private office suite, now being used by Duko.

"Has Fadawah discovered what we're up to?"

"Worse," said Jimmy.

"What?"

"Land's End was overrun by a Keshian company."

"Oh, gods."

"Yes," said Jimmy as they turned the corner and climbed stairs up toward Duko's offices. "And there are other reports coming in. It looks like Kesh has decided to punctuate her demands for concessions with a little show of force."

"Just what we need," said Dash.

Jimmy moved toward the door to Duko's office, knocked once, and opened the door without waiting to be bid enter. A clerk holding a large sheaf of papers, warned by the knock, jumped nimbly out of the way as the door opened.

The two brothers entered and found a half-dozen clerks and scribes writing orders and dispatchs. They made their way through the press of court officers and entered Duko's inner office. Dash was once again struck by the difference between his office when it was occupied by the Prince and his father, and as it was now, with Duko sitting behind the desk. Before it was the administrative center of the Western

Realm, now it was the headquarters of a military organization.

Dash and Jimmy now recognized most of Duko's remaining Captains, and all the Kingdom officers who now served. Wendell, a cavalry captain formerly of the garrison at Hawk's Hollow, now officially the Knight-Captain of the Royal Krondorian Horse, looked at a map and said, "I can have four hundred more men down there by the day after tomorrow, Your Grace."

Some of Duko's Captains glanced at one another; they were still having some problem with the protocols of the Kingdom and found the new title oddly unnerving.

Duko looked at Jimmy and Dash. "You two. You're familiar with this area, aren't you?"

Jimmy said, "We've spent the last few years here, Your Grace."

It suddenly struck Dash that the majority of the Krondorian garrison perished in the destruction of the city; the remaining fragments of the garrison were now serving to the east with Owen Greylock. Owen wasn't due in the city for another five days, just before the time selected to launch the offensive northward.

Duko pointed at the map. "We've got two or three hundred soldiers assaulting our position in Land's End. By this morning's dispatch, they're holding there, but hard-pressed. They may already have fallen. The five hundred foot soldiers I sent earlier this week won't get there for another five days, even if I send a galloper to order a forced march. We also have reports of some ships sailing along the coast toward Land's End, possibly in support of the assault."

Jimmy said, "That makes sense. If they bring up a large force across the Jal-Pur, they have logistics problems. But if they shock us with a smaller force, holding our men inside the citadel, while they land more troops by sea, they can quickly surround and siege."

"Who's in charge down in Port Vykor?" asked Duko.

"Admiral Reeves," supplied one of the Kingdom officers.

"Send him orders to intercept those ships and drive them off. I don't care if he sinks or captures them, just keep them from landing those men." The officer saluted and hurried to the outer office. Duko looked at Wendell. "Take your four hundred horse and leave at once. As soon as you overtake those foot soldiers, tell them to run." Captain Wendell saluted. Duko turned to one of his old captains and said, "Runcor, I want you to take a hundred or so of your best mother-killers and follow the coastline down to Land's End. If you see anyone coming ashore, kill them."

The old Captain said, "Yes, Duko . . . er, Your Grace."

Duko smiled and said, "Get out of here."

Duko looked at Jimmy and Dash. "Until your Lord Greylock gets here, I'm assuming command. I'll need your help, young sirs, as I am not all that familiar with this outlying area."

He pointed to a spot on the map. "But I'm guessing that if this Empire to the south is serious, here is where we will see their next push." His finger was on a small hill pass halfway between Shamata and Land's End. "It's a long run, but it's relatively flat land. If they only seek to put pressure on the negotiations in Darkmoor, then they'll withdraw at the first show of strength. If they are seeking to get into a serious fight, they'll launch a second assault through here about the time they land their ships at Land's End." Looking at another of his old captains, he said, "Jallom, get scouts down to that pass as fast as possible. I don't even know if we have any soldiers there."

"We don't," said the Captain named Jallom. "We assumed the Kingdom would take care of their southern flank and we wouldn't have to worry."

"Well, we're now the Kingdom, and we need to worry. And send word to Greylock about what is going on and ask him if he might consider sending troops that way if they can get there first."

Men hurried to carry out orders, and Duko said, "Gentlemen, we have a war on our hands. It's just not the one we wanted, and we don't know how big it is. It may be a little one, but if I were the Keshian General and I found out just how chaotic things were here, I might try to get into Krondor before Greylock, and then dare him to come dig me out with Nordan on his northern flank." Duko shook his head. "Let's hope that kicking them out of Land's End will teach them the error of their ways."

Jimmy looked at Dash and they both shared the same thought: What else could go wrong?

Twelve

Gamble

Arutha pointed.

Captain Subai motioned and the man behind him signaled. Another man pointed and nodded. He then started searching in the indicated area. The progress over the mountains had been slow, as the men on foot could cover only between ten and fifteen miles a day. But they were now in sight of the base of the mountain atop which perched the former Abbey of Sarth.

Three scouts were moving along the difficult trail, moving up tiny gullies worn by rainwater, small game tracks, anything that might lead to the entrance. They were looking for a large extrusion of rock that overlapped the face of the mountain, yet behind which was a long narrow passage, leading to the entrance to the tunnel under the abbey. Arutha remembered his father telling him that unless you were looking right at the entrance, end-on to the extrusion, you would only see what looked like mountainside.

They had been searching for days and had twice almost come into contact with Nordan's patrols. Only the fact that Arutha and Dominic were accompanied by the best woodsmen and trail scouts in the Kingdom kept them undetected. There were only six of them in this party. The one hundred and twenty Pathfinders and Crimson Eagles who were given the responsibility for taking the abbey waited miles away, in a tiny valley, just beyond the range of invader patrols.

Arutha took a drink of water from the skin he carried. The summer heat was oppressive, yet they could not tarry. His father had mentioned several other landmarks, but nothing in the area remotely looked like those features. The large oak may have burned in a fire, or been harvested for lumber. The three rocks piled one atop the other may have fallen, due to rain or an earthquake. After all, it had been over fifty years ago. Then a whistle alerted Arutha that someone had found something. He hurried to where Subai stood and saw a man below the Captain. He had jumped down into a depression where all but his head was hidden by brush; he would be invisible from the trail. Arutha glanced around and his eyes caught sight of a large oak tree, masked by other, younger trees, but directly opposite his position. He turned and saw a large boulder, the size of a wagon, and at the base were two others—instantly he knew. "We've found it!" he said quietly to Subai.

Arutha motioned to where Dominic stood and jumped down to stand behind the soldier. "There's something on the other side of this brush, Your Grace," said the soldier.

Without saying anything, Arutha took out his sword and started hacking away the brush. The soldier hesitated a moment, then pulled out his own. By the time Dominic arrived, they had cleared away a significant portion of the undergrowth. Behind the cleared brush was a passage. Arutha knew it was the place his father had described, because from end-on, it did indeed look like a hallway, between the face of the cliff and a wall of rock. To Captain Subai, he said, "Wait here until Dominic and I find the entrance."

The cleric and the Duke entered the narrow passage, which ran a full hundred yards along the face of the mountain. At the end, to their left, a cave large enough for one man to enter could be seen. Arutha said, "If this was discovered, it is as easy to defend as the access above."

Dominic looked into the darkness. "It is natural, but it has been 'improved' by the Brothers of Ishap. Notice, it's wide enough that a monk carrying books or pulling a handcart can negotiate the turn, but there's not enough room to turn a ram to break down the door.''

''What door?''

Dominic closed his eyes, chanted almost silently, then held up his hand. A nimbus of pale yellow light grew from his hand, casting enough illumination that Arutha could see a large oak door ten feet inside the entrance of the cave. It was without latch or lock. Across it three large iron bands showed it was heavily reinforced. Arutha said, ''You're right. You'd need a heavy ram to knock that down, and there's no room here to swing it.''

Dominic said, ''The latch—''

Arutha said, ''Indulge me a moment.''

He inspected the area, running his hand above a ledge, and then below another, and over the surface of the door. Finally he said, ''My father told me stories of his days as a thief. Often I imagined myself in his shoes, doing just this sort of thing, attempting to enter somewhere I was not welcome. I wondered if I would be equal to the task.'' He knelt and inspected the ground before the door. Off to one side, a small rock lay nestled against the overhanging stone wall. Arutha reached for the rock.

''I wouldn't do that,'' said Dominic.

Arutha's hand hesitated. He then said, ''I must concede I lack my father's gifts.'' Smiling, he stood and said, ''My grandfather tells me I have more of my mother in me than my father. Perhaps he's correct.''

''That's a trap, almost concealed. Over there is the true release.'' He moved to a small recess and put his hand inside. Feeling around he grasped a small latch, then moved it. ''Now pull that rock.''

Arutha did as he was bid and discovered the rock was attached to a steel cable, by a large bolt at the back. The rock traveled only a few inches, but as soon as he pulled it a deep rumble could be heard from the other side of the door. The door moved, ponderously, but it moved. Slowly it retracted to the left, leaving a narrow dark passage leading upward into the mountain.

Arutha turned and said to Captain Subai, ''It's open. Send a messenger and bring up the men!''

He followed Dominic into the passage. The cleric

pointed to a lever. "Don't touch that. It will close the door behind us." He continued walking up the passage. After nearly a hundred yards, the passage widened into a large gallery, where footprints and signs of recent passage could clearly be seen. Arutha inspected them and said, "These aren't boot marks. These look like sandals."

Dominic said, "We kept books, scrolls, and other tomes stored throughout the mountain, even this close to the escape route." He pointed upward. "But nothing was taken out that way. My brothers quit the abbey in good order, so whatever was kept here was hauled up the mountain, put aboard wagons, and taken to our new abbey, That Which Was Sarth."

"Where is the new abbey?" asked Arutha.

Dominic smiled. "For reasons that you may understand more than most, my order has decided that the information contained within that particular abbey is too dangerous in the wrong hands. Therefore, only those within our order know the exact location of That Which Was Sarth. All I may tell you is that while it is in Yabon, it is safe from Fadawah."

Arutha said, "As an officer of the Royal Court, I am not pleased to hear of this. As the grandson of Pug, I understand."

Boots upon the stone heralded the approach of the first band of Subai's raiders. The man in the van carried a torch and behind him came others holding bundles of supplies.

The timetable was critical. Greylock would begin his approach to Krondor in a week's time, but just before the city gates, he would wheel to the north and launch a flying attack up the road to Sarth, striking the first two defensive positions without stopping. They were relatively light positions, from Duko's information, and would provide scant resistance. It was at the southern border of Sarth they would meet the first major resistance.

From there the fight into the town would be difficult, but if Nordan's forces up in the abbey were to sally forth, Greylock's army would suddenly be caught between a stout defensive position and an army charging down a mountainside. If Greylock turned up the mountain road to attempt to seize the abbey, he would be fighting up a road that at several places narrowed so that only a single wagon or two men on horse could pass, with the town garrison at his back.

The Kingdom's only hope was for Subai's force inside the mountain to seize the abbey, or at least tie up the forces within long enough for Owen to take the town. Once the town was in Kingdom hands, the abbey could be isolated and its garrison starved out, or it would have already fallen to Arutha's forces.

Arutha considered this as the men started to filter into the chamber. It was possible they would be facing odds as high as four to one. No one knew how many men were billeted within. Nordan had not seen fit to share that information with Duko. Their only advantage was surprise.

The night before Greylock's assault from the south, the Kingdom forces below the abbey would launch their attack. Arutha knew he had the Kingdom's best men for the job, handpicked by Subai. The Pathfinders were trained for resourcefulness. To a man they were tough, resilient, and efficient. The Crimson Eagles were veterans of a series of brutal campaigns, men who would do exactly as needed and without hesitation.

At an hour past dawn in three days' time, they must either be in control of the abbey, or creating enough trouble the garrison would be unable to respond to any call for help from the town below. Arutha found a spot near the next tunnel leading up and sat down, conserving his energy until it was time to move. The balance of Subai's forces would be hours in reaching the cave, so there was nothing to do but rest, and wait.

Erik grunted and made some notes. John Vinci said loudly, "I'll need a larger storage room back here, and probably want to widen the gates so I can get bigger wagons in and out!"

Softly, Erik said, "Keep it down, John. We've been doing this for three days and no one has questioned us so far. Unless they're starting to think you're getting hard of hearing."

With a pained grin, Vinci said, "Just trying to be convincing."

"We're done," said Erik. "Let's get back to your shop."

They walked through the surprisingly bustling streets of Sarth. The town was always a fairly busy one, with many fishing villages bringing their catch to market. It was also an important secondary port between Ylith and Krondor, one which many traders and not a few smugglers from the Free Cities or Queg visited. Kingdom customs had been more lax there, and as a result the city had quite a large population of people who were enterprising, irrespective of who was governing, Kingdom or some recent invader.

Armed men were everywhere, yet the mood was relaxed. The mercenaries from Novindus who were billeted in Sarth obviously felt they were far enough behind the lines to not be taken unawares.

Erik and John hurried back to John's business, and moved through the front, then into the rear storage room, where a very bored Roo sat in a corner, half dozing. Without preamble, he said, "Are we leaving?"

Erik nodded. "Tonight."

John said, "I'll have a boat down at the smugglers' cove. You'll carry cargo, and the two men who we left down there will be happy to get back home."

Erik said, "Roo, look at this."

Roo stood and came to where Erik opened up his sketches. He moved them around until they formed a map of the region around the town of Sarth. "You'll need to memorize this, so if you get back and I don't, you can redraw it."

"What are you talking about?" asked Roo.

"I can't risk carrying these." He looked at Roo and John. "If we get stopped, and we're carrying these maps, we're going to be dead before anyone blinks. If we don't have them, we might be able to bluff our way out." He looked at John. "If you hear we are caught, John, you're going to have to try tomorrow night to get down to Krondor."

"Me?" said Vinci.

Roo said, "That's all right, John. It's not going to happen."

"But if it does," said Erik, "you're going to have to carry word to Duke Duko and Owen Greylock." He pointed to the assembled pieces of paper. "Look at this, and remember everything.

"Natural terrain is the enemy," said Erik. His finger showed a point where the checkpoint had been erected. "This is a bottleneck, this gap where the road runs atop the cliffs above the ocean and hard against the steep hill-side."

Sarth was built north of that gap, where the road swung suddenly westward and through the town. The southern edge of the town was hard against a cliff face, dropping down into a rocky beach where, even at low tide, there was no decent footing. The coast turned northwest after a while, and there Sarth's harbor could be found, with a long sandy beach and several fishing villages to the north.

"Even if we landed support troops at the smuggler's cove, we are still south of that gap," said Erik.

His finger indicated the harbor. "They've only got one ship in the harbor, but look where it is."

Roo said, "So if anyone sees a Kingdom fleet rounding the point south of town, they can move the ship to the mouth of the harbor and sink it."

Erik said, "I'm no sailor, but I don't think any ship we have can come from the south and make it through the harbor before they can move that ship and scuttle her."

Roo said, "Unless we take her first."

"We?" asked Erik.

"Figure of speech," said Roo with a grin.

Erik shook his head. "We can't get a message down to Krondor and return with a squad to take that ship. Owen will reach Krondor in three days' time. We need to be down there in two, so we can give him the latest intelligence."

Roo said, "If you stay and use that band of thugs John hired, you could take that ship."

Erik said, "No. Orders. I've got to be back day after tomorrow."

Roo looked at Vinci. "John?"

John held up his hands. "Not me!" He patted his ample gut and said, "I'm an old fat man, Roo, and I never was a fighter on my best day."

Then Erik looked at Roo and said, "Would you care to volunteer for one last mission for King and Country?"

Roo frowned. "To what good?"

"You might save the lives of a lot of good men, shorten the war, and regain your lost wealth that much faster." Erik pointed to the northeast end of town. "If we can chase Nordan's soldiers up the coast *and* get ships up from Port Vykor into that harbor, we can resupply and move north that much faster."

Roo said, "How many men do they keep on that ship, John?"

"A light crew, from what we can see. It's been sitting there since winter. Every once in a while someone rows back and forth between the ship and the town, and we think they've loaded some ballast on it, but we've never seen any significant cargo; just a box of provisions now and again. So maybe it is a blockade ship."

Roo scratched his head. "I'm an idiot for this, but I'll take that ship for you, Erik. When is Greylock supposed to get here?"

"If he turns northward at sundown in three days, he'll be here by dawn of the fourth."

"Three more days in that shed?"

"We've slept in worse," said Erik.

Roo nodded. "Don't remind me." He sighed. "Four days from now, just before dawn, I'll row out and take that ship."

Erik said, "Good. Now, John, you've got to memorize this map, because you're coming with me."

"Me?" said Vinci.

Erik smiled, and it was a smile filled with menace. "Your choice: come with me, or take the ship."

Vinci swallowed hard. "I'll visit Krondor."

"Wise choice," said Erik.

Roo said to John, "I need at least a dozen reliable men, twenty would be better."

John shrugged. "I can get a dozen. Twenty? I'll see."

"I'll need two large skiffs hidden nearby until it's time to leave."

"I have a warehouse near there. I'll have the boats taken there tonight."

Roo said, "Well, then, I guess it's decided. At least it will be over in five more days."

"With luck," said Erik.

His finger stabbed at the road leading from the town to the abbey. "If Arutha and his company can neutralize Nordan's forces up there. From the lack of troops down here I must assume he's got at least three or four hundred soldiers up there. If they come down that road and hit Owen from behind as he's trying to get into the city, they could throw us back south of the gap, and that would cost us dearly."

Roo sighed. "We can only hope. That's all we ever could do, even when we were running for our lives across Novindus: do our best and hope."

Erik was forced to agree. "A prayer might be in order, too."

Roo fell silent.

Arutha listened at the door. On the other side he heard voices. For the last day they had scouted out the lower basements of the abandoned library at Sarth. Dominic had estimated that as many as a thousand men could be housed at the abbey if they filled every empty chamber, even though the dormitory in the abbey itself was built for only forty monks.

They had calculated that stabling of horses dictated that the majority of soldiers in the abbey be foot soldiers, as no more than forty or fifty horses could be crowded into the courtyard of the abbey. The problem of providing fodder for the horses, and wagons full of hay or grain every week, probably kept the number down to a couple of dozen animals.

They had reached the second level of halls below the abbey proper before encountering any soldiers. Through the door at which Arutha listened they heard voices in casual conversation. Arutha moved back to where Dominic waited, and whispered, "Is there any way around this room?"

Dominic shook his head and quietly replied, "If we go back down two levels and return up the other side, we'll still come into that room, but through a different door. There are three doors, the third being to a stairway to the level above."

Arutha nodded. He had memorized the drawing Dominic

had made. "We'll wait here, then storm the room when it's time to take the abbey."

He glanced at one of Subai's soldiers, who carried a timing glass, filled with sand. At sundown the day before, he had turned it, starting the time-keeping. Within the dark confines of the basement under the abbey, there was no natural way to mark the passing of time. And timing was critical.

"I wish I could get a look and see how many soldiers were there."

Dominic said, "We could chance one late at night, when they're all asleep."

Arutha turned to a soldier and said, "Tell Captain Subai I want him to send half the men back down two levels, and up the other side, to the second door into this chamber ahead." The soldier saluted and hurried off to carry out his orders. To Dominic, Arutha said, "It occurs to me we've encountered no barriers to the lower chambers, but this door or the other may be blocked. I'd not want this raid to fail because someone moved a bunk in front of this door. Whoever gets in first can insure the other door is quickly opened."

Dominic nodded. He glanced over at the soldier holding the sand clock. "Another day and a half."

Roo waited impatiently. The last two days had dragged, moment by moment, second by second, until he thought he would lose his mind. Then suddenly it was time to leave.

He looked at the men John had rounded up. There were sixteen of them. All looked disreputable, but none looked particularly fearsome. Still, he had seen enough harmless-looking men who turned out to be killers in his days to judge too much on appearances. He said, "Do any of you know how to work aboard ship?"

Five of them held up their hands. Roo shook his head. Pointing to the first one, he said, "You, if you hear me shout, cut loose the anchor." To the second, he said, "If you hear me shout, raise whatever sail you can reach." To the last he said, "And you, head for the tiller and steer us for open water." Glancing at the other men, he said, "The rest of you, do whatever those three tell you. If we take that ship, I want to be able to get underway if anyone on shore tries to help.'' To himself he silently added, and get the hell away from Sarth if the attack fails.

''Ready?'' he asked, and the men nodded. ''Once we start moving, don't stop for anything unless I tell you or we're attacked.'' He opened the door to Vinci's store, and said, ''Let's go.''

The men followed Roo into the predawn gloom, down the street where Vinci's store sat, then around a corner that put them on the main street through the town, part of the King's Highway. They followed it, moving quickly without running, and when the road turned north again, they followed a smaller street that led down to the southern end of the docks. To Roo's mind, Sarth looked like nothing so much as a right hand slapped down on an otherwise northwest-running shoreline. The thumb was where the road turned west for a while, and the bulk of the town rested between, until the road turned north up the index finger. The docks started at the crook of the thumb and followed the highway for a distance, with several blocks of houses between the highway and the bay.

As they reached the docks, Roo found Vinci had instructed other men to leave the warehouse unbolted. It was the last one on the lower dock, the westernmost part of the thumb in Roo's imagination, and inside were two boats. Each boat was lifted by six men and quickly moved down a boat ramp, set in the water, and pushed off with eight men climbing into the first, and Roo and the other eight climbing into the second. They almost held their breath trying to be silent, but everything around them remained quiet.

Two men in each boat put oars into the water and rowed lightly, moving across the water to the ship, a dark silhouette against the grey of sky and water. As they neared, Roo felt a cold chill in his stomach. Softly he said, ''Damn.''

''What?'' asked a man nearby.

''It's a Quegan trader.''

''So?'' asked a second man.

''Nothing,'' said Roo. ''I'm in enough trouble with Queg that a little more won't make me any more dead if they catch me.''

A low cackle from a third man answered the remark, then the man said, "No, but it might make your dying a little nastier."

"Thanks," said Roo. "That makes me feel so much better."

The first boat reached the stern of the ship, a two-masted trading vessel. A man in the bow of the first boat leaped to a rear anchor line and nimbly climbed to the gunwale. He peeked over, turned, and nodded down to those in the boats below.

Silently, men started climbing aboard.

Up on deck, the sailor assigned the night watch sat against the rail sleeping. Roo motioned, and one of the men struck the sleeping sentry hard on the head with the hilt of a sword. The man slumped over, unconscious.

Roo motioned for the men to move fore and aft, and down into the ship they went. Things were quiet, then suddenly a shout from the bow of the ship sounded, answered quickly by the sound of blows. Other voices were raised, then it was quiet again. A minute later a group of downcast-looking sailors emerged from the fore hatch, followed a moment later by men coming up the aft. There were only twenty-two men aboard, including the Captain and mate. All had been asleep and had been easily roused from their berths to find themselves facing armed men.

Roo breathed a sigh of relief. The ship was his.

Roo looked at one of the men, who didn't look like a sailor. "Where did you find him?" he asked one of the smugglers.

The smuggler said, "In a little cabin next to the Captain's."

Roo came to stand before the man and said, "There's something familiar about you. Who are you?"

The man remained silent. Roo said, "Light a lantern."

One of the smugglers did so and brought it over. Roo held it close. "I know you! You're one of Vasarius's men. Your name is Velari."

The man politely said, "Mr. Avery."

Roo laughed. "Don't tell me this is one of Lord Vasarius's ships?"

"It is," said the high-placed servant. He had been the

first Quegan to meet Roo on his first visit to that island.

"Isn't that something," said Roo. "Well, I'm sure Vasarius is holding me personally responsible for every injury done him since I last saw him, so this additional offense won't surprise him."

Velari said, "He'll eventually find out, Avery."

"You can tell him," said Roo.

"Me? Aren't you going to kill us?"

"No reason to," said Roo. "In fact, we're doing you a favor. Sometime in the next few hours a full-scale war is about to erupt around here, and by that time I plan on being safely out of this harbor and on my way south."

"War?" said Valari.

"Yes, the very one you were told was the signal for you to sink this ship in the harbor."

"Sink this ship?" said Valari. "Why would we do that?"

"To keep Kingdom ships out of the harbor," answered Roo.

"We have no such orders," said Vinci.

"Then what are you waiting here for?"

The question was answered by silence.

Roo looked as if he was turning away, then he rounded hard and slammed his fist into Valari's stomach. The man collapsed to the deck, unable to breathe for a moment, then he crawled to his knees and vomited on the deck. Roo knelt and grabbed him by the hair, pulling his face up and saying, "Now, what are you waiting for?"

Again the man looked at Roo but said nothing. Roo pulled his dagger and held it before Valari's eyes. "Would you speak better if parts of you were missing?"

"We're waiting for another ship."

"What ship?"

The man was silent until Roo put the point of the dagger in the meat of Valari's shoulder and started to push, slowly increasing the pressure so that it became painful quickly, without doing serious damage.

Valari winced, then his eyes watered, then he cried out. "Stop it!" he begged.

"What ship?" asked Roo, letting the point dig deeper. He knew it was a light wound, but he also sensed that

Valari wasn't a man who knew that and was not used to enduring pain.

Valari sobbed, "My Lord Vasarius comes to Sarth."

"Vasarius! Here?" said Roo, wiping his blade and putting it away. "Why?"

"To escort us back to Queg."

Roo stood up, eyes wide. Turning to the leader of the smugglers, he said, "Get ready to raise sail. If I shout to get underway, I want to be moving by the time I'm back up on deck."

Roo hurried to a hatchway and half-jumped down the companionway to the lower deck. He ducked through a low door into the main cargo hold and saw crates and sacks lashed down along both sides of the hold. He grabbed a large sack and tried to lift it. It was too heavy to move. He used his knife to cut loose a small cord tied around the top of the sack, and gold spilled out onto the deck.

As loud as he could, Roo shouted, "Get underway."

Men shouted up on the deck, and the sound of a fist striking a jaw informed Roo the smugglers were insuring the captive sailors were obeying orders. He heard an ax fall and knew they had cut away the anchor and chain.

Roo found a pry bar and opened a crate. Inside, in the gloom, he had no trouble recognizing riches. Gems, coins, jewelry, a bolt of expensive silk, all had been haphazardly dumped into the chest and it had been nailed shut.

Roo knew what he had stumbled across; it was the booty of Krondor and Sarth, boxed and stored aboard this ship to send to Queg. As he made his way back up to the deck, Roo began to wonder. Why would General Fadawah be sending riches to Lord Vasarius?

He saw sails falling from the yards and his appointed man on the tiller as the ship slowly began to move forward, toward the mouth of the harbor. Roo moved to stand before Valari and said, "What is Fadawah buying from Queg?"

If Valari had any inclination to refuse to answer, it fled when Roo produced the dagger and showed it to him. "Weapons! He buys weapons."

"What weapons?"

"Swords, shields, pikes, and bows. Arrows, crossbows, and bolts. Catapults and ballistae. And fire oil."

"And it's being shipped here?"

"No, it is already delivered, to Ylith. But the gold was here and Fadawah arranged for it to be secretly stored on this ship."

"Why wasn't it guarded better?" asked one of the smugglers nearby. "I mean, if we had known, we'd have taken this ship ourselves, days ago!"

"Because guards would have called attention," said Roo. "They circulated a rumor it was a blockade ship, to be sunk in the harbor mouth." He grinned. "Lads, you're going farther than we thought. We're not going down the coast to the cove and then ashore to meet the army. We're heading down to Krondor itself."

"Why?" asked one of the smugglers.

"Because I'm claiming this gold for the crown, and the crown owes me gold beyond imagining, so I'm taking this cargo in partial payment of my debt, and because all of you will be paid a month's wages for each day we're at sea."

One of the men got a calculating look and said, "Why shouldn't we just split it up? We don't work for you, Avery."

Suddenly Roo's sword was out of its scabbard before the man could react. The point touched the man in the throat and Roo said, "Because I'm the only real soldier on this ship, and you copper-grubbing thugs are getting a chance for some real gold. Why die so a few of you can share this, when you can live and get enough to keep you drunk for the rest of your life?"

"Just asking," said the man, backing away.

"Besides," said Roo, "Vinci knows each of you, and if I don't make it alive back to Krondor and you show up anywhere in the West with gold, he'll know to send assassins after you."

That was a bluff, but Roo didn't think any of these smugglers were smart enough to suspect it was. He turned and shouted, "Get as much sail on as you can once we're out of the harbor! And find a Kingdom banner if there's one in the Captain's cabin and hoist it aloft! I don't want to get sunk by one of Reeve's attack ships before we can explain we're on their side."

As they exited the harbor, the lookout shouted, "Galley off the starboard bow!"

Roo raced to the fore of the ship and looked where the lookout indicated. Sure enough, heaving out of the morning mist came a Quegan war galley. Roo didn't hesitate, but dashed back to where the Captain of the ship still stood under guard. "How tight to the southern headland can you turn this ship without killing us all?"

The Captain said, "At this speed, not very."

"So we either slow down and get overtaken, or we turn south and shoal out."

"Yes," said the Captain with a smile.

Roo looked toward the canvas and saw the luff of the sail. He was not a true sailor, but he had served aboard ship on two long voyages down to Novindus. To those sailors aloft, he said, "I'll give every man here a thousand pieces of gold if we get away from that galley!"

Quegan sailors were often pressed into service, and none were known particularly for deep loyalty to their Emperor. Suddenly the activity above increased to a frenzied pace as Roo shouted orders. The Captain realized he was in the presence of a man who knew his way around a ship and said, "We can heel hard to port in a few moments and if we hold tight into the wind, make it clear of rocks, Mr. Avery."

Roo looked at the Captain and said, "Switching sides?"

"For twelve years I've sailed for my Lord Vasarius, and if I've made a thousand gold pieces in that time, it was barely."

"Good," said Roo. "For the Captain, two thousand. Now get us out of here."

The Captain shouted orders, and turned to take the tiller away from the man Roo had assigned to the job. Valari said, "What about me?"

Roo said, "Can you swim?"

"Yes, but—"

Roo nodded to the powerful-looking smuggler who had just released the tiller, and the man grabbed Valari by the collar and the seat of the pants, and with two steps pitched him over the side of the ship. As the man came to the surface, Roo called down, "Perhaps your employer will stop and pick you up!"

The galley bore down on them, and Roo stood on the quarterdeck, watching as it came straight at them, then to the side, and then to the stern, as the Captain turned southward. The men on the bow of the galley could be clearly seen, astonished expressions on their faces as the ship they were sent to escort seemed to be turning in the wrong direction.

A few moments later, the galley turned to pursue. "Can we lose her?" asked Roo.

The Captain said, "If we run out of wind before they run out of slaves, no. If they run out of slaves first, yes."

Roo said, "I hate to do it to the slaves, but let's pray for wind."

The Captain nodded.

"What's your name?"

"Nardini," said the Captain.

"Well, Captain Nardini, I used to have a fleet, and I expect to have one again. If we live through this, not only will you get your gold, I'll give you a job."

"That would be nice," said the Captain, a balding man of middle years. "I've never been farther into Krondor than the docks. I was last there about three years ago."

"It's changed since you were there," said Roo.

"So I hear," replied the Captain.

Roo looked rearward and saw the galley was holding steady about two hundred yards off their stern. They had come around the thumb, as Roo thought of it, and the coast fell away to the east, leaving them in relatively open water.

Roo knew that a support fleet was due to hit Sarth at noon, and hoped they reached it before Vasarius's war galley reached them.

Arutha whispered, "Try the latch."

The soldier nearest him quietly moved the latch up and the door opened. There was a faint squeak, but no one inside the room seemed to notice. He followed the first man into the room and glanced around in the dim light. A single candle burned on a table halfway across the long wall, opposite the stairway leading upward to the next level. The floor was littered with a dozen empty sleeping pallets, while another six were occupied. With a hand signal, Captain Subai indicated they were to be subdued and they were. Solders entered from the second door and Arutha smiled as he whispered, "Well, it seems I owe those soldiers an apology; that was a lot of stair climbing for no good reason."

Subai said, "They understand."

Arutha turned to locate Brother Dominic. The cleric wore a helm and breastplate, but carried no sword. He only sported a dull cudgel. He had said that his order would not permit him to spill blood. Breaking heads, Arutha had observed dryly, was permitted, however.

"What now?"

Dominic said, "There is something . . ."

"What?"

"I don't know. A presence . . ."

Arutha said, "A presence?"

"It's something I've felt before, but fainter, more distant."

"What?" urged Arutha.

"I don't know," whispered the cleric. "But whatever it is, it is not good. I should lead the soldiers up the stairs. If it is magical or mystic, I may be able to protect us."

Arutha nodded, frowning. Since the death of the Pantathian Serpent Priests and Pug's destruction of the demon Jakan, there had been no reports of any magical activity among the enemy. The possibility that some agency of darkness had hidden among them and was now about to manifest itself bothered him. But there was no turning back.

Dominic mounted the stairs and Arutha, Subai, and the soldiers followed. They entered a long hallway with doorways on either side, each leading into a large storage room, used to house books just a year earlier. Each doorway was open, and through the portals they could see more sleeping men. Arutha did a quick estimation and judged a hundred men between the two rooms. He signaled, and Subai placed archers at each end of the hall.

He then set about waking the invaders, quietly and one at a time, so that each man awoke to the sight of a naked blade before his face and archers behind drawing a bead. In less than a half hour, all one hundred mercenaries were herded down to the lowest chamber, to join the first six men captured.

"This can't last," said Subai quietly.

As if his words were prophetic, at the top of the next flight of stairs they were spied by two men walking down the corridor. As soon as they saw the black uniforms, the mercenaries knew there were Kingdom soldiers in the building. They raised alarm, and Arutha shouted, "Every man to his position!"

Each man knew his assignment. There were a dozen key positions throughout the abbey, and if the Kingdom forces could secure them, the invaders would be isolated from the town below. While Arutha and his men might be forced to eventually withdraw back down the stairs into the lower chambers of the abbey, they could keep the garrison up here from mounting a counterattack down the mountain to relieve the garrison at Sarth.

Sleepy mercenaries came stumbling through doors on both sides of the hall, and Arutha found himself fighting for his life. He had never fought in combat before, and until this moment had harbored a deep fear he would not be up to the task. He anticipated shame that he could not serve his King the way his father and sons already had. Yet now, without hesitation, he was coolly engaging a man intent on killing him. He had no time to think about his previous doubts, and without conscious effort, years of practice and drill took over and he began laying about him, using the sword once carried by his namesake, Prince Arutha.

Slowly they moved along the corridor, driving the forces of General Nordan before them. At the end of the corridor, another flight of stairs led upward. By the time Arutha reached them, the hall was littered with bodies, most of them invaders, and a trio of men stood at the bottom of the stairs. Fighting up the stairs would be difficult, as the advantage of height would make this a difficult contest.

From behind a voice shouted, "Down!"

Without hesitation, Arutha fell to the floor, ignoring the pool of blood in which he lay. A flight of arrows sped by overhead, and the three men upon the first step of the stairway fell. Before Arutha could rise to his feet, men were racing past him, their boots pounding on the stones of the steps as they hurried up to engage the enemy on the next level.

Arutha knew he was one flight below ground level. Above them stood the abbey, the stable, the outbuilding, and the walls. If they could get to the tower above the abbey, and command positions atop the walls, they could win the day.

Arutha took a deep breath and charged after the soldiers in front of him.

Thirteen

Calamity

ERIK CHARGED.

His company was second through the barricade, following hard on the heels of a unit of the Royal Krondorian Lancers led by Owen Greylock. The heavy cavalry rolled through the defenders effortlessly, driving a wedge through the invaders' line. Erik's unit was on Owen's right, following a hundred yards behind, and struck a deeply dug-in series of trenches supported by bow-fire from a clump of trees a dozen yards behind the last trench.

Erik had chosen this particular spot for himself and his men, for it was the sort of emplacement that was better attacked by mounted infantry rather than cavalry. As his men reached a point just beyond the enemy's bow-fire, Erik ordered a halt. The men reined in and dismounted, one man in five taking the horses to the rear. The rest formed up on Erik's command and ran the last hundred yards to attack the enemy lines.

Erik knew the key to taking this side of the line was to strike hard and fast at the upper portion that abutted the hillside. It was a series of shallow trenches and offered little protection for the defenders. Once they were in those trenches it would be easy to get behind the rest of the enemy line, root out the bowmen in the trees, and surround the men in the other trench locations.

As he had anticipated, it took his men less than an hour to completely subdue the defenders on the right flank. Seeing things were in hand, Erik returned to get his mount and ordered the rest of his men forward while a handful remained behind to escort prisoners back to the stockades being erected for holding captives.

Everywhere the first phase of battle was moving along without a hitch. Erik had expected stronger resistance on the left flank, the section of the defensive line between the road and the sea cliffs, but the rapidly advancing Kingdom forces had totally demoralized the advance position of Fadawah's army.

Realizing that things were in hand, Erik sent word back to bring up the second elements of Greylock's army, the heavy infantry that had been hiding in Krondor for the last week. They were a half-day down the coast and would be needed tomorrow morning if they had to dig out defenders at the gap or the southern boundary of Sarth.

As he motioned for his mounted infantry to form up to advance, Erik gave thanks that Sarth wasn't a walled town like some of the others in the Kingdom. He impatiently waited for his command to re-form, as the standing order was to move as fast into Sarth as possible. When they were mounted, he gave the order and they advanced.

Units of archers were hurrying along on either flank, their orders to flush out snipers in the woods. They were supported by squads of swordsmen.

Heavy pikemen, who would be critical to break any counterattacks, were hurrying along the road, and Erik had to order them to halt, so that his horsemen wouldn't be stuck behind the slower-moving footmen. When everyone was assembled, Erik signaled the advance, and the men moved out. The pikemen fell in behind the horses, and the march was resumed.

The hillsides echoed with the sounds of shouts and screams, the hum of arrows through the air and the sound of steel clashing. But it was obviously a mopping-up action here, and the heavy fighting would be ahead.

Erik motioned for his men to advance at a canter, and they began leaving the infantry behind.

Erik had reached Krondor without incident, he and John Vinci having slipped through the gap to the smuggler's cove, then by boat to a fast ship heading down to Krondor. They had reached the city in time to give Greylock the detailed layout he had needed.

The next morning advance scouting and infiltration units had been sent out to destroy Nordan's forward positions. The units Greylock had brought into Krondor under cover of darkness the previous night left two hours after and rode throughout the day, taking up positions a half-day's ride south of Sarth.

At dawn they had advanced on the city.

Erik glanced to where the sun hung in the sky and considered they were possibly an hour ahead of schedule. Any time gained in the first stage of the assault would be to their benefit. They would need as many men as possible in the town should Lord Arutha's infiltration of the abbey fail and Nordan launch a counteroffensive from up that road.

Glancing toward the sea, Erik saw sails in the distance, two ships heading south. He wondered if they might be invaders' ships or Quegans. Either way, they were about to run headlong into a fleet of ships from Port Vykor heading to Sarth to support the land advance.

Erik returned his attention to the matter at hand.

Roo said, "They're gaining."

Captain Nardini said, "Morning breeze is freshening, but whoever's in command of that galley is willing to kill slaves, that's the truth."

Roo said, "Any weapons aboard this ship?"

"Only what you brought with you. The plan always was to just look harmless and slip out of the harbor without anyone suspecting we had all that gold aboard." The Captain glanced backward and then returned his attention to the sails above. "We certainly have no ballistae or other war engines, if that's what you're asking."

"That's what I was asking," said Roo.

Slowly the galley pulled nearer Roo's ship.

"Sails ahead!" shouted the lookout.

"Where away?" questioned the Captain.

"Two quarters! Dead ahead and five points off the starboard bow!"

Roo hurried forward and squinted against the glare from the mist burning off in the morning light. Directly ahead he saw a dozen tiny dots of white, the sails of the fleet heading north from Port Vykor, while off to the right larger sails showed a fleet closer still.

Roo hurried back to the Captain. "We've got trouble."

"I know," said Nardini. "We need a much stronger wind, or that galley's going to catch us in less than an hour."

"Worse. It looks like we've got a Quegan raiding fleet heading this way, and it looks like they'll get to us before the Kingdom fleet does."

Nardini looked perplexed. "There shouldn't be enough ships in Queg to make up a raiding fleet. A few of the richer nobles, like Vasarius, have a single galley, one they didn't send on that big raid last year, but if there are five other warships left in Queg, I'd be shocked. A dozen or so are under construction in Queg, but they won't be ready to launch for at least another month."

"Then who belongs to that second fleet?" asked Roo.

Nardini shrugged. "We'll find out soon enough."

Roo said, "I wish I had your calm."

Nardini said, "Well, truth to tell, if you get free, I'm a rich man. If you get caught, I was your prisoner."

Roo had to admire the Captain's poise. But his perverse nature demanded he spoil it. "Well, if Vasarius catches us, I hope I live long enough to hear you explain to him how you managed to let us capture your ship."

The Captain's face drained of color. "Put on every inch of sail you can!" he shouted aloft.

Roo laughed.

The Captain continued calling out orders to the men aloft as the two fleets bore down on the ship. Roo called to the lookout, "As soon as you can identify that fleet off the starboard, sing out!"

"Yes, sir!" replied the man aloft.

Roo found it impossible not to look continuously astern, to attempt to measure in his mind the progress the galley behind was making. In his mind's eye he could see the hortator belowdecks slamming his wooden mallets onto the drum used to keep the rowers in unison. Roo knew that when they were close enough, and the Captain called for ramming speed, the beat would pick up and that huge ship would seem to leap forward, its heavy iron-clad ram striking this little ship in the stern. Then armed men would swarm aboard, and if Roo was lucky he'd die during the combat.

The galley drew nearer and Roo saw a man standing at the bow, watching intently. After a few moments, Roo said, "Well, it's Lord Vasarius himself."

Nardini said, "Then we had better pray that the wind picks up or more slaves die quickly, for we are unlikely to encounter mercy at his hands."

"I've found the man lacks any sense of humor, myself."

Nardini said, "I've never had the pleasure of any social encounters."

"With luck, you won't anytime soon," said Roo.

From aloft the lookout shouted, "Kingdom ships to the starboard!"

Roo raced to the bow of the ship and looked. After a few minutes, he could see that both squadrons heading toward him were Kingdom ships. He whooped in joy and turned to shout to the Captain, "Which can we reach first?"

From the rear of the ship, the Captain shouted back, "Those to the starboard are closer, but if we change course toward them, we will lose speed."

Roo didn't debate. "Just keep as much speed as you can and let Vasarius decide who he wants to fight first."

Roo heard a crash. He ran to the stern of the ship and saw the Captain cowering over the loose tiller, letting the high sterncastle shelter him. "What was that?" he asked Nardini.

"A ballista bolt! Vasarius seeks to slow us down."

"Or he's mad enough to sink his own treasure ship before he lets it get away."

Looking over his shoulder, where men worked frantically or watched in fear, he shouted, "Do we have a bow on this ship?"

Silence greeted his question. "Damn," Roo swore. "We can't even shoot back!"

Captain Nardini said, "A little more to the left and he'd have disabled our tiller."

As if listening, the officer in charge of the ballista fired more accurately, and Captain Nardini was almost cut in half by the tiller as it slammed hard into him. Blood flowed from his mouth and nose and his eyes were glassy before he collapsed to the deck.

Roo saw the tiller swinging loosely and knew the shaft connecting it to the rudder had been shattered. Roo knew it was possible to control the ship a little by trimming sails, but he had no idea of how one did that and was certain a high rate of speed was now out of the question. The ship began to drift to starboard and the sailors above frantically tried to trim sails. They looked down, awaiting orders, and a few of them could see the Captain lying dead on the deck.

Roo sighed in resignation. He pulled his sword and shouted, "Ready to repel boarders!"

Instantly those in the rigging above began sliding down sheets to reach the deck. Those who had no weapons grabbed belaying pins or large wooden tackles on rope which could be wheeled like a morningstar.

The Quegan galley bore down on them and another ballista bolt sped toward the ship's stern. A loud crack was accompanied by the entire ship shuddering with the impact.

From below a voice called out, "We're taking water."

"Wonderful," Roo said.

His ship began to turn sideways to the galley as the wind shifted quarter, and suddenly the huge galley's ram was angled at the starboard stern.

An arrow sped by and Roo realized he was standing exposed to any archers in the rigging of the other ship. He ducked low, behind the slight shelter offered by a hatch cover, knowing his chances for survival were very thin. If they could stay alive until the approaching Kingdom fleet reached them, Vasarius would be forced to withdraw. But the chances of this handful of sailors and smugglers holding off the Quegan crew were slim.

Obviously a couple of the sailors agreed, as they dove from the rigging into the water, attempting to swim to shore rather than face the wrath of a Quegan warship's crew. "Stand!" shouted Roo, hoping whatever note of authority he could muster might stiffen the spines of the remaining crew.

Suddenly the ship shuddered and shook like a rat caught by a terrier. The stern lifted as the huge iron-shod ram ripped into the starboard rear quarter of the ship. Roo held on for his life as more arrows sped past.

He kept as low as possible, waiting for the first boarder.

It seemed as soon as he thought of boarders, they were there. Quegan sailors swung down on ropes overhanging the bow of the galley. Similarly dressed in white trousers and shirts, with red headcovers, they were each armed with cutlass and knife. Roo gave a silent prayer that Vasarius wasn't accompanied by a squad of Quegan Legionaries. The men who swarmed his ship were little better than pirates, and might be held at bay.

Roo leaped at the first man near him, running him through before the boarder had a chance to defend himself. Roo ducked back, using the rear mast as cover from the archers above. Another pirate managed to step in the way of an arrow aimed at Roo, and fell to the deck screaming as the arrow protruded from his thigh.

Roo heard members of his own crew climbing the ladder from the main deck to the quarter, and saw the boarders hesitate. He launched a furious attack at the next man, who stepped back. This caused those behind to retreat, and suddenly there was a bunching of boarders on the rear of the quarterdeck. Arrows rained down from above indiscriminately, striking Quegans as well as Roo's men.

Another shout from above caused Roo to dive away as a second volley of arrows cut down men around him. Roo struck a dying man, who groaned as Roo rolled over him and came to his feet. One enterprising boarder was trying to hoist the dead body of a companion to use as a shield against the arrows, but Roo skewered him before he could get the dead man adjusted on his shoulder.

A shaft sped by Roo's face, close enough for him to feel the wind, and he moved backward, again trying to use the rear mast and the sails above as shelter from the bow-fire.

He glanced around and realized that only two of his own

men were standing and there were a half-dozen boarders advancing on him. He also knew that if he leaped to the main deck, he'd be exposed to even more fire from above.

Roo had not gotten to where he was by hesitating. Without looking back, he shouted, "Abandon ship!" and with a single step he dove over the side. Roo struck the water as he felt a hot sting in his shoulder, and he gasped involuntarily. Suddenly he had a mouth and nose full of seawater and he began choking.

Roo forced himself to the surface, choking and spitting water, and by sheer force of will he kept himself from panic. He managed a deep breath as arrows sped by him, and with a single gulp of air, he dove under the water again and started swimming toward the shore. After he had held his breath as long as possible, he broke the surface and turned, treading water.

Panic had erupted on both ships, as the sailors on the deck of his ship were frantically scrambling to gain the ropes they had just used to board it. The reason was that the galley was backing water, attempting to free the ram from the foundering ship. And the reason for that was the two Kingdom warships that were now bearing down on the galley.

The two ships were fast cutters. Neither alone could stand up to a Quegan war galley, but with the galley's ability to maneuver hindered by the sinking freighter, the two cutters were like hounds on a wounded bear with its muzzle stuck in a trap.

Men ran around on deck like ants after a stick had been jammed in their hill. The first cutter fired a ballista bolt that sheared rigging and fouled lines. The second fired a bolt that shattered several oars on the port side of the galley, probably killing a dozen slaves as the oars suddenly slammed around inside the hull.

Then the Kingdom ship closest to Roo blocked his view of the galley for several minutes. He heard ballistae fire several times before the ship passed and he could again see the galley. The galley was afire. The ship on the far side loosed another flaming bolt and the crew of the galley began to abandon ship.

Roo turned and swam toward the shore, memorizing

landmarks in the distance. After a few minutes another Kingdom ship appeared, bearing down on him, and Roo raised his hand, waving his arm back and forth. The ship lowered sail and armed men on deck stood ready to retrieve those in the water. Roo looked again at the two Quegan ships locked in a death embrace. The sinking treasure ship turned, and Roo could see the stern. There painted in red were the words, *Shala Rose*. Roo realized he hadn't even known the name of the ship until that moment. Now she was down by the stern and forcing the burning galley down by the bow.

Both ships were taking on water and men still swarmed off the decks of the galley. For a moment he wondered if anyone had unchained the slaves belowdecks, and said a silent prayer for those who wouldn't get abovedecks.

Then the Kingdom ship was upon him and a rope was lowered. He grabbed it and climbed aboard. Rough hands pulled him over the railing, and as he stood dripping sea-water upon the deck, one of the officers said, "And who might you be?"

"Rupert Avery of Krondor," he answered.

The name caused a visible shift in manners. "Mr. Avery," said the officer. "I'm Lieutenant Aker, second officer of the ship."

"Glad to meet you," said Roo. "A few of those swimming around may be my men, but most of them are Quegans."

"Quegans?" said the young officer. "Are they taking a hand?"

"Let's say it's a personal matter. Still, they were not kindly disposed to our cause."

"If you'd like, sir, I'll escort you to our Captain."

"Thank you."

Roo followed the officer to the quarterdeck, where they halted just before the ladder to the sterncastle. Roo knew that Kingdom navy tradition forbade anyone to climb the stairs to the Captain's domain without invitation.

The Lieutenant called up, "Captain Styles, sir!"

A grey-haired head peered over the railing and called down, "What is it, Mr. Aker?"

"This is Mr. Rupert Avery of Krondor, sir."

"Heard of you," said the Captain to Roo. "Forgive my lack of hospitality, but we have to rescue some drowning men."

"Understood, Captain," replied Rupert.

"Perhaps you'll dine with me this evening, after we reach Sarth," suggested the Captain. He turned away before Roo could answer.

Roo looked at the young officer. "Lieutenant, what ship?"

"You're aboard the *Royal Bulldog*, sir. If you'll come with me, we'll get you into some dry clothing."

As they crossed the deck, Roo saw other Kingdom ships racing northward, carrying soldiers to reinforce Sarth. "How many ships?" asked Roo.

"A dozen. Five carrying troops and the rest of us running screens. So far no enemy ships, until this one."

Roo said, "I'm confused a bit. Two squadrons of Kingdom ships?"

Aker said, "We're from the Far Coast, Mr. Avery. This is what's left of the command in Carse, with a couple of ships from Tulan and Crydee tossed into the bargain." He pointed to the rear. "The other squadron are the lads from Port Vykor."

Roo said, "Well, wherever you're from, I'm very glad you got here."

Roo went down belowdecks, to a small cabin he assumed belonged to the Lieutenant. The officer produced trousers and a white shirt, dry stockings, and small clothes. Roo quickly changed, and said, "When we get situated, I'll make sure these are returned."

"No rush, sir. I've another set."

Roo made his way back up to the main deck to find Quegan sailors being hauled up over the railing, then tied and forced to sit under the watchful gaze of armed Kingdom sailors. Sitting at the front of them, looking as much like a half-drowned rat as anything else, sat a dejected-looking figure familiar to Roo.

Roo came and knelt just beyond the guards, so that he was at eye-level with the man. "My Lord Vasarius, how pleasant to see you here."

"Avery," the man nearly spat. "Have the Gods selected

you to personally plague me for some affront?''

Roo shrugged. ''I wouldn't know. You just happened to be the unlucky conduit whereby I could achieve some gains for my King. Nothing personal.''

''It's very personal,'' said Vasarius.

''Then you better rethink things, for you are in no position to make threats.'' Roo looked up to where Lieutenant Akers stood, and said, ''This is a very important Quegan noble; he's a member of their Imperial Senate.''

The Lieutenant motioned to two guards to haul Vasarius up to his feet. They cut loose his bonds, and Lieutenant Akers said, ''I'll show you to private quarters, m'lord. You understand there will be a guard outside the door.''

With a curt nod, Vasarius acknowledged the courtesy and walked off behind the Lieutenant.

Roo took the moment to regard the captured Quegan sailors. The last time he had seen a lot that miserable had been in the death cell in the palace at Krondor. Turning to a guard, he said, ''What will happen to them?''

The guard shrugged. ''A work camp, I expect. If we ever get a treaty with Queg, maybe a prisoner exchange. Though the Quegans never release prisoners, so I guess we're stuck with these.''

Roo walked to the railing and again studied landmarks: the way the road turned, the odd clump of trees near a large boulder overlooking the beach. He glanced over his shoulder, across the deck where the Quegan galley slipped under the water with a burst of bubbles. Yes, he was certain he could find this spot again. Hire a magician from the Wreckers Guild in Krondor to raise the ship and offload the treasure, and he'd be the Western Realm's wealthiest man again. Roo grinned to himself.

Arutha ducked behind a door. An arrow sped through it, striking the hardwood floor of the main entrance to the abbey. Subai's men had control of the abbey and Nordan's invaders held the outer walls and the cookhouse. Subai had men on the roof of the abbey and they were exchanging bow-shots with those on the wall. So far both sides were being isolated.

Arutha said to Subai, "If we can keep them from getting out the gate, it's as good as a victory."

"If all is going according to plan, we need to hold them until dark."

Arutha glanced at the sun in the sky and judged it nearly noon. "Six, seven more hours."

Subai said, "I'm concerned, m'lord. I think I've seen some signals between those on the wall and those in the stable. If they risked lowering a man on the outside of the gate, he may already be down the hill asking for aid."

Arutha knew that if reinforcements arrived at the gate, they were done for. The abbey was originally an ancient warlord's fortress. The tower rose high above, seemingly touching the clouds. Kingdom soldiers were storming the tower from within, and once on the roof above, the abbey would be theirs. Around the tower a large citadel had been erected, with an outer wall and two outbuildings. Arutha had studied the plans alongside Captain Subai and Brother Dominic until he knew it like his own sons' faces. He knew that from the outside, it was a nearly impregnable fortification. Only by taking it from within would they gain control. Otherwise a long siege would ensue, requiring that a substantial number of men be diverted from the coming campaign.

"I'm not worried about that," said Arutha. "They'd have to risk getting shot to open the gate and let reinforcements in. Besides, if they can afford to strip men away from the defense of Sarth to rescue the men up here, we've lost this battle anyway."

Suddenly a shout heralded a charge from the stable. Arutha stood shocked a moment, as armed men raced toward the main door of the abbey, a flight of arrows over their heads forcing him to retreat from the door. Many of the attackers went down from answering shots from the abbey roof, but most made it to where Arutha, Subai, and a dozen men crowded the entrance. Arutha met the first man at the door and cut him down before he could step inside. As the man fell, Arutha looked past him to see men risking broken bones by jumping from the parapet, so they could unbar the massive wooden gates.

" 'Ware the gates!" Arutha shouted as he struck out at the next man to face him.

Then the sound of horses could be heard as a company of riders charged out from the barn, attempting to reach the gates as they opened. Without hesitation, Arutha shouted, "Follow me!" and charged out into the open. He knew that if he could keep the riders from fleeing the yard, he could prevent word reaching Nordan that the abbey was under attack. By denying them the gate, it would break the back of the last resistance in the abbey and force a surrender. Half the garrison was under guard in the basements below, and a full hundred lay dead or wounded throughout the compound. The hundred men trapped in the kitchen, the barn, and upon the walls were the only ones left.

Arutha felt a surge of energy, something akin to joy, mixed with nothing short of terror, as he dodged through the melee, striking up at a horseman who was attempting to engage another Kingdom soldier. Arutha's blade struck a glancing blow, not injuring the rider, but distracting him enough so the other soldier could unseat him.

Riders were milling around and horses were rearing and bucking, panic rising in the herd as the fighting swirled around them. Arutha glanced to his left and saw Subai signaling his men to fan out and, by pointing, to mount an unguarded set of steps leading to the upper wall.

Arutha looked toward the gate and saw two men, one wounded, were freeing the bar. He shouted, "The gate!" and charged.

Halfway between the main building of the abbey and the gate, an arrow struck Arutha in the neck, between breastplate and helm.

For a moment he thought someone had punched him with a fist, for he felt the impact of the blow and his legs go out from under him, but he didn't feel much pain. Then his vision seemed to contract, as if he were falling backward down a long tunnel, with darkness sweeping in from all sides. Still uncertain of what was happening, Arutha, Duke of Krondor, slipped into a void.

Subai was halfway to the steps to the top of the wall when he saw Arutha go down and shouted to two of his men, "Get the Duke back here!"

The two soldiers raced out in the middle of the fight, managed to grab the Duke, and haul him back to Subai's position. Subai knelt beside the Duke, but he had seen enough dead men before that he didn't have to take a second look at Arutha. He considered how ironic it was that this brave man had died in his first conflict, and then put aside all thoughts of the Duke; Subai had a battle to fight.

Erik signaled to Greylock and the two elements of the Kingdom army charged. Horsemen raced down the main street of Sarth, heading to the Trades Masters' Hall, the headquarters and final defense of the invaders. So far the retaking of Sarth had gone without a hitch. The entire city defense had been ordered south to deal with Greylock's center thrust. As had been the plan, Greylock stood and engaged, while Erik's right flank element pushed through light resistance on the treacherous hillside east of the road, and while ships were unloading soldiers at the dock.

Owen held a stable front, while Erik feigned a flanking attack from the right. The enemy shifted to face Erik, who withdrew just as soldiers under the command of the Duke of Ran struck them from the rear. Within minutes, it was a total rout.

Many men fled north along the King's Highway, but a few hundred had barricaded themselves in the large building that dominated the town's square. Erik's charging column wheeled to the right and flanked the building from the northeast, while Greylock's men stood on the southwest. Quickly the building was encircled.

Occasional arrows flew from windows in the upper floor, but otherwise the building was sealed. Windows and doors on the lower floor had been barricaded.

Erik turned to Duga, the mercenary Captain who had been among the first to switch sides during the war. "Keep the men back!" he ordered, then he set heels to his horse and rode around to Greylock's position. "Orders, sir?"

Greylock was sweating furiously under the midday heat, his hair hanging limply across his brow. "I'm lacking patience, Erik." He rode a little closer to the building and shouted, "You, in the guild hall!"

An arrow sped from an upper window, missing by a few feet.

"Damn it! I'm talking to you," shouted Greylock.

Erik said, "Let me," and switching to the language of Novindus, he shouted, "Our leader wishes parlay!"

After a moment, a voice from within shouted, "What terms?"

Erik translated.

Owen said, "Tell him, the terms are throw down weapons and walk out, or we'll burn the building down with them inside of it. They must decide now!"

Erik translated, and there was the sound of a sudden argument breaking out inside. Then the sound of fighting erupted, and Erik glanced at Owen, who nodded.

Erik shouted, "Charge!" and from all sides the Kingdom forces rushed the building.

Erik and Owen were closest, and reached the main door of the building. Erik turned and shouted, "Bring a ram!"

As men rushed to obey, other men were kicking at smaller doors or attempting to pry window shutters off their hinges. Suddenly the main door opened and a sword flew out, to clatter on the stone street at Erik's feet.

"We're coming out!" shouted a voice from within.

Erik and Owen stepped away from the door and a group of men came out, holding their swords by the blade. As they came into view of the Kingdom soldiers, they threw the swords to the ground, the Novindus mercenaries' sign of surrender. Duga came to stand beside Erik. "I know these lads. Most of them are pretty decent fellows if you give them a chance." Then he saw a few hanging back at the rear and added, "Though a few of them should probably be hung just to improve the air around here."

Erik said, "They're all going to be locked up for a while until we can get them sent back home."

Duga said, "Well, even after wintering with you, Captain, I can't say as I understand how you Kingdom folk think, but then nothing that's been happening for the last few years makes any sense to me. When this war is done, maybe you can explain things to me."

Erik said, "As soon as someone explains things to me."

Soldiers entered the building and took out the rest of the

invaders. A few were carried out bloodied and unconscious. One of the first to surrender said to Erik and Duga, "That lot didn't see any point to surrender. The rest of us didn't see any point in being roasted for Fadawah."

Duga grinned. "Nordan will fart flames when he hears this."

The soldier said, "He already did." He pointed to a man being carried out. "That's General Nordan."

Erik motioned for the two soldiers to take the unconscious general to one side. Owen nodded, a smile of satisfaction on his face. Reports started coming in that the town of Sarth was secure. Owen said, "Erik, take a company up the road and see if the abbey is secured. If you encounter any of the enemy, get back down that road as fast as you can." He turned to Duga. "You form up a barricade company at the bottom of the road, in case Erik returns in a hurry."

Erik saluted, and as he turned to find his horse, Owen said, "Captain."

Erik looked back at his old friend. "Yes, Marshal?"

"Your boys did very well on the right flank. Tell them I said so."

Erik smiled. "I'll tell them." He hurried to where his horse was being held and turned to find Jadow Shati. To his old companion, he said, "Bring second squad and follow me."

Jadow, who looked as if he had just finished a relaxing morning ride, nodded and signaled. "Second squad, follow me. The rest of you, help secure the area!"

Erik led his small company through the town of Sarth. There was occasional fighting in scattered locations, as a few hardcore members of Nordan's army refused to surrender, but mostly bands of disarmed prisoners being taken to the rear where a compound was being erected to confine them. A few townspeople, who had fled during the fighting, could be seen up in the hills surrounding the city, a few of the more courageous among them coming down into the town.

Erik and his men rode eastward, and rather than veering back along the King's Highway where it turned south, they moved along a smaller road heading upward, into the mountains. Atop the first of these, overlooking the coast, was the Abbey of Sarth, once home to the largest library on the world of Midkemia.

The horses were tired from the charge through the town, but Erik pushed them, anxious to find out if Arutha and Subai had been successful, or if a force of armed men was poised to strike down at Sarth. They had been so successful in retaking the southern end of Fadawah's holdings, Erik was certain something terrible must happen.

As they neared the summit, they heard the sounds of fighting from within. The road was narrow most of the way up the mountain, the men riding in pairs. At a point thirty yards before the gate, the road widened, allowing the men to spread out. Horse archers were ready and started firing upon the few men they could see on the wall. Erik signaled and a dozen riders dismounted and raced to the gate. They threw grapples up and secured them. Men climbed while the bowmen kept those on the wall busy. As soon as the first wave was across, other men followed, and fighting erupted along the parapet. Erik knew that had there been no Kingdom forces within, his own men would have died, never reaching the walls. A warning shout alerted Erik, and he formed up his men to charge. He gave the signal as soon as the gates began to open.

Erik and his men rode into the midst of a furious, surging battle, with horsemen and men on foot locked in a death struggle. Erik struck at the first horseman he faced, knocking him completely out of his saddle. The abrupt appearance of Kingdom soldiers riding in through the now open gate demoralized the remaining invaders. Quickly they started to back away and throw down weapons in surrender.

Erik caught his breath and took in the scene around him. Men lay all across the courtyard, as well as a few wounded or dead horses.

Erik motioned for Jadow Shati to move the prisoners over to the stable. Erik dismounted and led his horse to the entrance of the abbey building. He glanced up at the old keep tower and realized that with proper supplies, this fortress could withstand a year of siege. He counted himself lucky the Prince had agreed to launch the attack as soon as possible, rather than led Nordan get entrenched.

"Erik!" called a voice. Erik turned to see Captain Subai motioning for him to come over. Erik hurried to the abbey's main entrance. Just inside the door lay Duke Arutha. Erik glanced at Subai, who shook his head slightly. Softly the Captain of the Pathfinders said, "He tried to keep the raiders from opening the gates. If you had arrived a half hour earlier . . ."

Erik looked at the fallen Duke. He appeared to be asleep. "He fought well?" Erik asked.

Subai said, "Very well. He may not have been a warrior in life, but he died like one."

Erik said, "As soon as we've secured the abbey, I'll send word to Greylock. The Prince must be informed as soon as possible."

"Patrick will want to enter Krondor with his new Princess as soon as possible."

"Rillanon?" asked Erik, referring to the rumors circulated to mislead enemies about the Kingdom's intentions.

"No need," suggested Subai. "With Arutha dead, Patrick needs to be in Krondor, with or without a bride." Looking southward, as if seeing Krondor in the distance, Subai said, "There's our weakness, Captain. If Kesh learns we are committing all our soldiers to retake Ylith, and have only Duko's mercenaries along the border, without support troops within the city, they can wreak havoc."

Erik said, "Let us hope we can keep Kesh from discovering this before the war in the North is over."

Subai looked down at Arutha. "It was his task to see that they didn't." Looking at Erik, he added, "Now it is someone else's task. But it is the Prince's responsibility." With a gesture, he indicated the Duke's body was to be carried inside. To Erik he said, "As soon as Greylock has soldiers sent up here to secure this location, my Pathfinders will return to Krondor. We will return the Duke home."

Erik nodded. "And I will go north with Greylock." Erik turned and walked out into the courtyard, to bring order out of chaos and get the situation under control as quickly as possible. They had won a stunning victory, at far less cost than anticipated, and far quicker than they had imagined. Yet there was so very much to do still before them.

Fourteen

Consequences

JIMMY WEPT.

Standing at attention on the steps of the palace in Krondor, next to his brother, a step behind the Prince, his tears ran freely down his face. He could not imagine a life without his father. He had known those who fight might die, but his father had not been a warrior. He had studied arms and armor, like every noble in the Kingdom, but his life had been one of administration, diplomacy, and judgment. Only once had he chosen to fight, and that decision had cost him his life.

Dash had never imagined his father's return to Krondor would be on a wagon acting as a bier. He kept his features set in an unreadable mask as he watched the wagon carrying his father's body pass by. A day of mourning had been announced for Duke Arutha and the others who had fallen in retaking Sarth.

Dash wondered if it was worth it. He didn't feel anything, save a numb empty place within. Jimmy was expressing his anger and pain, yet within Dash something lay buried. Looking at the the assembled nobles and military captains of the Kingdom, all bowing their heads in respect as his father's body was returned to Krondor, Dash just couldn't make any sense of it.

His father had always been such a sensible man. He was a decent enough swordsman, at least for practice duels, and he kept himself fit, riding and swimming when the opportunity presented itself, but he had never fought in a military action. Then Dash realized he was thinking in present tense. He had been, from what Captain Subai said, a brave soldier at the last, but he should never have been allowed to go on that mission. Dash discovered tears forming in his eyes and he blinked them back.

Duke Arutha had been the practical member of the family. Their mother was always obsessed with the gossip of the royal court in Rillanon, and with long visits back to her own family in Roldem. The boys' childhood had been dominated by nannies, tutors, and their grandfather, who would teach them how to climb walls, pick locks, and all manner of outrageous behavior. Their grandmother had been a soothing presence and their father had been a rock, a calm, quiet man who had been affectionate and caring in little ways. Dash couldn't remember a time his father hadn't greeted him with a warm hug. He recalled the many times he would stand there, one hand upon Dash's shoulder as if making contact physically was important.

Suddenly Dash was aware he was mourning the loss of his entire family. His grandparents in Roldem were strangers, for the most part. He had a half-dozen visits to that island kingdom in his childhood—his maternal grandparents only came to Rillanon once, for his parents' wedding. His sister was married to the Duke of Faranzia in Roldem and had never returned to the Kingdom for a visit since her wedding. All that remained was his brother Jimmy.

As the wagon vanished into the stable area, Prince Patrick said, "Gentlemen, the entire nation mourns the loss of your father. Now, if you would join me in council in an hour, please." He nodded across the courtyard to where Francie stood with her father, and turned and mounted the broad palace steps. As soon as the Prince was out of sight, the rest of the assembled nobles in Krondor dispersed.

Jimmy took a deep breath, getting his emotions under control, and motioned for Dash to accompany him. They followed the wagon around the central palace to where an undertaker was overseeing the removal of their father's body from the wagon. Two soldiers gently removed the body of Duke Arutha, wrapped from head to foot in faded linen someone had found in Sarth. The undertaker turned to Jimmy and said, "You are Lord Arutha's son?"

Jimmy nodded, indicating with a gesture that he and Dash were the Duke's sons.

The undertaker attempted a compassionate pose. "The nation mourns with you, young lords. How will you wish to dispose of your father's remains?"

Jimmy stopped and looked at Dash. "I . . . never . . ."

Dash said, "What is usual?"

"As Duke of Krondor, your father is entitled to be interred in the palace vault. As the Earl Vecar, he is entitled to be interred in the Royal Palace in Rillanon. Or if you have family estates . . . ?"

Jimmy looked at Dash, who was silent. Finally the elder brother said, "My family's estates are this city. But my father was born and raised in Rillanon. That was always his home. Return him there."

"As you wish," said the undertaker.

Dash put his hand on Jimmy's shoulder and said, "Let's get a drink."

"Only one. We need to see the Prince in an hour. We can get drunk in Father's memory after."

Dash nodded as they walked back toward the main entrance to the palace.

Malar Enares was standing before the entrance when they reached it. "Sirs," he said. "Most regrettable. You have my sympathies."

The servant from the Vale of Dreams had found a hundred ways to make himself useful around the palace. When Jimmy had returned, expecting to find the servant still under guard, he had been both amused and surprised to discover him working frantically around Duko's headquarters. He seemed a wonder when it came to organizing, cleaning, and keeping things orderly. He had attached himself to Jimmy again when Duko rode south to take command of the Southern Marches and oversee the sentry forts along the Keshian border.

Malar followed the brothers inside. "May I do something for you, young lords?"

Jimmy said, "If you would bring a bottle of very good brandy to my quarters, I would appreciate it."

"I'll see what I can do," said Malar, rushing off.

Dash and Jimmy walked the long corridors of the palace, now restored to nearly the state they had enjoyed before the destruction of Krondor. Workers still scurried throughout the palace, repainting trim around windows and doors, laying tiles, and hanging tapestries. The rearmost stairs to the upper floors were still in need of repair, but the last of the cracked stones had been removed and replaced by masons, and the soot and fire damage erased.

"Do you remember how this place looked before?" asked Dash.

Jimmy said, "You know, I was just thinking the same thing. I know the tapestries are different, but I'm damned if I can tell you what the ones that hung on the walls before looked like."

"Patrick's having all the old war banners from the Prince's hall remade."

"It's not the same," said Jimmy, "but I can see the reason."

They reached Jimmy's quarters and entered. They sat in silence for a minute, then Dash said, "I am so mad at him." He looked up and his eyes brimmed with tears.

Jimmy's eyes watered as well, as he said, "I know. How bloody stupid was that? Going off and getting killed."

"You've written to Mother and the aunts?"

"Not yet. I'll do so this night. I'm still not sure what I'll say."

Dash let his tears flow. "Tell them he died bravely. For King and Country."

"Cold comfort," said Jimmy.

Dash wiped at his eyes. "He had to go."

Jimmy said, "No, he didn't."

"Yes, he did," said Dash. "All his life he has been in the shadow of Grandfather, and of the man for whom he was named."

Jimmy wiped his own eyes and said, "History will only acknowledge one Arutha of Krondor." He sighed. "Father will possibly be a small notation somewhere. The man named for a great prince who served admirably as administrator in Rillanon and Krondor. Isn't there more for him than just that?''

Dash said, ''Only to those of us who knew him and loved him.''

Jimmy stood as a knock came at the door. He opened it and found Malar Enares standing there, holding a tray upon which rested a bottle of brandy and two crystal goblets.

Jimmy stepped aside and allowed the servant to enter. Malar put the tray down on the table and said, ''I wish to express my deepest regrets, young sirs. While having not the pleasure of meeting your distinguished father, I have heard nothing of the man that was not salutary.''

''Thank you,'' said Jimmy.

Dash took the decanter and poured drinks as Malar left and closed the door behind him. Offering a goblet to his brother, Dash lifted his and said, ''To Father.''

''To Father,'' echoed Jimmy. They drank in silence.

After a minute, Jimmy said, ''I know how Father felt.''

''How so?'' asked Dash.

''No matter how good I am, no matter how high I rise, there will only be one James of Krondor,'' he said.

''Only one Jimmy the Hand,'' agreed Dash.

''Then, Grandfather would tell us it has nothing to do with fame.''

''He enjoyed the notoriety, though,'' said Dash.

''Agreed,'' said Jimmy. ''But he gained it from being so bloody brilliant at what he did. He didn't set out to be the most fiendishly clever noble in history.''

''Maybe that's what Father knew from the start; it's just getting the job done and let history decide what history will decide,'' observed Dash.

Jimmy said, ''No doubt you're right. Well, we'd better get to Patrick's office and see what the Prince will decide.''

Dash stood up, adjusted his tunic, and said, ''Do you think he'll make you Duke of Krondor? Eldest son and all that.''

Jimmy laughed. ''Hardly. He'll want someone with more experience in the office, as will the King.''

Dash opened the door. ''You're only two years younger than Patrick, Jimmy.''

''Which is exactly why Borric will want someone older

and wiser in Krondor,'' said Jimmy as he moved through the door. ''Had Father been the Duke of Crydee or Yabon, I most certainly would have gotten the title, with a strong Kingdom advisor on the first ship west, but Krondor? No, there's too much to be done and too many potential mistakes.'' As he moved down the hall, he added, ''Besides, there are too many headaches. Whatever Patrick offers me will be better than the office of Duke.''

They hurried along until they reached the side entrance to the Prince's quarters. Jimmy knocked and the door opened. A page stepped aside and allowed them to enter. Compared to the cramped offices endured in Darkmoor, these offices were spacious. The books and scrolls that their father had ordered hauled to safety were being returned to their appropriate shelves or cubicles. Malar was handing a bundle of scrolls to a clerk. ''Lending a hand?'' asked Jimmy as they passed.

''One helps where one can,'' said the servant with a smile.

They passed into the Prince's private chambers and Patrick looked up. Standing next to the Prince's desk was Duke Brian of Silden. He nodded at the brothers. They both knew that Brian and their father had been among the closest of friends at court, and that more than any other noble in the realm, Brian would share their sense of loss.

Patrick sat back in his chair and said, ''Gentlemen, first let me again express my sorrow at your father's death. His loss is not only to his family and friends, but to the Kingdom as a whole.'' Patrick looked around the room as if seeking something. ''It's as if I expect to see him at every hand. I know now just how much I've come to rely upon his counsel.''

Patrick let out a slow breath close to a sigh and continued, ''But we must, as ever, press on. Lord Silden will act as my counselor until the King sees fit to name a new duke in Krondor.'' Patrick looked at Jimmy and said, ''I know you well enough to know you didn't expect the office.''

Jimmy shook his head. ''Ten years from now, perhaps, but not now.''

Patrick nodded. ''Good, because we need you somewhere outside of Krondor.''

"Where, Highness?"

"I need someone dependable to keep an eye on Duko. You seem to get along well enough with him, and I need someone down there who will keep him in line."

Jimmy bowed his head. "Highness."

"I've sent a message to my father, Jimmy. Assume he'll accept my recommendation that you succeed your father as Earl of Vencar. It's a lovely little estate and your father would want you to have it."

Jimmy bowed his head in thanks. "Thank you, Your Highness." Vencar was where they had been raised. Like many of the estates on the original island Kingdom of Rillanon, it was tiny by mainland standards. A hundred acres of land, with a creek, meadows, and pastures. The tenant farmers had ceased to work the land centuries before as Rillanon had expanded its reach onto the mainland. But for its modest size, it was among the most beautiful estates in the Kingdom. Their grandfather had arranged for it to go to Arutha when the old Earl of Vencar had died without heirs. Jimmy had been born in the palace, as had his sister, but they had moved there when he was a baby. Dash had been born there. It was home.

"So unless my father writes back telling me I'm an idiot, from now forward, you are Earl James."

Jimmy said, "I thank His Highness."

Patrick said, "I have a special job for you, Dash."

"Highness."

"We have a problem here in Krondor. The army is in the North, and Duko's swords are down South. I've got the palace guard, and that's all. The city is returning to life and it's being overrun by thugs and ruffians, cutthroats and thieves. I need someone to bring order. I think of all those I have around here, you have the most affinity for the city streets. I am appointing you Sheriff of Krondor. Until we can create a true City Watch and Office of Constables, you are the law in the city. Recruit who you can, but keep this city under control until the wars are over."

Dash said, "Sheriff?"

Patrick said, "You object?"

"Ah . . . no, Highness. I'm just a little surprised."

"Life is full of surprises," said Patrick. He indicated

some parchments on his desk. "Reports from both fronts. The Keshians retreat before Duko at Land's End, but are raiding along the eastern front near Shamata. They won't get too close, for fear of the magicians at Stardock, I think, but they're harassing our patrols, which are thin to start with. In the North Greylock has consolidated in Sarth and is pushing northward." Patrick got a concerned look on his face. "Something is not right. The defense along the coast is weak. We know that Fadawah offered up Duko because he was fearful of Duko's loyalty.

"Now it appears he gave up Nordan in the same way, but by all reports Nordan was his oldest and most trusted ally."

"Perhaps his hold over his men is less secure than we thought," observed Jimmy.

Brian of Silden said, "All the reports indicate a difficult winter for the invaders, with many dying of injuries and starvation. But we also have word from our agents that they're trading with Queg and the Free Cities, food is plentiful, and they're established in Ylith."

Patrick ran his hand over his face. "Any word from Yabon?"

"None," said Duke Brian. "We've had nothing since the battle of Sarth. No ships can get past Queg's pirates to reach the Free Cities. All our ships from the Far Coast were used to support the raid. If word is coming, it is coming by runner, and the chances of a courier getting through the enemy to reach us is thin. Perhaps when we get closer to Ylith, we may hear of Yabon, but for now we must pray the young Duke is able to keep LaMut and Yabon intact."

Looking at Jimmy and Dash, Patrick said, "Dine with me tonight, both of you, and we'll discuss your duties. In your case, Jimmy, before you leave tomorrow."

"Tomorrow?" said Dash. "Patrick ... Highness, I thought we would accompany our father to Rillanon for his funeral."

"No time, sorry to say. You'll have to say your own good-byes after supper tonight. Perhaps we'll hold a little wake after supper ... yes, that would be fitting. But the requirements of this war don't permit any of us the luxury for our personal grief or joys. I had to lie to many nobles of the Kingdom about a state wedding, and my intended is not as happy about being married in the ashes of Krondor as she was at the thought of the King's palace. So we all make sacrifices."

"At supper, then," said Dash.

"You are dismissed," said the Prince.

The brothers bowed and left the Prince's office.

"Do you believe that?" said Jimmy.

"What?" said Dash.

"That business about 'we all make sacrifices.' "

Dash shrugged. "It's just Patrick. He never knows when he's ahead and when he should just shut up."

Jimmy laughed as they turned the corner toward their rooms. "You've got that right. Probably why he was always such a bad card player."

"Perfect," said Nakor.

Aleta stood still, but she said, "I feel silly."

"You look wonderful," said Nakor.

The young woman stood on a box, a linen sheet around her head and shoulders, otherwise garbed in her normal dress. A sculptor worked furiously in clay, trying to capture her likeness. He had been at it for three days, and stepped back and said, "It's finished."

Nakor walked around it while Aleta got off the box and came to look at it. "Do I look like that?" she asked.

"Yes," said Nakor. He continued to walk around it, and finally said, "Yes, that will do." Looking at the sculptor he asked, "How long will this take?"

"How big do you want it?"

"I want it life-sized." Pointing at Aleta, he said, "The same size as her."

"Then it will take a month for each one."

"Good. A month should be fine."

"Do you want me to bring them here?"

"I want one delivered here, to be put up in the wagon yard. The other one bring to Krondor."

"Krondor? Mr. Avery didn't say anything about trucking a statue all the way to Krondor."

"Do you want to let wagoners put up your statue?"

The sculptor shrugged. "Makes no difference to me, but it will cost extra."

Nakor frowned. "That's between you and Roo."

The sculptor nodded and carefully wrapped up the clay reference piece in oilcloth and moved it to his wagon, outside.

Aleta said, "Am I done now?"

Nakor said, "Probably not, but you don't need to pose anymore."

"What is this all about?" she asked, folding up the sheet she had worn. "I've felt very silly posing for that thing."

"It's a statue of the Goddess."

"You used me for a statue of the Goddess!" She seemed appalled. "That's . . ."

Nakor looked puzzled. "Something I don't understand. But it was the right choice."

Brother Dominic had been in the corner, observing the entire interaction, and he said, "Child, trust me, this strange man knows things, things he doesn't understand. But if he knows them, they are true."

The young woman looked as if that explanation caused her even more confusion. Dominic said, "If Nakor said it's proper for you to pose for the representation of the Goddess, then it is. Trust me on this. It's no blasphemy."

The girl seemed more reassured by that, and said, "Well, I have washing to do."

She left, and Dominic came over to Nakor and asked, "What is it you see in that girl?"

Nakor shrugged. "Something wonderful."

"Care to be more specific?"

"No," said Nakor. "Are you coming to Krondor with me?"

Dominic said, "My instructions from the home temple are to accommodate your plans to the best of my ability. If that means accompanying you to Krondor, then I will go."

Nakor said, "That's good. Things here will continue to operate without me. Sho Pi can oversee the feeding of the hungry and teaching the children. He's already begun training disciples in the basics of being a monk; the order of Dala is a good place to start, and that will weed out those looking for a free meal and warm bed from those who really want to contribute.''

"When do we leave?" asked Dominic.

Nakor shrugged. "In a day or two. The last detachments of the army will be leaving to journey to Krondor, to join the Prince, and we can tag along as escort.''

Dominic said, "Very well. I will be ready.''

As Dominic left, Nakor turned and regarded Aleta, who was hanging washing on a line across the courtyard. The sunlight struck her from behind, putting a golden nimbus of light around her head for a moment as she stood on her tiptoes to clip the clothing to the line. Nakor grinned. "Something very wonderful," he said to himself.

Dinner was quiet. Conversation had been subdued throughout the evening. Mostly it had been sporadic, on this or that issue before the throne, or a small remembrance of Lord Arutha, but long periods passed in silence.

As the last course was removed, waiters appeared with trays upon which rested crystal goblets and decanters of brandy. Patrick said, "As the sons of Lord Arutha are not permitted the relief of returning with their father to the capital for his funeral, I thought it appropriate to honor him with an informal wake. If you would be so kind, gentlemen, a word or two in remembrance would be appropriate.

"Lord Brian?"

The Duke of Silden said, "Since boyhood, Arutha and I were friends. If I was to name the one quality of his many that I found most remarkable, it was his unrivaled clarity of thought. Whatever opinion he gave, on whatever subject, it was the distillation of a remarkable mind. He may have been the most gifted man I have known.''

Jimmy and Dash exchanged glances, for they had never considered what his peers might have thought of their father.

The other nobles made their remarks, and last before the boys was Captain Subai. Not given to long speeches, he seemed uncomfortable, but nevertheless said, "I think of the Duke as perhaps the wisest man I've known. He knew his limits and yet was not afraid to challenge them. He put the welfare of others above his own. He loved his family. He will be missed.''

Subai looked at Jimmy, who said, "He was named for a great man." Jimmy nodded toward Patrick, who acknowledged the reference to his grandfather. "He was raised by a man who may be unique in our history. Yet he knew how to be himself." Looking at Patrick, he said, "I think about being the grandson of Lord James of Krondor, perhaps because I was named for him. I rarely thought what it must have been like to be his son." Tears gathered in James's eyes as he said, "I just wish I could have told him how much he meant to me."

Dash said, "I too. I think I may have taken him for granted. I hope I never make that mistake with anyone else who is dear to me."

The Prince stood, taking a glass from the servant. Others did as well. Jimmy and Dash each lifted a glass as the Prince said, "Lord Arutha!"

Everyone at supper, Lord Silden, Captain Subai, and the other nobles invited to Patrick's "intimate" dinner echoed the toast and drank. Then Patrick said, "This supper is now over, gentlemen." He withdrew from the hall, and the rest of the guests waited the appropriate time before themselves leaving the hall.

James and Patrick left the hall, a step behind Lord Silden and Captain Subai. They bid the other men good night and returned to their rooms. Jimmy was about to bid Dash good night when a page came running. "Gentlemen, please! Attend the Prince at once!"

They hurried after the page, who led them back to the Prince's office. Inside they found Patrick standing before his desk. His face was a red mask of rage and in his fist he held a message that he had crushed. He held it out to Lord Silden, who unfolded and read it. His eyes widened. "Gods!" he said. Looking stricken, he said quietly, "LaMut has fallen."

Patrick said, "A soldier escaped and made his way to Loriel, with half of Fadawah's army behind him. He died after delivering the message. It came south by fast courier from there to Darkmoor, then to here. LaMut has been in enemy hands for three weeks now." Patrick spoke bitterly.

"We congratulated ourselves on the ease with which we took Sarth, and it was all a trade. He gave us back a fishing town, a port of no importance, and in exchange he took the heart of Yabon! Yabon City is now at grave peril and we are no closer to retaking Ylith than we were at first thaw!"

The Prince looked close to being frantic. Suddenly, Jimmy and Dash were painfully aware of how the absence of their father was being felt. They both glanced at Brian Silden, who stood silently, looking afraid to speak. Patrick finally said, "I know, we must get word to Yabon! We must send word to Duke Carl to hold until we can get relief to him."

"What of Loriel?" asked Jimmy.

"It holds," said Patrick. "But we don't know for how long. Fadawah has massed a huge number of men outside the walls, and by this report the fighting is fierce. It may have fallen already. And the report says some sort of black magic is being directed at the defenders."

Jimmy and Dash exchanged glances. All reports from the previous year's campaigns said the Pantathian Serpent Priests were gone, but they may have been premature in their assessment. And there was nothing to prevent the magic being the product of human mages.

"We must get word to my great-grandfather," said Jimmy.

"The magician?" said Patrick. "Where is he?"

"He should still be in Elvandar, if things are as he planned them. He will return to Stardock in another month's time."

"Captain Subai," said Patrick. "Can you get messengers to Yabon?"

"It's difficult, Highness. We may be able to get one through the mountains to the north of Loriel. Perhaps reach some of the hillmen from Yabon. One of them could continue on to Elvandar."

Patrick said, "Subai, leave at first light for Darkmoor. Get whatever help you need and go north. I have no one else to spare for the task. Greylock and von Darkmoor will press on until they reach the invaders' positions south of Ylith. Jimmy, you will go south to Duko and apprise him of what we face. Krondor is now an empty shell and vulnerable. We must show a strong face to everyone. Dash, you must keep this city under control, by whatever means. Now, Lord Silden, please stay and help me compose the orders. Gentlemen, the rest of you are dismissed.''

Outside the Prince's quarters, Jimmy said, "Captain Subai, if I pen a message to my great-grandfather, would you see he gets it along with the other communications?''

"Of course," said the Captain. "I expect we'll both be at the city gate at first light tomorrow. Give it to me then. And I will have something for you. Until then, good night.''

Jimmy and Dash bid the Captain good night, and Jimmy said, "Well, Sheriff, help me compose a letter to Great-grandfather.''

Dash said, "Sheriff?" With a sigh he followed his brother.

The dawn was still hours away, but the sky was lightening in the east as Dash stood next to his brother. Upon another horse sat Malar Enares, the servant from the Vale of Dreams, who had somehow learned of Jimmy's journey. He had prevailed upon Jimmy to allow him to ride south with him, claiming that while work was plentiful in Krondor, payment wasn't, and that his former master's business holdings along the Keshian border might still be operating. As the man was harmless company in the main, and often useful, Jimmy agreed.

Captain Subai rode up with a company of his Pathfinders and handed a canvas-wrapped bundle to Jimmy. "This was your father's sword, Jimmy. I took it from him before they prepared his body to return it to Krondor. I knew as elder son it was to be yours.''

Jimmy took the bundle and unwrapped it. The hilt was worn, and the scabbard nicked and scratched. But the blade was immaculate. Jimmy drew the blade and saw the faint outlines of a miniature warhammer seemingly etched into the forte of the blade. He knew that this was where Macros the Black had empowered the blade with a talisman from the Abbot of Sarth Abbey when Prince Arutha had to face the moredhel leader Murmandamus. The sword had hung in the study in Krondor since the old Prince's death, and had been sent by Duke James to his son. Now Jimmy held it. "I don't know," said Jimmy. "This should go to Patrick or the King, I think."

Subai shook his head. "No, had the Prince of Krondor wished the sword to go to the King, it would have. He left it in Krondor for a reason."

Jimmy held it reverently for a while, then unbuckled his own belt, handing his sword to Dash. He put his father's sword belt around his waist. "Thank you."

Dash came to stand next to Captain Subai and said, "Would you see the courier who you're sending to Elvandar carries this message to our great-grandfather, please?"

Subai took the letter and placed it inside his tunic. "I am that courier. I personally will lead the Pathfinders who travel to Yabon and on to Elvandar."

"Thank you," said Dash.

Subai said, "If we don't chance to meet again, young Jimmy, it has been an honor."

Jimmy said, "Safe travel, Captain."

The Pathfinders rode out the gate, heading east at a relaxed trot. Jimmy looked at his brother. "Stay safe, little brother."

Dash reached up to shake Jimmy's hand. "You travel safely, too, big brother. I don't know how long it will be before we see one another, but you will be missed."

Jimmy nodded. "Letters to Mother and the rest of the family are in the pouch bound for Rillanon. When I know where I'm likely to be, I'll send word."

Dash waved as Jimmy and his company rode out the gate, then turned around to head back into the castle. He had a meeting in an hour with the Prince, Lord Brian, and others in the castle. After that he had to begin the process of bringing law and order to Krondor while Jimmy rode south to Port Vykor.

Fifteen

Betrayal

JIMMY HALTED.

The escort stopped behind him. The Captain of the company of Patrick's Royal Household Guards said, "This is as far as we're supposed to go, m'lord." He glanced around. "Leave it to those—"

"Captain?"

"I mean no disrespect to Lord Duko, m'lord, but after all, we were fighting him and those miserable bastards he calls soldiers just last year." He noted Jimmy's disapproving expression and said, "Anyway, they should be here, making a camp, before they start back to their patrol."

"Maybe they ran into some trouble."

"Possible, my lord."

They were at a fork in the road, the agreed-upon southern limit of Krondorian patrols—everything to the south was Duko's responsibility. The southwest fork in the road led to Port Vykor, while the southeast fork would start around the edge of Shandon Bay, eventually leading toward Land's End.

Jimmy said, "We'll be fine, Captain. We're halfway to Port Vykor and should be running into Lord Duko's patrols any time now. If they're not here today, they'll be here tomorrow, I'm sure."

"I'd still feel better if you'd wait here until one shows up, m'lord. We could linger here for another half-day or so."

"Thanks, but no, Captain. The sooner I get to Port Vykor, the sooner I can be about the Prince's business. We'll continue along the southwest road until sundown, then we'll camp. If Duko's patrol doesn't show up to escort us tomorrow, we'll find our way to Port Vykor alone."

"Very well, m'lord. May the gods watch over you."

"And you, too, Captain."

They parted company with the Krondorian patrol, who turned northward, while Jimmy and Malar continued southwest. They rode through quiet countryside, scrub grass, and what once might have been farmland, but which had known the tread of the conqueror's boot too often. Keshians on their way to the Kingdom, and Kingdom soldiers on their way to Kesh, had turned these rolling hills and sparse woodlands into a no-man's-land in the last hundred years. The rich lands of the Vale of Dreams to the east kept farmers and their families struggling despite the constant threat of war between two nations rolling over them. The lands through which Jimmy and Malar rode offered no such bounty. They might be the only two men for fifty miles in any direction.

As the sun sank low in the western sky, Malar asked, "What shall we do now, my lord?"

Jimmy looked around and pointed to a small dell near a clear-running stream. "Make camp for the night. Tomorrow we'll continue toward Port Vykor."

Malar had unsaddled the horses and brushed them down. Jimmy had discovered he was a competent enough groom along with his other talents. Jimmy said, "You feed the horses and I'll gather some firewood."

Malar said, "Yes, m'lord."

Jimmy moved around the campsite, finding enough small branches and sticks to make a reasonable fire.

After the fire was ready, Malar set about making an acceptable meal: hot trail biscuits, a mix of dried beef and vegetables chopped and mixed into a pot of rice, to which he added spices which made it quite flavorful. Malar produced a ceramic bottle of wine from Darkmoor. He even had a pair of cups.

As they ate, Jimmy said, "Port Vykor is a bit out of the way for you. If you're up to the risk, you may have that horse and ride on to the east. You're still north of the frontier and should be able to reach the vale safely."

Malar shrugged. "I will reach the vale eventually, my lord. My master is almost certainly dead, but perhaps his family has conspired to keep his business afloat and I can be of use to them. But I would rather spend a little more time in your company—the fierceness of your blade makes me more comfortable on the road than I would be alone."

"You managed well enough for those winter months you wandered in the wilderness."

"Of necessity, but not by choice. And most of that time was spent starving and hiding."

Jimmy nodded. He ate his meal and sipped his wine. "Is this off?" he asked.

Malar sipped his wine. "Not that I can tell, young lord."

Jimmy shrugged. "It's odd for this type of wine. Something metallic."

Malar took another sip. "Not that I can notice, sir. Perhaps you are just getting an odd aftertaste from the food. Maybe with the next drink it will taste differently."

Jimmy sipped again and swallowed. "No, it's definitely off." He set the cup aside. "I think some water would be better." Malar started to stand, and Jimmy said, "I'll get it." He started walking toward the creek and suddenly felt a wave of dizziness. He turned and looked to where the horses were tied. The horse seemed to be moving away from him, and then he felt as if he stepped into a hole, for he was now a great deal closer to the ground than before. He looked down and saw that he was on his knees, and as he tried to stand, his head swam. He fell hard to the ground and rolled over on his back. The face of Malar Enares moved into his view, and from a great distance, said, "I believe the wine *was* off, young Lord James."

The features of the man moved out of view and Jimmy tried to follow him. Jimmy rolled over and, lying with his head on his arm, he could see Malar move to Jimmy's horse, and open the pouches with all his messages to Duke

Duko. He glanced at several of them, nodded, and put them back into the pouch.

Jimmy felt his legs getting cold and felt a distant stab of panic. His thinking was growing foggy and he couldn't remember what it was he was supposed to do. His throat was tightening and his breathing was growing labored. Jimmy tried to force open his mouth with his left hand, which now felt as if he were wearing huge gloves. Dull sensations reached his brain, and suddenly he gagged on his own fingers, vomit rushing up through his mouth and nose. He gasped and choked, spat, and groaned aloud. His body wracked with pain as he felt his stomach heave again.

Malar's voice came from a great distance away. "It's a pity such a fair young lord has to come to such a messy and undignified end, but such are the necessities of war."

Somewhere in a dim evening, Jimmy heard a horse riding away, and then he was hit by another agonizing cramp and everything faded from view.

Dash looked across the faces of the men who had been recruited. Some were ex-soldiers, grey-haired men who remembered how to handle a sword. Others were street toughs, men who were just as likely to be brawling in a tavern as trying to keep the peace in the city. A few were mercenaries, looking for steady work, men who were clearly Kingdom citizens and who were not known criminals.

"We're presently under martial law in Krondor, which means just about any violation of the law is a hanging offense."

The men looked at one another, some nodding.

Dash continued, "This will start to change as of today. You are the first company of the new City Watch. You will be instructed in what that means in greater detail as we go, but unfortunately, we have no time to educate you before we begin. So, I will make a few things clear to you all." He held up a red armband, upon which a rough coat of arms, which looked like the Prince's, had been sewn. "You'll wear this at all times when on duty. It's what marks you as the Prince's men. You break a head while wearing this, you're restoring order; you break a head without it, and you're another thug I'll see behind bars. Is that clear?''

The men nodded and grunted agreement.

"I'll make this simple. This armband doesn't give you the right to bully, to settle old grudges, or to annoy the women in the town. Any man here who is convicted of assault, rape, or theft while wearing this will be hanged. Is that clear?''

The men were silent a moment, and a few nodded they understood. "Is that clear?" Dash repeated, and the men were more vocal in acknowledging the question.

"Now, until we can recruit a full-blown City Watch, the routine will be a half-day on, then a half-day off. One day in five, you'll work round the clock while the other half will get the day to themselves. If you know any men of arms-bearing age who can be recruited and can be trusted, send them to see me."

Using a chopping motion, he split the forty men in the room in half. "You," he said to the men on his right, "are the day watch. You," he said to the men on his left, "are the night watch. Get me another twenty good men and we'll go to three watches."

The men nodded.

Dash said, "Now, headquarters will be here in the palace until we can get the city courts and jail rebuilt. The prison here is the only one we have. We don't have a lot of room, so I don't want it filled with drunks and brawlers. If you have to break up a fight, send them home with a kick in the butt, but if you have to bring them in, don't be shy. I'll assume that if someone is stupid enough to not take a chance to get off with a warning, they need to talk to a judge.

"We're going to lift curfew at the Old Town Market; people are using it to trade now as the rest of the city rebuilds, and it's starting to be a trouble spot, but if we're going to have trouble, I want it in one place, not all over the city. So, pass the word, the market is open from sunset to midnight now. The rest of the city is still under curfew unless the person is on their way home from the market. And they better have the goods or gold to show they've been trading.

"Anyone causes you trouble, deal with it. We don't have enough swords to get you out of trouble if you get in over your head." He looked around the room at the faces of the men he now commanded and said, "If you're killed, I promise we'll avenge you."

One of the men said, "That's comforting," and the others laughed.

"I'll lead the first of you down to the market. You lot on the night shift, turn in. You're going to patrol the entire city, and if you see anyone outside the market after dark, bring them in for questioning.

"For today, anyone asks, you tell them you're the Prince's Law. Let's get the word out that order is returning to Krondor. Now, let's go."

The twenty men on the day shift rose and followed Dash outside the room. He moved through the large courtyard of the palace to the newly restored drawbridge over the still-dry moat. Some of the water system was still under repair and the palace wouldn't be isolated from the city by the moat again for a few more weeks. As they crossed the drawbridge, Dash said, "If no one causes any trouble and forces you to haul them back to the jail, I want you to keep moving. I want you everyplace you can reasonably reach. I want the citizens seeing lots of those red armbands . . . let them think we've got a dozen men for each one of you. If anyone asks, you don't know how many watchmen there are, just lots of them."

The men nodded, and as they walked toward the market square, Dash began splitting off pairs of constables and sending them along different routes, directing their activities for the first day of his new responsibility. More than once he silently cursed Patrick for his choice.

Dash was down to four men when he reached the market square of Krondor. Shortly after the original keep of the castle had been built, when the first Prince of Krondor had declared this city the capital of the Western Realm of the Kingdom of the Isles, the traders and local fishermen and farmers who lived in the region began regularly gathering in this market to trade, barter, and sell their wares. Over the years the city had grown, developed, and evolved to the point where the vast majority of trade was conducted by businessmen in all quarters of the city, but the ancient market square endured, and it was the first place for the reviving city to find its financial soul. It was thronging with men and women of all stations: merchants, nobles, fishermen, farmers, traders, peddlers, whores, beggars, thieves, and vagabonds.

Several people cast a wary eye at the five men, for while there were swordsmen here or there, the majority of soldiers had departed the city with Duko heading south, or with the Armies of the West, heading north. Only the Prince's Royal Household Guard remained, and they remained in the palace.

A short distance from where they had entered, Dash spied a familiar face. Luis de Savona was unloading a wagon, helped by a woman who turned out, to a surprised Dash, to be Roo Avery's wife Karli. Dash turned to his men and said, "Start wandering through the crowd, but unless you see a murder in progress, just keep looking."

The men spread out, and Dash crossed to where Luis and Karli were unloading the wagon. A local trader was watching closely as Luis handed down boxes of freight to the trader's boy.

Dash said, "Mrs. Avery! Luis! How are you?"

Luis looked over and smiled. "Dash! It's good to see you."

"When did you arrive in Krondor?"

"Very early this morning," replied Luis.

They shook hands, and Karli said, "I was very sorry to hear about your father. I still remember the day I first met him, at our house." She glanced over in the general direction of where their townhouse had once stood, across the street from Barret's Coffee House, now a burned-out husk of a building. "He was very kind to Roo and me."

Dash said, "Thank you. It's very difficult, but . . . well, you've lost your father, so you know."

She nodded.

Luis fingered the armband and said, "What is this?"

"I'm the new Sheriff of Krondor, and it falls to me to uphold the Prince's peace in the city."

Luis smiled. "You'd be better off coming back to work

for Roo. You'd lose your noble office, but you'd make a great deal more money with far less work.''

Dash laughed. ''Probably you're right, but as it is, we're very short-handed and Prince Patrick needs all of us pulling our weight.'' He glanced at the freight. ''Goods from Darkmoor?''

''No,'' said Luis. ''We unloaded our cargo from Darkmoor when we got in early this morning. These are from the Far Coast, actually. The ships still can't get into the harbor, but they're anchoring off of Fishtown and we're ferrying the goods ashore with fishing boats.''

Karli asked, ''How is your brother?''

''He's fine; he's running an errand for Patrick. He should be halfway to Port Vykor about now.''

Luis finished unloading the cargo, and said, ''Give us a minute, then I'll buy us an ale.''

''That would be welcome, Luis.''

Karli counted out the gold the merchant gave him, under the watchful eye of the merchant's bodyguard, and then said, ''Luis, we can't get young Dash drunk, so maybe we should get him to share a bite.'' She looked at Dash. ''Hungry?''

Dash said, ''Actually, I am.''

They walked across the market to an open-air kitchen, where hot meat pies were being sold. Karli purchased three, then they moved to an ale wagon, where Luis got three jacks of cold brew for them. Like most of those eating in the market, they stood and made do with keeping out of the way of those walking through the aisle.

Luis said, ''I was only partly joking; I could use someone of your talents. Things are beginning to turn around and men of talent are going to get rich.'' He motioned with his bad hand while juggling the hot pie with his good one. ''Since Helen and I married, Roo has made me manager of all Avery and Jacoby business while he's gone.''

Karli said, ''It's Avery and de Savon, now. Helen insisted.''

Luis smiled slightly. ''It wasn't my idea.'' He put down the pie and picked up the pewter jack of ale. After he took a drink, he said, ''I'm so busy I don't know what I need to do next. The wagon builders in Darkmoor are getting our freight business back to where it was before the destruction of the city, and the orders for cargo are starting to come in.''

"What about the other businesses that Roo held?"

Luis shrugged. "I'm in charge of the Avery and de Savon business. Most of the other was Bitter Sea Company. Roo hasn't said much. I get the feeling most of that is gone with the destruction of the city. I know he had some holdings in the East, but I think he's borrowed a great deal to get this enterprise underway. I know much about his business, but there is more that I don't know." He looked at Karli.

"Roo has told me most everything about his business interests," said Karli. "Except some things to do with the crown. I think the Kingdom owes Roo a large debt."

"No doubt," said Dash. "My grandfather got several very sizable loans from the Bitter Sea Company." Dash looked around. "While I suspect they will eventually be paid, as you can see, the Kingdom has a great deal to repair here before debts are settled." He finished his pie. With a long pull he drained the jack of ale, and said, "I thank you for the meal—"

Before he could say more, a shout from the next aisle caused him to turn. "Thief!"

Dash was off, hurrying toward the source of the disturbance. He rounded a corner and saw a man running right at him, looking over his shoulder to see who was behind. Dash braced himself, and as the man turned to look ahead, Dash struck him hard across the chest with an extended arm. As Dash expected, the man's feet went right out from under him and he fell hard upon the ground.

Dash knelt, his sword across the man's throat before he could regain his wits, and said, "In a hurry?"

The man started to move, but at the gentle pressure of the blade against his neck he relaxed. "Not anymore," he said with a grimace.

Two of Dash's constables appeared, and Dash said, "Take him to the palace."

Dash stood as they hoisted the thief to his feet and took him away. Dash moved to where Luis and Karli were finishing their meal, and said, "I'm going to borrow your wagon a moment.'' He moved to where the Avery and de Savon wagon was tied and mounted it. He stood up on the driver's seat and shouted, ''My name is Dashel Jamison! I am the new Sheriff of Krondor! The men you see wearing red armbands like mine are my constables. Pass the word that the law is returning to Krondor!''

Several merchants gave a weak cheer, but the majority of those gathered in the quarter seemed indifferent or openly contemptuous. Dash returned to where Karli and Luis stood. ''Well, I think that went rather well, don't you?''

Karli laughed, and Luis said, ''There are many here in the square who would just as soon not see any return of law to the city.''

Dash said, ''And I think I just spotted another of them. Excuse me,'' he said, darting into the crowd after a youngster he saw stealing a trinket from a distracted merchant.

Karli and Luis watched him until after he vanished into the press, and Karli said, ''I always liked that young man.''

Luis said, ''There's a great deal of his grandfather in him. He's a charming rogue.''

Karli said, ''Don't call him that. He has far too deep a sense of duty to be a rogue.''

Luis said, ''I stand corrected. You are, of course, right.''

Karli laughed. ''Helen has you trained well, doesn't she?''

Luis laughed in return. ''It was easy. I would never wish to make her unhappy.''

''Scant chance of that,'' said Karli. ''Well, we have another load waiting at the docks. Let's go get it.''

As Luis mounted the wagon, Karli put her hand on her lower back and stretched. ''I won't be doing this much longer. I hope Roo finished up his business to the north and gets back soon.''

Luis nodded agreement as she climbed the wagon, then he flicked the reins, getting the horses headed toward the harbor.

Lord Vasarius glanced to his left and said, ''Have you come to mock me, Avery?''

"Not in the least, my Lord Vasarius. I came out to enjoy the night air, as did you."

The defeated Quegan noble looked at his former business associate and current enemy. "Your Captain has been almost gracious in allowing me some liberty from that cabin."

"As is befitting your rank. Had our positions been reversed, I suspect I would be belowdecks on a Quegan ship, pulling against an oar."

"As is befitting your rank," replied Vasarius.

Roo laughed. "You haven't entirely lost your sense of humor, I see."

"I wasn't joking," Vasarius answered flatly.

Roo's smile faded. "Well, as fate would have it, you will enjoy a far less dire fate than I would have, it seems."

"I would have had you killed," said Vasarius.

"No doubt." Roo was silent a moment, then said, "My Prince is almost certain to return you to Queg by the first Free Cities ship heading there, as he has no desire to further antagonize your Emperor. It seems to me we have this opportunity to reach an accommodation."

Vasarius turned to face Roo. "Accommodation? To what purpose? You've won. I am close to ruin. My last copper piece was tied up in those ships and the cargo we sold to Fadawah. It's now at the bottom of the sea, and I can't see how you can be of any help to me, considering you were the one who sank my treasure!"

Roo shrugged. "Strictly speaking, you sank the treasure. I was merely trying to steal it.

"In any event, that wealth was stripped from the citizens of the Kingdom, and perhaps some from those living across the sea. I can't feel much sympathy for you losing *that* fortune, if you can see my point."

"Barely. But it's entirely academic, now, isn't it?"

"Not necessarily," said Roo.

"If you're proposing something, propose."

"I had nothing to do with your greed, Vasarius. If you had been anything near cautious, you wouldn't have dispatched your entire fleet to the Straits of Darkness on the strength of a rumor."

Vasarius laughed. "Of course, it was a rumor you spread."

"Of course," said Roo, "but any decent investigation might have made you reconsider the plan."

"Your Lord James was far too clever, by half. I'm sure, had I checked, I would have found more rumors to support the story of a vast treasure fleet coming from across the Endless Sea."

Roo said, "There is that. James had the most facile mind I've ever encountered. But that's not the point. The point is you have something to gain as do I, and we need to agree to that before we reach Krondor."

"What is that?"

"The price of my life."

Vasarius studied Roo for a long moment, then said, "Say on."

"I was taking that treasure ship of yours to Krondor. I would have sent the ship back to you, for I would not be counted a pirate, but the gold was taken from the Kingdom and was to be returned to the Kingdom." He smiled. "As it happens, the crown is in debt to me, considerable debt, and I suspect I would have accounted much of that treasure to that debt, so in a sense, it was more my treasure than yours."

Vasarius said, "Avery, your logic astonishes me."

"Thank you."

"It wasn't a compliment. Besides, the treasure resides below a great deal of ocean at the moment."

"Ah, but I know how to get it," said Roo.

Vasarius's eyes narrowed. He said, "And you need me to get it?"

"No, actually, I don't need you at all. In fact, unless you have access to certain magicians, you're of no use to me. I can locate members of the Wreckers Guild of Krondor. They're actively clearing the harbor right now, but the Prince will let me borrow some for a small commission."

"So then, why tell me this?"

"Because here's my offer. I will take what I raise from the ocean's floor. I will need to give one part in ten to the crown for interrupting their clearing of the harbor. And I will be forced to account the rest toward the debt of the crown, I am certain. And I will have to pay the guild's fee. But I am willing to divide what remains equally, and ship that half to Queg.''

"In exchange for what?"

"For you not engaging the services of a highly trained assassin as soon as you return to Queg."

"That is all?"

"More, a vow that you will never attempt to harm me or my family, nor will you idly allow anyone over whom you have influence in Queg to trouble us."

Vasarius was silent for a very long time, and Roo resisted the impulse to speak.

Finally the Quegan noble said, "If you can do this and account to me half the money you raise less the Prince's cut and the guild's fee, then I will agree to seek no further reprisals against you or your family."

The night air was cooling, and Roo hugged himself. "That takes a great load off my mind."

"Is there anything else?" asked Vasarius.

"One suggestion," said Roo.

"What?"

"Consider that when this war with Fadawah's invaders is over, there will be many opportunities for profit. But not if a war erupts between Queg and the Kingdom. Both sides have suffered from the invaders' intrusion into the Bitter Sea, and more war would bleed us all white."

"Agreed," said Vasarius. "We are not ready to fight a war."

"That's not the point. The point is when you're ready to fight one, it still does neither side any good."

"That is for us to decide," said the Quegan.

"Well, if you don't see it my way, at least consider this: there is going to be a great deal of profit in rebuilding the entire Bitter Sea after the war with Fadawah is finished, and those who aren't fighting are going to be able to reap most of it. I could use associates in many of the undertakings I'll be contemplating."

"You have the effrontery to suggest an association, after I made that terrible mistake once already?"

"No, but if you should someday choose to make it, I will listen."

Vasarius said, "I have heard enough. I will return to my cabin."

"Think on this, then, my lord," said Roo as the Quegan walked away. "There will be a great many men needing transport across the sea to Novindus, and there are few ships able to carry them. The fees for such transport will not be trivial."

Vasarius paused the briefest instant, then continued walking, until he disappeared down the ladder to the main deck and the cabins below.

Roo turned and looked out at the star-filled night, watching the whitecaps on the water. "I've got him!" he whispered to himself.

Jimmy felt as if someone had kicked in his ribs. It hurt to breathe and someone was tugging at his collar. A distant voice said, "Drink this."

Something wet touched his lips and he felt cool water fill his mouth and he drank reflexively. Suddenly his stomach knotted and he spewed forth the water, convulsing as strong hands held him.

His eyes were stuck shut. His head rang and his back felt as if his spine had been hammered by a mace; his trousers were fouled with his own excrement. Again water was forced between his lips and a voice in his ear said, "Sip slowly."

Jimmy let the water trickle slowly down his throat, a few drops at a time, and this time his stomach accepted the bounty. Other hands picked him up and moved him.

He passed out.

Sometime later, he woke up again, and found that a half-dozen armed men had set up a camp. One sat near by and said, "Do you feel up to drinking some more water?"

Jimmy nodded and the man brought him a cup of water. Jimmy drank and suddenly was terribly thirsty. He drank more, and after the third cup, the man took away the waterskin, saying, "No more. For a while at least."

Jimmy said, "Who are you?" His voice sounded dry and distant, as if it was being used by a stranger.

"My name is Captain Songti. I recognize you. You're the one called Baron James."

Jimmy sat up and said, "It's Earl James now. I got a new office." He glanced around and saw the sun was rising in the east. "How long?"

"We found you an hour after sunset. We had been preparing to make camp a short distance from here, and as is my practice, I had a rider sweep the perimeter. He saw your campfire. When we rode over to investigate, we found you lying there. There was no blood, so we thought you might have sickened on food."

"I was poisoned," said Jimmy. "In wine. I drank little."

The Captain, a round-faced man with a short beard, said, "A fine palate. It saved your life."

"Malar wasn't trying very hard to kill me. He could have cut my throat easily enough."

"Perhaps," said the Captain. "Or he could have fled against our arrival. He may have been gone only minutes before we arrived. He could have heard us before we saw him. I don't know."

James nodded, then wished he hadn't. His head swam. "My horse?"

"There are no horses here. You, your bedroll, a low burning fire, and that empty cup you held, that was all that was here."

Jimmy held out his hand. "Get me to my feet."

"You should rest."

"Captain," Jimmy ordered. "Help me stand."

The Captain did as he was bid, and when Jimmy stood, he asked, "Have you some extra clothing you can spare?"

"Alas, no," said the Captain. "We are but three days from Port Vykor and ready to return."

"Three days . . ." Jimmy said. He said nothing a moment, then said, "Help me walk to the creek."

"May I enquire why?" asked the Captain.

"Because I need to bathe. And wash my clothing."

The Captain said, "I understand, but we would do well to return to Port Vykor as quickly as possible, so you may recover in comfort."

"No, because after I bathe I have other business."

"Sir?"

"I need to find someone," said Jimmy as he looked down the southeastern road, "and then I need to kill him."

Sixteen

Deception

Erik FROWNED.

Owen swore. "We were taken like bumpkins at the fair."

Subai, still covered with road dirt and exhausted from days of nonstop riding, said, "Patrick was correct. They let us have Sarth, and while they were taking LaMut, they built that."

"That" was an impressive series of earthen barricades running from a steep hillside that was impossible to scale by anything less surefooted than a mountain goat down to the cliffs overlooking the sea. The woods for almost a thousand yards had been cleared, with low stumps left to confound any attempt at organizing a cavalry charge. The only break in the structure was a huge wooden gate across the King's Highway, easily as big as the northern city gates in Krondor.

The first hundred yards rolled down to a tiny creek which crossed the roadway, and from that point to the barricade the terrain rose steeply. To charge that position would be to invite serious casualties, and any attempt at wheeling a ram would be undercut by the need to force the device uphill. The breastwork was built up to six feet in height, and as Erik could see helmets reflecting the sun behind it, he assumed steps had been built up behind so that archers could fire down upon anyone charging up the slope.

Erik counted. "I see at least a dozen catapults back there."

Subai said, "That's a nasty piece of work."

Greylock was forced to agree. "Let's talk about this."

They moved away from the forward position, past the arrayed companies of Kingdom soldiers ready to attack if the order was given. In a clearing a hundred yards behind the front lines, they gathered. Owen said, "I don't see any easy way through that."

Erik said, "Agreed, but what has me worried is how many more positions like that we may face as we travel up the coast to Quester's View."

Owen said, "We might ask our guest." He indicated a position to the rear where General Nordan and some other key captains of Fadawah's army were being guarded. Most of the captives from Sarth were still under guard in that town, but the officers were accompanying Greylock's command company. Owen and the others walked over toward a pavilion being erected for the officers and waved the guards near Nordan to bring him over.

Nordan reached the tent just as table and chairs were being placed for Greylock to sit. He did so, letting Erik and the very tired Subai also sit, but he kept Nordan standing. "Now," Greylock said, "how many of these defensive positions can we expect between here and Quester's View?"

Nordan shrugged. "I do not know. Fadawah did not see fit to keep me informed of what was occurring behind my lines." He glanced around. "If he had, I wouldn't be standing here talking to you, Marshal. I would be over there, behind the breastwork."

"Sold you out, did he?" asked Erik.

"Unless he has some masterful plan to swoop down on the back of a dragon and carry me back to Ylith, apparently."

"Duko told us Fadawah feared rivals for command of the army."

Nordan nodded. "I was sent to Sarth to watch Duko more than I was to achieve any sort of secondary defense here in the South." He glanced around. "May I sit?"

Owen waved for a chair to be brought over, and when it was, Nordan sat. "Once the assault on Krondor was underway, I was going to ride down, watch a bit of the battle, ride north, and make a decision on fortifying the town or withdrawing north. You neglected to assault Krondor, so of course, I never got to make that decision."

"Lord Duko thought a change in allegiance seemed propitious," said Subai. "Without his cooperation, we never would have taken Sarth so easily."

"Lord Duko," said Nordan, as if weighing the sound of it. "He is now a Kingdom man, then?"

"That he is. He has command of our southern border with Great Kesh," replied Greylock.

"Would it be possible," asked Nordan, "for another such accommodation to be made?"

Owen laughed. "Duko had an army and a city to offer. What do you bring to the table?"

Nordan said, "I was afraid it would be something like that."

"Well," said Erik, "if you think those on the other side of the barricade would surrender on your word, we might be able to find sufficient incentive to make your future here more pleasant."

"Von Darkmoor, isn't it?" asked Nordan.

Erik nodded. "You know me?"

"We were looking for you long enough when your Captain Calis took his Crimson Eagles and turned renegade. We knew of the one who looked like a Long Lived, and we knew of the big young blond sergeant who fought like a demon. The Emerald Queen may have been a servant of darkness, but she had clever men among her officers."

Nordan grew reflective. "Kahil was one of her men, yet he managed to insinuate himself into Fadawah's trust. I am Fadawah's oldest companion." He looked at Erik. "You served with us long enough to know how our ways differ from yours. A Prince is an employer, no more worthy of loyalty than a merchant. To a hired sword, he is but a merchant with more gold.

"Fadawah and I began as boys, from nearby villages in the Westlands. We joined Jamagra's Iron Fists and started fighting. For years we served together, and when Fadawah started his own company, I was his subcaptain. When he became a general, I was his second-in-command. When he met the woman known as the Emerald Queen and swore dark oath to her, I went along.''

Subai looked at Erik, who nodded, and said, ''I think we need to know of this man, Kahil.''

Nordan said, ''He was one of her captains. We met him when she sent for Fadawah and arranged for him to take command of her forces. I thought it strange that she would seek us out when she already had commanders, but the money was good and she proposed conquests that would do nothing but make us rich beyond imagining.

''Kahil specialized in sneaking inside of cities before we attacked them, gathering information and sowing discord among the populace. He spent more time with the Emerald Queen than anyone save Fadawah, and those men she called her Immortals, the men who willingly died in her bed to feed her hunger.''

''You knew of that?'' asked Erik.

''You hear things. You try to ignore anything that distracts you from the task at hand. I was her sworn Captain, and until I either was released from duty, captured or killed, I would not betray her.''

''Understood,'' said Erik.

''When the chaos around Krondor revealed that we had been somehow tricked by a demonic creature and that the Emerald Queen was no longer our true mistress, we were left to fend for ourselves. Fadawah is an ambitious man. Kahil is also an ambitious man. I suspect it was he who proposed to Fadawah that my fate be much the same as Duko's.

''I was led to believe that we would keep a soft center in Sarth, with a thousand men secreted in the lower halls of the abbey. When your army was safely up the road, I was to ride out and strike from behind while Fadawah was rolling your army south along the coast.'' Bitterly he said, ''I never got the men. I should have known that the third time twenty men showed up when I expected two hundred. Instead I got a long visit from Kahil, who inspected the abbey and told me all was going according to plan. I got less than four hundred men in total, most of them of questionable skills.''

Owen said, ''We'll have to decide what to do with you later, General. For the moment, I have the problem of getting up north and getting the Duchy of Yabon back for my King.''

Nordan stood. ''I understand, Marshal. I will by force of circumstances await your pleasure.''

Greylock signaled to a guard to return the captive General to the company of the other officers. After he was out of hearing range, Owen said, ''He said one thing that disturbs me.''

''What?'' asked Erik.

''That remark he attributed to this Kahil: 'All was going according to plan.' ''

Subai said, ''I came up through the basement of the abbey. I saw nothing we need to fear.''

''I don't think he meant the abbey,'' said Owen. ''I think he meant some larger scheme that Fadawah is hatching.''

Erik said, ''All of which we will learn in due time.''

Owen pointed his finger at his old friend. ''That's what has me fearful.'' He pointed at the tabletop. He motioned for food to be brought and servants hurried to comply. To one of the junior officers standing nearby he said, ''Let me know when all the commanders report their units are in place.''

Erik was silent a moment, then said, ''We could hit them at night.''

''At night?'' asked Subai.

Erik's tone indicated he didn't strongly advocate the idea, but was rather just speculating. ''If we could get close to the barricade before they spotted our advance units, perhaps we could force a breach before they started doing too much damage with those catapults and archery fire.''

Owen was dubious. ''I think we do this the traditional way. Order camp, and tell the men to rest. At first light we assemble, we march out and stand in ranks. I'll ride forward with Erik and ask for surrender, and when they say no, we'll attack.''

Erik sighed. ''I wish I could think of something very clever.''

"Subai, can you see any way to get some of our soldiers around the hillside end of the barricade?"

"A few maybe," answered the Captain. "But not enough to do more than get them all killed when they were discovered. If my Pathfinders were to do it, we could get up there and be in position before we were discovered, I'm certain."

"But you have to be on your way north, carrying messages," said Owen. "No, gentlemen, this time we must walk up and kick down the door. See to your men."

Erik stood up. "I'll inspect the deployment."

Owen motioned for Erik to stay, and when the other officers were gone, he said, "Can you get some men on the beach below those cliffs?"

"I can get them down to the beach, but I don't know if I can get them up the cliffs," said Erik.

"Then you'd better get down there and see, before you lose the daylight. If you can get a squad up those cliffs and over the top before they see you coming, you could spring that gate from the inside."

Erik considered it. "It is closer to the cliffside than the hillside by a hundred yards or so, isn't it?"

"Think you can do it?"

Erik said, "Let me go down and take a look. I'll be back as soon as possible."

He heaved himself out of the chair and moved to where his Crimson Eagles were camped. "Jadow!" he shouted, "bring a squad!"

The large lieutenant and a sergeant named Hudson fell in almost instantly, and by the time Erik had moved to where the horses were picketed, he had a dozen other men hurrying along to catch up. The horses were saddled and ready to ride in minutes, and Erik formed up his squad. He glanced around, astonished at how well the army was being encamped. The move from Sarth northward had been at a forced march and the quartermasters had been pressed to their limit to get provisions together and underway on short notice. Yet here was the bulk of the Armies of the West, nearly eight thousand men under arms in the van, with another ten thousand less than a week behind, moving into locations preselected by Owen's staff. Logistics was still more an abstract concept to Erik than a real one. His time on the road had been in Calis's small companies in Novindus, or in defensive positions in Krondor and Darkmoor. This was his first experience having responsibility for large numbers of men on the march.

The dust was almost overwhelming from the thousands of men, wagons, and horses moving along both sides of the road. He knew he could ride freely down the cliffs to the coast and no enemy spotter would be able to see anything that would give away his inspection of the beach area.

He found the path leading down to a cove a mile behind the lines and led the patrol downward. The road narrowed as it wound down to the beach, so they rode single file.

They halted while Erik looked up and down the coast. He turned to the men Jadow had gathered, and said, "Any good swimmers here?"

Two of the men held up their hands, and Erik grinned at Jadow. "Oh, no, man. Not since we had to swim that river to get to Maharta."

Erik jumped down and began removing his armor. "This time we won't have to wear eighty pounds of iron." Jadow dismounted and, muttering curses, also started stripping off his armor.

The two men who had volunteered were soon standing next to Erik and Jadow, all wearing only their undertunics and leggings. Erik said, "We swim in pairs. This current looks rough. And be wary of the rocks."

He led the men as far along the beach as they could go before encountering the finger of cliff that extended into the rocks. Wading out into the surf, he turned and said, "It's safer to swim, I think, than to risk wading through the surf as it pounds those rocks."

The men followed, and Erik led them out until the waves started to break. He dove under a breaking wave and came up behind it. He struck out away from the beach, and when the water was merely surging back and forth, turned on a course that ran along the beach. The water was cold despite the time of the year, and the going difficult, but after a few minutes, Erik saw that he had left his partner behind. He waited and let the man catch up, then started swimming again. They drew even with the first of a series of small coves, and stopped, letting the others catch up and tread water a moment. He said, "We need to swim about another mile, then head in." He pointed. "The beach seems to open up over there."

Jadow said, "I can't tell; all I see is breaking surf and rocks."

"Well, avoid the rocks," said Erik, setting out again with powerful strokes.

He led them around a second point of land and toward more rocks. He stopped and pointed. "There! A section of open beach."

He swam straight in toward the breakers, catching one to ride in, and stood up in knee-deep water. He looked around and saw the other three men also riding waves in, though Jadow seemed to have swallowed a fair amount of water on the way.

Erik glanced up to the cliffs. He motioned and said, "I think we're between our lines and theirs." Looking up and down the coast, he said, "It's difficult to tell."

After a moment to catch his breath, he continued, "Come on. We're going to have our work cut out for us to get back before dark."

Jadow groaned.

"What?" asked Erik.

"Man, I just didn't even think; we've got to swim back, don't we?"

Erik and the other men laughed. "Unless you want to stay down here."

As Erik started off at a trot up the beach, Jadow said, "I'm thinking a beach life might be the thing; I could fish, make a hut, you know."

Erik grinned. "You'd get bored."

They hurried along the base of the cliffs, Erik looking up from time to time. They found a long, winding beach, a series of tidal pools, and some large outcroppings of rocks, but Erik was at last convinced they were a safe distance behind the enemy fortification without being seen.

He looked upward and asked, "Jadow, what do you think about climbing that cliff?"

Jadow looked upward and finally said, "Not much."

"Can it be done?"

"Possibly, but it's a job for the Pathfinders. They are very good at that sort of thing."

"The Pathfinders are going around the eastern end of the line, up the hills and north; Subai's got messages to get to Yabon."

"Well, then, do we have anyone else in camp who might be foolish enough to swim over here and climb those rocks for a little hand-to-hand mayhem?"

Erik looked at Jadow, then said, "I think I may have just the lot."

Owen said, "Let me get this straight. You want me only to hit them with probing attacks tomorrow?"

Erik pointed along the line of defense freshly drawn on Owen's map. "We're going to bleed if we storm that wall. We can put that off a day or two longer. But if I can get up over the cliff, open the gate so you can get inside, we can shorten this attack by days. And we'll save a lot of men's lives."

"But if you don't get to the gate, you're going to get yourself chopped up," said Owen.

Erik said, "Last time I looked, no one promised a soldier he would live forever."

Owen closed his eyes, then said, "Life used to be much easier when you were shoeing horses and I was teaching Otto's other sons how to hold a sword."

Erik sat down and said, "I won't argue that."

Owen said, "So, who are you taking with you? Climbing those cliffs will be dangerous . . . or am I stating the obvious?"

"You are," said Erik with a smile. He took a mug of wine offered him by an orderly, then said, "Akee and his Hadatis just showed up this morning. They're the best climbers we have."

Owen nodded approval. "That they are. And a handy bunch with a sword, as I recall."

"Very."

"Well, I was going to send them along the ridge route, but if I give Subai all the Pathfinders, he stands a better chance of getting through to Yabon."

''I haven't read the rolls of the fallen. How many Path-finders have we left?''

''Too few. We have too few of everyone,'' said Owen. ''We lost more men of quality at Darkmoor and Nightmare Ridge than the Gods should fairly ask of us. We are moving with the heart of the Army of the West, and if we fall, there's nothing left.'' He sighed. ''Subai has fourteen Path-finders left in his entire command.''

''Fourteen?'' Erik shook his head and his expression was one of regret. ''He had over a hundred before the war.''

''Those trackers and scouts are rare men,'' said Owen. ''You don't train them overnight like your band of cut-throats.''

Erik smiled. ''My cutthroats have proven themselves more times than any other unit in this army. And we've lost more of the Eagles than I care to think about.'' For a moment he reflected on the men whom he had served with during two voyages to Novindus, Luis and Roo, Nakor and Sho Pi, and those fallen at the battles along the way—Billy Goodwin, who fell off his horse and broke his head, Biggo the pious brawler, and Harper, who was twice the sergeant Erik had ever been, among many others. And most of all, one man. ''As much as I wish Calis was still leading this bunch instead of myself,'' he said to Owen, ''more than any other, I'd give half my remaining years to have Bobby de Loungville back.''

Owen raised his wine cup. ''Amen to that, my boy. Amen to that.'' He drank. ''But he'd be proud of you, no doubt.''

Erik said, ''When this is over, and we start taking men down to Novindus, I want to find that ice cave and bring Bobby home.''

Owen said, ''Men have done crazier things before. But dead is dead, and buried is buried, Erik. Of all the men who fell, why Bobby?''

''Because he was Bobby? Most of us wouldn't be alive today save for what he taught us, we in the Eagles. Calis was our Captain, but Bobby was our soul.''

''Well, if you can get the Prince to release you from duty for a time, maybe you can do it. Me, I'll be asking him to promote you again to take some weight off my shoulders.''

"Thanks, but I'll refuse."

Owen said, "Why? You've got a wife, and I expect someday children, and a promotion means more money as well as rank."

"I'm not worried about money. I mean, I have enough, even if the investments that Roo's made for me don't work out. I'll take care of Kitty and any children, but I just don't want to become a staff officer."

Greylock said, "There won't be much need for captains once the war is over, Erik. The nobility will again come to the fore and start taking care of keeping the peace."

Erik shook his head. "I don't think that's wise. I think the Riftwar and this war show we need a larger standing army. With Kesh again making moves along the South, and with as many casualties as we've taken, I think the Prince needs more men under arms at all times than we've had before here in the West."

"You're not the first to say that," said Owen, "but the politics . . . the nobles will never stand for it."

"They will if the King orders it," said Erik. "And someday Patrick will be King."

"Now there's a chilling thought," joked Owen.

Erik said, "He'll grow up."

Owen laughed. "Listen to you. You're the same age!"

Erik shrugged. "I feel older than my years."

"Well, you are," said Owen, "and that's a fact. Now, get out and find those Hadati and ask them if they're crazy enough to do as you ask. If they say no, I will not be surprised, as they strike me as being a smarter than average bunch."

Erik rose, saluted casually, and departed. When he was gone, Owen looked at the map and said to the orderly, "Send for Captain Subai, please."

Jimmy pointed. "Up there." He had commandeered a horse and sent two men back to Port Vykor, riding double. He had ordered the other ten men to accompany him in his pursuit of Malar, and he knew the spy had only one possible destination.

Jimmy was certain now that Malar Enares was a Keshian spy. A simple thief would have taken Jimmy's weapons

and gold. He only took Jimmy's horse to have a spare as
he fled to Keshian lines. The fact he had first taken the
Prince's orders to Lord Duko was the single most indicting
evidence.

Captain Songti and the other men looked uncertain about
the young noble's orders, but they obeyed. As they stopped
to rest their horses, Songti said, "Lord James—"

"Jimmy. My grandfather was Lord James."

"Lord Jimmy," amended Songti.

"Just Jimmy."

With a shrug, Songti said, "Jimmy, you move with certain purpose, and don't seem to be following tracks. Can I
assume you know where this fugitive is heading?"

"Yes," said Jimmy. "There are few places a man can
safely travel between Kesh and the Kingdom, and there is
only one crossing point near enough where he stands a
chance of finding a Keshian patrol before running into ours.
It's up there"—he pointed to a distant range of low mountains—"in the high desert. It's Dulsur Pass. It's a very
narrow little defile that empties out at the oasis of Okateo.
Very popular with smugglers."

"And spies," suggested Songti.

"Yes," said Jimmy.

"If you know of this place, sir, why not keep a garrison
there?"

Jimmy shrugged. "Because we find it as useful to keep
open as the Keshians do."

"I don't think I'll ever understand this society of yours,
sir."

"Well, when the war is over, you may return to Novindus should you wish."

Songti said, "I am a soldier and I have served Lord Duko
most of my life. I wouldn't know what to do back in Novindus. None of us would."

Jimmy motioned it was time to resume riding. "Well, as
sure as the sun rises in the east, there are those down in
Novindus building their own little empires as much as Fadawah is here."

"Some of the younger men might wish to return," said
Songti as he remounted. "But most of us who have been

with Duko for a while will make lives here, in your Kingdom.''

''Then it's time for you to begin thinking of it as *our*
Kingdom.''

''So my lord Duko instructs,'' admitted Songti as he motioned the patrol forward.

They rode up a dusty trail, into plateau country, long
rolling vistas of dust, tough dry plants, and sun-bleached
rock. A dry wind struck, and grit collected in a man's eyes,
nose, and threatened to peel skin from bone. Even water
tasted gritty when drunk, as the fine, powdery sand got
everywhere.

They reached a high plateau and Jimmy pointed upward.
''The oasis is at the top of that.'' He pointed at another
plateau, easily a thousand feet higher than the one upon
which they stood. Looking backward, they could see the
lowlands leading down to Shandon Bay.

Songti said, ''From here on a clear day you can see the
bay, I think.''

''More,'' said Jimmy. ''On a very clear day I have been
told you can see the peaks of the Calasitius Mountains to
the north.'' He urged his horse forward and they continued,
moving upward.

Night found them resting in a large pass, sheltered from
the wind and sand. They sat on the rocks, their saddles
behind them or under their feet. The horses were staked out
a short way away. Jimmy ordered a cold camp against the
possibilities others were nearby, or that Malar was looking
over his shoulder.

Jimmy knew that he stood a fair chance of overtaking
the spy if he didn't know his way through these hills as
well as Jimmy. He might have been a boy in far Rillanon,
but his grandfather made sure he and his brother knew
every weakness along the border with Kesh: smugglers'
coves, trails, goat paths, creeks, and gaps in the mountains.
And Lord James's knowledge had been encyclopedic,
Jimmy remembered; he had made sure his grandsons knew
of every potential attack corridor into the Kingdom.

Chewing jerked beef, Captain Songti said, ''Are you certain we'll catch this spy?''

''We must. He stole orders to Duko and knows too much

about the lack of defenses in Krondor. The orders also detail our plan for dealing with the threat to Land's End.''

"We have encountered a few of these Keshians. They are determined fighters.''

"Keshian Dog Soldiers are not known for cowardice. Occasionally their leaders are, but if they're ordered to fight to the last man, they will.''

"If we catch this man, we avoid a big fight?''

"Yes,'' said Jimmy.

"Then we shall have to catch this man.''

"At first light we leave,'' said Jimmy. He gathered his cloak about him and said, "Wake me just before.''

Akee and his men spread out along the base of the cliff. Erik said, "What's the best way to proceed?''

They had carried bundles of weapons and dry clothing wrapped in oil-treated canvas, swimming the route Erik had previously discovered. The plan was to get to the top of the cliff in the darkness, and just before dawn, Subai's Pathfinders, as well as a few dozen Krondorian regulars, would make as much noise as possible at the far end of the defenders' wall, hoping to make them think the Kingdom forces were attempting to circle the barricades on the hillside. They would retreat as soon as engaged, with Subai and his Pathfinders climbing the steep hillside and up into the mountains. Once past this barrier, they'd start their journey along the western slopes of the mountains, making their way to Yabon. The Krondorians would retreat with a lot of noise, apparently in disorder.

The hope was this would allow the Hadati and Erik to slip in behind the defenders and reach the gate. If they could get it open, Greylock promised they only had to hold it for two minutes. He had two companies of cavalry, light bowmen who could cross the gap in less than two minutes, and a company of one hundred heavy lancers, who could sweep behind the line and clear the wall of defenders.

From above the cliffs came the sounds of men shouting as Greylock's probing attacks were withdrawn. The defenders had been dealing with them since noon, and as the sun set, Owen was quitting the attacks. Erik prayed the attacks had kept the defenders busy enough not to peer over the cliffs. Otherwise there might be a very nasty reception waiting for them at the top.

Akee looked upward and said, "Pashan is our best climber. He goes first and carries a cord. If he reaches the top, we will tie the cord to a rope and he will pull it up." With a slight smile, Akee added, "Even you should be able to reach the top of the cliffs with a rope to hang on to, Captain."

Erik said, "I am flattered by your confidence in me."

The man named Pashan took off his weapons, the long blade most Hadati carried over their backs, and the short blade carried at the belt. He was short, compact, and his arms and legs looked powerful. He stripped off his soft buckskin boots and handed everything to a companion. He took the light cord and carefully coiled it around his chest and shoulder, so he wore it like the plaid most Hadati wore when sporting clan dress. The bulk of it trailed behind him to a coil resting on the sand. Akee had instructed the men to be careful it uncoiled without any hitch, lest Pashan be pulled off balance by unexpected resistance.

Pashan adjusted his kilt and started to climb. Erik glanced to the west. The sun had set a few minutes earlier, and now they were watching a brave man carefully scale a cliff face in failing light. It would be dark before he safely reached the top.

The minutes dragged by and upward the man climbed, each hand and foot moved carefully, testing the grip or footing. Like a fly on a wall, he moved slowly upward, slightly to the right of his starting point.

Erik was amazed. At first he was twenty feet above, then thirty, then forty. At fifty feet he was a third of the way to the top. He did not stop to rest, and Erik decided that hanging on the face of the rocks was no more rest than climbing would be. At no time did Pashan's rhythm change. A step, a grip, a shift of weight, and up he would move.

As darkness descended, it became more difficult to see him moving among the rocks. Erik lost sight of him in the inky shadows between the rocks, then he caught sight of movement; Pashan was now two-thirds of the way to the top of the cliffs.

Again he vanished into the gloom and the minutes

dragged by. As the night deepened into darkness—no moons would rise until near dawn this night—finally the cord began to jerk up and down.

"Tie the rope," instructed Akee.

The remaining cord was cut and tied tightly around the end of a much heavier rope. When it was secured, they tugged three times firmly on the cord. Pashan rapidly pulled the rope upward.

The rope continued to pay out, then jerked up and down again. The first jerks had been the signal Pashan had reached the top of the cliffs and to tie the rope. The second signal indicated either he had tied off the rope, or he was now digging in to hold it. The second man up the rope would be the smallest remaining. He would join with Pashan and hold the end. Each man after would add his strength as the larger men climbed.

The second man had his weapons tied in a bundle slung over his back and started up hand over hand, using his feet to boost him along the surface of the rocks. Erik was amazed at how fast he climbed.

Then the third man went up.

The night's silence was cut by the distant sounds from the enemy's camp, but not alarms or the sounds of fighting. Slowly the squad of fifty Hadati hillmen reached the summit, and at last Erik and Akee were alone on the beach.

"I'll go after you," said Erik.

Akee nodded and was up the rope without a word.

Erik waited, then gripped the rope. He was never a good climber, so he wanted to be last in case he slipped. If he was going to fall to his death, he wasn't about to knock Akee off the rope behind him.

Erik found his feet to be of little aid to him as he struggled up the rope. He was a powerful man, with a huge upper body, yet he was also a heavy man. His arms were burning and his back cramping with pain as he reached a point near the summit. Suddenly the rope began to move and for an instant Erik felt a stab of panic before he realized he was being pulled up.

Akee reached over the edge of the cliff, took Erik by the wrist, and with a yank hauled him up to safety. With a whisper, he said, "Someone comes."

Erik nodded, pulling his belt knife out and looking around. They were in a sparse stand of trees, pines and aspens, and as far as he could tell, he and Akee were alone. The other Hadati had somehow managed to vanish into the woods.

Akee quickly moved to cut off the rope tied to a tree nearby and cast the remnants off the cliff. Then he pulled Erik away and they slipped off into the woods.

From a short distance he heard men walking, and one spoke in the language of Novindus. "I don't hear nothing."

"I tell you, I thought I heard something, like someone moving around."

"There's no one here," came the first voice.

Erik hugged the side of a small oak, glancing through the lower branches of a pair of star pines as two figures emerged from the other side of the clearing. One carried a torch. "This is a fool's errand."

"Then you're just the man for the job," said the other.

"Very funny." They reached the clearing before the cliffs and the first man said, "That's a long way down, so don't get too close."

"Don't need to tell me, lad. I have no love for heights."

"Then how did you get up the wall at Krondor?"

"Didn't," said the second man. "I waited for them to blow up the walls and walked in."

"You were lucky," said the first man. "See, no one here. What did you think? Someone was sending monkeys climbing them cliffs, or some sort of magic thing?"

"I've seen enough weird magic things to last me my lifetime, that's a fact," said the second man as they turned to retrace their steps to the camp. "What about that demon thing and the Queen, and them snake priests? If I never see magic again in this life, it's fine by me."

"Did I tell you the time I met that dancer in Hamsa? Now that was magic."

"Only six or seven times, so spare me . . ."

The voices faded off into the night. From behind Erik heard a voice say, "They think the woods empty."

"Good," said Erik to Akee. "Then we can wait until just before first light to make our move."

Erik said, "Spread the word. Have the men stay where they are, out of sight. We gather an hour before dawn."

Akee vanished into the gloom without a word.

Seventeen

Assaults

JIMMY POINTED.

Captain Songti said, "I see them."

They were scouting out the well at Okatio oasis, and lounging in the shade of the desert willows was a patrol of Keshian soldiers.

"Those are Imperial Borderers," whispered Jimmy. "See those long lances?"

Leaning against the rocks near where the horses were staked out, rested twenty long slender spears with banners attached. Songti said, "Looks like we want to get in close, fast."

"Yes," said Jimmy. "No archers."

"Is that your man?" asked Songti, pointing at a figure on the far side of the campfire.

"That's him," said Jimmy. Malar was sitting next to a Keshian officer, who was examining the bundle of dispatches Jimmy had been carrying to Duko. "We've got to kill them all before they leave in the morning."

Songti said, "They're pretty lax at camp."

"They're arrogant bastards, but they've earned it. They're among the best light cavalry the world has seen. Those fellows with the long hair they pile up under their helmets when they ride"—he pointed to six men who were slightly apart, relaxing around a large pot of food, speaking quietly—"are Ashunta horsemen, from deep within the Empire. Man for man they are the best riders in the world."

"Some of my lads might take exception to that," said Songti.

Jimmy grinned. "The best horsemen in Triasia?"

"Not since we got here," said Songti. He turned and signaled. His men were hanging back down the trail. They slowly moved forward.

Jimmy said, "As soon as you attack, Malar is going to jump on the nearest horse and ride that way." He pointed to a pass to the south, leading down into the borderlands of Kesh. "Let me get over there, and if he does, I'll jump him from those rocks."

Songti said, "I'll go with you. He might bring a friend."

"Ignore the friend unless it's that officer looking at those documents. First thing we must do is get them back and kill any man who reads them."

"That makes it easy," said Songti. "We'll just have to kill them all."

Jimmy admired the man's confidence. There was a full patrol of twenty Keshian Borderers taking their ease around the well, and only ten Kingdom soldiers with Jimmy. Jimmy said, "Hit them fast." He got up and in a crouching run skirted the rocks above the oasis until he was poised above the point he had indicated.

Songti communicated with his men using hand signals, then came and stood beside Jimmy.

Suddenly chaos erupted at the oasis and men shouted. While outnumbered, the Kingdom soldiers were given the advantage of surprise. Without looking, Jimmy knew men were dying before they reached their weapons. The sound of bows was reassuring as only Songti's men had them.

As he predicted, Jimmy heard a shout and a rider coming fast through the defile. He readied himself.

Malar rounded the bend riding bareback, having taken time only to slip a bridle on his horse, and carrying only the bundle of messages. As he passed, Jimmy leaped out, sweeping the man from his horse. The bundle went flying and Jimmy tucked his shoulder, rolling on the ground and coming to his feet with a grunt of pain. He had struck a rock outcropping and could feel his left arm going numb. He knew instantly he had dislocated his shoulder.

Another horse appeared and Songti jumped out, sweeping a rider from his saddle, and Jimmy barely dodged the second horse as it raced by. He turned, trying to find Malar, and saw the spy attempting to flee down the trail after the horse.

Clutching his sword in his right hand, his left dangling limply at his side, Jimmy ran after him, past Songti, who was sitting astride the chest of a Keshian, choking the life from him.

Malar reached a bend in the trail, and Jimmy lost sight of him. He hurried after, and as he rounded the bend, pain exploded in his left shoulder.

Malar had climbed aboard a boulder and had kicked him hard, aiming for his head, but striking his shoulder instead. The effect was nearly the same, for the pain in Jimmy's left shoulder nearly rendered him unconscious. An involuntary cry escaped his lips as he staggered to his right.

Jimmy managed to keep enough wits to put his sword up, and Malar almost impaled himself on its point as he jumped off the boulder. Instead, he hit the ground and backed away a step. The spy said, "Well, young lord, it appears I should have used a stronger poison."

Jimmy shook his head to clear it, and said, "But then you wouldn't have been able to drink any."

Malar grinned. "Building up a resistance was a most unpleasant process, but over the years I've discovered it was worth it. I would love to continue our discussion, but I hold no confidence that your men will be delayed much longer, so I must leave." He was holding only a dagger, but he advanced as if confident Jimmy and his sword would be no match.

Years of training, back to when he was a boy learning at the knee of his grandfather, took over, and Jimmy leaped to his right, just as Malar let loose an underhand cast, lightning swift, with his left hand, and a previously unseen dagger glanced off the rocks where Jimmy had stood a moment before. Jimmy knew this man would have several blades secreted upon his person. As Jimmy expected, when he turned to confront Malar, the spy was already hurling himself at Jimmy, daggers in both hands.

Jimmy fell over backward, enduring further searing agony in his left shoulder as he avoided Malar's assault. Jimmy kicked out with his right leg as Malar closed on him, knocking him off balance. The spy's leg was rock hard and Jimmy was certain he'd find the man's slender build had been misleading; this was not a skinny weakling he fought. Wasting no time, Jimmy rolled upright and struck hard with his sword. Malar barely avoided the blow and rolled away, ignoring the sharp rocks that littered the trail.

Jimmy pressed on, not allowing this dangerous foe the chance to collect himself, not while Jimmy had only one good arm. He swung down again with his sword, almost cutting the Keshian spy. Malar scrambled backward, halfway up a rock face, then rather than retreat, he used the momentum to hurl himself forward, inside of Jimmy's sword.

Jimmy felt a blade slide across his ribs, and he gasped in pain, but he twisted enough that the point didn't dig in. He contracted with his chest and stomach, striking Malar's face with a vicious head-butt. Malar staggered backward, blood streaming from his broken nose, and Jimmy's vision swam a moment.

Suddenly a horse almost ran Jimmy down, hooves flying, as it raced by. Jimmy got up as quickly as he could and realized he no longer held a sword. The bleeding Keshian spy grinned like a crazed wolf as he crouched low, holding his remaining dagger in his right hand. "Don't move, young noble, and I'll make this quick and painless."

He took a step toward Jimmy, who countered with a handful of dirt to Malar's eyes. Malar turned away, blinded by the dust, and Jimmy leaped to grip Malar's wrist with his good right hand. Summoning as much strength as he could, he tried to crush Malar's wrist by sheer willpower. Malar grunted in pain, but didn't let go of the dagger. As Jimmy had suspected, the Keshian's slight build hid steel-like strength, and nothing as trivial as a broken wrist would distract him.

Malar pulled back, Jimmy still holding his right wrist in his own right hand. With his left fist, Malar struck a back-handed blow to Jimmy's shoulder. Jimmy cried out in pain and felt his knees buckle.

He nearly lost consciousness as Malar struck him in the left shoulder again, and felt the strength draining out of him. Malar drew back and wrenched his wrist free of Jimmy's grasp, and in one motion deftly tossed his dagger from left to right hand. For an instant Jimmy looked up as Malar stood above him, poised to deliver a death blow, a vicious backhand stab with his left hand.

Malar's eyes widened in shock, and he looked down. The dagger fell from his fingers and his hand went around behind his back, and he turned, as if to get a better angle on something. Jimmy saw an arrow protruding out of the spy's right shoulder, and suddenly a second struck him with a loud thud.

Malar went to his knees, then his eyes rolled up into his head as blood flowed from his nose and mouth, and he fell face forward onto the stones before Jimmy.

Jimmy turned to see Songti and one of his men, armed with a bow, hurrying toward him. Jimmy sat back on his heels, then fell over backward, banging himself against the rocks.

Songti knelt and said, "Are you hurt?"

"I'll live," Jimmy croaked. "My shoulder's dislocated."

"Let me see," said the Captain. He gently touched the shoulder and pain shot through Jimmy's body, from waist to jaw. "Just a moment," said the Captain, then with a sure move, he gripped the upper portion of Jimmy's arm and clamped his other hand down on the shoulder and shoved the arm back into position.

Jimmy's eyes widened and watered and he could barely catch his breath, then the pain passed.

Songti said, "Better to do it soon, before things swell and you can't get it back in. Then you need a healer or priest, or a great deal of brandy. You'll be better tomorrow."

"If you say so," Jimmy replied weakly.

"I got the second rider, but there was a third."

"He almost ran me down," said Jimmy as Songti helped him to his feet.

"It was the officer."

Jimmy swore. "Are the messages to Duko still over there?"

The archer looked around and saw the leather pouch, reached down, and held it up. "It's here."

Jimmy waved the man over, and he handed the bundle to the Captain. Songti pulled out the documents and said, "There are seven papers here."

"That's all of them," said Jimmy. He looked down at the dead spy and said, "That was too close."

Songti motioned for the archer to give Jimmy a steadying hand. "We must bury the dead. If there's another patrol nearby and they see vultures circling, they might come to investigate in the morning."

Jimmy shook his head. "It doesn't matter. Before first light, we're down that trail back across the border. We may kill horses, but we've got to get back to Port Vykor, and I've got to get up to Krondor as fast as possible.

"Because that officer escaped?"

Jimmy nodded yes. "I don't know how closely he read these, or what Malar told him, but he'll carry word back to his masters that Krondor is being held by a handful of palace guards and every fighting man not tied up at Land's End or in the vale is up north facing Fadawah."

"These Keshians would press the advantage?"

Jimmy said, "Indeed they would. One quick strike up to the city and they hold Prince Patrick. The King would grant them much to reclaim his son."

Songti said, "It was simpler when we lived in Novindus."

Jimmy laughed, though it hurt him to do so. "No doubt," he said as he leaned on the archer and hobbled back to the oasis.

Erik heard the Hadati moving before he saw him appear out of the gloom. Akee said, "It's almost time."

They had remained hidden through the night in the woods behind the barricade blocking the highway. Twice mercenaries had wandered close to where Erik waited, but none bothered to check the woods on the cliffs.

Erik nodded. The sky to the east was getting lighter.

Soon, if all went according to plan, a feint at the far end of the barricade would give Erik his opportunity to strike from behind and open the gate. "Let's look around a little," said Erik.

He crouched low and moved through the trees until he reached the clearing south of the highway. He gauged the distance to the gate at over a hundred yards, and counted a dozen low-burning campfires between his current position and the gate, and another score just the other side of the road. He felt Akee at his shoulder and whispered, "I expected more men here."

"I as well. If we can get through the gate, this battle will be over quickly."

He left unsaid what would be the result of not getting the gate open. Erik said, "I have an idea. Pass word that no man is to move when the alarm sounds. Tell them to wait until I signal you."

"Where will you be?"

Erik pointed. "I'll be somewhere out there."

Erik wore his black uniform, but without his Crimson Eagle tabard. To any casual observer he might pass as a mercenary given to wearing black. Glancing at Akee, he noticed a blue band around the warrior's brow. "Is that something I might borrow from you?" he asked, not knowing if it might have some sort of tribal significance.

Akee didn't answer. He reached up and untied the band, then stepped behind Erik and tied the headband in place. Now Erik looked even less like a Kingdom regular.

Erik cautiously stepped out between two campfires, walking carefully so as not to wake sleeping men. Soft voices from the barricade told him the guards on duty were gossiping or telling stories to keep awake.

Erik reached the edge of the road and his manner changed. He walked briskly as if he was about important business. He moved boldly down the road and reached the gate. As he approached, he noted the construction of the gate. It was simple, but effective. The gates each had one large iron bracket affixed to them by huge iron bolts. Through those brackets, an oak bar had been passed, and that was braced in turn by long poles driven into the ground. It should be easy to knock aside the poles and run the bar out of the brackets, but it would take a sizable ram to knock it open from the other side.

"Hey!" he said, before he could be challenged. He kept his voice deep, hopefully disguising his accent as he spoke the invaders' dialect.

"What?" asked the man in charge of the gate, a sergeant or Captain by the look of him.

"We're just down from the North, and I've got to find whoever's in charge."

"Captain Rastav is over there," said the man, pointing at a large tent barely visible in the predawn gloom. "What news?"

Erik growled, "Your name Rastav?"

"No," said the man in return, bristling a bit.

"Then my message isn't for you, is it?"

Erik turned and walked away before the man could respond. He made his way slowly but purposefully toward the command tent, then, just before approaching too closely, he veered away and walked between camps. Most of the men were sleeping; a few were rousing and stirring cooking fires, heading to nearby slit-trenches to relieve themselves, or already eating. He absently nodded or gave a slight wave of greeting to a few he passed, furthering the illusion he was a familiar figure known to someone in the camp; if not the person looking at him, perhaps the man across the way to whom he was waving.

Erik reached a particularly quiet camp where only one man stirred, one who was brewing up coffee by the smell of it. Crossing over, he said, "Have an extra cup to spare?"

The man looked up and nodded, motioning Erik over. Erik came over and knelt beside the warrior. "I've got a few minutes before I report to the gate, and can't find a hot cup anywhere."

"I know what you mean," said the soldier, handing an earthen mug filled with the black hot liquid to Erik. "You with Gaja?"

Erik recognized the name, a captain he had heard of before, but he knew nothing about the man. "No," said Erik, "we just got here. My captain is over there"—he indicated the command tent—"talking with Rastav, and I thought I'd sneak off and grab this.'' He stood. ''Thanks, I'll bring back the mug when my duty's over.''

The soldier waved off the remark. ''Keep it. We've looted enough crockery I'm thinking of opening a store.''

Erik strolled along, drinking his coffee, which wasn't too bad for camp fare, and inspected the area. There were no more than a thousand men behind the wall, and from the look of what he could see along the barricade, no more than twelve hundred total at this position. Another mystery. From the other side, it looked like half of Fadawah's army waited, yet from this side Erik knew that if he could get the gate open, this battle would be won in minutes, not hours.

When he was halfway back to the gate area, Erik heard a shout raised up at the eastern end of the barricade. Then more shouts as an alarm was raised. Erik paused, and counted slowly to ten, until he heard a horn sounded, a call to arms. Men sprang up from where they slept, and Erik tossed aside his cup and hurried along. In his most commanding voice he started shouting, ''They're hitting the east flank! Get to the east!''

Men who were half asleep started hurrying off toward the far end of the line. As he neared the gate, a man hurried over and said, ''What is this?''

Erik knew at once this was a sergeant or captain of some company, one not used to obeying mindlessly. ''Rastav's orders! Are you Captain Gaja?''

The man blinked and said, ''No, I'm Tulme. Gaja is due to relieve me in an hour.''

''Then get two men in three off the gate and rush them to the eastern end of the line! The enemy is breaking through over there!''

Erik hurried along, and kept shouting, ''Get to the east! Hurry up!''

Men saw other soldiers rushing off to where they were ordered, and hastened to obey. Erik ran back to where he could be seen by Akee and signaled. Instantly the Hadati hillmen were running from the trees.

Erik ran to the gate and shouted, ''Orders! Open the gate. Get ready to sally!''

''What?'' said a man. ''Who are you?''

Erik had his sword out and killed the man before he could react. "My luck couldn't run forever," he said to Akee as the Hadati reached his side.

The Hadati killed every man standing before the gate before anyone more than twenty-five yards away noticed. The supporting poles were kicked aside, and before they hit the ground Erik and Akee, along with two other men, were lifting the heavy oaken bar out of the brackets that held it in place.

As they carried the bar aside, others opened the gate.

"Two minutes!" Erik cried. "We have to keep it open for two minutes."

Seconds slipped by slowly, as shouts up and down the line demanded answers and suddenly it was clear to Erik that those to the north of him on the defenders' side of the barricade knew something was amiss.

Suddenly men were charging at the Hadati, who were to a man armed with long swords and short swords, held in right and left hands respectively. They moved out to keep enough room between each that they could do a maximum of damage. Erik hesitated only a moment, then ran and leaped atop a pile of grain sacks, and pulled himself up on the ramparts behind the breastwork. He could not afford for bowmen to get above the Hadati. If he did, the fight would be over.

Erik glanced to the south and saw the Kingdom cavalry was already on its way. One more minute and the day would be won.

Erik charged along the ramparts, and the first man he encountered looked confused, still trying to see what was occurring to the east. Erik grabbed him and threw him off the rampart. He landed on top of a pair of men running along, and those behind stopped. A crossbow bolt sped past Erik's head and he ducked.

He retreated, weapons ready, and when he saw soldiers heading toward him, he halted. The first man to face him slowed, uncertain of what was before him. Erik was happy to wait, and let the Kingdom cavalry reach the gate.

Abruptly a sense of alarm passed through those near the gate, as if they finally realized what had happened. They charged the waiting Hadati, and the man opposite Erik let out a howl of rage and charged him.

Erik took a step back when the man swung, letting him overbalance himself, and with a swift kick, Erik sent the man tumbling over the side of the rampart. The second man approached a little more cautiously, if just as intently, and struck out. Erik took the blow on his sword and parried, then unexpectedly, he stepped into the man, slamming him in the face with his sword hilt. The man stumbled backward into another man behind him and both fell back.

Erik glanced over the wall and saw the first pair of Kingdom horsemen was near, lowering their lances as they started up the last part of the incline toward the gate. Erik had a sudden impulse, and shouted at the top of his lungs: "Throw down your swords! It's over!"

The man opposite him on the barricade hesitated, and Erik shouted, "This is your last chance! *Throw down your sword!*"

The man looked at the huge blond man before him, as lancers raced through the gate behind the Hadati hillmen whose whirling blades were inflicting terrible injury on any who closed on them. With a look of disgust, he threw down his blade.

A band of horsemen rode up from behind the line and were charged by Krondorian lancers as the second unit of cavalry swept in. A scaling ladder slammed against the wall near Erik and he realized that Greylock had hedged his bet by getting men close under cover of darkness. He glanced to his right and saw footmen racing across the open ground ahead.

Erik leaned out over the edge of the wall and almost got his head split open as thanks. "Hey!" he shouted down to a Kingdom soldier halfway up the ladder who had just swung his sword at Erik. "Slow down! You might fall off and hurt yourself!"

It was not what the soldier expected. He stopped, and the man behind him on the ladder shouted, "Keep moving."

Erik said, "You can climb back down and walk through the gate."

The man on the top of the ladder shouted, "Sorry, Captain von Darkmoor."

Erik looked to the left and saw mercenaries throwing down their swords and backing away as a line of lancers slowly advanced on them, the points of their heavy weapons pointed at chest height.

Erik saw the light cavalry entering behind the lancers and recognized Jadow and Duga. He signaled to get their attention. Jadow rode closer and Erik shouted, "Get things organized, and send word back to Greylock to move up. Quickly."

Jadow signaled that he understood and turned to carry word to Owen himself. Duga jumped down from his horse and boldly walked past the line of lancers, and started separating mercenaries from their weapons. Erik glanced at the rear of the enemy camp where a running fight had erupted between the lancers and the invaders' cavalry units, and realized the enemy didn't know they'd lost yet. Given what he knew of enemy horsemen, he knew a few heads would be broken before word reached them if he didn't intervene. He shouted for messengers to carry the word to the fight, before men died needlessly.

Erik jumped off the wall as the first Kingdom foot soldiers entered the gate. He pushed through the press of prisoners, and sought out the senior lieutenant of the light cavalry. "Go give the lancers a hand with that lot at the rear, then I want a sweep of the woods on both sides of the road for the next five miles. If anyone's cut and running north to tell Fadawah this position is fallen, I want them overtaken."

The rider saluted, gave orders, and rode off, then Erik sought out Akee. "How are your men?"

"I have some injuries, but no one dead," said the leader of the hillmen. "Had they a few more minutes to get organized, I think we would have seen otherwise."

"I think you are correct," said Erik.

He left the hillmen and turned as Jadow and Owen rode through the gate, and as he approached, he turned to a passing soldier and said, "Find a Captain among the prisoners, a man named Rastav, and bring him here."

Owen looked around and said, "Another illusion?"

Erik said, "Almost. If we hadn't gotten the gate open, we would have bled, but not as badly as we thought."

Owen glanced northward, as if to see over the horizon. "What is he doing?"

Erik said, "I wish I knew."

Erik looked to the south. "And I wish I knew what was going on down there, too."

Owen said, "That's Duko and Patrick's problem, not ours. Now, let's get things here under control, then start moving north again."

Erik saluted, then turned and began organizing the chaos behind the barricade.

Dash could barely contain his rage. A dozen of his constables were standing around the room, looking from one to another, a few openly frightened.

Two of his men lay dead before him. Sometime during the night they had been waylaid and killed, their throats cut and their bodies deposited before the door of the New Market Jail.

Whispering, Dash said, "Someone's going to bleed for this."

The men were two recent recruits, Nolan and Riggs, and they had just finished their training. The last month had been difficult for Dash, but as order returned to Krondor, he found that larger portions of the city were slowly getting back to a rhythm not unlike that known before the war.

The Prince had authorized the purchase of a building just off the Market Square, and the cells had just been installed by an iron monger. A near riot down near the docks the night before had taken the jail to its limit and Dash had been busy dragging malefactors off to the city court, established by the Prince the week before; two eastern nobles were serving as judges, and a lot of drunks were finding themselves sentenced to the labor gangs in a hurry. Most got a year, but a few were pulling five-and ten-year sentences, and the citizens of the more unruly areas of the city were loudly protesting. So far the protest had been vocal, with insults hurled at watchmen as they made their rounds. Until last night.

"Where were they scheduled to patrol?" asked Dash.

Gustaf, the former prisoner, had turned up looking for work a few days before and Dash had made him a corporal. Gustaf had the duty roster. "They were working down near the old Poor Quarter."

"Damn," said Dash. The old Poor Quarter of the city was now a shanty town of huts and tents, and people living in the lees of partial walls. Every vice imaginable was available there and, predictably, the Thieves Guild was establishing its power there faster than the crown. "Now all bets are off."

Since taking the office of Sheriff of Krondor, Dash had managed to keep hanging to a minimum. Two murderers had been publicly hanged five days before, but the majority of crimes had been relatively petty.

"What were these two doing down there anyway?" asked Dash. "They were both new to the job."

Gustaf said, "The draw just came up that way." Lowering his voice, he said, "There's no one here with what you might call a great deal of experience, Dash."

Dash nodded. The two dead men weren't downy-cheeked youths by any stretch of imagination. "Four to a squad down there, starting tomorrow."

"What about tonight?" asked Gustaf.

"I'll take care of tonight," said Dash, leaving the small squad room.

He hurried down the street and made his way through the open market, heading toward what had been the Poor Quarter. He kept his wits about him and his eyes open. Even in the daylight he could count on nothing but trouble in this part of the city.

Reaching a burned-out two-story building, he ducked inside. Quickly he removed his red armband and ducked out the back of the building. He hurried down a narrow alley and climbed a wooden fence that was still somehow standing between two stone walls while everything nearby had been reduced to ash. Ducking under a low-hanging arch of stone he reached his goal.

He crept through an open building, a small former business on the edge of the Poor Quarter. He hung inside, staying hidden in shadow, while watching the view out in the quarter.

Men and women moved through the tents and shacks, dealing trade goods and food, as well as illicit goods. Dash was looking for a certain face and would be content to wait until he saw it.

Near sundown, a small man came hurrying toward the building, intent on some errand, lost in thought. As he passed the open door, Dash reached out and grabbed him by the collar of his dingy shirt, hauling him inside.

The man yelped in terror, and started to beg, "Don't kill me! I didn't do it!"

Dash put his hand over the little man's mouth and said, "Didn't do what, Kirby?"

When he saw he wasn't going to be instantly killed, the little man relaxed. Dash removed his hand. "Whatever it was you think I did," said the little man.

"Kirby Dokins," said Dash, "the only thing you do is trade in information. If you weren't so useful, I'd squash you like the bug you are."

The vile-smelling little man grinned. His face was a patchwork of scars and blemishes. He was a beggar by trade, and an informant when opportunity presented himself. Like the cockroach he was, he had crawled into a crack in the stones and survived the destruction of the city. "But you have use of me, don't you?"

"For the moment," conceded Dash. "Two of my men were dumped on the jail steps last night, their throats cut. I want those who did it."

"No one's bragging."

"See what you can find out, but at midnight tonight, I'll be here, and you better be as well, with names."

"That might prove difficult," said the snitch.

"Make it happen," said Dash, hauling the little man up so that Dash's nose almost touched Kirby's. "I don't need to make up crimes to get you hung. Keep me happy."

"I live to keep you happy, Sheriff."

"Exactly." He let go of the little man's shirt. "And pass word back to that old man."

"What old man?" asked Kirby, feigning ignorance.

"I don't have to tell you who," said Dash. "Tell him if this murder lands at his feet, any faint affection I might feel toward his merry band of mummers will be gone forever.

If they're his pranksters cutting throats, he better serve them up to me, or the Mockers will be crushed, root and branch.''

Kirby swallowed hard. ''I'll pass that along, if it becomes appropriate.''

Dash pushed the little man outside the door. ''Go. Midnight,'' he ordered.

Dash saw that he still had an hour of daylight and imagined there were many tasks waiting for him back at headquarters. He turned to retrace his steps back to the New Market Jail, and cursed Patrick for giving him this thankless task of beating obedience into his subjects. But as long as it was his job, vowed Dash, he would do it properly. And that started with keeping his constables alive.

Dash hurried through the failing light into the shadows of Krondor.

Eighteen

Revelations

OWEN SQUIRMED.

He didn't seem able to find a comfortable position in his camp chair, and yet the situation demanded he sit for hours reviewing reports and communiqués.

Erik approached, looming up out of the evening darkness against the campfires burning in every direction. He saluted. "We've interrogated the captains, and they're as ignorant as the swordsmen they've hired."

"There's a pattern here, somewhere," said Owen. "I'm just too stupid to see it." He indicated that Erik should sit.

"Not stupid," said Erik, sitting next to his commander. "Just tired."

"Not that tired," said Owen. His old leathery face wrinkled in a smile. "I've gotten three good nights' sleep, truth to tell, since you opened the gates. In fact, it's been too good." He leaned forward, looking at the map as if there was something in there to see, if he just stared at it long enough.

Companies of regular soldiers were arriving from the south. The prisoners were being kept in a makeshift compound, fashioned of freshly felled trees. Erik said, "The best I can come up with is Fadawah has some men he

305

wasn't really happy with, so he thought he'd turn them over to us to feed.''

''Well, if you hadn't opened that gate, we would have bled a bit getting over that wall,'' said Owen, hiking his thumb over his shoulder at the large earthen breastwork behind his command pavilion.

''True, but we would have taken it in a day or two.''

''I'm wondering why Fadawah is going to all the trouble of making us think he's down here and then letting us discover he isn't.''

''I'm guessing,'' said Erik, ''but if he's taken LaMut, he might be moving south of Ylith now, getting ready for a counterattack.''

''He can't ignore Yabon,'' said Owen. ''As long as Duke Carl is up there with his army, Fadawah has to keep a strong face northward. Carl can get men in and out of there if Fadawah doesn't keep the pressure on. Even so, there are Hadati hillmen still up there who can probably sneak through his lines at will. And I'm sure the dwarves and elves aren't proving hospitable neighbors if his patrols wander too far from their current position. No, he must take all of Yabon before he turns south.''

''Well, he can't hope to slow us down with these little sham positions.''

Owen's face showed concern. ''I don't know if these are shams as much as they're just . . . irritations, to make us proceed slowly.''

Erik's eyes narrowed. ''Or maybe they're designed to make us go fast.''

''What do you mean?''

''Say we find one or two more of these lightly defended positions?''

''Okay, so we do.''

Erik pointed to the map. ''Let's say we hit Quester's View and find another fortification like this. We get all excited and strike out toward Ylith.''

''And run into a meat grinder?''

Erik nodded. He pointed to details on the map. ''There's this line of unforgiving ridges north of the road from Quester's View to Hawk's Hollow. He holds both ends of the road, and if he keeps us off the ridge, he can dig in here.'' Erik's finger showed a particularly narrow point in the road about twenty miles south of Ylith. "Let say he sets up a series of fortifications, tunnels, catapults, arrow towers, the entire bag of tricks. We stick a boot into that mess too fast and we may draw back a bloody stump.'' His finger traced a line from that point up to the dot on the map representing Ylith. "He's got thirty-foot-high walls, and a single weak point, an eastern gate by the docks. That he can fortify, and if he sinks ships in the harbor mouth, he can sit inside the city like a turtle in its shell.'' The more he spoke, the more Erik was certain of his analysis. "We can't land on the western shore; that's Free Cities land, and if we try it, Patrick risks alienating the only neutral party left on the Bitter Sea. Besides, to get there we'd probably run up against whatever warships Queg has in the area.''

Owen sighed. "More to the point, our fleet needs to support the army on its western flank to make sure we're supplied and to carry the wounded south to Sarth and Krondor.''

Erik scratched at his chin. "I'm willing to bet if we had the eyes of a bird we'd see a very heavy set of fortifications being built along that stretch right now.''

"It all makes sense,'' said Owen. "But then I've seen too many things in war that make no sense to count too heavily on theory. We'll have to wait to see what Subai says when he gets word back to us.''

"If he gets word back,'' said Erik.

"Let's cover our bet,'' said Owen.

"What?'' asked Erik.

"I'm going to send an order to Admiral Reeves to send a fast cutter up the coast from Sarth. I want to see how far north he can get before someone tries to discourage him.''

Erik sat forward. "Care to bet it's about there?'' he said, his finger stabbing at a point on the coast due west of Quester's View.

"No bet,'' said Owen. "I've come to appreciate your instincts.''

Erik sat back in the chair. "I actually hope I'm wrong and Fadawah's all tied up outside of Yabon. I can imagine what I would do if I was building defensive fortifications along that route.''

Owen said, "You have too much imagination. Did any-one ever tell you that?"

Erik looked at his old friend and said, "Not often enough." He stood and said, "I have things to see to. I'll report in when I've done talking to the rest of the prison-ers."

"Supper is ready. Get back here before it's all gone." Owen added, "I'll be here," and went back to his reports as Erik walked off.

Dash waited, and as the darkness deepened, he began to fume. It was already a quarter hour past midnight and Kirby hadn't put in an appearance. He was about to start looking for him when he sensed someone was behind him. He slipped his hand over the hilt of his dagger and moved with a feigned casual motion, walking back toward the rear en-trance of the burned-out building.

As soon as he slipped through the door, he stepped side-ways, reaching toward an exposed roof beam with both hands, pulling himself up with a single fluid motion. Out came the dagger and he waited.

A moment later a figure emerged from the door and glanced around. Dash waited. The cloaked figure below him took a step forward and Dash dropped to the ground, his dagger going to the lurker's throat.

From beneath the hood, a voice said, "Going to bite me, Puppy?"

Dash spun the figure around. "Trina!"

The young woman smiled. "It's nice to be remem-bered."

"What are you doing here?"

"Put down that toothpick and I'll tell you."

Dash grinned. "Sorry, but I'll bet you're as dangerous as you are beautiful."

The woman pouted theatrically. "You flatterer."

Dash lost his smile. "I've got dead men and I want some answers. Where's Kirby Dokins?"

"Dead," said the women.

Dash put away his dagger.

"Am I suddenly less dangerous?"

"No," said Dash, pulling the woman back inside the

building. "But you wouldn't have been sent to tell me the Mockers killed my snitch."

"And?"

"That means you didn't kill my men."

"Very good, Puppy."

"Who did?"

"An old acquaintance of yours thinks there's a new gang moving into the city. Smugglers, maybe, though there doesn't seem to be a lot of new goods in the market, if you know what I mean."

"I do," said Dash. The woman meant there wasn't a noticeable increase in drugs, stolen goods, or other contraband.

"Another Crawler?"

"You know your history, Puppy."

"That's Sheriff Puppy, to you," said Dash.

She laughed. It was the first time he had heard her laugh without mockery. It was a sweet sound. She said, "We're left alone, so if someone is planning on moving into our territory, they're not ready to try yet.

"Our old friend said to tell you we don't know who killed your two lads, but you should know they weren't altar boys from the Temple of Sung. Find out who Nolan and Riggs were working for before they joined your gang and you might have a clue."

Dash was silent, then said, "So the Upright Man thinks these two knew their killers."

"Maybe. Or maybe they just happened to be at the wrong place at the wrong time, but either way, once the deed was done, someone wanted you to think was done it to defy your authority. That's why they were dumped on your doorstep. Had the Mockers killed those men, they would have been dumped in the harbor."

"Who killed Kirby?"

"We don't know," said Trina. "He was snooping around, being his usually pesky sclf, then suddenly about two hours ago, he turns up floating in the sewer."

"Where?"

"Five Points, near the big outfall below Stinky Street." Stinky Street was Poor Quarter's slang for Tanners Road, where many odorous businesses had resided before the war.

Five Points was the name of a large confluence of sewers, three big ones, two small ones. Dash had never been there, but he knew where it was.

"You working Five Points?"

"We're not up there, but don't ask me where we're working."

Dash grinned in the darkness. "Not yet, anyway."

"Not ever, Sheriff Puppy, not ever."

Dash said, "Anything else?"

"No," said Trina.

"Tell the old man thanks."

Trina said, "He didn't do it from love, Sheriff Puppy. We're just not ready to take on the crown. But he did tell me one other thing to tell you."

"What?"

"Don't make threats. The day you declare war on the Mockers, take your sword to bed with you."

Dash said, "Then tell my uncle that advice works both ways."

"Then good night."

"Lovely to see you again, Trina."

"Always a pleasure, Sheriff Puppy," said the woman thief. Then she ducked through the door and was gone.

Dash allowed her the courtesy of not leaving for five minutes, so she could be sure she wasn't being followed. Besides, he could find her any time he wanted. And more to the point, his mind was wrestling with the question: Who killed his men?

He slipped into the darkness, heading back to his headquarters.

Roo chuckled at the sight before him. Nakor was jumping around like a grasshopper, shouting orders at the workers as they tried to wrestle the statue upright. Roo moved his own wagon over to the side of the road and let those carts and wagons behind him pass. He jumped down and crossed the road to where Nakor's wagon was parked.

"What are you doing?" he asked with a laugh.

Nakor said, "These fools are determined to destroy this work of art!"

Roo said, "I think they'll get it where you want it, but

why do you want it out here?'' He made a sweeping motion with his hand, indicating a vacant field outside the gates of Krondor. A small farm had occupied this plot of land, but the house had been destroyed and now only a charred square of foundation stones marked its passing.

''I want everyone entering the city to see this,'' said Nakor as the workers got the statue upright.

Roo paused. There was something about the woman's expression that captivated the eye. He studied it for a long moment, then said, ''It's really very lovely, Nakor. Is that your goddess?''

''That's the Lady,'' said Nakor with a nod.

''But why not put her in the center of your temple?''

''Because I don't yet have a temple,'' said Nakor as he motioned for the workers to return to the wagon. ''I have to find a place to build one.''

Roo laughed. ''Don't look at me. I already sprang for one warehouse in Darkmoor. Besides, I don't own any buildings near Temple Square.''

A gleam entered Nakor's eyes. ''Yes! Temple Square. That's where we need to build!''

''Builders I have,'' said Roo. Then he fixed Nakor with a narrow gaze. ''But I'm a little short on charity these days.''

''Ah,'' said Nakor with a laugh. ''Then you must have money. You're only penurious when you have gold. When you're broke, you're very generous.''

Roo laughed. ''You are the most amazing man, Nakor.''

''Yes, I am,'' he agreed. ''Now, I have some gold, so you won't have to build me a temple, but I would like some, shall we call it discounts?''

''I'll see what I can do.'' He looked around so as not to be overheard. ''There is a lot of confusion in the city still. Many landowners are dead and the crown hasn't established a policy yet on who owns what.''

''You mean Patrick hasn't seized unclaimed land yet.''

''You catch on,'' said Roo. ''Squatters seem to have a certain advantage if the real owner doesn't press a claim. I happen to know that the empty lot on the northwest corner of Temple Square, over by the Temple of Lims-Kragma, was owned by a former associate of mine. It was always a difficult piece of land to dispose of, being located between the Death Goddess's temple and the Temple of Guis-wa. Old Crowley tried to sell it to me once, and I declined. As Crowley is now among those who didn't survive the war, that land is unclaimed.'' Roo whispered, ''He left no survivors. So it's you, some other squatter, or the crown who's going to get it.''

Nakor grinned. ''Being between the Death Goddess and the Red-Jawed Hunter doesn't bother me, so I'm certain it won't bother the Lady. I'll go check it out.''

Roo glanced back at the statue. ''That's really quite good.''

Nakor laughed. ''The sculptor was inspired.''

''I can believe it. Who modeled for it?''

''One of my students. She's special.''

''I can see that,'' said Roo.

As Nakor climbed back on his wagon, motioning for the workers to climb into the back, he said, ''Where are you bound?''

''Back to Ravensburg. I'm rebuilding the Inn of the Pintail for Milo. With his daughter living in Darkmoor now, he's going to sell me half interest.''

''You, an innkeeper?'' asked Nakor with a disbelieving laugh.

''Any business that can make a profit, Nakor.''

Nakor laughed, waved, and urged his wagon on into the press of traffic heading into the city.

Roo climbed aboard his own wagon and looked again at the statue. He saw there were people who were stopping to look at it or glancing at it as they drove past. One woman reached out and touched it reverently, and Roo admitted to himself that the sculptor must have, indeed, been inspired.

He flicked the reins and urged his horses into the traffic on the road, heading east. Things were still difficult, but since capturing Vasarius, life had taken a turn for the better.

He had discovered he really enjoyed his children, and Karli was quite a bit better company than he imagined when he married her. While no gold had been forthcoming from the crown since the winter, he knew that eventually he could use that debt to his own advantage. He needed a good base of liquid wealth, then he could turn the debt into licenses and concessions from the crown. Eventually peace between the Kingdom and Kesh would be achieved, and when that happened the profitable luxury trade would again be open, and now with Jacob Esterbrook dead, there would be no stranglehold on trade with the South.

"Yes," Roo said softly to himself as he drove his wagon back to his boyhood home. Things were certainly taking a turn for the better.

Jimmy said, "If it gets much worse, we're going to lose everything."

Duke Duko nodded. "Here we're locked up at Land's End." He pointed to the map. "It's as if they don't want to take the place, but they're reluctant to leave."

They occupied the largest room of the biggest inn in Port Vykor, a town that didn't exist five years before. Upon seeing the settlement, Jimmy was of the opinion that had the first Prince of Krondor wandered a little farther south those many years ago, this would be the site for the capital of the Western Realm, not Krondor.

The harbor was commodious, opening into a calm bay that was relatively safe for shipping during the worst weather in the Bitter Sea. The docks could be extended as needed, for miles if necessary, and a broad highway to the northeast provided easy access from land. Already traders were making their way to the military encampment and businesses were springing up around the wooden stockade erected around the port. In a dozen years, there would be a city here, thought Jimmy.

He had ridden to the town as fast as he could drive his horse, and had gotten to Duko with his dispatches two days prior. He had rested for an entire day, sleeping most of the time.

Duko had dispatched more patrols and now messengers were returning with the latest intelligence.

Jimmy had a very sore left shoulder, with a huge purple and blue bruise that was now turning green and yellow as it started to fade. Several small cuts had been dressed, and while feeling worse for the wear, he was on the mend and knew that in a few days he'd be fit once more.

He had come to appreciate the former enemy General.

Lord Duko was a thoughtful man who, had he been born in the Kingdom to a noble family, would have risen high, perhaps as high as to the very office in which a capricious fate had placed him. Somehow that reassured Jimmy, knowing that a very important position in the Kingdom was being occupied by a man of talent and intelligence.

Jimmy had not asked Duko what had been contained in the orders sent by Prince Patrick. He knew the Duke would inform him of what Jimmy needed to know, and nothing more.

Duko motioned Jimmy to another table, one which had been set with food and wine. "Hungry?"

Jimmy smiled. "Yes," he said, rising from his seat at the campaign table and moving to where the food was.

"I have no servants," said Duko. "The ease with which your Keshian insinuated himself into the palace at Krondor makes me dubious of anyone here I do not know. I'm afraid that has not endeared me to those officers who previously held posts here. Those that weren't called north, I've moved to posts at the harbor or down in Land's End."

Jimmy nodded. "Not very politic, but very smart."

The old General smiled. "Thank you."

"M'lord," said Jimmy, "I am at your disposal. Prince Patrick wishes me to serve you here in any capacity you see fit as well as serve as a liaison between Your Grace and the crown."

"So you're to be Patrick's spy in my court?"

Jimmy laughed. "Well, you can appreciate his being somewhat dubious and a little cautious in dealing with as prodigious a former enemy as yourself, my lord."

"I understand, even if I'm not terribly happy."

"I think you'll find me useful, sir. You are going to discover yourself subject to some scrutiny for the foreseeable future, and not all of it from the crown; many eastern nobles have sons and brothers whom they will wish to insert into vacant offices here in the West. Several will no doubt show up here unannounced. Some will be honest volunteers, younger brothers or sons looking to gain glory fighting Kesh, as did their ancestors. Others, however, will be seeking anything that can be used to discredit you, or another lord who is a rival to their lord, or simply to find such information to sell to interested parties. The politics of the eastern court is inherently lethal and complex. I can be of service in deflecting a great deal of such nonsense.''

"I believe you," said Duko. "I am first a soldier, but you don't become one of the top generals in my homeland without some facility at dealing with princes and rulers. They are in the main more concerned with their own vanity than in truly finding solutions to problems, and as often as not I had to guard against those who would work against my own interests within the court of my employer. We may not be all that unlike, after all.''

"Well, anyone who looks at the history of the Kingdom, Your Grace, and thinks that for every victor there wasn't a vanquished, or that all the lands of the West embraced the Kingdom with open arms, is a fool. It was the King's scribes who wrote history, and should you wish a slightly different perspective of our annexation of the West, I could recommend one or two histories published in the Free Cities that don't cast too kind a light on our rulers.''

"History is written by victors," said Duko. "But I have little use for history. It is the future with which I am concerned.''

"Probably a wise attitude given the present circumstances.''

"Right now I am very concerned about that Keshian officer and what his escape may portend.''

Jimmy nodded. "Malar was showing him the documents when we found them. He may have just been beginning to explain the significance of your orders. If it's nothing more than 'Krondor is vulnerable,' and the Keshians think we'll reinforce due to the discovery of the spy, we may avoid any problems up there. If he has any of the details of those messages memorized, he'll be able to tell his masters we can't reinforce Krondor.''

Duko said, "If I could chase the Keshians out of Land's End, that would help.''

Jimmy said, "Yes, it would, but without additional soldiers I can't see how you can accomplish that. Enduring a siege is one thing, but mounting an effective counteroffensive . . . ?" He shrugged.

"With all that desert at their rear, I'm impressed how

well the Keshians are resupplying the army facing Land's End,'' admitted Duko. "If we could get part of the fleet down to intercept their shipping out of Durbin, we might shake them loose, but short of that I have no idea how we're going to dig them out. I've asked the Prince for permission to dispatch Reeves and a squadron to raid off of Durban . . ." He shrugged. "The Prince seems reluctant."

"Compared to previous wars with Kesh, this is still a 'misunderstanding.' Patrick is understandably reluctant to expand it," Jimmy said. "I'm fresh out of ideas, my lord." He stood. "If you'll excuse me, I think I'm going to take a walk and clear my head a bit. Otherwise, I might find myself asleep at your table."

"Sleep heals," said Duko. "If you feel the need of a nap, you'll not hear me say no. I've seen those marks the Keshian left on you."

"If I still feel the need after my walk, my lord, I'll sleep a bit before supper."

Duko waved his permission to withdraw, and Jimmy left. The inn converted to headquarters was busy, with many clerks supporting the demands of a headquarters command. Jimmy was amused at how the clerks and functionaries were rapidly overwhelming the far more casual approach traditional to the mercenaries from across the sea. At most a Captain from Novindus had to worry about organization and logistics on the same level as a baron, a few hundred men at most. A general such as Duko rarely had more than a few thousand men under his command. Now, suddenly, these disorganized swords-for-hire were being forced into acting like a tradition-bound, massively organized army. Jimmy suspected more than one clerk would earn a black eye or broken head from a frustrated soldier from Novindus before this campaign was through.

If this campaign was ever through, thought Jimmy as he left the building to get a good look at Port Vykor.

The crack of whips echoed through the evening air. Subai recognized the sound, even at a distance. He had heard it often enough as a child, living in the hills outside of Durbin.

His grandfather had been a member of the nearly legendary Imperial Keshian Guides, the finest scouts and trackers in the Empire. He had taught his grandson every trick and skill he could, and when the slavers raided the villages for boys and girls to take to the slave blocks, Subai had used those skills to hide.

Then one time, after a raid, he had returned to find his entire family dead, his father and grandfather's bodies hacked to pieces, his mother and sister missing. Only eleven years of age, he had taken his few possessions and set out after the men who had done this.

By the time he had reached the Durbin docks, Subai had killed three men. He had never found those who had taken his mother and sister, and Durbin was, if anything, more lethal an environment than the hills nearby. He stowed away on a ship bound for Krondor, and had stayed hidden for the entire voyage.

Knowing nothing else, he had found his way to a village outside the city, where he worked as a servant for a family who fed him and clothed him in exchange for work. At sixteen, he returned to Krondor and enlisted in the Prince's army.

By the time he was twenty-five, Subai was the leader of the Pathfinders. But now, ten years later, he still remembered the sound of the slaver's whip as it cracked through the air.

There were still five Pathfinders with him as they reached the area east of Quester's View. Two had been dispatched south already, carrying back intelligence to Marshal Greylock. There had been no fortifications like the one halfway between Sarth and Quester's View. There had been two observation towers, with relay riders ready to carry word when the Kingdom forces reached a certain point in their journey north. Subai had drawn detailed maps showing them, and Erik's best avenue of approach was to take them out before they could send warning north. Subai had faith in von Darkmoor, and knew his Crimson Eagles would take those positions quickly.

Subai had left four of his Pathfinders high in the hills above where he and his companion worked their way down steep hillsides to oversee the sounds coming from the highway. Their horses were far enough above them now that they didn't worry about being discovered unless the two men blundered into a sentry.

Given the treacherous footing on the hills as they made their way down toward the coast, Subai doubted there even was a guard up here. Each step was made slowly, so as not to dislodge stones and send a man rolling down the mountain to his death.

The trees were thick enough there were ample handholds, but the going was difficult.

When they reached the edge of a high ridge, with a veritable cliff below them to another steep slope fifty feet below, Subai knew the effort had been worth it. Without speaking he withdrew a roll of fine parchment from within his tunic and removed a tiny box, along with some writing sticks. With economy, he sketched what he saw before him and added a few notes. At the bottom he wrote a short commentary, then he put away his writing implements. To his companion he said, "Study what you see below."

They remained for a full hour, watching as slave gangs of Kingdom citizens dug deep trenches along the route Greylock's army would have to take. Walls were being built, but unlike the earthen barricade down south, these were huge constructions of stone and iron. A forge had been constructed near the front, and its hellish glow cast a reddish light over hundreds of poor wretches laboring for the invaders. Guards walked along, many carrying whips which they used to keep the miserable workers hard at their labor.

The sound of sawing also reached them, and they saw a lumber mill had also been constructed near the coast. Riders came down the road and wagons pulled by oxen slowly made their way toward the construction.

As night fell, Subai said, "We must be back up the hill, else we're stuck here through the night."

He stood and, as he took a step, heard his companion say, "Captain, look!"

Subai looked where the man pointed and swore. Along the road, as far as the eye could trace, in the evening gloom, other lights burned brightly; more forges and torches and tantalizing hints that told Subai one cold fact. The Kingdom could not win this war fighting the way it was. He started up the hill, knowing that he would have to wait until first light, then begin a long report to Greylock. Then he would have to race north and reach Yabon before it fell. With LaMut, Zūn, and Ylith in enemy hands, Subai realized the King and Prince of Krondor did not realize how close they were to losing Yabon Province forever.

And should Yabon be lost, it would only be a matter of time before the invaders turned south again and attempted to retake Krondor and the West.

Nineteen

Decisions

WIND SWEPT THE beach.

Pug walked hand in hand with Miranda as the sun rose in the east. They had been walking and talking all night and were close to agreement about several critical issues facing them.

"But I don't see why you have to do anything *now*," said Miranda. "I thought after relaxing in Elvandar for those weeks and getting rid of all that anger you had directed at the Prince, well, I thought you could just ignore Patrick's stupidity."

Pug grinned. "Ignoring stupidity in a merchant or servant is one thing; ignoring it in a Prince is quite a different thing. It's not the simple question of the Saaur. That's merely a symptom. It's the entire issue of who is, at the end, responsible for my power, me or the crown?"

"I understand," she said, "but why rush this decision? Why not wait until it's clear that you're being told to act against your conscience?"

"Because I want to avoid a situation where I'm faced with two evils, and must act to prevent the greater evil by embracing the lesser."

Miranda said, "Well, I still think you may be rushing things."

"I'm not about to fly to Krondor and explain my stance to Patrick until I've taken care of a few other things," Pug said.

They climbed over some rocks and picked their way among some tidal pools. Pug said, "When I was a boy in Crydee, I used to beg Tomas's father to let me go to the pools south of town, where I looked for rockclaws and crabs; he made the best shellfish stew."

Miranda said, "Seems like a long time ago, doesn't it?"

Pug turned, a youthful grin on his face, and said, "Sometimes it seems like ages, but other times it's as fresh in my mind as yesterday."

"What about the Saaur?" asked Miranda. "That problem won't go away by dwelling in the past."

"For several nights, my love, I have been spending some time with one of the oldest toys in my collection."

"That crystal you inherited from Kulgan?"

"The very one. Fashioned by Athalfain of Carse. I've been scouring the globe and think I may have found a place to which we can move the Saaur."

"Care to show me?"

Pug extended his hand and said, "I need to practice that transport spell, anyway. Put a protective shell around us, please."

Miranda did so, and suddenly a bluish, transparent globe surrounded them. "Don't materialize us inside a mountain again and we won't need this."

Pug said, "I'm trying." He put his arm around her waist, and said, "Let's try this."

Instantly the scene around them swirled, resolving itself into a vast grassy plain.

"Where are we?" asked Miranda.

"The Ethel-du-ath, in the local tongue," said Pug.

The blue globe vanished, and they were struck by a hot summer wind. "That sounds like Lower Delkian," said Miranda.

"The Duathian Plain," said Pug. "Come here."

He walked her a few hundred yards south and suddenly they were peering down the face of a towering cliff. Pug said, "Sometime ages ago, this part of the continent rose up while that down there fell. There's no portion of this cliff face less than six hundred feet high. There are two or three places you might climb, but I wouldn't recommend it."

Miranda stepped off into the air and continued walking. She turned and looked down. "That's quite a drop."

"Show-off," said Pug. "The lower portion of the continent was settled by refugees from Triasia, during the purging of the Ishapian Temple of the Heretics of Al-maral."

"That's the same bunch that settled down in Novindus," said Miranda, walking back to solid ground. "No people up here?"

"No people," said Pug. "Just a million or so square miles of grassland, rolling hills, rivers, and lakes, with mountains to the north and west, and cliffs to the south and east."

"So you want to put the Saaur here."

"Until I come up with a better solution," said Pug. "This place is large enough they can live here for several hundred years, if need be. Eventually, I'll go back to Shila and rid that place of the remaining demons. But even then it will take centuries to get enough life back on the planet to support the Saaur."

Miranda said, "What if they don't want to live here?"

"I may not be able to afford them the luxury of a choice," said Pug.

Miranda put her arms about Pug's waist. Hugging him, she said, "Just getting the feel of how much these choices are going to cost, aren't you?"

"I never told you the story about the Imperial Games, did I?" he asked.

"No," she said.

He held her, and suddenly they were back on the beach on Sorcerer's Island. "Now who's being a show-off!" she demanded, halfway between amusement and anger.

"I think I have the hang of it now," he said with a wry smile.

She playfully punched him in the arm. "You're not allowed to 'think' you have the hang of it. You damn well better know, unless you want to see how quickly you can erect a protective spell when you're materializing inside of rock!"

"Sorry," he said, his expression clearly showing he wasn't. "Let's get back to the house."

"I could use some sleep," she said. "We've been talking all night."

"Lots of important things to discuss," he said, putting his arm back around her waist. They walked quietly for a short distance, up to the path that led over the hill and back to the villa.

"I was a new Great One," Pug began, "and Hochopepa, my mentor in the Assembly, persuaded me to attend a great festival the Warlord was orchestrating to honor the Emperor. And to announce a great victory over the Kingdom." He fell silent, in remembrance. After a moment, he continued. "Kingdom soldiers were pitted against soldiers of the Thruil, my wife's people. I became enraged."

"I can understand that," said Miranda. They continued to walk the path upward.

"I used my power to tear apart the imperial arena. I caused the winds to blow, fire to fall from the sky, rain, earthquakes, the whole bag of tricks."

"Must have been impressive."

"It was. It scared hell out of many thousands of people, Miranda."

"And you saved the men condemned to fight and die?"

"Yes," replied Pug.

"But what?"

"But to save two score of soldiers wrongly condemned, I ended up killing hundreds of people whose only crime was to be born on Kelewan and choose to attend a festival for their Emperor."

Miranda said, "I think I understand."

"It was a temper tantrum," said Pug. "Nothing more. I could have found a better way to deal with it had I remained calm, but I let my anger consume me."

"It's understandable," she said.

"It may be understandable," replied Pug, "but it is no more forgivable for being understandable." He paused at the top of the ridge that separated the beach from the interior of the island and looked out at the vista. "Look at the sea. It doesn't care. It endures. This world endures. Shila will eventually endure. When the last demon starves to death, something will happen. A bit of life will fall from the sky, in a meteor or on the winds of magic, or by means I don't understand. Maybe it will be a single blade of grass hidden behind a rock the demons missed, or some other tiny life that lingers at the bottom of the oceans will emerge and eventually that world will again see life thrive, even if I never return to it.''

"What are you saying, my love?"

"It's tempting to think of yourself as powerful when those around you are far less so, but compared to the simple fact of existence, to the power of life and how it hangs on, we are nothing." He looked at his wife. "The Gods are nothing." He looked toward their home. "Despite my years, I am nothing more than a child when it comes to understanding these things. I know now why your father was always so driven to seek out new knowledge. I know why Nakor revels in each new thing he encounters. We are the same as children encountering a tiny bauble."

He fell quiet, and Miranda said, "Talking of children makes you sad?"

They walked down the sloping path, through a glade of trees, and approached the outer garden of their estate. They could see students gathered around in a circle, practicing an exercise Pug had given them the day before.

"When I felt my children die, it took all my willpower to keep from flying to confront the demon again," said Pug.

Miranda lowered her eyes. "I'm glad you didn't, my love." She still blamed herself for goading him into attacking the demon prematurely and almost losing his life in the process.

"Well, perhaps my injuries taught me something. Had I challenged Jakan when he was still in Krondor, I might not have survived to defeat him at Sethanon."

"Is that why you avoid helping remove this General Fadawah from Ylith?"

"Patrick would be pleased for me to simply show up and burn the entire province of Yabon to the ground. He'd happily move settlers in from the East and replant trees, claiming a great victory.

"I doubt the people living there would agree, and neither would the elves or the dwarves who live nearby. Besides, most of those men are no more evil than those serving Patrick. I find matters of politics are of less interest to me every day.''

"Wise," said Miranda. "You are a force, as am I, and between the two of us we could probably conquer a small nation."

"Yes," said Pug with a grin, his first smile since telling of the arena. "What would you do with it?"

"Ask Fadawah," suggested Miranda. "He obviously has plans."

Entering the main building of the estate, Pug said, "I have larger concerns."

"I know," she replied.

"There is something out there," said Pug. "Something I haven't encountered for years."

"What?"

"I'm not sure," said Pug. "When I know, I will tell you." Pug said nothing more. Both knew of the existence out in the cosmos of a great evil, the Nameless One, who was at the root of all the troubles they had been facing for the previous century. And that evil had human agents, men whom Pug had encountered more than once in the past. Pug kept his thoughts to himself, but there had been one agent of Nalar, a mad magician named Sidi, who had created havoc fifty years before. Pug thought the man dead, but now he wasn't sure. If it wasn't Sidi he sensed out there, it was another like him, and either possibility left Pug feeling dread and fear. Dealing with these forces was a task beyond any Pug had imagined while he was a Great One of the Assembly, or during his early days of creating Stardock.

It was a task that more than once left Pug feeling defeated before he had even begun. He thanked the gods that he had Miranda, for without her, he would long before have given himself up to despair.

Dash looked up and saw a face he knew. "Talwin?"

The former prisoner walked past the two constables sitting at the table drinking coffee and getting ready for their next patrol. "Can I speak to you in private?" asked the man who had vanished right after Dash escaped from Krondor.

"Sure," said Dash, standing up and waving the man to a far corner of the converted inn. When they were out of earshot of the constables, Dash said, "I wondered what happened to you. I left you and Gustaf outside a tent when I went in to report, and when I came back out I found only Gustaf."

Talwin reached inside his tunic and pulled out a faded parchment, obviously old. Dash read:

To whoever reads this:

   The bearer of this document will be identified by a mole on his neck and a scar on the back of his left arm. He is a servant of the crown and I request all aid and assistance asked be given to him without question.

                              Signed,
                              James, Duke of Krondor

Dash's eyebrows rose. He glanced at Talwin and saw the man pointing to the mole on his neck, then rolling up his left sleeve to show the scar on his arm.

"Who are you?" Dash asked quietly.

"I was your grandfather's agent, and your father's after him."

"Agent?" asked Dash. "One of his spies, you mean."

"Among other things," said Talwin.

"And I don't suppose Talwin is your real name," said Dash.

"It serves," said Talwin. Lowering his voice he said, "As Sheriff of Krondor you need to know that I am responsible for intelligence within the Western Realm, now."

Dash nodded. "Knowing my grandfather, he didn't hand out a lot of cartes blanches, so that makes you a very important spy. Why didn't you show this to me before?"

"I don't carry it on me; I had to go dig it out of its hiding place. If I'm searched and it's found on me by the wrong people, I'm dead."

"So why now?"

"This city is barely intact, and while it appears to be crawling back from oblivion, it's very vulnerable. Your job is to insure order, and my job is to ferret out enemy agents."

Dash was silent for a moment. "Very well. What is it you need?"

"Cooperation between us. Until the palace staff is restored and I can work out of there unseen, I need to work someplace where I can be seen poking around in all parts of the city without people asking too many questions."

"You need a job as a constable," supplied Dash.

"Yes. When the present danger is over and the city more secure than it is, I'll move back to the palace and get out of your hair. Right now I need to be a constable."

"Do you report to me?" asked Dash.

"No," said Talwin. "I report to the Duke of Krondor."

"There is no Duke of Krondor," said Dash.

"Not at present, but until there is, I report to Duke Brian."

Dash inclined his head to show that made sense. "Have you alerted him to your existence?"

"Not yet," said Talwin. "The fewer people who know of me, the better. Rumor has it the King is sending Rufio, Earl Delamo, from Rodez to take the office. If true, I'll let him know who I am as soon as he arrives."

Dash said, "I'm not happy with having a constable here under false colors, but I know the business. Just make sure if there's anything going on out there I should know about, you tell me."

"I'll do that," said Talwin.

"Now, what else do you need from me?"

"I need to know who killed your two men."

Suddenly Dash had an insight. "You mean who killed your two agents, don't you?"

Talwin nodded. "How did you guess?"

"The Mockers. Someone told me I needed to find out what Nolan and Riggs did before joining up."

"They spent a lot of time working the docks for your grandfather and your father. We kept low during the fall of the city and managed to stay alive. I was captured and stuck on the damn work gang until you showed up. I couldn't risk showing anyone I knew the way out, and I couldn't get free of guards and other prisoners, but when you organized that break, it was a godsend. Getting us past the Mockers was a bonus.''

"Glad to be of service," Dash said dryly.

"Nolan and Riggs were also in work gangs, and they got sprung when Duko made his deal with the Prince. I put them into your service because I need to get my network reestablished." He looked pained as he said, "They were my last two agents in this city."

"So you have to start from scratch."

"Yes," said Talwin. "It's the only reason you're being told all this."

Dash said, "I understand. Look, circumstances say we must work together. Someone killed one of my better snitches when I started asking about who murdered your men."

"Someone in Krondor doesn't want us too close," said Talwin.

"Anyway, we don't have enough warm bodies to do all the jobs that need to be done. Sniff around and I won't bother you with a regular beat. If anyone asks, you're my deputy and on errands for me. I think we'd better quickly get another man in on this."

"Who?"

"Gustaf is as rock-solid as he can be."

"Not my idea of an agent," said Talwin dubiously.

"Not mine, either," admitted Dash, "but we can't all be sneaky bastards. I want a third person knowing what's going on so if we both end up dead he can run off to Brian Silden and let him know why. I don't think we want him crawling through the sewers."

"Agreed, but we need some people crawling through the sewers."

Dash grinned. "Not really. We just need to make a deal with the right people."

"Mockers?"

"They think another gang is trying to move in, but you and I know better."

Talwin nodded. "Agents from Kesh or from Queg."

"Or both."

"But whoever they are, we have to root them out and quickly, because if word gets out to either of those nations that we're sitting here with less than five hundred men under arms in the entire city, we could all be dead before the snows fall next winter."

"I'll take care of the Mockers," said Dash. "You find yourself some agents. I don't want to know who they are, unless you stick them in here as constables."

"Agreed."

"I assume you're using intermediaries."

"Safe assumption."

"Make a list and give it to me. I'll hide it in my room in the palace." He grinned. "I actually manage to get back there once a week to change clothes and bathe. I'll leave a scaled message with Lord Brian, an 'open upon my death' message telling where the list is."

Talwin said, "When the network is reestablished, I'll want the list destroyed."

"Gladly," said Dash, "but what good are agents out there going to do if you and I are both gone and there's no one to get the information to the crown?"

"I understand," said Talwin.

"Come with me," said Dash.

He took Talwin back to the center of the room. To the two resting constables, he said, "This is Talwin. He's been appointed the new Deputy. He'll work the desk when I'm not here. You two, take him around and show him what things are like, then do what he tells you."

Talwin nodded, and Dash fetched him a red armband. When the agent left, Dash sat down and returned to work. He idly wondered how many other little surprises were out there, left in place by his grandfather and father.

Jimmy said, "The fancy fellow on the very hot stallion is a gentleman named Marcel Duval, Squire of the King's Court, and a very close friend to the eldest son of the Duke of Bas-Tyra."

"Hot" stallion appeared to be correct, for the black stud snorted and pawed the ground and appeared to be ready to dump his rider at any moment. The Squire didn't attempt to get off until an orderly ran over and took the animal's bridle. Then he dismounted quickly, putting distance between himself and the horse.

Duko laughed. "Why did he pick that fractious creature?"

"Vanity," said Jimmy. "You see a lot of that east of Malac's Cross."

"And what company is that?" asked Duko.

"His own private guard. Many nobles in the East indulge themselves with such companies. They're very pretty on parade."

Looking at the company of soldiers that accompanied the Squire, it was obvious it was a unit designed for parade, not combat. Each man sat astride a black horse, nearly identical in size, and all without a marking. Each soldier wore buckskin-colored leggings tucked into knee-high black cavalier boots, the large knee flaps of which were rimmed in scarlet cord. The color was an exact match to their red tunics, which were trimmed in black whipcord at shoulders, sleeve, and collar. Their polished steel breastplates appeared to be trimmed in brass, and each man had a short yellow cape slung over the left shoulder. Atop their heads they endured steel round helms, trimmed in white fur, with polished steel neck chains. Each man carried a long lance of lacquered black wood tipped with brilliantly polished steel.

Duko couldn't resist laughing. "They're going to get dirty."

Suddenly Jimmy started to laugh, and he could barely contain himself as the Squire walked up the steps of the inn to the front door. As the door opened, one of Duko's old soldiers said, "A gentleman to see you, m'lord."

Duko walked over to Duval, his hand extended, saying, "Squire Marcel. Your reputation precedes you."

It was protocol for the Squire to introduce himself to the Duke, and Duval was taken completely off guard. He stood there, unsure of whether to take the Duke's proffered hand or bow, so he gave a rapid and awkward bow, and reached out to take the Duke's hand just as it was being withdrawn. Jimmy almost hurt himself trying not to laugh.

"Ah . . . Your Grace," said the flustered squire from

Bas-Tyra. "I've come to place my sword at your disposal."
He saw Jimmy standing off to one side, and said, "James?"

"Marcel," Jimmy said with a slight bow.

"I didn't know you were here, Squire."

"It's Earl, now, actually," said Duko.

Marcel's eyes widened, which heightened his comic appearance. For while he was dressed exactly like his men, he had elected to wear a larger helm, with stylized wings on each side. He had a round face, with a large waxed mustache that stuck out on either side.

"Congratulations," said Marcel.

Jimmy couldn't resist. "I received the office upon my father's death," he said seriously.

Marcel Duval had the decency to blush a furious red color, stammer and appear close to tears over the gaffe. "I'm so sorry . . . m'lord," he said with a tone so apologetic it bordered on the comical.

Jimmy swallowed a laugh and said, "Glad to see you, Marcel."

Duval ignored the remark, totally defeated socially. He turned to Duko and, mustering as military a manner as he could, said, "I have fifty lancers at your disposal, m'lord!"

Duko said, "I'll have my sergeant get your men billeted, Squire. As long as you're in my command, you'll carry the rank of lieutenant. Join us for supper." Duko shouted, "Matak!"

The old soldier who opened the door, said, "Yes?"

"Show this officer and his men a place they can pitch their tents."

"Yes, m'lord," said the old soldier, holding open the door to allow Duval to flee.

When he was gone, Jimmy laughed, and Duko said, "I take it you didn't get along with him before?"

"Oh, Marcel is harmless, if a bore," said Jimmy. "When we were boys in Rillanon, he was always trying to intrude into social situations to which he had not been invited. I think he was trying to get on Patrick's good side." Jimmy sighed. "It was Patrick who couldn't stand him, actually. Francie, Dash, and I got along well enough with him."

"Francie?" asked Duko.

Jimmy's expression clouded over, as memory of her suddenly inserted itself in his consciousness. "The Duke of Silden's daughter," Jimmy supplied.

"Well, he has fifty men. We'll get them into shape, and if nothing else, they'll be *very* obvious on patrol, so the Keshians will know they're around."

"They'll be hard to miss in those scarlet tunics," said Jimmy.

A knock came at the door and it opened, and a messenger hurried in. Handing a packet to Jimmy, he said, "Messages from Land's End, m'lords."

Jimmy took them, opened the packet, and Duko waved the messenger outside. Jimmy quickly sorted out those messages that were urgent and other communiqués that could wait, then opened the first. "Damn," he said as he skimmed the letter. The Duke was learning to read the King's tongue, but it was more efficient to let Jimmy read and sum up for him. "Another raid and this time two villages south of Land's End were sacked. Captain Kuvak is withdrawing from patrolling there, as the villagers have fled and they no longer require the Earl's protection."

Duko shook his head. "Some protection. Had he been protecting those villages, they wouldn't be sacked!"

Jimmy knew the static front was wearing on everyone's nerves, especially the Duke's. Kuvak had been one of Duko's most trusted officers, which is why he had been selected to oversee the defense of the castle at Land's End. Jimmy jumped to the end of the report. "They still give the castle wide berth, and he's routed two other raids in the area."

Duko walked back to the window and looked out at his rapidly growing town. "I know Kuvak's doing the best he can down there. It's not his fault." He looked at the map. "When will they come?"

"The Keshians?"

"They're not going to do this forever. There's a reason behind the raids and the probes. They will eventually show us what their intent is, but it may be too late."

Jimmy was silent. While ambassadors were negotiating at Stardock, men from both nations were dying. Jimmy knew that the strike would come if and when the Keshians

decided they could strengthen their negotiating position by
doing so.

A strike at the Vale of Dreams, an attempt to seize the
western coast from Land's End to Port Vykor, or a strike
directly at Krondor, all were possible. And they were only
able to defend two of those three locations, so they had a
one in three chance of being wrong, tragically wrong. And
lingering in the back of his mind was that escaped Keshian
officer, and what he knew.

"Up here," said Dash.

Turning and looking up, Trina smiled, and Dash was
again struck with how attractive she could be should she
ever decide to play up her looks. "You're getting better,
Sheriff Puppy."

Dash leaped down from the roof beam upon which he
had rested, landing lightly on his feet. "I found out who
Nolan and Riggs worked for," said Dash.

"And?"

"So I know whoever killed them is neither friend to the
crown nor the Mockers."

"So the enemy of my enemy is my friend?"

Dash grinned. "I wouldn't go that far. Let's say that it
suits our mutual interest to cooperate in discovering who
else is using the sewers as a highway, besides the thieves."

Trina leaned back against the wall and looked Dash up
and down in an appraising fashion. "When we were told
you were to be in charge of the city's security, we thought
it a bit of a joke. I guess not. You're more like your grandfather than not."

"You knew my grandfather?" asked Dash.

"Only by reputation. Our old friend held your grandfather in awe."

Dash laughed. "I have always understood how special
my grandfather was, but I never thought of him that way."

"Think on it, Sheriff Puppy. A thief who became the
most powerful noble in the Kingdom. That's a tale."

"I guess," said Dash. "But to me he was always Grandfather, and those stories were always just wonderful stories."

"What do you propose?" asked Trina, changing the topic.

"I need to know if you catch sight of any of these strangers in the sewer, especially if you discover where they're hiding."

Trina said, "You know who they are?"

"I have my suspicions," said Dash.

"Care to share them?"

"Would you in my place?"

She laughed. "No, I wouldn't. What is in it for the Mockers?"

Dash said, "I should think you'd just want them gone if they're causing you problems."

"They are causing us no problems whatsoever. Nolan and Riggs we knew because they've bought information from us before, and they've set up a few deals. We always suspected they were working for some businessmen in the city, like Avery and his bunch, who didn't wish to conduct business in the usual fashion, or a noble who wasn't entirely aboveboard in paying taxes. That sort of thing."

Dash realized she was fishing for information. "Whoever Nolan and Riggs were working for prior to the war, they were *my* men when they got their throats cut. I don't care if it was over some old grudge or because they happened to wander into the wrong place at the wrong time. I cannot afford to have people running around this city thinking they can kill *my* constables. It's that simple."

"If you say so, Sheriff Puppy. But there's still the matter of price."

Dash had no illusions. It was a waste of his time to make any sort of offer. "Ask the old man what he wants, but I won't compromise the city's security or look the other way about a capital crime. I'll get what I want without your help."

"I'll ask him," said Trina. She started to leave.

"Trina," said Dash.

She stopped and smiled. "You want something else?"

Dash ignored the double entendre. "How is he?"

Trina lost her smile. "Not well."

"Is there anything I can do?"

Her smile returned, this time a small one without any

hint of mockery. ''No, I don't think so, but it's good of you to ask.''

Dash said, ''Well, he is family.''

Trina was silent for a long minute, then she reached out and touched Dash's cheek. ''Yes, more than I thought.'' Then, with a sudden turn, she was out the door and down the street into the darkness.

Dash waited a few minutes, then ducked out the back of the old building. He felt an odd sensation inside. He didn't know how much of it was concern for the old man's health, worry over the possible infiltration of Keshian agents into the city, or the woman's touch on his cheek. Muttering to himself, Dash said, ''If only she wasn't so damned attractive.''

Putting aside the distractions of a beautiful woman, he turned his mind back to the problems of protecting the city of Krondor.

Twenty

Clash

MEN SHOUTED.

Erik motioned the third element of the infantry forward and they marched out into the killing zone. The heavy ram had breached the door, and the first and second waves had swarmed the gates and were now inside the barricade. Resistance had been heavier this time, but as with the first two barricades they had encountered, the defense was more for show than for real resistance.

The messages from Subai had Erik and Greylock worried, for his picture of the defenses ahead had Erik concerned that they simply were not equal to the task of breaking through in time to rescue Yabon. The summer was nearly half over, with the Festival of Banapis only a week away. If there were heavy fall rains, or an early winter snow, they could lose Yabon Province for good. And if they lost Yabon this year, it was possible they would lose Krondor again the next.

If not sooner.

Erik could not escape the feeling that Krondor lay naked and ready for the taking if Kesh should simply realize that fact. He hoped the negotiations at Stardock were proceeding well.

He pushed aside his worry and looked at Owen. The

Knight-Marshal of Krondor nodded, and Erik spurred his own horse forward. For whatever reasons, Owen had ordered Erik to remain behind at the headquarters tent, rather than lead the first assault as was Erik's desire.

The fighting was fierce for an hour, then suddenly the defense collapsed. Erik moved his horse through the gate and realized that, once again, they were facing an enemy that lacked the resources for a sustained defense.

Erik rode around, and saw that everything was now under control. As before, he dispatched light cavalry to ride up the road, seeking those fleeing northward, preventing any from reaching their own lines.

Greylock appeared at the gate of the barricade, and Erik rode toward him. "This is pointless," he said. "If what Subai says is true, we should have sat outside the wall and starved them out."

Owen shrugged. "The Prince's orders didn't give us leave to tarry." He looked about the scene unfolding around them, and said, "Though if you put a dagger to my throat, I'd be forced to agree with you." He stood up in his stirrups. "My backside longs for a comfortable chair by the fire at the Inn of the Pintail, a jack of ale in my hand, and your mother's stew in front of me."

Erik grinned. "I'll mention that to Mother when next I see her. She'll be flattered."

Owen returned the smile, then seemed to leap out of his saddle, backward, spinning over the rear of his horse and landing hard on his back. His horse sprang forward.

Erik looked in all directions, and all he could see were mercenaries throwing down their swords, putting their hands in the air, and being herded to rear positions. A few signs of struggle could still be seen, and there was sporadic combat in the distance, but whoever shot the crossbow bolt that had felled Greylock was nowhere to be seen.

"Damn!" Erik leaped from his horse, and raced to where Greylock lay. Before Erik's knee touched the ground next to his old friend, he knew the dreadful truth. A crossbow bolt protruded from above the breastplate Owen wore, and it had smashed the upper portion of his chest and lower throat to pulp. Blood flowed everywhere and Owen's eyes stared lifelessly at the sky above.

Erik felt a cold stab of anger and hopelessness. He felt like screaming, but resisted the impulse. Owen had always been a friend, even before Erik had become a soldier, and they had shared a love for horses, an appreciation of the great wines from the Darkmoor region, and the fruits of honest labor. Looking down at the lifeless form of his old friend, Erik's mind was awash with images, laughter over jokes, losses endured together, and the approval of an old teacher who was generous in his praise and frugal in his criticism.

Erik turned and his eyes sought out Owen's killer. A short distance away, he spied two Kingdom soldiers arguing. One held a crossbow and the other pointed in his direction. Erik leaped to his feet and ran to face them. "What happened?"

Both men looked as if the Killer God Guis-wa had appeared before them. One of them looked as if he was ready to vomit. Perspiration appeared on his brow as he said, "Captain . . . I was . . ."

"What?" demanded Erik.

The man appeared close to tears as he said, "I was about to shoot when the order to hold was called out. I put the crossbow over my shoulder, and it went off."

"It's true!" said the other man. "He fired it backward. It was an accident."

Erik closed his eyes. He felt a shaking in his body start at his feet and run up his legs to his groin and up through his chest. Of all the jokes he had endured in his short life, this was the most cruel. Owen had died at the hands of one of his own men, by accident, because the man had been lazy and sloppy.

With a hard swallow, Erik forced back his frustration and rage. He knew there were other officers in the army who would hang this man for not unloading his crossbow and costing the Kingdom the life of their commander in the West. He looked at the two men involved in the accidental shooting, and said, "Go away."

They didn't hesitate, but ran as if wishing to be as far away from the giant young Captain as possible when his rage finally erupted. Erik stood motionless a moment, then turned back to see soldiers gathered around the body of

Owen Greylock, Knight-Marshal of Krondor. Erik calmly moved through them, gently but firmly pushing them aside until he was once again beside his old friend.

He knelt next to Owen and scooped him up in his arms, as if carrying a child, and turned toward the gates. The battle was not quite over, but the situation was well in hand, and Erik felt a need, a duty, to carry his old friend back to his command pavilion; he would not trust the task to another. Slowly, he walked back down the road, holding his dear friend.

The officers had assembled and the silence was awkward. Erik stood beside Owen's empty chair of command. He glanced around the room. There were a dozen captains senior to him, but none holding the unique position of Captain of the Prince's Crimson Eagles. The nobility in the tent was also senior to him, but none of them were part of Patrick's command structure.

Erik self-consciously cleared his throat, then said, "My lords, we are faced with a dilemma. The Knight-Marshal has fallen and we are in need of a commander. Until Prince Patrick appoints one, we need to be united in our duty." He looked around the tent. Many eyes regarded him suspiciously. "If Captain Subai were here, I would easily accept him as leader, given his years of service to the Principality. Or if Captain Calis, my predecessor, were here, he also would easily ascend to the office of commander. But we have a situation both dangerous and awkward."

Erik looked at one old soldier, the Earl of Makurlic, and said, "My Lord Richard."

"Captain?"

"Of those here you are senior in service and age. I would be honored to follow your command."

The minor Earl, from a small corner of the Kingdom located outside Deep Taunton, appeared both surprised and pleased. He glanced around the tent, and when no one seemed to object, he said, "I will serve as interim commander until the Prince names another, Captain."

There seemed an almost palpable sigh of relief in the tent as the conflict between the Prince's handpicked Captain and the more traditional nobles was avoided for the time being. The Earl of Makurlic said, "Let us get the Knight-Marshal on his way back to Krondor, then I want a meeting of all senior staff immediately after."

Erik von Darkmoor saluted and said, "Sir," and left the tent before anyone could say another word. He hurried in search of Jadow Shati, for he needed to make sure his own men knew what they must do before any other officer could find them and send them off on another mission. He might give public acknowledgment to the new commander, but he wasn't about to turn his own men over to the whim of a man who a year before had been hosting parties at his peaceful seaside estate a half-continent away.

Save those soldiers guarding prisoners, the entirety of the Kingdom's Army of the West stood at attention as the wagon carrying Greylock's body rolled south. Men who barely knew the Knight-Marshal of Krondor stood side by side with men who had served every step of the way with Owen.

Despite the previous day's victory, there was a grim mood in camp, as if everyone sensed that the easy victories were behind them now, and that the future held only more loss and suffering.

Drummers beat a slow tattoo and a single horn blew farewell, and as the wagon passed each company on parade, they dipped their banners and the men saluted, fist over heart, head bowed, until the wagon moved on.

When the last company on parade was left behind, a company of Krondorian lancers, twenty handpicked men, fell in, ten on each side of the wagon, to escort the leader of their army back to the capital.

Each company commander dismissed his men, and Richard, Earl of Makurlic, sounded an officer's call. Erik hurried to the command tent, putting aside his discomfort at seeing someone else sitting in Owen's old chair.

Earl Richard was an old man, grey hair and blue eyes his dominant features. His long face seemed worn by years of duty, but his voice was strong and without hesitation when he spoke. "I am appointing Captain von Darkmoor my second-in-command, gentleman, to keep as much continuity as possible. For that reason, I'm asking all of you to return to your previous assignments, and to funnel all communications through Captain von Darkmoor. I will instruct my son, Lelan, to assume command of our cavalry units from Makurlic. That will be all.''

The nobles and other officers departed, and Richard said, ''Erik, stay a moment.''

''Sir?'' asked Erik when they were alone.

''I know why you chose me, son,'' said the old officer. ''You've a fair grasp of politics. I appreciate that. What I don't appreciate is any thought you might have of using me for your own gains.''

Erik stiffened. ''Sir, I will follow your orders and offer you the best counsel of which I am capable. Should you find my service lacking, you may remove me at your pleasure and I will not voice objection, even to the Prince.''

''Well said,'' replied the Earl, ''but now I need to know your heart. I've seen you lead men in the field, von Darkmoor, and the reports of your actions last year at Nightmare Ridge do you credit, but I need to know I can depend on you.''

''My lord,'' said Erik, ''I have no ambitions in this. I am a reluctant Captain, but I serve to my utmost. If you wish to replace me and have me serve at the van of my men, I will acknowledge your orders and depart immediately to fulfill whatever mission you name.''

The old man studied Erik a while longer, then said, ''That won't be necessary, Erik. Just tell me what's going on.''

Erik nodded. He outlined his fears and Greylock's, that they were being lulled by a series of modest defenses to have them charge foolishly into Fadawah's real southern position. Erik pointed to a stack of parchments. ''Subai's messages are there, sir, and I suggest you read them.'' Erik pointed to the map on the table before Earl Richard. ''We're here, and about here''—his finger jumped up the map about sixty miles—''we should hit the first serious defensive position. If what Subai writes is accurate, it's going to be hell to pay getting to Ylith.''

''I assume you've considered all the alternatives, landing

on Free Cities soil and attacking from the west, attempting to land outside the harbor, and the rest?''

Erik nodded.

"I'll want you to cover those discarded options for me later, just in case I might think of something you and Owen missed, but I'm certain you didn't miss anything. Assuming that's true, what do we do next?''

Erik said, "I want to take a patrol and go north, and see how far I can get before things get nasty. I want to see what Subai saw, my lord.''

Richard, Earl of Makurlic, said nothing for a long moment, his mind weighing options, then he said, "I sent a letter to Prince Patrick, asking him to relieve me of this command, but until he does, I suppose I should act like a commander.

"Here's what you do. Send those Hadati hillmen ahead up the right flank. They can move through the hills better than anyone we have. Have them leave at once. Then send a company of your Crimson Eagles up the left flank, along the coast but out of sight.

"Then at first light tomorrow, I want you and my son to lead a patrol of cavalry up the highway. Be as loud and careless as you wish.''

Erik nodded. "That should flush out anyone looking to lay an ambush.''

"If the Gods were kinder, you'd all ride into Ylith at the same time and hoist an ale. The Gods, however, have been short on kindness toward the Kingdom of late.'' He looked up and saw Erik still standing there. "Well, go, dismissed, whatever it is I'm supposed to say.''

Erik grinned at the old man. "Yes, sir,'' he said with a salute, and he was off.

Talwin signaled from outside the building and Dash waved a reply through the open front door. He then motioned with his hand indicating Talwin and the men next to him should circle around the next block of buildings and come up behind the men they stalked. Their targets, four men who had been waiting for a fifth for the last half hour, were gathered together in a workyard behind an abandoned shop in the poor quarter. Talwin vanished into the night with his men.

It had taken Dash, with the help of the Mockers, a week to discover this meeting place. Talwin had identified three men who were very likely to be Keshian agents, and the fourth was either another agent or their employee. Dash had overheard enough snippets of conversation to know they were getting restless waiting for someone and would soon leave if that person didn't show up.

Dash wanted Talwin and the two constables with him ready to come in from the other side of the yard, through a broken-down fence next to an alley. Dash and his men were in an old shop, hiding by hanging above the main floor in the rafters. A glance into the murk of the shop's ceiling showed his three men crouched uncomfortably on the roof beam. He'd better get them down soon, he thought, or they'd be too stiff to move.

Dash motioned and the three men hung from their fingers, then dropped quietly to the floor. Dash crouched low so as not to alert the men out back, as he was closest to the open door.

"He's not coming," said one of the four men, a muscular man dressed like a common laborer. "We should split up and meet somewhere else tomorrow."

"Maybe they got him," a second man said; he was thin and dangerous-looking, and bore a sword and dagger at his belt.

"Who?" asked the first man.

"Who do you think?" offered the first man. "The Prince's men."

"They'd have to be quicker than they've been so far," came the voice of a man ducking into view from the next building. "You almost got nicked," he said.

"What do you mean?" asked the first man.

"I saw constables hurrying away from just in front of this building. They looked like they was looking through the door. They must have just missed you all."

Dash decided it was time. He pulled his sword and ran from his hiding place, his three constables behind him. The first man turned and fled, running right into Talwin as he climbed through a large hole in the fence. "Put down your weapons!" Dash commanded.

Four of the men put down weapons, but the one slender man, the one Dash had judged dangerous, pulled his. "Run!" he shouted to his companions, and as if to buy them time, he launched a two-weapon attack on Dash.

Dash had practiced against this style of fighting before, but this man was very good at it. One of his constables tried to come to his aid but only managed to almost get Dash killed. "Back off!" Dash commanded after he slipped aside of a thrust, while his constable moved away.

Talwin walked up behind the slender man and slammed him in the back of the head with the hilt of his sword. Dash, frustrated at the long wait, turned to his constable and shouted, "That's how you do it! You hit them from behind! You don't leap in and almost get someone killed! Got it?"

The constable nodded, looking embarrassed, and Dash turned to inspect the other prisoners. The fifth man, the one who arrived last, looked familiar to Dash. Dash studied him for a moment, then his eyes widened. "I know you! You're a clerk from the palace!" The man said nothing, looking terrified.

Talwin said, "Let's get this bunch to the palace for some questioning . . . if you agree, Sheriff."

"Good idea, Deputy," said Dash.

The other members of the constabulary knew something odd was going on with Talwin, but no one had voiced any concerns, or at least not within Dash's hearing. Dash, Talwin, and the other five constables ordered two of the prisoners to pick up their unconscious comrade and started them on their way to the palace.

"They're not Keshian," said Talwin as he closed the door behind them.

"Then who are they working for?" asked Dash.

They were in Dash's room, unused since he had been given the office of Sheriff. "I think they're working for the Keshians, but they may not know that."

Dash had appropriated five rooms in the palace in which each of the prisoners was isolated. He didn't want them talking to one another before questioning each in turn. Talwin had briefly spoken to each man, before beginning intensive questioning. He said, "We've got one interesting case, Pickney, a clerk from the Prince's office. The rest of them are . . . odd. One vagabond swordsman, one baker, a stablehand, and a journeyman mason."

Dash said, "Hardly the lot I'd pick for conspiracy."

Talwin said, "I think they're dupes. Not one of them has the wits of a bug. Pickney worries me."

"I'd worry a little about that swordsman—"

"Desgarden," supplied Talwin, "is the happy blade who tried to kill you."

"Desgarden," repeated Dash. "He was willing to try to fight his way out rather than be captured."

"Either he has an inflated sense of his own ability with a sword, or he's just as stupid as I think he is."

"Stupid he may be," said Dash, "but unlike the other three, he's not what I would consider a 'stand-up' citizen. He has the look of someone who knows his way around the back alleys and sewers. He may be part of those who are causing some troubles in the Poor Quarter."

Talwin nodded. "Well, let me squeeze them and see what I can find out."

Dash said, "Good. I think I'm going to sleep in my own bed tonight. It's been a month."

Talwin said, "By the way, I should be leaving your service at the end of the week."

"Oh?" said Dash, with a slight smile. "Have I been that difficult an employer?"

"Duke Rufio arrives."

"It's been confirmed he's to be Duke of Krondor?"

"Not publicly," said Talwin. "You didn't hear that from me."

Dash waved away the man, who closed the door while Dash took off his boots. He lay back on his own bed and marveled at how soft his heavy down mattress was compared to that straw thing in the back of the jail.

He was wondering if he should take this one back with him when he fell asleep.

He came awake suddenly when someone pounded on his door.

"What?" he said sleepily, opening his door.

Talwin said, "We need to talk."

Dash waved him inside. "How long was I asleep?"

"A few hours."

"It wasn't long enough," said Dash.

"We have a grave problem."

"What?" asked Dash, coming awake.

"Those five are dupes, as I suspected, but they were working for someone inside the palace, and from what I can tell, he's an agent for Kesh."

"Inside the palace?"

Talwin nodded. "The clerk believes him to be someone connected with a business concern—he thinks it might be your old employer, Rupert Avery."

"Hardly," said Dash. "Whatever Roo needs to know, he simply asks. The crown owes him so much gold, we usually tell him."

"I know. He's well connected with you, von Darkmoor, and others. But that's what Pickney believed. Desgarden on the other hand, thinks he's working for a band of smugglers from Durbin."

"Cut to it, what's going on?"

"These five, and others I'll warrant, were gathering information on the deployment of resources, soldiers, the condition of defenses, every potentially valuable bit of information an enemy might want. They were feeding it to someone here in the palace."

"Now I'm confused. I could see someone in the palace feeding the information to someone outside, but from outside in?"

"That's what had me puzzled for a bit, but the fact is, the person inside the castle they were reporting to wasn't part of Patrick's staff."

"Who was it?"

Talwin said, "A man who was working here when Patrick arrived, but who stayed on when Duko left. A man who seemed to be everywhere when someone needed help with documents or messages. A man named Malar Enares."

Dash said, "Gods! He's that servant we met out in the woods last winter. He claimed to be from the vale."

Talwin shook his head. "If we had access to your grandfather's documents, I bet we'd find his name amongst those on a list of agents of Great Kesh.''

Suddenly Dash was concerned about his brother. ''I need to see if there are any messages in from Duko down at Port Vykor in the last few days.''

''Enares left with your brother, right?''

''Right,'' said Dash. ''If he's a Keshian agent, he's either already left for Kesh, to let them know how bad things are in the city, or he's down in Port Vykor doing more harm.''

''Send word to Duko, and if your brother has arrived there safely, let me know.''

''Are you quitting the constabulary today?'' asked Dash as he pulled on his boots and moved to the door.

''I think so. Once the new Duke is in his office, I need to repair the damage done during the war. There are agents who reported to me who don't know I'm still alive. There are agents I don't know are dead yet. Your grandfather had a marvelously devious mind and created a thing of beauty. It may take me the rest of my life, but eventually I'll get the intelligence network he made back in place.''

''Well, as long as I'm the Sheriff of Krondor, if you need help, let me know.''

''I will,'' said Talwin, following Dash through the door.

Talwin turned without another word and moved back toward the rooms in which the prisoners were kept, while Dash hurried toward the Knight-Marshal's office, where all incoming military messages would be logged before being sent to Prince Patrick, or north to Lord Greylock. If Jimmy had sent word, it would be there. Dash picked up the pace and was almost running when he reached the door.

The sleepy-looking clerk looked up and said, ''Yes, Sheriff?''

''Has there been a message from Port Vykor in the last day or two?''

The clerk looked over a long scroll upon which the most recent messages were logged. ''No, sir, none in the last five days.''

Dash said, ''If one arrives anytime soon, inform me at once. Thank you.'' He turned around and started back toward his room. Then he glanced outside and saw the sun was rising. Putting aside fatigue, he turned and started to-

ward the door to the courtyard and the way back to the
New Market Jail. He had a great deal of work to do and it
couldn't wait on worrying about his brother.

"Sheriff Puppy," came the voice through the window.

Dash came awake. He had spent a long day keeping the
city under control and had retired to the little room in the
rear of the old inn he used for sleeping.

"Trina?" he asked as he stood up to look through the
shutters. Opening them, he saw the young woman's face
illuminated by moonlight.

Grinning, he stood there in his under-trousers. His shirt,
trousers, and boots lay in a heap beside his straw mattress.
"Why do I doubt you came to my window because you
couldn't bear to be away from me?"

She smiled back and took a moment to look him up and
down, then said, "You're a pretty enough boy, Sheriff
Puppy, but I like my men with a little more experience."

Dash started getting dressed. "I feel like I've got enough
experience for a man three times my age," he said. "As
much as I enjoy bantering with you, why did you wake
me?"

"We've got a problem."

Dash grabbed his sword, handed it to Trina, then with a
single vault, grabbed the upper sill of the window and
hauled himself through. Landing on the ground next to her,
he said, "We as in 'you and me,' or as in 'the Mockers'?"
as he took back his sword and buckled it around his waist.

"As in the entire city of Krondor," she replied. Suddenly, and apparently impulsively, she leaned over and
kissed him on the cheek. "I wasn't mocking you about
being pretty."

Dash reached out and put his hand behind her head,
drawing her to him. He kissed her deeply and lingeringly.
When he let her go, he said, "I've known a lot of women,
despite my youth, but you're unique." He looked into her
eyes a moment, then said, "Let me know when I've got
enough experience."

Softly she said, "I'm a thief and you're the Sheriff of
Krondor. Wouldn't that be a match?"

Dash grinned. ''Have I ever told you about my grand-father?''

She shook her head in irritation. ''We don't have time for this.''

''What's the problem?''

''We've found that bunch who've been using the sewers, and who probably killed your men.''

''Where?''

''Near that point where Kirby was found, over by Five Points. There's a big tannery that was burned to the ground during the battle, but it's got a subbasement, a big one, and a long water entrance to the bay, as well as the usual sewer dumps.''

''I want to see this.''

''I thought you would.'' He started walking away when Trina said, ''Dash?''

He stopped and turned around. ''What?''

''The Old Man.''

''How is he?''

She shook her head slightly. ''Not much longer.''

''Damn,'' said Dash, and he surprised himself at how sad knowing that his grandfather's brother was dying made him. ''Where is he?''

''Someplace safe. He won't see you.''

''Why?''

''He won't see anybody but me and one or two others.''

Dash paused, then said, ''Who's going to take over?''

The girl grinned. ''I would tell the Sheriff?''

Seriously, Dash said, ''You will if you get into enough trouble.''

''I'll think on this,'' said Trina.

They hurried through the night, and when they reached the abandoned northern quarter of the city nearest to the old tanneries and slaughterhouses, Trina led Dash through a series of back alleys and abandoned buildings. Dash memorized the route and realized that it had been cleared by the Mockers so they would have a fast avenue of escape.

They reached a burned-out row of shanties, barely more than a few charred walls and portions of roofs, bordering a large watercourse, a stone-lined channel that would flood during the rainy season, or that could be fed by water gates off the river that bordered the northeast corner of the city. In summer, with the gate destroyed, only a little water ran through the very center of the manmade stream. Trina jumped over it nimbly and Dash followed her, marveling at just how lithe she was. She wore her usual man's shirt and black leather vest, tight leggings and high boots. Dash could see she was both strong and fast.

She headed straight toward a large open pipe in the far bank. It was old, fire-hardened clay, circled by a heavy iron band. Pieces of the clay had fallen away over the years, where the pipe extended from the bank, and a three-foot length of metal could be seen at the upper lip of the pipe. With a prodigious leap, she vaulted to where she could grip the bar and swung herself into the pipe, vanishing from view.

Dash waited a moment to let her get clear, then duplicated her leap. He discovered why as he swung over broken crockery, glass, and jagged metal. Landing behind Trina, he said, "Not the normal garbage one expects."

"It discourages the idly curious."

She moved on without another word, and Dash followed her.

They moved deeper into the sewer network, the woman leading the way surely, though there was almost no light filtering down through the burned-out buildings above. At the first turn right, she turned and stopped, felt around, and produced a lamp. Dash smiled, but remained silent. The system still hadn't changed.

She lit it and shuttered it. The tiny bit of light that was allowed to escape would provide ample illumination for their purposes, and someone more than a dozen feet away would have to be looking directly at the light source to notice it.

Trina led Dash deep into the sewer system until they reached a confluence of two large pipes entering a third, with two smaller—though big enough for a person to crab-walk through—emptying into the large circular cavern. This was Five Points. Trina pointed at the upper left of the two smaller pipes. As he poised to jump, she whispered, "Trip wire."

Dash pulled himself up and moved slowly and quietly in

the dark, feeling around before him in case there might have been any additional alarms added. Trina would have warned him had there been one she knew about, but Dash's grandfather had impressed on him that people who took things for granted in these situations were called corpses.

As he inched along, he found himself thinking of Trina. He had known many women since the age of fifteen, being handsome, noble, and the grandson of the most powerful man after the King in the nation. Twice he had been infatuated to the point of thinking he might be in love, but both times the notion had quickly passed. But something about this woman thief, with her mannish clothing, unkempt hair, and piercing stare caught his imagination. It had been quite some time since he had known a woman and that was part of it, but there was something more, and he wondered if circumstances would ever permit more than a casual flirtation.

Dash froze. He was alone in the dark looking for traps, and he was daydreaming about a woman. He scolded himself and heard his grandfather's voice in his mind. The old man would have had a great deal to say about this sort of inattention.

Dash took a deep breath and began moving again. After a few minutes he heard a sound ahead. It was little more than a whisper, but Dash waited. It came again, and with effort he made out what appeared to be a low conversation.

He inched forward again. Suddenly he halted. Ahead of him he sensed something. He put his hand out and felt a line. He didn't move when his palm came into contact with it. He waited, listening for an alarm, a sound, a voice, anything that would tell him he had alerted whoever had placed this line across the duct. When silence continued unbroken for a long while, he moved his hand back, waiting again.

He touched it again, as gently as possible, and ran his finger to the right. He encountered a metal eye, driven into the side of the duct, and there the line was tied. He moved his finger to the left and found another eyelet, but this time the line was threaded through and ran forward in the direction he was heading.

He felt over and under the line to make sure there wasn't a second, and when he was satisfied this was the only line across the way, he moved back. With a little squirming, he got on his back and crawled under the line. When he was past the line, he again got up into his kneeling position and continued his careful progress.

Soon he saw a dim light ahead and he worked toward it. Again he heard voices and again the conversation was just below his ability to hear it. He moved slowly forward.

He reached a large catch basin, with a big grating overhead, and above him he could hear boots on the stone. From the stench at this end of the pipe, it was obvious the men had been using the catch basin to relieve themselves and didn't have enough water to flush the pipe easily.

"What is that?" came a voice from above and Dash froze.

"It's a baked meat roll. It's got spices and onions, baked into a bread crust. I got it at the market."

"What kind of meat?"

Dash moved closer.

"Beef! What do you think?"

"Looks like horse to me."

"How could you tell by looking at it?"

"You better let me taste it. Then I can tell."

Dash moved around and craned his neck. He could see movement, and a pair of boots. Much of his view was cut off by a chair, near the catch basin grate, and the man who sat on it.

"Cow, horse, what does it matter?"

"You just want some because you didn't bring anything to eat."

"I didn't know we'd be spending our lives waiting here."

"Maybe the others ran into some trouble?"

"Could be, but orders are clear enough. Wait here."

"Did you at least bring some cards?"

Dash settled in.

Near dawn, Dash lowered himself out of the large pipe at Five Points. He found himself disappointed that Trina wasn't waiting. He knew she probably left a moment after he entered the pipe, but he still wished she had lingered.

He found that feeling irrational alongside the distress he was experiencing over what he had found.

Not wishing to stay too long, he hurried through the pipes and back toward the New Market Jail. He knew that as soon as he got there, he was going to have to change clothing, then hurry to the palace. This wasn't a matter for the Sheriff and his constables, but Brian Silden and the army.

Dash forced himself to calmness, but if what he had overheard was any indication, someone was readying a staging area. Inside the city itself, a nest of soldiers was being prepared, soldiers who would appear within the walls of Krondor at some future date, and Dash was certain that date was not far off.

Twenty-One

Mysteries

T HE DOOR OPENED.

Nakor entered, shaking his head as he said, "No, no, no. This won't do."

Rupert Avery looked up from the plans unrolled before him. He was standing on the newly refinished floor of what had once been Barret's Coffee House, watching workers repair the walls and roof above. "What won't do, Nakor?" he asked.

Nakor looked up, surprised at being addressed. "What? What won't do?"

Roo laughed. "You were the one muttering that something wouldn't do!"

"Was I?" asked Nakor, looking surprised. "How odd."

Roo shook his head in amusement. "You, odd? Perish the thought."

Nakor said, "Never mind. I need something."

"What?" asked Roo.

"I need to get a message to someone."

"Who?"

"Pug."

Roo motioned Nakor away from the workers and said, "I think you need to start at the beginning."

"I had a dream last night," said Nakor. "I don't have

many of them, so when I do, I try to pay attention.''

''All right,'' said Roo. ''I'm with you so far.''

Nakor grinned. ''I don't think so. But that's all right. There's something going on. There are three pieces here, all seemingly separate, but they're all the same thing. And they all look to be about one thing, but they're about another. And after the odd thing that happened, I need to talk to Pug.''

Roo said, ''I am no longer with you.''

''That's all right,'' said Nakor, squeezing Roo's upper arm in a reassuring fashion. ''Anyway, do you know where Pug is?''

''No, but I can ask at the palace. Someone there might. Don't you have some sort of magic . . . trick you can do that would get Pug's attention?''

''Maybe, but I don't know if the damage would be worth it.''

''I don't want to know,'' said Roo.

''No, you don't,'' agreed Nakor. He looked around, as if noticing the work for the first time. ''What is this, then?''

''No one's seen the old owner since the fall of the city, so either he's dead or not coming back. Even if he shows up, we'll work out a deal.'' Roo waved his hand around in an arc. ''I'm trying to restore this exactly as it was before the war. I'm very fond of this place.''

''As you should be,'' said Nakor with a grin. ''You made a great deal of wealth here.''

Roo shrugged. ''That's part of it, but more importantly, this is where I made myself.''

''You've come a long way,'' said Nakor.

''More than I could have imagined,'' said the one-time death cell prisoner.

''How is your wife?''

''Getting large,'' he said, motioning with his hands as he grinned.

''I heard a rumor that you arrived in town with Lord Vasarius of Queg as a prisoner.''

Roo said, ''He wasn't my prisoner.''

''Is it a good story?''

Roo said, ''It's a *very* good story.''

"Good, then you can tell me sometime, but first I need to ask about Pug."

Roo put down his plans and said, "Tell you what. I could do with a bit of a stretch, so let's walk over to the New Market Jail and visit with Dash Jamison."

"Fine," said Nakor, and they left the coffeehouse.

Everywhere they looked the city was slowly returning to the life they had known before the war. Each day another building was restored and another shop opened. More goods were coming into the city via the ferry outside of Fishtown, or over the caravan routes. Rumor had it a large caravan from Kesh would arrive within the week, the first since before the fighting. As war hadn't formally been declared, trade between the Kingdom and Kesh was resuming. If the Wreckers Guild could continue raising ships, the harbor would be navigable the following spring, and fully restored within a year after that.

Moving through the crowd, Nakor said, "This city is like a person, don't you see?"

"It was beat up pretty badly," agreed Roo, "but it's coming back."

"More," said Nakor. "There are cities that have no . . . I don't know what to call it, an identity perhaps. A sense of being someplace different. Lots of those in the Empire. Very old cities with lots of history, but one day is much like the next. Krondor is a very lively place in comparison."

Roo laughed. "In a manner of speaking."

They reached the market and saw the New Market Jail, now sporting a fresh coat of paint and bars on all the visible windows. Entering the door, they found a harried-looking clerk, who looked up and said, "Yes?"

"We're looking for the Sheriff," said Nakor.

"He's out in the market, somewhere, and will be back here, sometime. Sorry," he said, returning to his paperwork.

Roo motioned for Nakor to move outside. They stood on the porch looking at the press of people in the market. Vendors had organized themselves into a rough series of aisles, with the outer edge of the market a sort of random pattern of blankets with goods laid atop, carts overloaded with produce, men carrying boards covered with trinkets, and the furtive denizens who offered less than legitimate wares. Roo said, "He could be anywhere."

Nakor grinned. "I know how to get his attention."

Before Nakor could step down from the porch, Roo put a restraining hand on his shoulder. "Wait!"

"What?"

"I know you, my friend, and if you think you're helping out by starting a riot so that every constable in the market comes running, think again."

"Well, it would be effective, wouldn't it?"

"Do you remember an old proverb?"

"Several. Which one do you have in mind?"

"The one about not using an ax to remove a fly from a friend's nose."

Nakor's grin broadened, and he laughed. "I like that one."

"Anyway, the point is, we should be able to find Dash without starting a riot."

"Very well," said Nakor. "Lead on."

Roo and Nakor entered the press of humanity in the market. Roo knew that Krondor still had less than half its former population, yet it seemed even more crowded than before, mostly due to the largest portion of that population thronging to the market. While work was underway throughout the city, in every neighborhood, the business of daily life was confined for the most part to the market.

Roo and Nakor made their way past wagon after wagon with late spring and early summer harvest: squash, corn, grain in sacks, and even some rice up from above Land's End. Fruit was offered and so was wine and ale. A number of prepared food vendors filled the air with aromas both savory and pungent. Nakor sneezed as they passed one vendor of *pakashka*, a bread pocket filled with meats, onions, peppers, and pods. "That man has so much spice on that meat my eyes want to pop!" he said, hurrying by.

Roo laughed. "Some people like their meats hot."

"I learned a long time ago," said Nakor, "that too much spice often masks bad meat."

"As my father said," returned Roo, "if there's enough spice on it, it doesn't matter if the meat's bad."

Nakor laughed. They turned the corner and saw a group of men standing before a large wagon being used as make-shift tavern. Two barrels had been set up at each end of the wagon, and a board was set atop them to serve as a bar. Two dozen men idly stood around, drinking and laughing. As Nakor and Roo drew near, they quieted down and watched the two men pass.

After they had moved down the street, Nakor said, "That's odd."

"What is?"

He motioned over his shoulder. "Those men."

"What about them?"

Nakor stopped and said, "Turn around and tell me what you see."

Roo did as he was asked, and said, "I see a bunch of workmen drinking."

Nakor said, "Look closer."

Roo said, "I don't see . . ."

"What?"

Roo scratched his chin. "There's something strange, but I can't quite tell what it is."

Nakor said, "Come with me," and led Roo off the way they had been heading. "First of all, those aren't workers."

"What do you mean?"

"They're dressed like workers, but they're not. They're soldiers."

"Soldiers?" said Roo. "I don't understand."

"You have more work than you have workers, correct?"

"Yes," said Roo. "That's true."

"So what are workmen doing standing around at this hour of the day drinking ale?"

"I . . ." Roo stopped. After a moment, he said, "Damn. I thought they were simply having their midday meal."

"That's the second thing, the midday meal isn't for an-other hour, Roo. And did you see how they stopped talking when we got too close? And how everyone around them gives them a wide berth?"

Roo said, "Yes, now that you point it out. So the ques-tion is, what are soldiers doing standing around dressed like workmen getting drunk in the morning?"

Nakor said, "No, that's not the question. They're standing around dressed like workmen getting drunk in the morning so that people will think they're workmen getting drunk in the morning. The question is *why* are they trying to make people think they're workmen—''

"I get the point," interrupted Roo. "Let's find Dash."

It took them only a half hour to spy a band of men wearing the red armbands, and when they overtook them, they found Dash leading them. Dash told his men to continue their patrol, and said, "Nakor, Roo, what can I do for you?"

Nakor said, "Tell your great-grandfather I need to talk to him. But before that, there are men at a wagon bar over there"—he pointed to the general area where they had passed the wagon—"dressed like workmen, but they aren't."

Dash nodded. "I know. They are one of several bands like that throughout the market."

"Oh?" said Roo. "You know?"

Dash said, "What sort of sheriff would I be if I didn't?"

"The usual sort," said Nakor. "Anyway, if you know about those men, we can talk about Pug."

"What about him?"

"I need to see him."

Dash's eyes narrowed. "And you want me to do what?"

"You're his great-grandson, how do you contact him?"

Dash shook his head. "I don't. If Father had means, he never told me. Or Jimmy, else I'd know. Grandmother merely had to close her eyes."

Nakor nodded. "I know that. Gamina could talk to him across the world at times."

Dash said, "I thought you'd have the means."

Nakor said, "I don't see him that much, except when we're both on the island. Maybe he's there." Nakor turned toward Roo. "Can I borrow a ship to go to Sorcerer's Island?"

Roo said, "If you haven't noticed, there's a full-blown war going on out there!" He pointed toward the ocean. "A Free Cities ship might sail out there without being accosted, but a Kingdom ship is either going to run into Quegan pirates, Keshian pirates, or Fadawah's pirates, unless you have a fleet. I might be tempted to lend you a ship, but I'm not lending you a fleet.''

Nakor said, ''I don't need a fleet. One ship will be fine.''

''And the pirates?''

''Not to worry,'' said Nakor with a grin. ''I have tricks.''

''Very well,'' said Roo, ''but what's the problem?''

''Oh, I didn't tell you?''

''No,'' said Roo. He looked at Dash, who shrugged.

''You have to see this,'' said Nakor, setting off without bothering to see who was following.

Roo looked at Dash, who said, ''We'd better see what this is all about.''

They hurried after Nakor, so as not to lose sight of him, and the little man walked briskly through the city, all the way to the eastern gate, the one which opened on the King's Highway.

By the time they got to this destination, Roo was almost out of breath. ''We should have ridden.''

''I don't have a horse,'' said Nakor. ''I had a horse once, a beautiful black stallion, but he died. That's when I was Nakor the Blue Rider.''

Dash said, ''What did you want to show us?''

''That,'' said Nakor, pointing to the statue he had erected a week earlier.

A dozen people were gathered before the statue looking and gesturing.

Dash and Roo left the road and moved to where they could see what the travelers were looking at. Roo asked, ''What is that?''

Down the face of the statue, two red streaks could be seen below the eyes, marring the otherwise perfect face.

Dash pushed his way past the onlookers, and said, ''It looks like blood!''

''It is,'' said Nakor. ''The statue of the Lady is crying blood.''

Roo hurried over and said, ''It's a trick, right?''

''No!'' said Nakor. ''I wouldn't stoop to cheap tricks, at least not where the Lady is concerned. She's the Goddess of Good, and . . . well, I just wouldn't.''

''All right,'' said Dash. ''I'll take your word for that, but what's causing this?''

"I don't know," said Nakor, "but that's nothing. You've got to see the other thing."

He hurried off again. Dash and Roo exchanged glances, and Dash said, "I can't wait to see what this other thing is."

Again they followed the hurrying little man. Once more they entered the city gates, crossed through the eastern quarter of the city and back across the city toward the market. Only this time, they skirted the market to the south and headed over toward Temple Square.

Roo was laughing as he struggled to keep up with Nakor. "Why couldn't he have two marvels across the street from one another?"

Dash said, "I have no idea."

They reached the empty lot between the Temples of Lims-Kragma and Guis-wa. Clerics from several other temples were gathered nearby, peering at the crowd gathered before a tent that was erected there.

Where Nakor had found the tent, Dash had no idea. One day it wasn't there, the next day it was—a huge pavilion with enough room under it to comfortably accommodate a couple of hundred people.

Dash firmly shoved his way through the crowd. Some people began to object until they saw the red armband. When they got to the entrance, Nakor and Roo a step behind, Dash stopped, and his mouth fell open.

"Gods," said Roo.

Directly before them, his back toward them, in a meditative position, sat Sho Pi and a half dozen other acolytes of this new temple. In the center of the tent was the young woman, Aleta. Only she was neither standing nor sitting. She was in a position identical to Sho Pi's: legs crossed, hands in her lap. And she was bathed in a nimbus of pure white light which seemed to emanate from within her, suffusing the tent with light. But she floated six feet above the ground.

Roo put his hand on Nakor's shoulder, and said, "I'll give you a ship."

Dash whispered, "Why my great-grandfather? Why not ask the other temple clerics?"

"Because of that," said Nakor.

Directly below the woman something hovered. Dash and Roo hadn't noticed it when they first entered, because of the startling sight of the young woman afloat. But now they could see there was a blackness hanging in the air, a cloud of something vile and terrifying. A clear certainty struck both Dash and Roo at the same time: the light from the young woman was confining that black presence, keeping it penned up.

"What is it?" whispered Dash.

Nakor said, "Something very bad. Something I didn't think I would see in my lifetime. And it's something Pug must know about as soon as possible. The temple clerics will know about it soon enough, and they have an important part, but Pug must know about this." He looked Dash in the eyes. "He must know soon."

Roo grabbed Nakor by the arm. "I'll take you out to Fishtown myself, right now. I'll put you aboard a ship and you just tell the Captain where you want to go."

"Thank you." To Sho Pi, Nakor shouted, "Take care of things. And tell Dominic he's in charge until I get back."

If Sho Pi heard Nakor, he said nothing. As they left the tent, Roo said, "I didn't think you went anywhere without Sho Pi going with you."

Nakor gave a slight shrug. "That used to be true. But I am no longer his master."

Roo dodged along the street. "When did that happen?"

Using his walking stick to point over his shoulder, Nakor said, "When she started floating in the air a couple of hours ago."

"I see," said Roo.

"And that's what I meant."

"What is what you meant?"

"When you asked me what was I talking about."

Roo said, "When? I seem to be asking you what are you talking about nearly every time we meet."

"When I first walked into the coffeehouse, and I said, 'This won't do,' that's what I was talking about. That blackness."

Roo said, "I don't know what it is, and I don't think I want to know what it is, but 'it won't do' is a rather mild way of putting things. Just looking at it scares me."

"We'll fix it," said Nakor. "As soon as I reach Pug."

They got to the docks and Roo only had to wait a few minutes to commandeer one of his boats. He had them row Nakor out to one of his fastest ships.

"What do you do if Pug's not on the island?"

Nakor said, "Don't worry. Gathis will find him for me. Someone on the island will."

Nakor climbed a net ladder, and Roo shouted, "Captain! Shove off as soon as you can and take him where he wants to go!"

A disbelieving Captain said, "Mr. Avery! We're only half unloaded."

"That will have to do, Captain. Have you supplies for two more weeks at sea?"

"Aye, sir, we do."

"Then you have your orders, Captain."

"Aye, sir," said the Captain. He shouted, "Get ready to cast off! Secure the cargo!"

Men started scrambling, and Roo instructed the boat crew to turn around and take him back to shore. As he reached the docks he saw the sails unfurling on his ship and he bid Nakor a fair voyage. With good winds he'd reach Sorcerer's Island in a week or less, and knowing Nakor's "tricks," he was certain Nakor would see good winds on this voyage.

Reaching the docks, Roo couldn't shake the feeling that whatever was occurring in Krondor, it was now something far beyond his plans for wealth and power. The game that was about to unfold would be beyond the powers of even the richest man in the Western Realm, and that frightened him. He decided to let the workers leave early tonight and return to his estates. Karli was overseeing the rebuilding there, and Roo had a powerful desire to spend the night with his wife and children.

Jimmy reviewed the reports until his eyes couldn't focus. He stood up and said, "I have to get some air."

Duko looked up and said, "I understand. You've been reading since dawn." Duko's own command of the written King's Tongue was improving, so he could now read along with Jimmy or someone else reading aloud, but the messages they were getting were too critical for him to trust he wasn't making a mistake.

The net effect of this was twofold: first, Jimmy didn't think he could see anything more than two feet away right now and, second, he was starting to develop an overall appreciation of the strategic situation along the Kingdom's southern frontier.

Kesh had a plan. Jimmy wasn't sure what it was, but he was almost certain that it required a large commitment of Kingdom forces in two places, in Land's End and near Shamata to the east. At times he almost felt as if he understood what Kesh was going to do next, but he just couldn't quite make it come together in his mind.

A rider came galloping toward the headquarters building and reined in his lathered horse. "Sir!" he said. "Messages from Shamata!"

Jimmy stepped off the porch and took the packet. He brought it inside and Duko said, "That wasn't much time."

"Messages from Shamata."

Duko said, "More messages. You'd better read them."

"The messenger was in a hurry," said Jimmy as he unwrapped the package.

He read the single paper that was in the packet and said, "Gods! One of our patrols caught sight of a fast-moving Keshian column moving rapidly northeast through Tahupset Pass."

"What's the significance?" asked Duko.

"Damned if I know," said Jimmy. He motioned for one of the orderlies in the room to bring over a particular map and spread it out before the Duke. "That's a pass that runs along the western shore of the Sea of Dreams. It's part of the old caravan route from Shamata to Landreth."

"Why would the Keshians threaten Landreth, when we have a garrison in Shamata that can take them from behind?"

Jimmy stared into space and for a moment he didn't answer, then he said, "Because they're not going to Landreth. They just want us to think they are."

"Where are they going?"

Jimmy studied the map. "They're too far east to support any move at Land's End." His finger traced a line, and he said, "If they cut west here, they could come straight at us, but we're too well defended with all the support units for Land's End here."

"Unless they want to draw us off before they push at Land's End?"

Jimmy rubbed his tired eyes. "Maybe."

Duko said, "Isolating us from Land's End would make sense."

"If they could, but they'd need more than a single cavalry column. Maybe if they were sneaking other units through . . ." Jimmy said, "I have a hunch, m'lord, and I don't like it."

"What?"

His finger traced lines across the map. "What if the column doesn't go northeast to Landreth, but goes due north instead?"

"That would bring them here," said Duko. "You said you didn't think they were trying to draw us off."

"They aren't. If they go straight north from here"—his finger marked a spot on the map—"they're fifty miles east of our usual patrol route."

"There's nothing out there," observed the Duke.

"There's nothing out there to defend," replied Jimmy. "But if they keep moving north, they intercept a trail here that runs through the foothills. It's part of an old caravan route from the dwarven mines at Dworgin that runs to here." His finger stabbed at the map.

"Krondor?"

"Yes," said Jimmy. "What if they've been slipping columns and soldiers through there for weeks? We just caught a glimpse of this one." He reexamined the communiqué. "No word of banners or markings. The soldiers could be from anywhere within the Empire."

"They hold us static with units we're used to facing, then bring up units from farther down in the Empire . . ."

"And they take Krondor in a flash attack."

Duko was on his feet. He headed to the door of the headquarters and was shouting orders just as the old soldier, Matak, got the door open.

"I want every unit ready to move in an hour!" He turned to Jimmy. "My orders instruct me to defend and protect the Southern Marches. So I'm keeping the garrison intact, but if you're correct, the Prince will need every soldier we can spare back in Krondor.''

With efficiency born of experience, he had the entire garrison moving within minutes. ''Jimmy, you will lead the column, and I hope you're in time. For if you are correct, Kesh will strike at Krondor any time now, and if they take it . . .''

Jimmy knew probably better than Duko what that would mean. It would leave the Kingdom split in half. Greylock's army would be locked in struggle south of Ylith, Duko's army would be forced to hold against the aggressors at Land's End, and the garrison at Shamata would be forced to hold a defensive position to prevent a strike past them at Landreth. If Kesh held Krondor, Greylock would lose all support by land from the south, as well as any chance of retreat. He would be caught between two hostile armies. And if the Armies of the West were lost . . .

Jimmy said, ''I'll have them on the road within the hour.''

Duko said, ''Good, for if Krondor falls, the West is indeed lost.''

If that observation from one of the men attempting to overthrow the West just a year prior struck Jimmy as ironic, he was too busy to register it. He hurried back inside the headquarters and shouted to the nearest orderly, ''Get all my things together, and get my horse out of the stable!'' He grabbed a parchment and leaned over the writing desk. He almost pushed the scribe out of his seat.

Jimmy couldn't very well order the Knight-Marshal of Krondor to do anything, nor could Lord Duko, but he could make a suggestion. A strongly worded suggestion.

He wrote:

> *Reports indicate a strong likelihood of a major offensive against Krondor by Kesh, striking along old Dorgin mine road. Urge you detach whatever units can be spared and send them south by fastest means.*
>
> *James, Earl of Vencar.*

He grabbed a stick of sealing wax, heated it, and affixed his ring seal to it. He folded the parchment and inserted it into a message pouch.

The scribe whom he had displaced was sitting in his chair, watching the entire thing. Jimmy turned and said, "What's your name?"

"Herbert, sir. Herbert of Rutherwood."

"Come with me."

The scribe glanced around the room at the other orderlies and scribes, but all returned only astonished or blank expressions.

He hurried past Duko, who was still watching over the unfolding spectacle of his entire command, save the resident garrison, getting ready to mobilize. Jimmy led the scribe down to the docks and hurried to the far end, where a Kingdom cutter lay at anchor.

He hurried up the gangplank, and when he reached the top shouted, "Captain!"

From the quarterdeck, a voice replied, "Here, sir!"

"Orders!" shouted Jimmy. "Take this man north."

The scribe stood on the plank behind Jimmy. Jimmy reached around and grabbed him by the front of his tunic, hauling him forward and depositing him on the deck. Jimmy said, "Herbert, take this pouch. Sail north, find our army, and give this to Lord Greylock or Captain von Darkmoor. Do you understand?"

The scribe's eyes were round and he couldn't speak, but he nodded.

"Captain, get this man to Lord Greylock. He's somewhere south of Quester's View!"

"Sir!" replied the Captain, who turned and shouted, "Make ready to get underway!"

Jimmy left the stunned Herbert standing on the deck and ran from the docks back through the town of Port Vykor toward where he hoped his gear was ready. He was impatient to leave, and impatient to reach Krondor. His only brother was still in Krondor, and unless Greylock could get units south faster than Jimmy could go north, all that stood between Dash and destruction was a few palace guards, the city militia, and a barely repaired city wall.

*　　*　　*

Erik shouted, "Get into that breach!"

Catapults on both sides of the line fired rocks and bundles of burning hay. Large ballista bolts flew overhead and men lay screaming and dying.

The fighting had been underway since dawn the previous day, and night turned the scene hellish. The enemy had dug a series of trenches backed by a high wall, upon which platforms held war engines. Thousands had died building these fortifications, and the dead had been left outside the wall, unburied. The stench could be smelled miles before the first trench could be seen. The trenches had been filled with water, atop which oil had been floated. The oil had been fired and was sending a black blanket of smoke across the ground.

Earl Richard had reviewed the defensive position and had been forced to agree that the only approach was a direct one. Erik had supervised the construction of a set of massive wooden bridges, set up to roll over logs cut from the nearby woods. The first set of trenches had been difficult, because of the bow-fire from the wall above, but once he got his men underway, the trenches were quickly bridged. Soldiers frantically shoveled dirt across the top of the oil, banking the fires as the bridges were run across.

Fortunately for the Kingdom forces, when they reached the wall, they found a wooden stockade. It was brilliantly fashioned, and as stout as could be imagined, but being wood it could be cut. Men had died wielding axes at key locations, and when finally their work was done, chains with large iron bars had been thrown through the gaps. The iron bars snapped sideways when pulled back and the chains were tied to draft horses.

They had pulled down a twelve-foot-wide section of the wall, and the Kingdom forces were now pouring through. Erik waited for the huge gates across the highway to be opened so he could lead his cavalry through.

The gates suddenly shuddered, then swung open, and Erik ordered the advance. He kicked his horse, and the large chestnut gelding leaped forward and was up to a comfortable canter immediately.

Erik's eyes watered from smoke and the stench of blood and death, but he could clearly see what lay on the other side of the gates. He frantically shouted for a halt.

Moving slowly forward, he saw his footmen were upon the battlements and locked in hand-to-hand fighting. "Dismount!" he shouted to his men.

They did, and Erik said, "Follow me!"

He ran through the gate and the men behind him saw what had made him stop the advance. Just behind the gate lay a pit ten feet deep, with sharpened wooden stakes. The gate was only six feet wider than the pit, three on each side, so men could move around the pit, but a horse could not pass.

Erik urged his men through the smoke and blinked tears from his eyes. "Where is all that smoke coming from?" he shouted.

"Over there," came the familiar voice of Jadow Shati.

Erik looked where his old friend pointed, and said, "Damn."

"Yes, man, damn and damn again."

Four hundred yards up the highway, thousands of men were lined up in ranks, with officers and cavalry mounted to the flanks and rear. More catapults, mangonels, and ballistae were apparent. This was not a defensive position. This army was making ready to attack.

Suddenly Erik saw what was about to happen. He glanced at the wall through which he had fought and realized that if it were knocked down from behind it provided a massive bridge over the trenches on either side of the pit.

"Back!" shouted Erik, and the order was passed.

"Get back and get ready!" shouted Jadow.

Erik raced back to where his horse was waiting, and he leaped into the saddle. The sound of horns and the shout of men up the highway told him that at last he was going to join battle in the field with General Fadawah. And Erik's only thought now wasn't on victory, but rather on survival.

Twenty-Two

Realization

Men stalked the woods.

Subai moved quietly but with purpose, following the river. Most of his men were dead, though two might have gotten over the ridge to make their way along the eastern face of the mountains down to Darkmoor. He prayed it was so.

He had made it through a murderous journey lasting weeks. His Pathfinders had skills unmatched by any on Midkemia, save the elves and the Rangers of Natal. But Fadawah's defenses were bolstered by something far more terrible than mere human ability: they were aided by dark magic Subai did not understand.

It became noticeable when they passed the first of the true southern defenses. Besides the death and destruction, there had been a feeling of despair everywhere, as if a miasma of pain and hopelessness hung in the air. The farther north they traveled, the worse the feeling became.

They saw little of the coastal defenses for a while, as they moved north while the road to Quester's View turned northwest. When they reached the road from Quester's View to Hawk's Hollow, they encountered more indications of dark powers.

Not only had the northern ridge above that road been

fortified, the southern ridge had been decorated with a grisly set of corpses. Wooden Xs had been erected along the ridgeline, with a human prisoner nailed to each. All had expressions of horror on their faces, showing they died from wounds, rather than exposure and crucifixion. Most had their throats cut, but a few had their hearts removed, their chests showing gaping wounds.

And the dead were not just men. Women and children had also been murdered for this hideous display.

Two of his men had died an hour later, as terrible-looking men wearing scars upon their cheeks and seemingly possessed of inhuman strength and determination had chanced upon Subai's camp. From what intelligence Subai had read on the Emerald Queen's army, he knew these men were most likely Immortals. Originally the honor guard of the Priest-King of Lanada, they were ordinary soldiers turned into murderous fiends by black rites and a diet of drugs. The Emerald Queen had further degenerated them, using one a night in death rites to continue her eternal youth.

It had been thought they had fallen out of favor with Fadawah, but they seemed very evident on the approaches to Yabon.

For the next week they had been hunted, and two more men had died, leaving it to Subai to order to his two remaining companions to turn east and find their way to Loriel, which was still held by the Kingdom. He hoped they would lead away the pursuing warriors.

Subai had effectively isolated himself in the hope that one man might slip by where two would be noticed.

For a week he had journeyed past patrols and encampments, and each time he saw another enemy band, his confidence in the Kingdom's chances of regaining Yabon was eroded. The theory that only a core of twenty or twenty-five thousand soldiers remained under Fadawah's command was in error. Given the numbers he knew to be deployed down near Sarth and estimates of what it would have taken to overrun LaMut, Subai was now convinced Fadawah had at least thirty-five thousand soldiers under his command.

Subai knew that if it were true, and if Kesh continued to probe the southern border, freezing soldiers along the frontier, Greylock did not have enough men to dislodge Fadawah. It might be possible to retake Ylith, but the price would be grim.

Subai had failed to reach Yabon. The city was besieged and there was no way he could get close enough to attempt to sneak in. He had considered trying for Tyr-Sog, but found himself behind the enemy's lines and realized his best bet was to strike for the Lake of the Sky, and around the northern tip of the Grey Towers and down into the elven forests.

Subai had no illusions. He had been chased for two days, since almost reaching the Lake of the Sky. He didn't know if the men who were behind him were fanatics of Fadawah's or renegades, but either way he knew he needed to find a place to rest and something to eat.

He had had no provisions since a week after leaving the vicinity of Yabon City. He had foraged and found nuts and berries, as well as snaring a rabbit, but he hadn't eaten in the last two days, since being spotted by his pursuers. He was losing weight and energy, and was in no condition to fight more than one or two men. If five or six were after him, to be caught was to die.

He was following the southern bank of the River Crydee, which began at the Lake of the Sky. He knew that soon he would be opposite woods that were claimed by the elves, and that to enter them he would need permission. He also knew that it was his only chance of safety. There was no way he could continue to follow the rift down to the castle at Crydee, or risk moving south through the Green Heart to the Jonril garrison.

Subai stopped and looked back. Cresting some rocks a mile back, he saw dark figures moving. He looked ahead and saw a ford.

It was never going to be a better time, he told himself.

Subai entered the water and found it rose to his knees. At the height of summer the water level was lowest, and he knew that at thaw, or after fall thundershowers, he could not cross here.

He was halfway across when he heard shouts behind and knew his pursuers had sighted him. That renewed his determination and he forced himself to move faster.

He was ashore when the men following him reached the ford. He didn't look back, but dodged into the woods, wishing he still had a bow. He had watched it fall into a rocky crevasse when he was still in the mountains, two weeks before. With a bow he could have stopped those after him.

He ran on.

The light was falling and Subai was disoriented, but he knew he was moving generally toward the west. Suddenly a voice from ahead challenged him. "What do you seek in Elvandar, human?"

Subai halted. "I seek refuge and I bring messages," he said, leaning over with his hands on his knees as fatigue swept up over him.

"Who are you?"

"I am Captain Subai of the Royal Krondorian Pathfinders, and I bring messages from Owen Greylock, Knight-Marshal of Krondor."

"Enter, Subai," said an elf, who seemed to step out of nowhere.

"There are men following me," said Subai, "agents of the invader, and I fear they will be upon us in minutes."

The elf shook his head. "None may enter Elvandar unbidden. Already they are being led away from us, and should they finally escape the woods, they will be miles from here. Else they may wander until they starve."

Subai said, "Thank you for inviting me in."

The elf smiled and said, "I am called Adelin. I will guide you."

"Thanks," replied Subai. "I am almost done."

The elf reached into his belt pouch; removed a piece of food, and said, "Eat this. It will restore you."

Subai took the offering, a square piece of what looked to be a thick, hard bread. He bit into it and his mouth filled with flavors: nuts, berries, grains, and honey. He chewed it greedily.

Adelin said, "We still have far to go." He led the Pathfinder to the west, toward Elvandar.

Erik washed the blood from his face and hands, while outside the tent trumpets blew and horses rode by. Richard, Earl of Makurlic, looked at the map and said, "We're holding."

Erik said, "We're losing."

The counteroffensive had rolled the Kingdom army back

in confusion, until Erik could order up reserves to blunt the assault. Now they were five miles south of the original point of contact, and night was falling. Leland, Richard's son, entered the tent and said, "We're routing them." He was a likable young man, nineteen years old, with a shock of blondish brown hair and wide-set blue eyes.

Erik said, "Hardly. They're withdrawing to their own lines until morning. They'll hit us again."

The young soldier was eager, and Erik had been pleased to discover he kept his wits about him in the midst of battle. He officially was a junior officer attached to a company of soldiers from Deep Tauton, left to bolster the Army of the West when the Army of the East withdrew. But with his father in command of the army, he was acting in an un-official capacity as Lord Richard's adjutant and had picked up the responsibility of relaying orders to outlying units.

"What do we do next?" asked Richard.

Erik wiped his face with a towel and came over to look down at the map. "We dig in. Jadow!" he shouted over his shoulder.

A moment later, Jadow Shati appeared and said, "Erik?" Seeing the Earl sitting there, he changed that to "Captain? Hello, m'lord."

Erik waved him over. "I want three diamonds dug in, here, here, and here," he said, pointing to three points across the front. Jadow didn't wait for further explanation, turning and leaving without even bothering to salute.

"Diamonds?" asked Leland.

Richard looked on in curiosity, too. Erik explained, "It's an old Keshian formation. We build up three breastworks, each with two hundred men inside, but rather than try and build a huge one across the road, which we wouldn't be able to finish by sunrise, we build three small, diamond-shaped ones across the front. Inside we place pikemen and build up the berm with shields and let them form defensive positions. The enemy's horsemen can't overrun them eas-ily, and the tendency will be for men to move around the points of the diamond."

Richard said, "That funnels their men into these two constricted areas between the center and the sides."

"Yes," said Erik. "With luck they get jammed up in

those constriction points and our archers here''—he drew
a line with his finger across the map behind the diamonds—
''can wither any of the enemy who get trapped there. We'll
put a wall of swordsmen with shields in front of them in
case the enemy gets past the diamonds in quantity.''

''What about our horse?'' asked Leland.

''They hold to each side of the outer diamonds. If we're
lucky they can prevent any flanking, and if the enemy re-
treats, we can unleash them to harry the enemy.''

''Then what?'' asked Richard.

''Then we lick our wounds, reorganize, and see if we
can do something about that mess up the road.''

Reports were filtering back from men who had been cut
off and lost for a while behind enemy lines, and who returned to fill in gaps in Erik's knowledge of what was ahead
of them. Along with Subai's reports, carried back by his
first two couriers, Erik wasn't optimistic. The fact that no
more Pathfinders had returned from Subai's journey was
also a part of that pessimism. With no firm picture of what
lay closer to Ylith, Erik's cautious nature turned his imagination to the darkest possibilities.

As best as they could determine, not only was there a
vast network of fortifications at the crest of each hill and
rise, but tunnels had been dug, so that reinforcements could
be rushed from one location to another without being exposed to enemy attack. Erik recognized the trap inherent in
the design: to attempt to bypass the fortifications left an
unknown number of enemies at his back, and to stop and
dig them out one at a time meant no hope of relieving the
siege of Yabon.

Erik shook his head. ''I'm too tired to think. At this point
it seems possible that our only choice is in the manner of
our defeat: either ride home and dig in at Krondor, or get
butchered as we continue to push north.''

''Can we not get support from the sea?'' asked Lord
Richard.

Erik said, ''Perhaps, up here, if we get past Quester's
View. There're a number of coves and beaches where we
could land men, but we lack enough ships to get the men
there, don't have the proper boats for a landing, and if

Fadawah positions men on the bluffs above, none of our men would reach the road.''

Leland said, ''You make it sound hopeless.''

Erik said, ''Right now, that's how I feel. Some sleep and a meal, and we'll see how I feel in the morning, but either way, I'm not going to conclude anything on the basis of my feelings.''

Richard said, ''For one so young, you've seen a great deal of war, haven't you?''

Erik nodded. ''I'm not yet twenty-six years of age, m'lord, yet I feel old in my bones.''

''Get some rest,'' suggested Richard.

Erik nodded as he left the tent. He saw a soldier in the black tunic of the Crimson Eagles, and said, ''Sean, where is our camp?''

''Over there, Captain,'' answered the soldier as he hurried past.

Erik moved in the indicated direction and found a dozen members of his old command setting up their tents. ''Bless you, Jadow,'' he said when he saw his own tent already up. Erik flung himself down on the bedroll waiting for him and was asleep within seconds.

''Ring the alarm,'' said Dash.

''What?'' asked Patrick, a look of incredulity on his face.

''I said ring the alarm. Spread word that a Keshian army is advancing on the city, and those soldiers hidden within the city will leap to attack the positions they're supposed to. Only instead of taking our soldiers from behind, our soldiers will be waiting for them.''

''Isn't that extreme?'' asked Duke Rufio, recently arrived from Rodez. Dash knew him slightly from his time at the King's court in Rillanon, and knew him to be a no-nonsense sort of fellow. He was a competent administrator, an adequate military advisor, and a fair rider and swordsman, exactly the wrong man for Krondor on the brink of a crisis. Rufio would prove a fine administrator for a talented monarch served by a brilliant general, thought Dash. Unfortunately, he had only Patrick and Dash to depend on, and Dash was now certain he would have to improvise and be dazzling else Krondor would be lost.

"Yes, Your Grace, it is extreme," answered Dash, "but it's better to flush them out when we're ready for them than to have them appear behind us at the height of an attack. I've seen enough proof there are weapons and food caches in the sewers so that armed insurrection inside the city can commence with any attack from outside."

"If there is any attack," said Patrick. He remained dubious about the entire possibility. He was convinced that negotiations underway at Stardock would eventually yield a solution. Even the revelation that Malar Enares had been a Keshian spy, and the lack of response to an inquiry about Jimmy's arrival at Port Vykor, didn't persuade him there was the risk of a surprise attack against the capital of the Western Realm.

Dash had never been close to Patrick. More of an age with Jimmy and Francie, Dash had always been the "tag-along" as children, and during the period when Dash and Jimmy had been tossed out of the palace to learn in the rough and tumble of the docks at Rillanon, Patrick had been visiting the eastern courts, learning diplomacy. Even as young men, Dash and Patrick had felt little affinity for one another. Dash was sure Patrick had redeeming qualities, but at this moment, he couldn't begin to think what they were.

"If you know who these men are," suggested Patrick, "the ones who are secreting all these weapons and food, why don't you just arrest them?"

"Because presently I have less than one hundred constables, and I believe there are close to a thousand enemy soldiers scattered throughout the city. As soon as I arrest the first bunch, the rest will go to ground. And I don't know who all of them are. I think I've got some lying low aboard ships off the coast, and there may be some in the caravansary outside the gate, and who knows how many are lurking down in the sewers.

"But if I ring the alarm bell, and you have the soldiers in the city placed at key locations, between them and my constables, we can eliminate this threat."

Duke Rufio said, "I have two hundred soldiers en route from Rodez who should be arriving here within the week. Perhaps when they arrive?"

Dash tried mightily to hide his aggravation. He almost

succeeded. "At least let me employee more men," Dash pleaded.

Patrick said, "The treasury is low; you'll have to make do with what you have."

"What about volunteers?" asked Dash.

"If anyone volunteers to serve, swear them to duty. Do whatever you have to. Perhaps after the war we might pay them." Patrick looked as if he had run out of patience. "That will be all, Sheriff," said Patrick.

Dash bowed and removed himself from the office. Stalking down the hall, he was lost in thought when he turned a corner and almost ran into Francie. "Dash!" she said, sounding pleased to see him. "It's been so long."

"I've been busy," he said, still feeling nettled over Patrick's dismissal of his idea.

"Everyone has. Father tells me your job is probably as thankless as anyone's in the palace, yet he thinks you're doing it well."

"Thanks," said Dash. "Are you staying here in Krondor, now that Duko Rufio has assumed office?"

"Father and I leave for Rillanon in a week," said Francie. "We have to make plans . . ."

"For the wedding?"

Francie nodded. "No one is supposed to know; the King will announce it after things calm down. . . ." She looked troubled.

"What is it?"

Lowering her voice she said, "Have you heard anything from Jimmy?"

"No," he said.

"I'm worried about him," said Francie. "He left in such a hurry and we really had little chance to talk . . . about things."

Dash had no time for this. "Francie, he's fine, and as for talking about things, well, perhaps after the wedding, when Patrick's returned and you're Princess of Krondor, you can order him to come to a garden party . . ."

"Dash!" said Francie, looking hurt. "Why are you being so mean?"

Dash sighed. "Because I'm tired, angry, frustrated, and because your future husband is being . . . well, he's being

Patrick. And if you want to know, I'm worried about Jimmy, too.''

Francie nodded. ''Is he really upset by my marrying Patrick?''

Dash shrugged. ''I don't know. I think in a way, yes, but in another way he knows things have to be what they are. He's . . . confused, like the rest of us.''

Francie sighed. ''I just want him to be my friend.''

Dash tried to force a smile. ''You shouldn't worry about that. Jimmy's very loyal. He'll always be your friend.'' He bowed slightly. ''Well, milady, I must be off. There's too much to do and I'm already late.''

''Good-bye, Dash,'' she said, and Dash detected a note of sadness in her voice, as if they were parting forever.

''Good-bye, Francie,'' he said as he turned and walked off. Here he was trying to keep the city intact, and she was concerned with hurt feelings. Dash knew he was in a bad mood, but he also knew it was well earned. And he knew he was likely to be in a worse one if he didn't come up with some way to neutralize those forces hostile to the crown already secreted inside the city.

Subai was astonished, as was every human upon first viewing Elvandar. He had been led through the glades to the large clearing surrounding the heart of the elven forests, and when he had spied the giant trees of luminous colors he had been moved to his most expressive exclamation in years. ''Killian! What joy!'' he had whispered.

Adelin said, ''Of those beings you humans worship, we revere Killian most.''

He led the tired and hungry Captain to the Queen's court, and by the time Subai reached it, he felt far better than he had any reason to expect. He suspected it had something to do with the magic associated with the place, according to legend.

He bowed before the two beings sitting upon the dais, a woman of stunning if alien beauty, and a tall, powerfully built but young-looking man. ''Your Majesty,'' he said to the Queen. ''My lord,'' he said to the man.

''Welcome,'' said the Elf Queen, and her voice was soft and musical. ''You have come a great distance, and at great peril. Take your ease and tell us of your message from your Prince.''

Subai looked around the Queen's Council. Three elderly-looking, grey-haired elves stood to her right hand, one wearing rich-looking robes, the second an impressive-looking suit of armor with a sword at his side, and the third a simple blue robe with a corded belt.

Next to Tomas, Prince-Consort of Elvandar, stood a young-looking elf, one who bore a resemblance to the Queen, and Subai deduced this to be her older son, Calin. To his left stood a familiar figure: Calis. Next to Calis was a man wearing leathers and a long grey cloak.

Subai said to the Queen, ''The message is this, Fair Queen: an enemy of great evil lies between our realms. Calis as much as any man knows this evil. He has faced it more than anyone, and knows it wears many faces.''

''What would you have of us?'' asked the Queen.

Subai looked from face to face. ''I do not know, Great Queen. I had hoped to find the magician Pug here, for it may be we are at the mercy of powers only he might face.''

Tomas stood and said, ''Should we have need of Pug I can promise you a quick passage to him. He has returned to his island and can be found there.''

Calis said, ''Mother, may I speak?'' The Queen nodded, and Calis said, ''Subai, the Emerald Queen is dead and so is the demon who destroyed her. Surely the Kingdom can deal with the remaining invaders.''

''I wish that it were so, Calis,'' said Subai. ''But on my way here I saw things that make me think we have again encountered more than we've suspected. I've seen the return of those men you told us of, the Immortals, and other drinkers of blood. I've seen men, women, and children sacrificed up to dark powers. I've seen bodies piled in pits, and mystic fires burning in villages. I've heard chants and songs that no human should hear. Whatever help you have to give, please, we need it now.''

The Queen said, ''We shall discuss this in council. Our son has spoken at length of the invaders from across the sea. They do not trouble us, but they do patrol near our borders.

''Go now and rest. We shall meet again in the morning.''

Calis and the man in grey came down to stand before Subai. Calis shook hands with the Captain. "It is good to see you," said Calis.

The Pathfinder said, "You can't imagine how good it is to see you, Calis. And I'm betting that Erik wishes you were back in command of the Eagles."

Calis said, "This is Pahaman of Natal."

The man in grey put out his hand, and Subai said, "Our grandfathers were brothers."

"Our grandfathers were brothers," returned Pahaman.

Calis said, "An odd greeting."

Subai smiled. "It's a ritual. The Pathfinders and the Rangers of Natal are of like spirit. Never in the conflicts between the Free Cities and the Kingdom has a Ranger or Pathfinder spilled the other's blood."

Pahaman said, "In ancient times, when Kesh ruled, our ancestors were Imperial Guides. When the Empire retreated, many who were left behind became Rangers, and those who lived near Krondor founded the Pathfinders. All are kin, Pathfinder, Ranger, and Guide."

Calis said, "Would that all men knew they were kin. Come, let us feed you, Subai, and find you a place to sleep. While you dine, tell me what you've seen."

They departed.

Tomas turned to his wife and said, "More than anytime since the Riftwar I fear we may not be free of involvement."

The Queen looked at her eldest counselor and said, "Tathar?"

"We will wait upon Calis's return. After he has spoken to the human he will tell us how grave is the risk."

Prince Calin said, "I will join my brother and listen, as well."

The Queen nodded, and the old warrior, Redtree, said, "What good would it do for us to leave Elvandar? We are few in number and could not tip the balance."

Tomas said, "I don't think that will be the question." He looked at his wife and said, "The question becomes, should *I* depart Elvandar?"

The Queen looked at her husband and said nothing.

Twenty-Three

Decisions

T HE MEN WALKED softly.

Dash led his detachment through the cellar, each man carrying a large billy club and a dagger. The order was simple. If they resist, subdue them; if they draw weapons, kill them.

All over the city, raids were being conducted, by constables and members of Patrick's Royal Household Guard. Patrick would not permit the sounding of the city's alarm, and the only concession Dash could wring from the Prince was the use of two hundred of his guards for a coordinated raid.

Seven different hideouts had been discovered, as well as three ships in the harbor. The ships were being left to the Royal Navy, which had enough presence in the area that the sudden boarding of the target ships should be unexpected.

But Dash was unhappy. He knew there were other agents in the city, and that a significant portion of the caravan guards at the caravansary were probably Keshian soldiers. The only comfort he drew from their going uncaught was that they were outside the wall and would remain so. He had established checkpoints at the gate, on the pretext of needing a better census with the rebuilding of the city.

They had reached a cellar in the northeastern portion of the city; the building was still burned-out, but Dash knew the door to the cellar had been restored. It had been scorched to look burned.

He had debated the best way to approach this task with himself all day, and had finally elected to take the shock approach.

The upper cellar was deserted, but he knew the rear door led to a ramp down to the lower cellar, the one which opened onto the sewers. He tested the door handle and found it unlatched. Gently he lifted it and moved the door open. He whispered to the men behind him, "All right, silently until I say different."

He crept down the ramp to a landing opening up on a large cellar, once previously used to house large casks of ale and wine. The building above had been an inn. On the far side of the room a score of men were lying around on bedding on the floor, or sitting on barrels. Dash said to his own men, "Spread out and don't stop."

He walked purposefully toward the nearest man who looked in surprise at the men approaching. Then he saw the red armband and started to stand up. Dash shouted, "In the name of the Prince, surrender!"

The man lying on the nearest pallet started to rise, but Dash lashed out with his billy club and knocked the man senseless. The other constables hurried forward, and one man who started to pull his sword was struck unconscious by three constables. Others raised hands in surrender, though one tried to run down a passage. One of the constables flung his billy along the floor, sending it skipping over the stones to strike the man in the back of the legs. He fell hard and before he could rise two other constables were on him.

Dash had the prisoners roped together with their hands tied behind them before they could organize a resistance. One of the newly deputized constables said, "That went easily enough, Sheriff."

Dash said, "Don't get too comfortable. The rest of the night won't be this easy."

At dawn Jimmy rose to find a worried-looking Marcel Duval standing over his sleeping roll. "Earl James," said the Squire from Bas-Tyra.

"What is it?" asked Jimmy, getting up and trying to stretch at the same time.

"Some of the horses are footsore, sir, and I was wondering if we might take a day to rest them."

Jimmy blinked, not sure he was entirely awake. "Rest them?"

"The pace has been punishing, sir, and some of these animals are going to be lame by the time we reach Krondor."

Jimmy came wide awake. "Squire," said Jimmy in as calm a voice as he could muster. "You may play at being a soldier all you wish back at the court in Bas-Tyra. Here you *are* a soldier. Now, by the time I get my horse saddled, you and your men had better be ready to ride. Today, your gallant troop rides in the van."

"Sir?"

"That is all!" said Jimmy far too sharply. He closed his eyes a moment, then counted slowly to ten. He took a deep breath, then shouted, "Mount up!"

Everywhere men scrambled to get their horses saddled. Part of what made Jimmy irritable was that he knew the horses were being punished. Duval's pretty bunch wouldn't be the only ones limping into Krondor, but he knew that by pushing this company, he'd reach the city in three more days. He just hoped that would be soon enough.

When the column was ready, Jimmy looked back and did a mental calculation. Five hundred cavalry and mounted infantry. The men were eating dried rations in the saddle, and already a few could be seen showing signs of illness. But sick or well, tired or rested, he was going to get them all to Krondor. They could tip the balance if the city was still intact when they got there. Fighting back hunger and fatigue, he shouted, "Get something in your bellies while you can. In ten minutes we pick up the pace." Turning to the head of the line, he shouted, "Squire Duval, lead the column at the walk!"

"Sir!" came the reply, and Duval led his fifty lancers out in the van.

As the sun crept above the horizon in the east and rose and yellow hues bathed the landscape, Jimmy was forced to admit Duval's company did cut a dashing appearance.

The attack came at dawn, before the sun had risen over the mountains, at the time when men were the least ready to fight and the most likely to react slowly. Erik was already awake and had eaten, seen to the fortifications he had ordered constructed, and had called for the camp to be made ready.

Richard stood at the command tent, watching the advance in the grey of the morning, and said, "They seek to roll over us."

"As I would in their place," said Erik. He held his helmet under his arm and pointed with his right hand. "If we hold the center, we can win the day. If either flank falls, I can plug the flow, but if the center falls, we must retreat."

Leland stood beside his father and said, "Then we will make certain the center doesn't fall." He donned his own helmet and said, "Father, may I join our men?"

His father said, "Yes, my boy." The lad ran off to where a groom held his mount. Leland leaped into the saddle as his father said, "Tith-Onanka guide your blade, and Ruthia smile on you." The invocation of the War God and Goddess of Luck was appropriate, thought Erik.

The invaders marched in irregular rhythm, without drummers or the other time-keepers Erik would have expected from Keshian or other Kingdom units. He had fought alongside most of the men he now faced, and while he had been a spy in their midst, he felt little kinship for them. Still, he respected their individual bravery, and it was clear that Fadawah had forged them into an army instead of the disorganized bands of mounted infantry and foot soldiers they had been in Novindus. Now he saw heavy infantry, companies of men with pikes advancing, supported by men with shields and swords, bucklers and axes. Behind sat men on horseback, cavalry units from the look of them, half with spears, the others armed with sword and buckler. Erik gave a silent prayer of thanks that horse archers had never been common in Novindus.

A thought occurred to Erik and he turned to a message

runner. "Send word to Akee and the Hadati. I want them moving into those trees to the right of our position. Look for flanking bowmen trying to infiltrate the woods."

The messenger ran off, and Erik turned to Richard. "Nothing to do now but fight." He put on his helm and walked to where a groom held his horse. He mounted and rode quickly forward, inspecting the position of the three diamonds. As he had known would be the case, Jadow had the men positioned as well as could be, and they were his hardest troops, with the Crimson Eagles holding the center diamond. Jadow waved from the center of the middle diamond and Erik saluted him. As an officer he could have delegated command to a sergeant and remained with the horse units, but Erik knew that, at heart, Lieutenant Jadow Shati from the Vale of Dreams would always be a sergeant.

"Tith-Onanka strengthen your arm!" Erik shouted.

The men in the diamond cheered their commander.

Then the invaders broke formation and charged, and the battle was on.

Tomas watched as Acaila meditated. Tathar and another elf sat with him at three points of a triangle. Tomas had asked for their wisdom and Acaila had agreed to use his mystic powers to provide guidance.

At the end of the Riftwar Tomas had vowed to never leave Elvandar unprotected. Now Tomas wondered if that oath would ultimately lead to the destruction of the thing he had sworn to protect.

Tomas knew ancient lore, lived through the memories of the being whose powers he had inherited. Ashen-Shugar, last of the Valheru, had become for a time one with Tomas, and much of his power resided still in the former kitchen boy from Crydee. With but a few others, Tomas understood the powers behind much of what had shaped his life.

In days past, beyond numbering, Ashen-Shugar and his brethren had flown the skies on the backs of dragons. They had hunted like the predators they were, both creatures without intelligence, and creatures with. In their arrogance they counted themselves among the mightiest beings in creation and had no concept of their own delusions.

Tomas had over the years come to understand that what

he knew from Ashen-Shugar was truth as Ashen-Shugar knew it. He knew how the ancient Valheru felt, thought, and remembered, but because the Valheru believed it true didn't make it so.

Alone of his kind, Ashen-Shugar avoided the influence of Drakin-Korin, who Tomas now knew was a pawn of the Nameless One, the god whose name alone invites destruction. The human in Tomas considered it ironic that the Nameless One used Valheru vanity and their own certainty of their omnipotence to destroy them eventually. The Valheru portion of Tomas's nature felt rage at the thought his race had been nothing more than a tool, and one used and discarded when it was no longer effective.

Tomas looked at the three elves and knew it would be a while before Acaila had wisdom to share. He left the contemplation glade and walked through Elvandar. Across the way he noticed Subai and Pahaman of Natal talking. Rangers rarely talked to anyone besides other Rangers and occasionally the elves, so Tomas knew that in Subai, Pahaman had found one he considered kin.

The laughter of children pulled Tomas like a lodestone. He found a dozen little ones playing a game of tag. Tomas saw his son, Calis, sitting next to the woman from across the sea, Ellia. They sat close, her hand in his, and Tomas felt a warmth toward his son. He knew that he would never father another child, for it was a special magic that gave life to his son. He had played his part in destroying the great threat to all life on Midkemia, the Lifestone, and now his fate was his own. But Calis would never father children, so Tomas's line ended with his son. Yet at play were two elven children, Tilac and Chapac, who seemed family. Yet even the names of the boys, alien on the ears of those born in Elvandar, reminded Tomas that there would never be a place in the world where he entirely belonged. He smiled at Calis. Like his son, he had forged a place for himself, and was content with it.

Calis waved at his father and said, "Join us."

Ellia smiled at Tomas, but it was a smile tempered with uncertainty. Rid of Ashen-Shugar's Valheru mind during the Riftwar and cleansed of many of the lingering effects of that meld of human and Valheru by the Lifestone, Tomas nevertheless bore the Valheru stamp upon him. To any of the edhel—the elven races—there would almost be an instinctive response, a subservience that bordered on fear. Tomas knelt next to his son. "There is much to be thankful for."

Calis said, "Yes." He glanced at the woman at his side and she smiled. Tomas was almost certain eventually they would wed. The boys' father had died during the war in Novindus that had led to the invasion of the Kingdom. With a very low birthrate and a high percentage of marriage by those who underwent the "recognition," the instinctive knowledge of who their mates were, there was little hope for a widow to find a second husband. As Calis had lived most of his life among humans and was half-human himself, there was no mate for him among his mother's people. Tomas felt that fate had chosen to deal kindly with his son by bringing this woman and her sons to Elvandar.

Tomas said, "There is much to concern us with the news Subai brings."

Calis looked down. "I know. I feel as if it might be wise for me to return to the Kingdom and to again serve."

Tomas put his hand on his son's shoulder. "You've done your share. I think it's time for me to return to the Kingdom."

Calis looked at his father. "But you said—"

"I know, but if this threat is what you and I both know it could be, then if we do not deal with it now, down near Ylith, we will deal with it someday, only we will be fighting here."

Ellia said, "This is the same madness that destroyed my village across the sea." Her accent was odd by elven standards, but she was mastering the tongue of her ancestors. "They are evil beyond measure. They are black of soul and have no hearts." She glanced at her sons playing. "Only a miracle sent Miranda to save us. They had killed all the other children in the village."

Tomas said, "I'm waiting for Acaila's wisdom on this, but I think I must fly to Sorcerer's Island and take council with Pug, as well."

Calis said, "With the demon destroyed, I thought it but an issue between men."

Tomas shook his head. "If I understand a tenth of what I have been told, it will never be merely an issue between men. There will always be far greater powers behind those men, and at each turn those powers must be balanced."

Tomas stood up. "I will see you at supper?"

Calis said, "I dine with Ellia and the boys."

Tomas smiled. "I will tell your mother."

He wandered through Elvandar, home for most of his life, and as he did every day, he marveled that he was allowed to live here. If there was a more beautiful place in creation to live, he couldn't imagine it. This was part of his reason for vowing to never leave, to always be here to protect it, for he couldn't imagine the world without Elvandar.

He continued and found himself returning eventually to the contemplation glade. Acaila had roused himself from his meditation and was walking toward Tomas. His expression was clouded with worry. Tomas was surprised, as the ancient leader of the Eldar rarely revealed his thoughts this casually.

Tomas asked, "You've seen something?"

To Tathar and the other elf, Acaila said, "Thank you for your guidance." He took Tomas by the elbow and said, "Walk with me, my friend."

He led Tomas through a quiet part of the woods, away from the kitchens and shops, near the edge of the inner circle of Elvandar. When he was certain they were alone, Acaila said, "Something dark still lingers in Krondor." He looked at Tomas. "Something wonderful, too. I cannot explain it, but an old power for good verges upon returning. Perhaps the universe is trying to put itself right."

Acaila led the Eldar, the ancient line of elves who had been closest to the Valheru. Tomas had come to value his counsel. He had a perspective unique and vast.

"But whatever force for good there is, the evil unleashed by the demon before it was destroyed is still stronger," Acaila continued. "That dark agency has servants, and they are building power in Ylith and Zūn and now in LaMut."

"What Subai said about human sacrifice?"

Acaila said, "It is a thing of great evil and great power, and it grows by the day. The servants of such evil often are dupes and have no idea of what they bring upon themselves as well as others. They do not know they destroy their own souls first. As soulless men they feel no remorse, no shame, no regret. They merely act on impulse, seeking what they think they want, glory, power, wealth, the trappings of might. They do not realize they have already lost and anything they do serves only waste and destruction.''

Tomas was silent for a while, then said, "I have Valheru memory, so those impulses are well known to me.''

"Your Valheru forebears lived in different times, my friend. The universe was ordered differently. The Valheru were natural forces, serving neither good nor evil.

"But this thing is a thing of evil, apart from any other consideration, and it must be rooted out and destroyed. And to do so, the forces which strive to endure and survive the onslaught will need help.''

Tomas said, "So I leave to lend my strength.''

Acaila said, "Of all of us here, you alone have the means to tip the balance to good.''

"I will leave and find Pug," said Tomas. "Together we will do what we must to save the Kingdom and prevent the rise of this evil in Krondor.''

"Go to the Queen," said Acaila, "and know whatever you do, you do for her and your son.''

Tomas gripped Acaila's hand and left.

Later that night, after dining with his wife and a lingering good-bye, Tomas returned to the clearing north of the center of the forest. He was now dressed in his white-and-gold armor. A legacy of an ancient past, the armor was without blemish or scratch. He had reclaimed his golden sword with the white hilt when his son had unraveled the mystery of the Lifestone. His hand rested on its hilt, and he wore his white shield with the golden dragon emblazoned on it over his shoulder. He looked to the sky and sent forth a call. He waited.

Men lay dead and dying on all sides. Erik stood exhausted, a mound of dead enemies before him. Sometime during the afternoon his horse had gone out from under him courtesy of a stray arrow.

Twice he had been tempted to order retreat, but on both

occasions his men had rallied and the enemy had been thrown back. He vaguely recalled a lull during the afternoon in which he had greedily drunk from a waterskin and eaten something; he couldn't remember what.

Horns had sounded from the other side a few minutes before, and the enemy withdrew. The diamonds had held, and a thousand or more men had died trying to take them. Erik couldn't begin to guess how many defenders had died as well. He knew he'd get a body count in the morning.

Leland rode up and said, "My father's compliments, Captain."

Erik nodded, trying to get his thoughts organized. "I'll be along presently, Lieutenant."

Erik bent and cleaned his sword on the tunic of a dead man before him, then put it in his scabbard and looked over the field. He had ended up in the gap between the center diamond and the one on the right. The bodies before him were waist-high. He turned toward Jadow Shati, who yelled, "I hope we don't have to do that again anytime soon, man!"

Erik waved. "Not until tomorrow." He headed toward Earl Richard's tent. When he got there he found two bodies being dragged out of the tent by guards, and the old Earl sitting at his table, an orderly bandaging his arm.

"What happened?" asked Erik.

"Some of the enemy got loose on your left flank, Captain, and actually got here. I finally got to use this sword."

"How do you feel?" asked Erik.

"Like hell, Captain." He looked at the orderly, who finished tying off the bandage, and waved him away. "Still, I can at last feel like a soldier.

"You know," he said, leaning back, "I once rode a patrol, and we saw some Keshians who ran across the border when they saw us, and until today that was as close as I had come to being in an actual battle." He got a distant look. "That was forty years ago, Erik."

Erik sat. "I envy you."

"I don't doubt that," said Richard. "What next?"

"We wait until they withdraw a bit more, then I'd like to put some scouts up in the hills to get a sense of how they're deploying. Our men did well this day."

"But we didn't break them," said Richard.

"No," said Erik. "And each day we fight out here in the middle of the road, our chances of reaching Ylith diminish, and our hope of freeing Yabon becomes faint."

"We need some sort of magic," said Richard.

"I'm short of magic right now," said Erik, standing up. "I had better see how the men are." He saluted and left the tent.

He encountered Leland outside and said, "Your father's fine; his wound is slight."

Leland's face reflected his relief. Erik's estimation of the boy rose; he had gone about his business not knowing how his father fared.

Erik asked, "How are the reserves?"

"They stand ready," said Leland.

Erik was relieved. "I lost track in the afternoon and didn't remember if they had been called up."

"They were not, Captain."

"Good, order the men inside the diamonds relieved and tell the cavalry to stand down. Get the men fed. Then come back. I have a job for you."

Leland saluted and hurried off. Erik made his way to his own modest tent among the Crimson Eagles and sat down. Commissary soldiers hurried with water and food and one approached Erik with a wooden bowl of hot stew and a water skin. He took the bowl and a spoon and dug in, ignoring the heat.

Jadow Shati and the men from the center diamond came walking slowly back and Jadow half-sat, half-collapsed next to Erik. "Man, I don't want to do that again."

"How did we do?"

"We lost a few," said Jadow, fatigue making his speech slow and his tone somber. "It could have been worse."

"I know," said Erik. "We've got to come up with something brilliant and unexpected, or we're going to lose this war."

"I thought it was something like that," said Jadow. "Maybe if we could bleed them enough tomorrow we could launch a counteroffensive and punch through their center, leaving their forces divided."

Erik was almost finished eating when a messenger found

him. "Earl Richard's compliments, sir. Would you attend him at once?"

Erik rose and followed the youngster and returned to the command tent. There he found a terrified-looking scribe standing next to Earl Richard. "This just came in a few minutes ago," Richard said to Erik.

Erik read Jimmy's message and said, "Gods!"

Richard said, "What do you think we should do?"

"If we take any of our forces south, we lose Yabon. If we keep them here, we lose Krondor."

Richard said, "We must preserve Krondor. We can hold here and, if we must, postpone the campaign to retake Yabon until next year."

Erik said, "This is impossible." He was silent for a minute, then said, "My lord, if you'll allow me?"

The Earl said, "I always do, Erik. You haven't made a mistake so far." The old Earl had come to recognize Erik's talents and his utter lack of personal ambition and would ratify any decision Erik made.

Erik said, "Send for Jadow Shati."

While the messenger was gone, Erik questioned the scribe and found the man completely ignorant of most of the things Erik wanted to know. He did, however, impress upon Erik the level of concern and agitation in Earl James, enough that Erik felt he must heed Jimmy's warning.

When Jadow showed up, Erik said, "We have a change in plans."

"Don't we always?"

"I want you to start now on building a barricade. I want a fort by the end of this week."

"Where?"

"Here," said Erik. "Across this road. Put a squad up in the hills to the east with Akee's Hadati and kill anything that comes south. This is our new northern border until I tell you otherwise."

"What sort of fortifications?"

"I want a six-foot-high earthen breastwork a hundred yards north of the three diamonds. When that's done, start building a wall. Fell trees to the south and get on it. I want it twelve feet high, reinforced, with an archery platform every twenty yards. I want two ballista ports every hundred feet, and a clear line of fire to the rear for catapults, so they can launch stones without knocking our own men off the walls.''

"Man, how long is this thing to be?"

"From the cliffs overlooking the sea to the steepest hill you can find."

"Erik, that's more than two miles!"

"Then you'd better start now."

Leland of Malkuric appeared. "The cavalry is standing down, sir."

"Good," said Erik. "At first light I want you leading them down the coast, back to Krondor."

"Krondor?" said the youth, looking at his father.

The old Earl nodded. "It appears our old friends the Keshians are about to launch an assault on the city. Earl James of Vencar requests reinforcements."

"But what about the fight here?" asked the youth.

"You just get south and save Krondor, lad," said Erik. "Leave this area to me."

"Yes, sir," said the lad. "Which units, sir?"

"Every horseman we have. We can dig in and hold here for the rest of the summer with the footmen, but they can't reach Krondor in anything under three weeks.

"Now, listen carefully. Don't start off galloping down the coast. You'll kill half your mounts in the first three days. Start off forty minutes at a trot, then get off the horses and lead them for twenty. At noon, switch to a half hour trotting and a half hour leading the horses. And give them plenty of grain and water each evening. If you do that, you'll save most of them and get thirty miles a day out of the troops. That should put you in Krondor in a week."

"Yes, sir!" said Leland. He turned and left to carry out his orders.

Erik balled his fist and looked skyward. "Damn!" he said. "I just thought up a way to dig those bastards out from behind that fortress to the north, and this has to happen."

Jadow, who had been about to leave when Leland appeared, said, "You know they say Tith-Onanka runs a soldier's life, but I got to tell you, man, Banath seems to run my little corner of the world." He left.

Erik nodded. "Banath runs mine too, it seems." The God of Thieves was also known as "The Prankster," and was commonly given credit for everything that went wrong.

Erik looked at the old Earl, who said, "We do what we can."

Erik nodded, and silently left the tent, feeling as defeated as he had ever felt in his life.

Dash roused himself and rubbed his eyes. He had given up on staying awake during the afternoon unless an emergency occurred. There was too much to do after darkness fell.

He began his day at sundown and worked throughout the night, with his mornings spent at the palace or sorting out problems around the city. About noon, if the gods were kind, he would collapse into his bed at the rear of the New Market Jail and fall into an exhausted sleep. Six or seven hours later, he would be roused.

He had received unexpected help from the Mockers in locating the infiltrators. He had put at least two hundred of them behind bars, and had forced Patrick to build a temporary stockade to the north of the city over the Prince's objections. Should Kesh attack—*when* Kesh attacked, in Dash's mind—they would be freed by the Keshians. At least, thought Dash, they would be unarmed and *outside* the city.

It was the ones still armed and inside the city that he worried about.

As Dash entered the former inn's common room, used as a squad room by the constabulary, he realized he had overslept, and it was at least an hour after he had planned to be up. He asked one of the constables, "What time is it?"

"Eight of the clock about fifteen minutes ago. He's been waiting here an hour. We wouldn't let him wake you."

The constable was pointing at a court page. "What is it?" he asked.

The lad handed him a note. "The Prince wishes you at the palace at once, sir," said the boy.

Dash read it and winced. He had completely forgotten he had been invited to dinner this evening at the palace and had agreed to go. "I'll be along shortly," said Dash.

Lately he was unhappy with Patrick even more than usual and probably that was the reason he had forgotten the invitation. Dash realized that the Prince could certainly operate in any fashion he wished, with or without Dash's approval, but given that the city's security was Dash's responsibility, he resented those decisions of Patrick's which made security that much more difficult to insure.

Dash wanted things from Patrick, and making the Prince angry wasn't a good way to do that. He had to make Patrick understand how dangerous things were right now.

Dash couldn't seem to impress upon Patrick the mere fact that having had two Keshian agents inside the palace walls was a major source of concern. Dash knew his grandfather would have had both men singing out the names of every contact they had from Krondor to the Overn Deep. Patrick, on the other hand, seemed oblivious, and Duke Rufio felt that as both men were *absent* from the palace— one gone and the other in custody—things were in hand. Dash wondered if Talwin had put in an appearance as yet and what his view on the matter was. Dash was certain his late father's spy wouldn't share Rufio's equanimity on the matter.

Dash gave instructions on the night's raids and put Gustaf in charge of the most delicate one; he had come to trust the former mercenary as a steady influence on the other men. Dash got his horse and rode to the palace.

As he rode through the city, Dash registered the rhythm of the place, becoming more familiar by the day. Krondor was reviving and it angered him to the point of irrationality that anyone, Keshian or Fadawah, might return to undo the work he had done. Rillanon had been his home until three years before, when his grandfather had brought Dash and his brother to Krondor. Since then he had worked for a while for Roo Avery, though he was always in his grandfather's employ. And against any reasonable expectation he had made the city his own.

As he neared the palace, Dash conceded there was more of his grandfather in him than he might have once been willing to admit. Dash rode in past a pair of guards at the main gate who saluted the Sheriff. A groom hurried forward to take his horse. Dash moved quickly up the palace steps and past guards standing in the entrance hall.

He was hurrying to the point of almost running as he rounded the corner that would take him directly to the great hall. Instantly he knew something was wrong.

The great doors were open and a pair of guards stood just inside, as if inquiring over something. A servant was running from the hall, toward the rear of the palace, shouting something.

Dash ran. He pushed past the two guards at the door and saw people in agony or unconscious. The hall had been set up with a giant U-shaped table, allowing jugglers and entertainers to perform before the entire court. The Prince, Francie, Dukes Brian and Rufio were at the head table. Dash noted an empty chair at the far end on the Prince's left.

The other two tables were occupied by the remaining nobles of the area and most of the important citizens of Krondor. Half of them appeared unconscious, slumped down in their chairs or on the floor, while a few others were attempting to stand, and one or two were sitting, a vacant disoriented expression on their faces.

Dash ran across the room to the head table and vaulted over it, swinging his legs over the prone form of Duke Brian. Francie was slumped over the table between her father and Patrick, and Duke Rufio had fallen to the floor and was lying on his back, eyes open and vacant. The Prince sat back in his chair gasping for air, his eyes wide and unfocused.

Dash stuck his finger into the Prince's mouth, and Patrick vomited the contents of his stomach. He repeated the action with Francie, who also threw up what she had eaten. He turned to see startled-looking servants and guards standing around, unsure of what to do. "Make them vomit!" shouted Dash. "They've been poisoned!"

He reached Duke Silden and got him to gag up food, but far less than Dash would have liked. He reached Duke Rufio and could not force a response. The Duke's breathing was shallow and his face was clammy to the touch.

Dash jumped up and saw that three of the servants were attempting to get those still conscious to throw up. He shouted to a guard, "Get a horse! Ride to Temple Square! Bring back any clerics you can find. We need healers!"

Dash organized the servants and had more come bringing fresh water. He had no idea what poison had been used, but he knew that some of them could be diluted. "Make those who can drink swallow as much as they can!" he shouted. "Don't force those who can't; you'll drown them."

Dash grabbed a sergeant of the guard and said, "Arrest everyone in the kitchen."

Dash realized that whoever had poisoned the entire royal court was probably gone by now, but perhaps he had not had time to flee. He certainly hadn't expected the Sheriff to be late and avoid being among those afflicted.

The room stank and Dash set some of the staff to cleaning up as others attended those ill. It took nearly a half hour for the first cleric to arrive, a priest of Astalon. He set about doing what he could do for the stricken, starting with the Prince.

Dash did a mental inventory of those in attendance: of the nobles in Krondor, only he had been absent from this meal. Every other titled lord from Duke to Squire in the area was at that table. Of the town's wealthy and powerful merchants, only Roo Avery was absent, being out at his estate with his family.

Soon other priests of the various orders appeared, including Brother Dominic, the Ishapian who now served at Nakor's temple. They tended those in the room throughout the night, and Dash interrogated the kitchen staff. Near sunrise he returned to the great hall, which now resembled an infirmary. Dominic was near the door and Dash called him over. "How do we stand?" he asked.

"It was a close thing," said the monk. "Had you not acted as you had, you would be the only noble in the city still breathing.

"The Prince will live, though he will be sick for a long time, as will the Lady Francine." He shook his head. "Her father is touch and go. I don't know if he'll pull through."

Dash said, "Duke Rufio?"

Dominic shook his head in the negative. "It was the wine that was poisoned. He drank a great deal of it."

Dash closed his eyes. "I tried to tell Patrick that if we had one spy in the palace . . ."

"Well," said Dominic, "while the loss is terrible, at least the Prince will survive."

"There is that." Dash looked at those dead who were being carried away. "But we've lost too many already to have to endure this insult. It could have been worse, but not by much," said the exhausted young Sheriff.

Then the alarm bell began to ring and Dash realized the city was under attack.

Twenty-Four

Attacks

Dash RACED DOWN the street.

People ran through the streets while soldiers raced to the walls. The gates were closing and a panic-stricken constable in charge of the gate check said, "Sheriff! A rider raced in claiming there's a Keshian army coming up the road."

"Bar the gate," said Dash. He grabbed the constable and said, "What's your name?"

"Delwin, sir," said the agitated young man.

"You're now a sergeant, understand?"

The man nodded, then said, "But we don't have sergeants in the constabulary, sir."

"Right now, you're in the army," Dash shouted. "Come with me." He led Delwin up the steps to the ramparts on the wall above the gate and looked to the east. The sun was rising over the distant mountains and caused him to squint.

Movement caught his eyes and he held his hand up to shield them from the sun. He squinted, and there, along a road running along the base of a distant hill, he saw movement, nothing more than the appearance of a long line undulating along the side of the hill.

"Gods," he whispered. To the newly created sergeant he said, "Send word to the New Market Jail. I want every constable up on these walls with the solders. We have an army coming to visit.''

Sergeant Delwin hurried off. Dash looked to his right and his left and saw a sergeant of the Palace Guard hurrying toward him. Dash grabbed him and said, ''What's your name?''

''McCally, sir.''

''Your Captain is either dead or very sick; I do not know which. Are there any other officers around?''

''Lieutenant Yardley has the duty, sir, and should be above the palace wall.''

''Go fetch him and tell him I need him here at once.''

The Sergeant ran off and returned a few minutes later with the Lieutenant. ''Sir,'' said the Lieutenant, ''what are your orders?''

Dash said, ''As Baron of the court and Sheriff of Krondor, I find I am the only functioning noble in the city. How many officers escaped the poisoning last night?''

''Four, sir, of which I am senior.''

''You are now an acting Captain, Yardley. How many men have we?''

Yardley spoke without hesitation, ''We have five hundred members of the Prince's Household Guards, and fifteen hundred members of the city garrison, spread out around the city. I don't know the current number of your constables, sir.''

''Slightly better than two hundred. What about guards who came with the nobles last night?''

''Maybe another three hundred, honor guards, personal retinues,'' replied the newly made Captain.

''Very well, have them support your men on the palace walls. Have whoever's in charge of the city garrison find me here and report.''

Yardley ran off, and a short time later a grey-haired old sergeant appeared. ''I'm Sergeant Mackey, sir. Lieutenant Yardley said to report to you.''

''Where's your officer?'' asked Dash.

''Dead, sir,'' replied the stocky old man. ''He was dining with the Prince last night.''

Dash shook his head. ''Well, Sergeant,'' said Dash dryly,

"for the next few days, you're going to play the part of Knight-Marshal of Krondor."

The old man smiled and came to attention. With a glint in his eye, he said, "I had hoped for a promotion before I retired, sir!" He then lost his smile. "If I may be so bold, who then are you to be?"

"Me?" said Dash with a bitter laugh. "I get to play the part of the Prince of Krondor until Patrick's strong enough to stand."

"Well, then, *Highness*," said the Sergeant in a semi-mocking tone, "I respectfully submit we better quit larking about and get ready to defend this city." He pointed to the advancing column in the distance. "That lot doesn't appear very tender to me."

"Right you are," said Dash with a tired smile. "I want you to deploy three men in four on the walls. I want the remaining men held in reserve."

"Sir!" said Mackey with a salute. As Mackey ran off, Gustaf and the constables ran down High Street toward the main gate. Dash yelled down, "How did the raids go last night?"

Gustaf shouted, "We netted another score of the bastards, but I know there are more out there."

"Here's the duty: call martial law and tell everyone to remain in their houses. Then I want the constables to check all the places we've talked about." Gustaf knew exactly what Dash meant: those places within the city vulnerable to attack from within. "Then sweep the city and arrest anyone on the streets. Then report back to the jail and wait."

"Wait for what, Sheriff?"

"Wait for word the Keshians are breaching the defenses, then come fast."

Gustaf saluted. He turned and gave orders to groups of constables, who ran off in different directions, shouting, "Martial law! Get inside! Get off the streets!"

Dash turned and watched as the sun continued to rise in the east, and the enemy continued their advance.

Erik leaned over, perspiration dripping off his brow, as the enemy retreated once more. He stood at the point of the center diamond, the dead piled outside the shield wall to chest height. He turned when someone touched his shoulder and saw Jadow behind him, his face a mask of red from the splattered blood. "We held," said the Lieutenant. "We did it."

The attack had been unrelenting; a wave of soldiers who had simply pushed themselves upon the waiting defenses of the Kingdom. Erik had been able to repulse them without having to rely on horses which he no longer had. The left diamond had threatened to collapse at one point, but a reserve company had been thrown in and the enemy pushed back. Archers had continued a slaughter between the diamonds and two flying companies had been able to respond to threatened flanking attacks from either side. On the whole, it had been a masterful defense.

Erik said to Jadow, "I'm worried about arrows. Get scavengers out there picking up as many as can be salvaged."

Jadow hurried off and Erik waved over another soldier, named Wilks. "Run to the command tent and inform Earl Richard I'll be along presently, and ask him if any supply trains have caught up with us. Then come back here and report."

Erik was handed a waterskin by a commissary and he drank greedily. He then poured water over his face and wiped off whatever blood and dirt he could.

Around him men were pushing bodies outside the diamonds. The enemy showed no interest in removing their dead, and Erik was worried: beyond the obvious problems of the stink and the danger of disease, there was the added burden of his men having to clear the positions so they could be defended.

Erik directed the cleanup, and Jadow returned saying that the scavengers were hard at work recovering any arrows that could be used again. Even some that were damaged would be repaired by a trio of fletchers hard at work at the rear of their position. But Erik was nearly out of supplies and was concerned, because a baggage train due to arrive the previous day was overdue. He had dispatched a patrol to the south to find them and hurry them along. While a smith's apprentice, Erik had tended mules and donkeys and knew they were even more fractious and difficult at times than horses, but now he was concerned that something beyond a difficult team or two was slowing down the supplies.

Jadow said, "Man, that was some fight."

"Not much in it, save stand and slaughter."

"Nightmare Ridge all over again."

Erik hiked his thumb at the enemy. "They're not very smart, but they are fearless."

"I've been thinking," said Jadow. "We know that those we faced before were under some spell or another, a demon or what have you, according to the rumors, and that's why they fell apart after the battle at the ridge, but they don't seem to have learned anything over the winter."

"I know what you mean," said Erik. "From everything we know about Fadawah, I'd expect something different. He must have discovered by now that we're not going to chase him." Erik rubbed his hand over his face as if he could wipe away the fatigue.

Wilks returned and said, "Captain, Earl Richmond awaits your report and told me to tell you the baggage train has arrived."

"Good," said Erik, "I was beginning to worry." To Jadow, he said, "Relieve the men in the diamonds and get something to eat."

"Sir," said Jadow with a casual salute.

Erik left the diamond and paused to inspect the three positions for a minute. The shields were damaged, as he expected, and he had ample replacements, but the spears were almost used up. He turned to a soldier. "Johnson, get a squad and move south to the woods near the road. Start felling trees that we can use to make long spears." The soldier saluted, and Erik could tell from his expression he had no wish to be doing anything but eating and sleeping, but during war few got to do what they wished for.

Erik knew they'd not have spearpoints, but sharpened, fire-hardened stakes would serve to keep enemy horse at bay. And other weapons would be in the baggage, machine parts for constructing catapults, oil for burning out underground tunnels and firing wooden defensive positions. Erik began to feel optimistic about being able to hold the position. He had no thought at this moment about advancing, not with his entire detachment of horse soldiers dashing toward Krondor.

He reached the command tent and found the Earl sitting at his command table. "How is the arm, sir?"

"Fine," said Richard. He smiled. "Do you want to know why our baggage is late?"

"I was wondering," admitted Erik as he poured himself a mug of ale from a pitcher on the table.

"Leland forced them off the road," said Richard, "so he could get down to Krondor. Some of the wagons got stuck in the mud and it took a half-day to get them out."

"Well," said Erik with a laugh, "I'd have rather had them here yesterday, but as long as they're going to be late, I'll settle for that reason; I was afraid they'd been ambushed."

Hot wet towels were provided and Erik washed up. A servant went to his tent and returned with a fresh tunic, and Erik sat with the Earl, the teeth-gritting pressure of the day beginning to slip away slightly as the ale relaxed him.

Food was provided, and while plain camp fare, it was hot and filling, and the bread was fresh baked. Erik bit off a large hunk of the hot flavorful bread, and after he had swallowed, said, "One good thing about holding a defensive position is our commissary has time to set up their ovens."

Earl Richard laughed. "Well, there you have it; I was wondering if there was even a hint of good in all this, and you found it."

Erik said, "Unfortunately, that may be about all the good there is to wring out of this situation. I would trade all the hot bread in the world to be outside the gates of Ylith, ready to storm the city with our army."

"Someone once said that you can make all the plans you wish, but they all go to naught as soon as the first elements in your army encounter the enemy."

"My experience is that is true."

"The truly great field commanders can improvise"— Richard looked at Erik—"as you do."

"Thank you, but I'm far from being anyone's notion of a great general."

"You underestimate yourself, Erik."

"I wanted to be a smith."

"Truth?"

"Truth. I was apprenticed to a drunk who failed to register my name with the guild, and had he, I would probably have been moved from Darkmoor before I killed my half-brother." He went on and outlined the story of how he had become a soldier, from murdering Manfred while in a rage over Manfred's rape of Rosalyn, the girl who had been like a sister to Erik, and being tried and convicted of murder. He told him of being pulled from prison by Bobby de Loungville, Lord James, and Calis, and the journeys to Novindus.

When he was done, Lord Richard said, "A remarkable story, Erik. We had heard things in the East of some of those things Lord James did, but only rumors and conjecture." Lord Richard said, "My son will follow me in my office, and perhaps rise even higher as a result of this service, but you stand poised for greatness should you choose to take advantage, Erik. With Greylock dead, it is but a short step for you to take command of the Armies of the West."

Erik said, "I am unsuited for it; there is so much I don't know about strategy, long-range planning, the political consequences of things."

"The fact you know those issues exist places you ahead of most of us who might be selected for the position on the basis of who our fathers were, Erik. Don't underestimate yourself."

Erik shrugged. "I don't think I am, Richard. I'm Captain of the Crimson Eagles, and a Court Baron as a result. That's far more than I wished to be. I thought I had everything I wanted when I was named Sergeant. I only want to serve as a soldier."

"Sometimes we have no choice," said Richard. "I wanted to grow roses. I love my gardens. I don't think I'm happier than when I'm showing guests through them. I amuse my wife and annoy our groundskeeper no end by puttering around out there, on my hands and knees, pulling weeds."

Erik smiled at the image of the old man out there in the dirt. "Yet you do it."

"It makes me happy. Find what makes you happy, Erik, and hold to it."

"My wife, doing a good job, the company of friends," said Erik. "I can't think of much more."

"You'll do, Erik von Darkmoor. You'll do very well, should fate tap you for greatness."

They talked late into the night.

Nakor pointed. "That way."

The Captain said, "I can't see anything in this fog. Are you sure?"

"Of course I am," said Nakor. "The fog's an illusion. I know where we're going."

"I'll remember you said that, sir." The Captain appeared dubious.

Nakor had tried a couple of "tricks" to contact Pug, but nothing seemed to work. He was almost certain new defenses had been erected around Sorcerer's Isle, and upon entering the region of fog he was certain that was the case.

Pug didn't want to be bothered by casual travelers, it seemed. When Nakor had been in charge of the island, he had relied on the reputation of the place, coupled with a menacing-looking castle with blue light flickering in the tower windows.

Now the defensive magic was stronger. Nakor had to correct the Captain's course, because while in the fog the tillerman was letting the ship curve away from the island.

In the distance he heard the sound of surf and said, "Get ready to lower sails, Captain. We're almost there."

"How can you—"

Suddenly they were out of the fog, in brilliant daylight. Members of the crew looked over their shoulders and saw a wall of fog which circled the island like a fortress.

The castle still stood atop the cliffs, a looming black presence that seemed to cast a pall over the area. "Should we move farther down the coast?" asked the Captain.

"This is very good," said Nakor. "They've added some new tricks." He looked at the Captain. "Everything is fine. You just lower a boat, drop me on the beach, then you can go back to Krondor."

The relief was obvious on the man's face. "How do we plot our course?"

"Just sail through the fog, that way." Nakor pointed. "If you're turned around a little in the fog, that's fine, because it will want to turn you away from the island anyway. You'll come out more or less pointed east, and you can get your bearings off the sun or stars. You'll be fine."

The Captain tried to look reassured, but failed.

The sails were hauled in and a boat lowered, and within an hour Nakor stood on the beach of Sorcerer's Island. He didn't bother to watch the ship depart, as he knew the Captain would be raising sail even as the boat that had dropped Nakor off was rowing furiously back. Pug had done a wonderful job of casting a pall of woe and despair over anyone sitting off the coast.

Nakor hiked the path up from the beach, and where it split toward the castle and down into the small valley, he chose the valley path. Nakor didn't even bother using the energy needed to shift his perceptions, as he knew that when he reached the limit of the illusion he would pass from the seemingly wild woodlands into a lovely pasture, dominated by a rambling villa.

When the illusion finally did shift, Nakor almost tripped in surprise. For while the landscape was as he had expected it to be, there was one feature that was totally unexpected. A golden dragon rested comfortably next to the house, apparently asleep.

Nakor hiked up his faded orange robe and hurried on spindly shanks until he was before the dragon. "Ryana!" he shouted.

The dragon opened one eye and said, "Hello, Nakor. Is there a reason you're waking me?"

"Why don't you change and come inside?"

"Because it's more comfortable sleeping like this," said the dragon, her voice revealing her mood as less than pleased.

"Late night?"

"Flying all night. Tomas asked me to bring him."

"Tomas is here! That is wonderful news."

"You may be the only one in Midkemia to think so," rejoined the dragon.

"No, I don't mean the reason he's here, I mean the fact he's here. That means I don't have to explain things to Pug."

"Probably for the best," said the dragon as a nimbus of golden light surrounded her. Her form shimmered, the edges blurring, and the light seemed to shrink until she was human size. Then she resolved into the form of a striking woman with reddish blond hair, enormous blue eyes, and a deep tan of gold.

"Put some clothing on," said Nakor. "I can't concentrate when you run around naked."

With a slight movement, Ryana created a long blue gown, which accentuated her coloring. "How you can be the age you are and still act like such an adolescent at times is beyond me, Nakor."

"It's part of my charm," said Nakor with a grin.

Ryana slipped her arm in his and said, "No, I don't think that's it. Let's go inside."

They walked into the house and headed toward Pug's study. When they got there, they heard voices inside, and when Nakor knocked, Pug's voice said, "Come in."

Ryana entered first, and Nakor came in behind her. Pug's study was large, with a broad windowseat upon which Miranda sat. Tomas sat uncomfortably in a chair that was obviously a little too small for him, while Pug sat facing the two of them. If either Tomas or Pug were surprised to see Nakor, neither showed it. Miranda grinned. "Why am I not surprised to see you here?"

"I give up," said Nakor sitting down. "So, what are we to do?"

All eyes turned toward him, and Pug said, "Why don't you tell us?"

Nakor opened his sack and reached in, up to his shoulder, as if feeling around. Everyone in the room had seen him do the trick before, but the effect was still comic. He fished out an orange and said, "Anyone want one?"

Miranda held up her hand and Nakor tossed it to her. He got another one for himself. Nakor began to peel the orange. "Something amazing happened in Krondor last week. A terrible thing and a wonderful thing. Or they were both the same thing. Anyway, one of my students, a very special woman named Aleta, was studying with Sho Pi—meditation, just the basics—when suddenly a light gathered around her. She rose in the air, and below her, trapped, was a very black thing."

"A black thing?" asked Miranda. "Could you be a little more specific?"

"I don't know what to call it," said Nakor. "It's energy, perhaps a spirit of some sort. Maybe by now some of the other clerics from the different temples have figured out what it is. But it's something very bad. Maybe it's left over from the demon. I don't know, but I think it was in place so that something could happen in Krondor, later."

"Later?" asked Miranda, then she looked at Pug, who shrugged.

Tomas said, "I have just been telling Pug that Captain Subai of the Pathfinders reached Elvandar. It seems Greylock's army is stalled south of Quester's View. And from what Subai reported, there is dark power being used again."

Nakor said, "Yes, that makes a great deal of sense." He was about to say something, then hesitated. "A moment." He made a broad gesture with his hands and waved over his head, then the room crackled with energy.

Tomas smiled. "Don't lower the barrier prematurely this time."

Nakor grinned in embarrassment. The last time he had used this mystic shield to protect them, he had lowered it too soon and the demon Jakan had located them. "I put the field around the room. I'll just leave it up permanently. No agency of Nalar's will ever be able to spy on this room. Now we can talk without falling under his sway."

At the mention of Nalar's name, Pug felt a prickling sensation in his head for a moment, and suddenly barriers to his memory were lowered. Images and voices swam in his consciousness, and things he had placed apart in his mind were now accessible to him. "We must assume the Nameless One has more servants."

"Obviously," said Tomas. "The human sacrifices and other slaughter are means for gathering power."

"What fascinates me," said Nakor, "is what is happening in Krondor."

Pug smiled at his occasional companion. "Obviously this new faith of yours is having a direct effect."

"Yes, but that's what I find odd and fascinating." He pulled a section from his orange and ate it. "I am no expert on issues of faith, but I had the distinct impression it would take a few centuries or longer for our new temple to have any effect."

Miranda said, "Don't give yourself too much credit, Nakor. It may be the power was already there, and your little temple just happened to be the convenient conduit."

"That makes more sense," agreed Nakor. "In any event, we have this issue to discuss. When we fought the demon, we mistakenly thought we had defeated the Nameless One's agents. What we did was destroy their most current weapons, nothing more."

Nakor waved out the window past Miranda. "Out there," he said, "is at least one more evil agency doing very bad things, and it is gathering power.

"That is who we must defeat."

Tomas said, "Subai leads me to think that Elvandar will soon be at risk if we do not stop this army now."

Nakor leaped out of his chair. "No! You are not listening." He stopped, then said, "Or I am not saying this right. We are not trying to save Elvandar, or Krondor, or the Kingdom." He looked from face to face. "We are trying to save this world."

Ryana said, "Very well, Nakor. You now have my undivided attention. These petty human wars are nothing to dragonkind, but we share this world with you. What is the threat to us all?"

"This Mad God, this Nalar, whose very name is a danger, he is the threat. When you look at everything that has occurred since the Chaos Wars, remember this. When you once again forget the very conversation we have this hour, when your memories are locked away to prevent you from falling under Nalar's sway, remember this much: there is always something deeper behind what you see on the surface."

"All right," said Pug. "So what we see on the surface, the invasion and the conquest by Fadawah, they hide a deeper truth."

"Yes, Fadawah is a dupe. He was before and he is still. He is just the next to be placed at the head of this murderous army. We must identify whoever it is that stands behind him, in the shadow. There is something evil growing in Krondor. It is there against the time Fadawah's army arrives. Whoever is behind Fadawah—an advisor, or servant, or a member of his guard—must be destroyed. Somewhere is a being who was there when the my old wife, Jorma, became Lady Clovis, when she was controlling Dhakon, and when she sat the Emerald Throne. He was there when the demon ruled, and now when Fadawah is the leader. This creature, man, or spirit, this thing is the agent of Nalar who is orchestrating the war. It is this being who seeks no conquest, but rather destruction. This is the creature who doesn't wish to see one side or the other win, but rather seeks to let the suffering linger, let innocents die. This is the creature we must find."

Tomas said, "Do you suspect another Pantathian?"

Nakor said, "I don't think so. Maybe, but it may also be a man, or a dark elf, or any other manner of creature. It may be a spirit in the body of one such as Fadawah. I just don't know. But we must seek out this creature and destroy it."

Pug said, "This sounds as if we must fly to the heart of the enemy and confront their leader."

Nakor said, "Yes, and that is dangerous."

Pug winced in memory of the trap the demon had laid for him, the one that in his arrogance he had overlooked, the trap that had almost cost Pug his life.

"Why don't we just . . . I don't know," said Miranda, "just burn everything within a mile of Fadawah's headquarters? That should end this creature, shouldn't it?"

Pug said, "Probably not. Years ago I faced another of Nalar's creatures, a mad magician named Sidi. A few of the older members of the temples know the story, for we strove to control the Tear of the Gods."

Ryana said, "Tear of the Gods?"

Pug said, "It is a powerful artifact, used by the Ishapians to channel power from the controller gods." He looked at Miranda. "You could burn this house down around Sidi and he would have been standing there laughing at you when the ashes cooled.''

''How did you destroy him?'' asked Miranda.

Pug looked at his wife. ''I didn't.''

Miranda said, ''Are you saying this person controlling Fadawah is this Sidi?''

''It could be. Or it could be one of Sidi's servants, or another like him.''

Nakor said, ''Nalar has many agents. Most do not know they serve the Mad God. They just do things because they feel the need.''

Tomas said, ''What must we do?''

Pug said, ''We lure this agent of Nalar into showing itself.''

''How?'' asked Miranda.

Pug nodded. ''Me. I have to be bait. Fadawah's true master must know that at some point I will act. I have in the past. And we can assume there's some sort of surprise waiting for me if I show up.''

Miranda said, ''No! The last time I goaded you into acting prematurely, you almost got killed. Since then I think I've changed my mind about kicking down doors and walking into rooms. Let's sneak around some first.''

Nakor said, ''I've snuck around in the enemy's camp, back when I went to Novindus with Calis and his friends, and I stood close to the Emerald Queen. I couldn't tell who was running things. Pug is right. We must find a way to force this person or creature or spirit or whatever it is to reveal itself to us.''

Miranda said, ''No! And I'm going to keep saying 'no' until you get it through your head.'' She stood up. ''I've snuck around behind the lines, too. Let Nakor and me do it one more time. We can go to where Greylock's army is, and I know we can sneak into the camp. Let me get close to Fadawah and see what I can see. If we can't find anything, I'll agree to go in and let them throw everything at you. But I don't want to risk it just yet. All right?'' She touched his face.

''Your temper is going to get you killed,'' he warned her.

''I can keep it under control when I have to.''

Pug looked at Nakor. "I want you to promise me you'll tell her when it's too dangerous and it's time to come back here." He looked at Miranda. "And I want you to promise you'll listen to him, and when he says so, you'll transport yourself back to this room."

They both agreed. Pug said, "I don't like this anymore than you like my idea." He kissed Miranda and said, "It's better if you go now, while it's still dark over there."

Miranda held out her hand. "Nakor, where do we want to go?"

"Last I heard, Greylock was somewhere south of Quester's View."

"I know a village on the coast. We'll transport there, then we can fly up the coast."

Ryana said, "I'm going to go sleep. Wake me when you have someone worth fighting."

Nakor said, "A moment, please." Pug and the others felt their memories shut off again, hiding knowledge of Nalar, and then the mystic barrier was lowered.

Tomas said, "Sleep well, friend." The dragon in human form left the room.

Miranda took Nakor's hand and they vanished from sight, leaving Pug and Tomas alone.

Tomas removed his golden helm and placed it on Pug's desk. "Well, old friend, there's not much for us to do but wait."

Pug said, "I'm not very hungry, but we should eat." He rose and led his friend out of the study, down the hall, and toward the kitchen.

"You better land soon!" shouted Nakor. "My arms are getting tired."

They were flying to the east of the highway, just above the treetops, with Nakor dangling from his staff, which Miranda held below her as she flew. They had appeared at a fishing village near Quester's View. It had been deserted. Miranda had picked up Nakor and had flown across the highway, some distance away from a few campfires, and then had turned northward. They had flown past the campfires of both sides, past a large static position that had Nakor puzzled. He knew something significant had occurred for Greylock to have halted his northward march.

Miranda came in for a landing, letting go of Nakor's staff. He landed with an audible "oof," as he struck the ground hard. "Sorry," she said as she landed. "My wrists were starting to hurt."

"When you said we could fly together, I thought you had a spell that would carry both of us," Nakor said as he stood up, brushing himself off. "I almost hurt myself on my staff."

"Well, if you'd left the thing behind like I told you to it wouldn't have happened." She sounded very unsympathetic.

Nakor laughed. "You will be an excellent mother someday."

She said, "Not until Pug and I feel the world is a safer place than it is right now."

"Being alive is being at risk," said Nakor as he adjusted his garment and recovered his staff. "Now, let us see if we can sneak into the enemy camp."

"How do you propose to do it?"

"Like I always do: act like I belong. Just stay close behind me and, please, one thing."

"What?"

"Don't lose your temper."

Miranda's expression clouded and she said, "I don't have a temper!"

Nakor grinned. "There, you're doing it now."

"You insufferable little man!" she said, walking off ahead of him.

"Miranda!"

"What!" she shouted, looking over her shoulder.

Nakor hurried to catch up, and said, "For a woman of your experience, you can be very childish."

Miranda seemed on the verge of saying something. She stood still for a moment, then finally said, "You don't know me, Nakor. You may have been my mother's first husband, but you know nothing of me. You don't know what my childhood was like. You don't know what it was to be raised by imperial agents. If I'm childish, it may be because I had no childhood."

"Whatever the reasons, please try to keep from getting

us killed," said Nakor as he walked by her. Softly he said, "And for a woman your age, you are very concerned about things that happened a very long time ago."

She hurried to stay up with him. "What?"

Nakor turned to face her, and for the first time since she had met him, there was not one shred of humor in the man's expression. He gazed at her with an expression that could only be called intimidating. And for a moment, she glimpsed the power he had within him. Softly he said, "The past can be a terrible weight bound to you by an unbreakable chain. You can drag it with you, forever looking over your shoulder at what holds you back. Or you can let it go and move forward. It's your choice. For those who live centuries, it's a very important choice."

He turned and walked away from her.

Miranda stood a moment, then caught up with him again. This time she said nothing.

They worked their way down through trees on the western face of the Calastius Mountains. They had passed the battlelines several miles to the south, where Greylock's army had established a fixed front. Nakor said, "Something strange has happened. Greylock is dug in down south, at least that's what it looked like from up there"—he pointed skyward—"as you sped along. It looks like he's digging in, perhaps against a counterattack."

Miranda said, "I don't know. Maybe they're going to wait for supplies sent up to that fishing village where we landed."

"Maybe, but I don't think so." From the battlefield the stench of the dead filled the night air. Thousands of bodies littered the field. "This is very bad. To leave the dead unburied is an evil thing."

North of the battlefield a structure was being built. It appeared to be a fortress of some type, but as they neared it, they could see it was actually a series of large buildings linked together by huge wooden fences a uniform twenty feet high. Men were camped around fires scattered around the periphery. "Look," said Nakor, "they don't camp too close."

"What is it?" asked Miranda as they came near the edge of the sheltering trees.

"Something very bad I think. A temple, maybe."

"Temple to what?"

"Let's go find out." He glanced around. "Over there."

He led her through the trees to a place close to a collection of tents of all sizes and colors. They scurried through the heavy boles until they found a gap between two campfires, where they could slip in without attracting undue attention.

They passed by unchallenged. Nakor led Miranda past a series of campsites, where they were just two people among several walking about on some errand or another. But as they passed a large camp, a man walked toward them. His head was shaved, save for a single fall of hair, tied up to cascade behind him. The hair looked to be cinched by a ring of bone. He wore deep scars on each cheek. He was bare chested and wore a vest of what appeared to be human skin. His trousers were dyed leather and Nakor didn't inspect them too closely. He was massively muscled and carried a huge curved blade known as a flasher. It was a two-handed weapon, but he looked capable of wielding it with one hand.

He walked up, weaving slightly, to Miranda, and looked her over in a very frank fashion, then turned to Nakor and said, with a drunken slur, "You sell her to me."

Nakor grinned. "No, I can't."

The man's eyes grew wide and he looked as if he was about to erupt into a rage as he said, "No? You say no to Fustafa!"

Nakor pointed at the building and said, "She goes there."

Instantly the man's expression changed, and he looked at Nakor and backed away. "I don't ask," he said, hurrying away.

"What was that?" asked Miranda.

"I don't know," said Nakor. He looked at the building, less than a hundred yards away. "But I think it means we need to be careful in there."

"We're going to walk in?" asked Miranda.

"You have a better idea?" replied Nakor, walking toward the building.

"No," said Miranda, hurrying after him again.

They both felt a strange energy as they neared it. As they got closer, it grew stronger. Miranda said, "That makes me feel like I need to take a bath."

"If your husband doesn't object, I'll join you," said Nakor. "Come this way." He motioned toward an opening in the fence, between sections of the building, and they entered.

Once they had entered, Nakor saw what the structures were. A huge square had three small buildings at each corner. In the center rose six large stones, each one carved with runes that set Miranda's teeth on edge to view. "What is this place?" she asked.

"It's a place of summoning, a place of dark magic, a place from which something very bad will come," said Nakor.

They saw movement in the dark, in the middle of the ring of stones. They moved forward quietly. A band of men, all wearing dark robes, stood around a large stone. Behind the stone was a man who stood with arms outstretched, one who chanted something to the sky.

"Now we know why that man was so afraid," whispered Nakor. "Look!"

Upon the stone lay a young woman, her eyes wide with terror, a gag in her mouth. Her hands were tied to rings of iron in the stone and she was dressed in a short black sleeveless shift.

Nakor's eyes widened as he considered this. "We must leave!" he said urgently.

Miranda said, "We can't leave her there to die."

"Thousands will die soon if we don't leave," he whispered, holding her elbow and steering her back toward the exit.

Then there came a rumbling in the air, and Nakor said, "Run!"

Miranda didn't hesitate, and followed Nakor out the doorway. The soldiers nearby ignored the two who ran from the building, for their eyes were riveted on the scene before them. A faint blue-green light was gathering around the building, swirling as if being stirred by a giant invisible stick.

Nakor stopped a few yards before Miranda and held his staff overhead. "Fly!" he shouted.

Miranda halted, closed her eyes, and gathered her own powers to fly. She leaped forward, as if diving, but rather than falling, she rose. She grabbed Nakor's staff and hauled him into the sky.

She flew in a straight line, up the hillside, then began a gentle turn. When she could look down upon the building, she said, "Oh, gods of mercy!"

Up the coast, a dozen lights like the one before them had blossomed, evil green and blue lights that filled the night with a terrible illumination. Then down the coast came a line of power, moving from each of the constructions, starting somewhere near Ylith and ending below where Miranda flew.

A note painful to hear rang and below those soldiers camped nearest the building reeled back from the sound. A faint light spread out in a fan from the building, toward the Kingdom camp, growing fainter as it went. It shifted through the spectrum, going to red, then back to green, then to violet. A last deep indigo wave faded from view, and the grinding sound suddenly stopped.

Then, on the battlefield, the dead began to rise.

Twenty-Five

━━━━━━━━━

Confrontation

MEN SCREAMED.

Erik raced from his tent, barely dressed, holding his sword. Battle-hardened soldiers were fleeing in terror, while others struggled at the front. He grabbed one man, and shouted, "What is it?"

The man's eyes were wide with horror and he could only point to the front of the line as he pulled free of Erik's grasp and ran. Erik hurried to the front of the line, and for a moment he couldn't understand what he saw.

His men were fighting a vicious action against the invader, and he leaped forward, shouting, "All units to the line!"

Then he saw one of the men locked in struggle with a Kingdom soldier who wore the tunic of a different Kingdom unit. For a second he wondered if they had been infiltrated. Then he saw the man's face, and the hair on Erik's neck and arms stood up. He felt revulsion unlike anything he had known in his short life.

The soldier trying to kill his former companion was dead. His lifeless eyes were still rolled up in his head and the flesh of his face was pallid and slack. But his movements were deliberate as he swung his sword.

Erik jumped forward and severed the thing's head from

its body with a single blow. The head rolled away, but the body kept swinging the sword. Erik hacked again and severed the creature's arm, yet the creature pressed forward.

Jadow Shati leaped past Erik and cut the creature's leg out from under it. The corpse toppled over.

"Man, they won't stop."

Erik recognized the danger. Beyond the horror of facing men already dead, which had caused one man in four to run in fear, the dead were unrelenting. They could not be stopped unless they were hacked to pieces. And while one was being butchered, another would strike and kill a Kingdom soldier.

Then Erik saw a freshly killed Kingdom soldier rise up, his eyes rolled up in his head, and turn to attack his former companions.

"How do we fight them?" shouted Jadow.

"Fire!" said Erik. He turned and shouted, "Hold them here!" and ran to the rear. Men were running forward to answer the alarm, and Erik held up his hands, halting a score of them. "Go to the rear and get all the hay the cavalry left." He pointed to where the road narrowed. "Lay it from there, to there." He indicated another point opposite it across the road. Then he ran to another squad who were about to run to the front, and shouted, "Strip the tents! Get everything that will burn and pile it on the hay."

"What hay, Captain?" asked one soldier.

"When you get back with the tents, you'll see the hay."

Erik hurried to the rear, where the engineers had been sleeping under their partially completed catapults. They were up and buckling on weapons, ready to defend their war engines if necessary. "Are any of these finished?" asked Erik.

The Captain of Engineers, a stocky man with a grey beard, said, "This one is ready, Captain, and that other over there is just about ready to go. What is going on?"

Erik grasped the man's arm. "Go to the front. See where our forward positions are. Return here and aim your catapult at that location."

The Captain of Engineers ran off, while Erik turned to the rest of his crew. "How many of you will it take to finish that other catapult?"

One of the engineers said, "Just two of us, Captain. All we have to do is install the locking clamps on the arm. We could have finished last night, but we wanted to get supper."

"Go finish it. The rest of you, come with me."

He led them to the baggage train and shouted to the soldiers guarding it, "Get to the front and hold!"

They ran off, and Erik pointed to a pair of wagons sitting on the side of the road. He asked the engineers, "Can any of you hitch up those horses?"

All of them answered they could, so Erik said, "Get half that oil to the front, where you'll see them building a barricade, and the other half to the catapults."

He ran back to the front. The plan would only work if they could keep the dead soldiers outside the barricade. And until that task was finished, Erik could serve his cause best by using his power to hack apart each dead soldier trying to get past the diamonds.

Miranda said, "We must get Pug and Tomas!"

They watched from a vantage point among the trees upon the hillside, as the Kingdom forces rallied to repulse the first wave of undead soldiers. Then Nakor heard horns blowing at the rear of Fadawah's army. Men under arms gathered and formed up behind the struggle taking place at the diamonds. "Yes," said Nakor. "Get Pug and Tomas, and Ryana if she's there."

Miranda vanished.

Nakor heard a trumpet sound, and the Kingdom forces at the diamonds retreated to a barrier wall that had been building rapidly behind them. They leaped over it and those who were wounded were dragged up and over it by their comrades. No man wished to die and turn against his comrades.

Then a fire was ignited and another. Suddenly the barricade was ablaze. Von Darkmoor, he thought. Young Erik was thinking fast on his feet.

The dead stumbled into the flames and noiselessly they flailed about, until they collapsed upon the ground. The few that managed to gain a purchase on the burning barriers were pushed back by spears and poles.

Then Nakor heard the sound of a war engine firing and in the darkness he could see something flying over the camp to land near the diamonds. A minute later another missile came flying overhead and landed closer to the barricade. Nakor could see a barrel explode upon impact, sending oil in all directions, which ignited when some struck the barricade. The pool of fire engulfed those corpses stumbling toward the barricade and soon they were falling.

Pug, Tomas, Ryana, and Miranda suddenly appeared next to Nakor.

Pug said, ''Gods!''

Nakor said, ''Those corpses aren't the problem, Pug. Erik von Darkmoor is taking care of them as needed, but there is where you must go!'' He pointed northward. ''Find the source of that energy, and you'll find the one you need to destroy.''

Battle horns sounded, and Fadawah's army started to march forward as the fires began to abate.

Tomas asked, ''Where can I best serve?''

Nakor said, ''Killing those soldiers here does no good, but ending the problem up there may save the West.''

Ryana shifted her form and suddenly the huge dragon towered over them. ''I will carry you all.''

They climbed on her back and she launched herself skyward. Those soldiers who happened to be glancing toward the treeline as Ryana struck a mighty beat of her wings and gained altitude were astonished, and many shouted and pointed, but as the battle built in fury and the advancing army of Fadawah bore down on the abandoned diamonds, most were too preoccupied with survival to notice the dragon.

She circled once and headed north.

Dash heard the drums from the Keshians in the field. He knew he'd see what they had in store later; the darkness hid the Keshians' deployment as sunrise was still hours off. As best the watchmen on the walls could tell in the dark they were facing only cavalry and mounted infantry, with no heavy foot or war engines; Dash assumed they had infiltrated fast-moving companies for weeks now, and that slower-moving units had been avoided. With even half the normal garrison here, Kesh would never risk an attack on this scale. So the news was mixed good and bad: they were only facing swordsmen and horse archers, but they were facing a lot of them.

Dash expected this meant the escaping Keshian officer Duko wrote of in his message to Patrick had successfully reached his army with the news of Krondor's weaknesses. The only good news in the message had been the fact of Jimmy being alive and Malar being dead.

The word from the palace was equally mixed. Patrick, Francie, and her father would recover—though Lord Brian might have lasting effects from the poison. Lord Rufio was dead, and several of the other nobles of the area as well. Two officers had recovered enough to take up positions on the walls, but Dash knew they were woefully undermanned to hold off the Keshian army for more than a few hours, a day or two at best.

There were still too many weaknesses in the defense of the city. There were ways into the city that you didn't have to be a Mocker to find. The dry aqueduct along the north wall had more than a half-dozen entrances if one simply took the time to probe. Dash wished he could have repaired the sluice gates and flooded it, but he would have filled a hundred cellars full of water by doing so. Suddenly an idea struck Dash. He called out, "Gustaf!"

The mercenary appeared and said, "Sheriff?"

"Take two men and run to the city armory. See if we have any Quegan fire oil. If we do, here's what you do with it." Dash outlined his plan, then called to Mackey, "Hold things here while I'm gone. I'll be back as soon as I can."

Dash hurried off the wall and ran down High Street, to the intersection of the North Gate road. He cut through burned-out buildings until he reached the cleverly cleared alley and he hurried through it, despite the predawn darkness.

He jumped fences and ducked under obstacles, risking injury to reach his goal in as timely a fashion as he could. He found the door he sought, a root cellar entrance from all appearances, but really a cover to one of the Mocker-controlled tunnels leading toward their headquarters.

He hurried down stone steps, as lightly as he could while

keeping up a good rate of speed. He grabbed a stone wall corner with his left hand, steadying himself as he swung around.

A man turned with a startled expression on his face, and without breaking strike, Dash hit him as hard as he could, dropping him to the stone floor without a sound. Dash hurried along a wide walkway which ran above the watercourse. There was a slow trickle of water flowing through it. Dash knew that would change if Gustaf found the oil and used it as directed.

Dash reached a section of wall that appeared identical to the adjacent sections, but which yielded to pressure, swinging open on a shaft, perfectly balanced so as to pivot with ease. Down a short tunnel Dash hurried, reaching a plain door. Dash knew that here he stood the biggest risk of being killed before he could speak.

He tripped the locks from his side, but instead of opening the door he stood back. The audible clicks alerted someone, for after a moment the door swung open and a curious face peered through. Dash grabbed the thief and hauled him forward, spinning him around while off balance, and propelling him back through the door before he entered.

The man careened into two others who were standing on the other side of the door, knocking all of them over in a heap.

Dash stepped through. He held his hands out so anyone could see he wasn't armed. But to insure that he made things as clear as possible, he shouted, "I'm not armed! I came to talk!"

The denizens of Mother's, the headquarters for the Mockers, turned in astonishment at the sight of the Sheriff of Krondor standing before them, his sword still at his side. From across the room, Trina said, "Why, Sheriff Puppy, to what do we owe this honor?"

Looking from face to face, most of which were shifting from surprise to anger, he said, "I came to warn you."

"Of what?" said one man. "Keshians in the tunnels?"

"They're your worry," said Dash. "The ones outside the gate are mine. No. I came to warn you that in less than an hour this entire room and the rest of Mother's is going to be under water."

"What!" shouted one man.

"It's a lie," swore another.

"No, it's not a lie," said Dash. "I'm going to flood the north aqueduct and the bypass channel below Stinky Street. The culverts above the main passage"—he pointed to the door though which he had just entered and the passage beyond—"are shattered and all that water is going to come flooding down here. This entire section is going to be underwater by noon."

Trina walked over, two very large menacing-looking men accompanying her. "You wouldn't be saying that to flush us out, would you, Sheriff Puppy? It could be useful to have us running through the sewers and tangling with some Keshians you haven't managed to find yet."

"Maybe, but that's not it."

"Or maybe you want us to be standing up in the streets for the Keshians to run over when they break down the gate?" said a man nearby, pulling his dagger.

"Hardly," said Dash. "There are enough bumps in the roads as it is. I don't need more."

"I would believe you," said Trina, "if I didn't know the north sluice is damaged from the war and can't be opened until it's repaired."

"I'm not repairing it," said Dash. "I'm going to burn it."

Several men laughed. "You're going to burn a gate that's half underwater!" said one. "How you doing that?"

"Quegan fire oil."

Suddenly a man said, "It burns underwater!"

Trina turned and shouted orders, and men began to grab packages, bundles, and sacks. She came to stand before Dash and said, "Why warn us?"

He grabbed her arm and looked her in the eyes. "I've grown fond of certain thieves over my life." He kissed her. "Call me an idiot," he said after she stepped back. "Besides, you may be a bunch of ragged good-for-nothings, but you're *my* ragged good-for-nothings."

"Where should we go?" she asked, and Dash knew she wasn't referring to the Mockers in general.

"Take the old man to Barret's Coffee House. It's almost rebuilt, and Roo Avery already has stocked it with some

food. There's a tunnel off of the sewer under Prince Arutha's Way that leads to a landing by his basement. Lie low
there.''

She looked him in the eyes and said, "You're going to
cause me more trouble than you're worth before we're
done, Sheriff Puppy, but for now I am in your debt.''

He started to turn away, but she grabbed him and kissed
him back. Whispering into his ear, she said, "Stay alive,
damn you."

"You as well," he whispered. Then he turned and hurried back down the tunnel. He stopped to revive the man
he had knocked unconscious and was glad he hadn't tried
a stunt like walking into Mother's uninvited when the
Mockers were at the height of their power; there would
have been a dozen guards in that tunnel instead of one.

The groggy man didn't quite understand what it was
Dash was telling him, but he pieced together enough of the
message to know he had to get to high ground in a hurry.

Dash ran along the major waterway that passed Mother's
and reached a place where the culverts above had broken
through. He leaped and grabbed the jagged edge of a heavy
hard-clay pipe that protruded out of the wall above his
head. He pulled himself up and stood on it, working his
way along to a break in the wall, barely large enough to
permit him entrance. He risked getting stuck as he wiggled
through the break to a place where a large hole appeared
above his head. He pulled himself up and stood outside in
the bed of the northern watercourse. He looked around in
the predawn grey and saw no one in sight. He ran toward
the east.

As he reached the end of the aqueduct, he saw Gustaf
and his men standing before the large wooden gate. Two
men were already slamming axes into the supports on either
side of the jammed gate.

Dash said, "How goes it?"

Gustaf smiled ruefully. "If those supports don't give way
before we want them to and drown us all, this might work."

"How much oil did you find?"

"Several casks. I've got some of the lads pouring it into
clay jugs like you said."

Dash hurried over to the place Gustaf indicated, where

two men were pouring sticky, foul-smelling naphthalene from small casks into large clay jugs. "Only about a third of the way," said Dash. "And leave the stoppers off. We want the air to get to it."

The men nodded. As Dash started to return to Gustaf, he said, "And you want to be as far away from fire as you can get until you wash that stuff off. Use lots of soap. Remember, it burns underwater."

The two men who were swinging the axes jumped back as one when a loud crack sounded, accompanied by a flexing of the wooden gate. Small jets of water spurted through cracks in the wood, and a bit of dirt and gravel washed down the bank.

"Looks like it's going to go under the weight of the water," said Gustaf.

"Eventually, but we can't wait until the next big rain. Did you bring the rags?"

"Over there," said Gustaf, pointing to a man standing over a box up on the bank.

"Good," said Dash, hurrying over to inspect the damage. To one of the men with an ax he said, "Crack this beam here some more."

The beam was a huge one, a foot on each side, that had been stuck between foundation stones and held the right side of the sluice gate. The man set to with his huge ax, smashing into the wood, almost as hard as rock with age. Yet each time he struck, chips flew and the wood splintered more.

Dash waved his men out of the way and indicated that the rags and what was left of the naphthalene in the casks should be brought over and the jars should be taken to the top of the bank. The men hurried up the stone bank of the aqueduct. Dash motioned the ax-wielder aside and said, "Get up there." He set two casks down on the stones and picked up the third. Carefully, he laid out a long run of the rags, tied it into a knotted cord, and dribbled naphthalene on it. He then tucked one end of the rags into a cask and set a third atop the two on the bottom, forming a little pyramid right below where the beam had been chopped by the ax.

Dash hurried to the far end of the rag and pulled a piece of flint from his pocket. Using his knife blade, he struck sparks until one caught on the naphthalene–soaked rag.

Dash wasn't entirely sure what to expect. He had heard stories from his grandfather, but had only seen the results of the use of this oil distillation mixed with powdered lime-stone and sulfur.

With a *whoosh* the flame sprang up the rag. Dash ran.

He reached the bank of the aqueduct as the flame burned quickly along the rag. He stood next to Gustaf and said, "If it burns as hot as it's reputed to burn, it should eat through the rest of that wood quickly. The water pressure should shove over the—"

The flame reached the casks. They exploded.

The force of the blast was far more than Dash had expected, thinking he was going to get more of a large fire. Instead, men were thrown to the ground and two were struck by wood splinters.

Gustaf picked himself up off the ground, saying, "Gods! What was that?"

"I'm not sure," said Dash. "My grandfather told me something about too much air on the stuff, and I guess that's what he meant."

"Look!" said one of the constables.

The blast had cut through most of the large beam, which now was being bent back by the gate under the pressure of millions of gallons of river water trapped behind it. With a loud groan the entire sluice gate began to move as water started to pour through several gaps in the wood. As the force of the water increased, the wood started to move more rapidly. Creaking and groaning sounds were replaced by a crack, the beam sheared in two, and suddenly the entire gate was swept away before a wall of water.

Dash sat on the bank, watching the wall of water move down the aqueduct. When it hit the break in the stones that would send water pouring into the lower sewer, he could barely see a pause as the wave swept on past it.

Gustaf said, "Well, that should drown some rats."

"We can hope," said Dash, taking the constable's of-fered hand and pulling himself to his feet. Thinking of the Mockers, he said, "As long as it isn't our rats that get drowned."

"What do you want us to do with these clay jugs, Sheriff?" asked one of the constables.

Dash said, "I was going to have you throw them at what I thought would be a nice little fire down there. Bring them along. I think we can find a use for them." As the man reached down to grab the jugs, Dash added, "And handle them gently." He motioned to the water surging through the destroyed sluice.

They hurried back through the city, and as they turned the corner to High Street, Dash shouted to Gustaf, "Get some barricades up here." He then pointed back another block and said, "And there. When they break through, I want them turned before their cavalry hits the market. As soon as the gate goes, get archers up on the roofs there, there, and there." He pointed to three corners of the intersection.

Gustaf nodded. "I notice you didn't say *if* they break through."

"It's just a question of when, and if help can get here before they do. I think we're in for some nasty days ahead."

Gustaf shrugged. "I'm a mercenary, Sheriff. Nasty days are what I get paid for."

Dash nodded as Gustaf hurried off to carry out his orders and the rest of the constables carried the jugs of naphthalene to the gate. He glanced around the city streets, now deserted as people hid in their houses hoping against hope that somehow they would be spared another destructive rampage such as they had endured the year before. Dash shook his head. Mercenaries, soldiers, and constables might get paid to endure such as this, but citizens didn't. They were the ones who suffered, and in his time as Sheriff he had forged a bond with the people of Krondor he couldn't have imagined before. Now he was starting to understand why his grandfather had loved this city so much, both the noble and the base, the exalted and the low. It was *his* city. And Dash would be damned to the lowest hell before he'd see another invader take it again.

Dash hurried toward the gate when he heard horns. He knew a Keshian herald was approaching under a flag of truce to announce under what conditions his general would accept the surrender of the city. Dash climbed the steps in the gatehouse and reached the battlements as the Keshian herald approached, the rising sun peeking over the mountains behind him. He was a desert man, and on each side accompanying him rode a Dog Soldier, each holding a banner. One was the Lion Banner of the Empire, and the other was a house flag; Dash knew his grandfather and father would both disapprove his not recognizing it at once.

Sergeant Mackey said, "They want to talk."

Dash said, "Well, it would be rude not to listen."

Dash would be tempted to drop a jar of the naphthalene on the herald before the man was through, he thought, but each minute that passed before the attack bought them a little more time to prepare.

The herald rode before the gate and shouted, "In the name of the Empire of Great Kesh and her great General Asham ibin Al-tuk, open the gates and surrender the city!"

Dash looked around and saw that every man on the wall was watching him. He leaned out between two merlons on the wall and shouted back, "By what right have you come to claim a city that is not yours?" He glanced at Mackey and said, "Might as well go through the formalities."

"We claim these lands as ancient Keshian soil! Who speaks for the city?"

"I, Dashel Jamison, Sheriff of Krondor!"

With contempt in every word, the herald shouted, "Where is your Prince, O jailer of beggars? Hiding under his bed?"

"Still sleeping, I think," said Dash, not wishing to reveal to this man anything about the poisoning. "If you care to wait, he may show up later today."

"That's all right," came a voice from behind Dash.

Dash turned and saw a pale Patrick standing there, being held erect by a soldier. Patrick had donned his royal armor, golden trimmed breastplate and open-faced helm, with a gold-trimmed purple sash of office over his shoulder. As he passed Dash, Patrick whispered, "Should I lose consciousness, tell them I've left in outrage."

He reached the wall and steadied himself, and Dash could see how difficult it was for him to stand, even with the strong soldier holding onto him from behind. Yet Patrick found it within himself to shout out with power, "I am here, dogs of Kesh. Say what you will!"

The herald barely hid his surprise at seeing the Prince of Krondor on the wall. He obviously had believed the poisoner successful. "Most gracious Prince!" said the herald. "My . . . master bids you open your gates and withdraw. He will escort you and your retinue to your nation's borders."

"Just this side of Salador," said Dash quietly.

Patrick shouted, "My nation's borders! I am standing on the wall of the capital city of the Western Realm!"

"These lands are Ancient Kesh, and are being reclaimed."

Dash whispered, "I know we're buying time, but why bother?"

Patrick gulped for air and nodded. Then, with his last strong breath, shouted, "Then come you on and do your worst! We reject your claim and scorn your master."

The herald said, "Act not in haste, fair Prince. My master is kind. He shall make his offer three times. At sundown tonight we return to hear your second answer. Should you say again nay, we shall come one last time, at dawn tomorrow. And that shall be the last of it." The herald turned and spurred his mount forward.

Dash turned to see Patrick barely conscious, still being held up by the soldier. "Bravely done, fair Prince," Dash said without sarcasm. To the soldier he said, "Take him back to his quarters and see he rests."

Turning to Mackey, Dash said, "Get the men down from the wall and fed. Keep a few to watch, but the Keshians will probably be as good as their word and not attack us until dawn tomorrow." He sat down and suddenly felt bone-tired. "At least now we know when their spies inside the city will attack." Looking at the old sergeant, he said, "They'll try to open the gate tonight."

The dragon sped through the sky while in the east the sun rose above the hills. The mystic energy along the coast was a map for them to follow. Tomas's arts, the lingering heritage of the Valheru, allowed them all to ride upon Ryana's back without falling.

"You know," said Nakor, speaking loudly to overcome the wind noise as he sat behind Miranda at the base of the dragon's neck, "as much as being an engine of death, this display is set to lure us to some sort of confrontation."

Pug, who sat directly behind Tomas, said, "I expect as much."

"There," said Tomas, pointing down and to the left.

Below them stretched the coastline, a southwest-facing shoreline from Quester's View to Ylith. The harbor of Ylith showed a frenzy of ships, most of them hauling anchor and sailing out of the port.

Nakor said, "Those ships' captains didn't like what they saw last night and are catching the morning tide out."

"Ryana," said Tomas, "down there."

He indicated the eastern gate of the city, outside of which a great building had been erected, and it was that building that was the source of the energy which had flowed down the coast, fueling the evil magic that had animated the corpses.

As the dragon landed, armed men ran in all directions, uncertain of what to do. "Let me go first," said Tomas.

Pug said, "Let's not shed any blood until we have to."

Miranda said, "We will have to."

Pug said, "But until then . . ." He gestured toward the ground just before Ryana touched down. They all could see a ripple, as if water had been troubled by a stone, causing the earth to undulate. A deep rumbling could be heard and dust shot into the air following the course of the quickly expanding circle. As they touched down, the circle was now large enough to easily encompass the dragon. The soil below their feet was motionless.

But where the expanding circle's wave struck, it was as if an earthquake raged, for each advancing soldier who stepped upon the ripple was thrown down to the ground, then mercilessly tossed into the air several times.

Many turned and fled, leaving only the bravest of the invaders to confront the dragon and her riders.

Then Ryana bellowed and their ears rang, and she shot a blast of fire into the heavens, and the rest of the soldiers fled. No sane man would face a great golden dragon.

As the four of them dismounted, Miranda said, "Thank you. That should buy us some time."

Ryana said, "You are welcome." To Tomas she said, "When the danger has passed, I shall leave, but until it has, call me should you need me. I will be nearby." The dragon launched herself into the sky, and with a powerful beat of her wings was gone, speeding to the north.

Tomas walked purposefully toward the building. Pug, Miranda, and Nakor followed.

With the departure of the dragon, some of the bolder warriors near the city gate ran to intercept the four. Tomas unstrapped his shield from across his back in a movement so fluid and natural it looked impossible to Pug. No mortal man could have duplicated the feat. His sword was out before the first warrior had closed.

The man was big and carried a large sword in two hands. He ran at Tomas shouting an inarticulate battle cry, but Tomas continued to advance at his normal pace. The man struck a powerful blow downward and Tomas moved his shield slightly, causing the blade to skid off the surface. The man saw sparks explode from the contact, but no mark sullied the surface of the shield. Tomas swung lightly, as if flicking a fly from his shoulder, and the man died before he hit the ground.

Two men behind him hesitated. One then shouted and charged while the other showed fear, and turned and ran. The one who charged died like the man before, and Tomas again looked as if he were disposing of annoying pests, not battle-hardened warriors.

Tomas reached the building, a thing of black stones and wooden facades. It squatted, a terrible black sore on the landscape; there was nothing about it pleasing to the eye or harmonious in any fashion. It reeked of evil.

Tomas walked to the large black wooden doors and paused. He drew back his right fist and struck the rightmost door. The door exploded inward, as if there had been no hinges.

As they walked in, Nakor looked at the shattered iron hinges and said, "Impressive."

Miranda said, "Remind me never to get him mad."

"He's not mad," said Nakor. "Just determined. If he was mad, he'd pull the walls down."

The building was a giant square, with two rows of seats set hard against the walls. There were two doors: the one through which they had entered and another opposite.

In the center of the room a square pit yawned at them, and from deep within a red glow could be seen. Above it hung a metal platform.

"Gods!" said Miranda. "What a stench."

"Look," said Nakor, indicating the floor.

Before each seat, on the floor, lay a body. They were warriors, men with scars upon their cheeks, and each was openmouthed, their eyes wide, as if they had died screaming in horror.

Nakor hurried over to the pit and looked in. He stepped back. "Something is down there."

Pug looked up at the platform and said, "That appears to be a way down."

Indicating the dried blood and gore on it, Miranda said, "And now the way up."

Tomas said, "Whatever caused that necromancy last night is down there."

Nakor said, "No, it is a tool, like all those dead fools."

"Where is Fadawah?" asked Miranda.

"In the city, I think," said Nakor. "Probably in the Baron's citadel."

A strange keening sound echoed from deep within the pit. The hairs on Pug's neck stood up. "We can't leave this here."

Nakor said, "We can always come back."

Miranda said, "Good. Let's leave this place."

She walked to the closed door, opposite the one through which they had entered, and threw it wide.

As soon as she did, they saw the soldiers arrayed on the other side, their shields in a wall, their bows poised, and cavalry behind them.

In the moment it took for the scene to register, they heard the order given and the bowmen fired.

Dash swore. "We've got twelve, eighteen hours to ferret out the rest of the infiltrators or risk a breach."

Thomas Calhern, a squire in Duke Rufio's court, had recovered enough from the poison to serve; Dash had named him an acting Captain. "What matter?" he asked. "Gods, man, you saw the army outside the gate."

Dash said, "Never been in a battle before?"

"No," said the young man, about the same age as Dash. "If the walls are intact, those outside must bring ten men against the wall for every one we have on top of it. We should be able to hold them for a few days, perhaps a week, and if my brother is as clever as I know him to be, a force from Port Vykor should arrive within days.

"But if some band of Keshian thugs gets a portal opened, and the Keshians get inside the walls, this battle is over before it starts."

They were sitting in the Prince's conference room, and Dash turned to Mackey. "Send a message to the lads at New Market Jail: I want the constables sniffing around the streets."

"That takes care of the streets," said Mackey. "But what about below them?"

Dash said, "I'll take care of that part."

Dash slipped through a door and a dagger was suddenly at his throat. "Put that away," he hissed.

"Sheriff Puppy," said a happy-sounding Trina. "I would have been very upset had I killed you."

"Not as much as I," said Dash. "How is he?"

She nodded toward the corner. A score of thieves were huddled in a far corner of the cellar. Dash smelled coffee and food. "Raided the kitchen, have we?"

Trina said, "It's a coffeehouse. We were hungry. There was food up there. What did you think?"

Dash shook his head. "I don't know what I'm thinking these days."

Trina walked with him over to where the old man lay upon a low bed, one that had been used as a stretcher to bear him to Barret's. She whispered, "He's not doing well."

Dash knelt beside the old man, who looked at him but didn't say anything. The old man held up his hand and Dash took it. "Uncle," he said softly.

The old man gently squeezed, then let go. His one eye closed.

She leaned over, and after a moment said, "He's sleeping again. Sometimes he speaks, other times he can't."

Dash stood up and they went to a relatively uncrowded corner of the basement, between stacks of crates. "How much time?" asked Dash.

"A few days, maybe less. When he was recovering from his burns the priest said only a great wish or the gift of a God would save him. He's known this day was coming since then."

Dash looked at this odd woman who had come to captivate his attention. "How many of you are left?"

She started to make a quip, then said, "I don't know. There are maybe another two hundred scattered through the city. Why?"

"Pass the word; we can use every sword we can find. The Keshians will sell you all into slavery, you know that."

"If they can find us," said Trina.

"If they take the city and hold it more than a week, they'll find you."

"Maybe."

"Well, anyone who shows up with a sword and fights, I'll see they're pardoned for their crimes."

"Guaranteed?" she asked.

"You have my word on it."

"I'll pass the word," she said.

"I've got more pressing matters now. The Keshians have given us until dawn tomorrow to surrender, else they'll attack. We assume that means they're going to try to open one of the gates between now and then."

"And you want us to watch the gates and let you know?"

"Something like that." He stepped closer to her, looking deep into her eyes. "You've got to slow them down."

She laughed. "You mean defend the gates until you get there."

He smiled. "Something like that," he repeated.

"I can't ask my brothers and sisters to do that. We're not warriors. Sure, we have some bashers among the Mock-

ers, but most of us don't know which end of a sword is
which."

"Then you better learn," said Dash.

"I can't ask them."

"No, but you can order them," said Dash slowly.

She said nothing.

Dash said, "I know the old man has been unable to run
things for a while. I'll bet my inheritance you're the current
Daymaster."

She remained silent.

"I won't ask anything from you without fair trade."

"What do you propose?"

"Hold the gate, whichever they attack. Defend it until I
can get a flying company there, and I will pardon everyone."

"A general amnesty?"

"The same deal I made originally with the old man."

"Not enough."

"What more do you want?" asked Dash.

She pointed around the room. "Do you know how we
came to be, the Mockers of Krondor?"

Dash said, "I've heard stories since I was a boy from
my grandfather about the Mockers."

"But did he ever tell you how the guild came to be?"

"No," Dash admitted.

"The first leader of the guild was called the Square Man.
He was a fence who settled disputes between different
gangs in the city. We were killing ourselves more than the
citizens. We were stealing from one another as much as
from the citizens. And we were getting hung for it.

"The Square Man fixed that. He started making truces
between gangs and getting things organized.

"He made a place for us called Mother's and he paid
bribes and bought some of us out of jail and off the gallows.

"The Upright Man took over before your grandfather
was born. He consolidated the Square Man's power and
made the guild the place it was when Jimmy the Hand was
running roofs.

"A few of us enjoy the dodgy path, Dash. Some of us
like breaking heads and there's no excuse for us. But most

of us just got dealt a bad hand. Most of us have nowhere else to go.''

Dash looked around the cellar. Men and women of all ages gathered there, and Dash remembered the stories his grandfather had told him of the beggar gangs, the urchins running the streets, the girls working the taverns, and the rest of them.

''If we get amnesty, we're back on the streets the next day, and most of us are breaking laws and we're right back where we started. There was only one Jimmy the Hand who had a prince reach down and raise him up to the heights.''

Trina gripped Dash's arm. She said, ''Don't you see? If your grandfather hadn't saved the Prince that one night long ago, he would have lived out his life with these people. It might have been him lying on that bed over there instead of his brother. And you might be over there with the other young men, thinking of how to survive the coming war, find a meal, and keep out of the Sheriff's clutches instead of being the Sheriff.

''You're only a noble by a quirk of fate, Dash.''

She looked into his eyes, then she kissed him, long and hard. ''You've got to make a promise, Dash. Make a promise and I'll do whatever you ask.''

''What is the promise?''

''You've got to save them. All of them.''

''Save them?''

''You've got to see they are fed and clothed and warm and dry, and out of harm's way.''

Dash said, ''Oh, Trina, why don't you ask me to move the city?''

She kissed him again. ''I've never felt anything for any man like I feel for you,'' she whispered. ''Maybe I'm finally acting the lovestruck girl after all these years. Maybe in my foolish dreams I see myself living in comfort as the wife of a noble. Maybe tomorrow I'll be dead.

''But if we fight for Krondor, then you must save us all. That's the deal, not some meaningless amnesty. You must take care of the Mockers. That's the promise.''

He looked at her for a long time, studying every detail of her face, as if memorizing it. Finally he said, ''I promise.''

She looked at him and a tear formed in each eye. As they ran down her face, she said, "The deal is done. What do you want us to do?"

Dash told her and they spent another moment together. Then he tore himself away from her, the hardest thing he had ever had to do in his life, and he left Barret's, knowing that his life would never be the same.

In his heart, Dash knew that he had made a promise that would be impossible to keep. Or, if he kept it, he would be betraying his duty to his office.

He tried to tell himself that the expediency of the moment required this, that saving the city came first, and that should Krondor fall and they all die, the promise was nothing anyway. But deep inside, Dash knew that he would never look at himself or any oath he gave the same way.

Twenty-Six

Discovery

P UG'S ARM SHOT forward.

A rippling energy wave exploded forward, a wall of moving forces that distorted the air as it passed. Bowmen who had just released their arrows saw them shattered by it an instant before the wall struck them.

As if a giant child's arm had swept aside a table full of toys, the soldiers were thrown back. Horsemen died as their mounts were seemingly picked up and tossed back a dozen feet, landing upon their riders. Horses screamed in terror, and those that managed to land on their feet bucked and kicked as they fled.

Pug, Tomas, Miranda, and Nakor walked through the avenue cleared by Pug's magic, past men who lay groaning upon the ground. One more hearty warrior rose to his feet, his sword in hand, and lunged toward them. Tomas's sword snaked out of his white scabbard silently and took the man's life before he had taken a step.

They walked to the gates of Ylith.

A guard on the gate had witnessed the assault and had frantically ordered the gates closed. Men were pushing furiously on the gates as Tomas reached them. They swung ponderously toward him but he reached out, placing his shield against the left gate and his sword against the right and with one massive push, the gates swung inward, knocking dozens of men aside.

Nakor said, "I wish he'd left Elvandar earlier."

Pug nodded. "But a vow is a vow. He couldn't see the threat to his home until now."

Miranda said, "Having power doesn't free one from being short-sighted."

"Not short-sighted," said Pug. "Just a different appreciation of the situation."

"Where to now?" asked Miranda.

"If I remember the layout of Ylith," said Nakor, "straight down this street to the High Road, turn right, and we walk straight up to the citadel."

Archers on the wall loosed a barrage of arrows, and Pug erected a protective barrier. "Ignore those," he said to Tomas. "We have weightier matters to address."

Tomas smiled at his boyhood friend. "Agreed."

They walked calmly through the city of Ylith, and the depredation of the occupation was visible on every side. Some buildings had been rebuilt, but others still lay abandoned, their doors off their hinges and windows shattered, looking like nothing so much as empty faces.

Men ran from the sight of the four people encompassed by a sphere of flickering blue energy. From nearby alleys and streets, archers peered out and fired arrows at them; they bounced harmlessly off the magic shell.

They reached the corner where they needed to turn and found another company of archers waiting. Dozens of arrows struck the barrier and bounced off, and when Tomas reached a position a dozen feet before the first rank of archers, they broke and ran.

Nakor said, "These men are not dangerous to us as long as we pay attention to them, but somewhere ahead is someone who is *very* dangerous."

"Do you know this as a fact," asked Tomas, "or are you conjecturing?"

"Conjecturing," said Nakor.

"But you suspect something," said Miranda.

"What?" asked Pug.

"Nothing I care to talk about yet," said Nakor. "But yes, I have a suspicion."

"I've learned over the years to take those seriously," said Pug. "What do you suggest?"

They were nearing a large intersection where soldiers were rolling wagons across the street in a barricade. Nakor said, "Only to be careful."

Arrows rained down upon them, and even knowing the defense was in place, Miranda and Nakor flinched. "This is irritating," said Nakor.

Pug said, "I agree. And as you observed, it could be dangerous if I let my concentration slip." He said, "Stop a moment."

They did and Pug raised his hand. He pointed up in the air, and outside the protective sphere, directly over the tip of his finger, a spark of white light appeared. Pug twirled his finger a moment, and the tiny white hot point of light spun. "Protect your eyes!" Pug warned.

Abruptly the scene became a harsh contrast in white and black, as the point of light erupted to the brilliance of the sun at noon, then brighter. The pulse of light lasted only for a moment, but the effect was literally blinding.

Pug and his companions opened their eyes to see men crying in panic and terror, some reaching around, while others fell to their knees, their hands to their eyes.

"I'm blind!" was repeated on all sides by panic-stricken men. Tomas walked through a gap between two wagons, the defense of the city forgotten by men made blind. "How long will it last?" asked Miranda.

"No more than a day for some, hours for others," said Pug. "But this particular group will not be any further trouble to us."

They made their way around the last of the barriers and moved up the street toward the citadel. The remaining soldiers who had retained their sight ran at the vision of the four powerful beings walking purposefully down the street.

A panic-stricken sentry had called for the drawbridge to be raised, and as they came within a hundred yards of the bridge, they saw it starting to rise. Tomas broke into an effortless run, his sword drawn, and Pug realized he had left the containment of the defensive shell. Pug let it lapse, for while it didn't take a considerable level of concentration to maintain, it required energy he might need later.

Tomas leaped atop the rising bridge as it reached a height of six feet above the road. With a quick swing of his sword he severed the massive iron chain on the right, links the size of a man's head shearing with an explosion of sparks and a deafening clang.

Then he severed the left chain and the bridge crashed back into place. The soldiers inside the citadel cut the restraining ropes on the winch that raised the portcullis, and the heavy iron gate slid down before them, the iron points slamming into the stones with a loud crash. "I can raise it and you can all slip under," said Tomas.

Miranda said, "No, let me." She waved her hands in a series of gestures and raised her right palm, then extended her right arm toward the gate. A ball of scintillating white-and-silver light formed around her hand, then flew off, like a ball lazily tossed by a child, arching gracefully to strike the center of the portcullis. The energy ran along the bars, sparking and sizzling, and the iron in the gate began to smoke. Then it heated up, turning first red, then white-hot. Even standing yards away, they could feel the scorching heat of the metal as it began to melt and crumble before them. The men in the gatehouse above the portcullis began to shout and flee the structure, due to the tremendous heat rising from the burning gate.

Where the molten metal struck the wood of the gate, it flamed and smoke rose. In minutes a hole more than adequate to allow them to pass had been melted through the gate. "Watch where you step, Nakor," said Miranda.

"You watch, too," said Nakor.

"I'm not the one wearing sandals," she said.

They entered the courtyard and no one was in sight. Whatever fight may have resided in the garrison was driven from them by the destruction of the portcullis. They crossed the small bailey and entered the keep.

A simple tower keep had dominated the harbor at Ylith for years, for the original rulers had been little more than pirates and traders and their harbor was everything. But after the Kingdom had annexed Yabon, the new Baron had decided to build this citadel at the north end of the city to protect the city from goblins and Brothers of the Dark Path from the Northlands, raiding down into Yabon. Here, for five generations, the business of the Barony had been conducted.

They walked up a broad set of steps to a daunting set of oak doors. Tomas pushed them open, and they parted with a shattering crack as a bar the size of a man's arm behind the doors splintered and broke.

Before they crossed the threshold, Nakor said, "Ware this place. It is a seat of power."

Tomas said, "I can feel it. It has an alien feeling, something no Valheru has encountered."

Pug said, "That's saying something. If a Dragon Lord hasn't encountered what's on the other side of that door . . ." He closed his eyes and sent out his senses. At the portal a ward existed; had they passed through without protection, they would have been incinerated. Pug quickly ascertained the nature of the ward and countered it. "It's safe to pass," he said.

Sword at the ready and shield before him, Tomas entered the room first. Pug followed with Miranda and Nakor.

As soon as they entered the old baronial great hall, it was as if they had stepped into anther world. The hall reeked of death and the floors were stained with blood. Skulls and bones were scattered around the room, and a faint haze darkened the air. Torches burned in sconces, their light angry and red, as if something had sucked the light out of the flames.

Men who were no longer human stood on either side of the great hall. Their eyes were glowing jewels of luminous red, their muscles unnaturally enlarged and straining at the skin. They all wore facial scars and expressions of madness. Some twitched and others drooled, and they all had mystic tattoos covering their upper bodies. Some carried double-bladed axes and others had swords and buckler shields.

They seemed poised to attack, yet appeared to be waiting upon something. The great vaulted windows of the room had been painted in red and black, passing only the faintest illumination from outside. The runes upon them were alien and repugnant to view.

Nakor glanced from window to window. "These are wrong," he whispered.

"What do you mean?" asked Miranda.

"Whoever painted those is trying to do something very . . . very bad. But they didn't do it . . . correctly."

"How do you know?" asked Tomas, holding his sword ready and watching first one side then the other as he advanced slowly up the center of the room.

"Years of sleeping on the *Codex of Wodar-Hospur* . . . I remember things when I need to know them. If I thought about that too much, it might make me upset."

As they crossed the hall, they confronted a figure on the right-hand side of the baronial throne that caused them all to pause. It was clearly not human. It looked roughly human, though its skin had a pale blue tinge. Upon its back large wings with brilliant white feathers sprouted. On the left-hand side of the throne stood a man, dressed in black robes with runes embroidered upon them. He had a silver collar around his neck.

Sitting on the throne was an old warrior, still strong-looking despite his age. His grey-shot hair was cut short, though he retained the long fall common to those who had chosen to serve dark powers. And upon his cheeks the ritual scars clearly showed.

He regarded the four intruders with a wary gaze and said, "One of you must be the magician named Pug."

Pug stepped forward and said, "I am Pug."

"I was warned that eventually you would be troubling me."

"You are General Fadawah," said Pug.

"King Fadawah!" said the man with an anger that didn't mask his fear.

Nakor said, "Your claim to that title seems to be at the root of our dispute."

Fadawah's eyes drifted to Tomas, and he said, "What is that?"

Tomas said, "I am Tomas, Warleader of Elvandar."

The being to Fadawah's left smiled. His features were cruel and evil, despite being stunningly beautiful, and twice as terrifying for that beauty: a high brow framed in golden ringlets, a straight regal nose. The mouth was full, sensual, and the eyes were a pale blue. His body looked powerful, heavily muscled, and there was an aura of danger about him even as he sat motionless.

He spoke and the room rang with despair upon every word. "The Valheru!" he said. The creature stepped forward and said, "Stand aside, Your Majesty."

Fadawah stood up and moved behind the other man, who silently watched the exchange.

Crossing to stand before Tomas, the entity was his equal in stature. The creature's voice boomed out in laughter. "Long have I ached to face one of the Dragon Host," he said. Suddenly he lashed out with his bare fist, striking Tomas's shield. Tomas flew back across the room, and the dozens of guards who had stood motionless erupted into action.

Miranda reacted before either Nakor or Pug. She spun full circle, her hand held palm downward, and spoke a word of power: a diamond of energy flew from her hand, shrieking through the air to strike the wall behind one of the warriors. It ricocheted off the wall and struck another warrior in the back. Like the finest blade slicing butter, it cut the man in half. Across the room it flew, as Miranda shouted to Tomas, "Stay down!"

Pug ignored Miranda's destructive energy blade and turned to face the monster. Pug made a single motion, both hands circling like an open-handed fighting monk's. But rather than striking a blow, he pulled both hands back before his chest and shouted a word. A single blast of energy came from both his hands, invisible but parting the air like a thousand fists. The winged creature was physically picked up and slammed back into the throne. Fadawah and the man with the silver collar both jumped away, to avoid being struck by the thing's wing.

Nakor ran forward, as if to attack, but rather than strike with his staff, he confronted the being. "What are you?" he demanded.

Laughing as it stood, the creature pushed Nakor aside, as if he was too trivial a being to warrant violence. "I am the One Who Was Called!"

"Who are you?" Nakor repeated, sitting on the floor.

Leaning over, his beautiful face mere inches from Nakor, he said, "I am Zaltais of the Eternal Despair."

Nakor shouted, "Tomas! You must vanquish him."

With a gesture of his finger, Zaltais seemed to lift Nakor

up and propel him in an arc across the hall, letting the old Isalani gambler slam into the wall. Nakor slumped to the floor.

Tomas lay below the flashing mystic blade that Miranda had cast, as it rebounded from wall to wall, carving through those warriors still standing.

Pug held his hand palm-out toward Zaltais, and an explosion of energy slammed into the winged being, propelling him backward into the throne one more time.

The mystic weapon that Miranda had cast faded suddenly, and Tomas leaped to his feet. The dozen remaining warriors surrounded him, and he struck out with his sword. Possessed by senses beyond human, he moved to avoid every blow. His golden sword, not wielded in battle since the Riftwar, struck out, and each blow took a limb or a head.

Miranda ran past the struggle in the middle of the room to see how Nakor fared. The ancient gambler lay stunned. Miranda couldn't tell how serious his injuries were.

Pug advanced on Zaltais, who sat with eyes blinking a moment, as if stunned, then his eyes focused and he grinned. Pug felt only hopelessness on seeing that smile.

"I underestimated you, Pug of Crydee, Milamber of the Assembly! You are no Macros the Black, but you are a power! Too bad you're not worthy of your mentor's legacy!"

Pug faltered a moment, suddenly unsure of his next act. That hesitation cost him as Zaltais flicked his hand and sent coils of black energy snaking toward Pug. They struck, and each time they hit, Pug felt pain unlike any he had known; beyond the pain of flesh ripped by cruel fangs, each bite made him doubt his own ability. He hesitated, then fell back.

"Pug!" shouted Miranda, seeing her husband retreating.

Tomas swung his golden sword and killed the last of the warriors as Nakor started to rouse.

As Pug fell back, Tomas leaped past him, and the golden sword swung down. Zaltais raised his arm, taking Tomas's blade on a golden bracer upon his wrist. The blade showered golden sparks and Tomas overbalanced, leaving himself open to a blow from the winged creature. Zaltais leveled a backhand strike with his right fist, slamming into Tomas's face, and the warrior in white-and-gold staggered from the blow.

In thirty years Tomas had never faced a creature of this power. Not since facing the combined mind of the Valheru had Tomas known such doubt. Even the demon Jakan seemed a trivial test compared to this creature.

Tomas fell to the floor and tasted blood on his lips. "What are you?"

"I?" said Zaltais. "I am an Angel of the Seventh Circle! I am an agent of the Gods!"

Nakor stood up and said, "Get back! He is not what he seems! He is a creature of lies and misdirection!" Nakor shook off Miranda's hand as she tried to steady him. The old man hurried over to the bloody bodies that littered the floor, and said, "These are dead because this thing convinced them their only hope was to do as he bid and he treated them thusly. He will deceive and mislead, and raise doubts that will strike to the root of your being. If you listen to him, he will eventually convince you to serve him."

Tomas rose up, the blood from his lip dripping onto his breastplate, where it ran off, without stain. "I will never serve this creature," he said.

"First he'll make you doubt your ability. Then he will make you doubt your purpose. Then he'll make you doubt your place in the universe. Then he'll convince you where that place is!"

The self-proclaimed Angel from Hell said, "You talk too much, old man!" He withdrew the black coils that had struck Pug and pointed his hand at Nakor. A blinding flash of white-hot energy flared, and Nakor leaped aside as it shot across the hall. It shot out the doorway as Miranda also leaped aside.

Tomas jumped to his feet, drawing back his sword, and struck down at the crown of the creature's head. Zaltais pulled away, so the tip of the blade struck him in the face. He reeled back, screaming in rage and pain. A red gash cut him from crown to chin. As if the muscles below his skin were pushing outward, the crack down his face widened, then split, runnning down his throat to his chest and stomach, and he shrieked, an inhuman sound.

It was a keening sound, and it made Pug's teeth ache as if they were being ground together. Pug saw the red gash splitting Zaltais from crown to groin. Like a pea pod being cracked open, Zaltais's skin and wings fell away.

The thing that emerged from within that shell looked like a giant praying mantis, with a black chitinous exterior, and large diaphanous wings.

"That is no more its true shape than the last!" shouted Nakor from his position on the floor. "You cannot kill it. You can only hold it. You must confine it and return it to that pit outside."

"And that you will never do," said the thing that was now Zaltais. It buzzed an angry sound and the wings blurred as it launched itself from the dais. Tomas lashed out again with his sword and sheared through one of the wings.

Zaltais slammed hard into the stones and Nakor stood up, moving back as Miranda came forward incanting a spell. Pug also was attempting a spell.

Nakor hurried around the confrontation now in the center of the room. He didn't want to get in the way. He looked over to where General Fadawah stood, his own sword at the ready as if he sought to join in the fight on the side of his infernal servant. The other man crouched down beside the throne and Nakor approached them, his staff ready if he needed to defend himself.

Miranda and Pug's spells were completed within seconds of one another. Crimson bands materialized around the insect and clamped down hard upon it. It chittered in rage and pain. Then Pug's spell manifested, a nimbus of white light which caused Zaltais to go limp. It crashed to the stones.

"Quickly!" shouted Nakor. "Take it back to the pit and cast it in. Then seal the pit."

"How?" asked Miranda.

"Any way you can think of!" Turning to face Fadawah and his companion, Nakor said, "I'll take care of these two."

Tomas picked up the imprisoned creature, while Pug cast a backward glance at Nakor. Miranda said, "Go, now!"

Nakor advanced on Fadawah, his staff before him, while

the General stood poised with his sword. "I don't need demons from hell to best an old fool like you," sneered the leader of the invading army. "I was killing better men than you when I was a boy."

"No doubt," said Nakor, "but you'll find that for my obvious shortcomings, I'm still very difficult to kill." He glanced at the man beside Fadawah. "Ask your companion there; he knows."

"What?" asked Fadawah, glancing to his left at Kahil.

That slight distraction was all Nakor needed. Lightning-swift, his staff shot forward, the butt striking Fadawah's sword hand with a knuckle-crushing blow. The sword fell from fingers gone numb and the General fell back, knocking over Kahil.

Fadawah tried to pull out a belt dagger with his left hand, but Nakor smashed it with his staff, and the General cried out in pain, as he now held out two useless hands.

Nakor's staff shot out a third time, and the General's kneecap shattered. He fell, crying in agony as Nakor said, "For too many crimes to measure, beyond what the Emerald Queen and the demon Jakan forced you to do, you have earned death. I shall be merciful and spare you the suffering you deserve." Suddenly the staff shot forward again, striking the now helpless Fadawah in the center of his forehead. Nakor heard the man's skull crack. The self-styled King of the Bitter Sea's eyes rolled up into his head and he died.

Nakor moved around Fadawah's body and knelt next to the man who crouched next to the throne. He was a thin man, his cheekbones the most prominent feature of his face. "Hello, my love," said Nakor.

"You recognize me?" he whispered.

"Always," said Nakor. "Who are you in this body?"

"I am Kahil, Captain of Intelligence."

"The power behind the throne, eh?" said Nakor. "So this is where you went when the demon took your place?"

"No, before," said Kahil. "I sensed something wrong with that body when I wore the Emerald Crown. My powers were being subverted . . . in any event, Kahil had been with Fadawah before and was trusted. He was clever, but he was greedy. It took little for me to take over this body.

For a while the Emerald Queen was nearly mindless, but no one seemed to notice. Then that damned demon showed up and ate it." Kahil shrugged. "I was the only one who could see through the illusion and knew a demon ruled in my place. I bided my time, knowing eventually I would have a chance to rule again."

"There have been things working beyond your most ambitious dreams. Do you now realize what a dangerous game you played?"

Weakly, the man said, "Yes, Nakor." Then a light came into his eyes and he said, "But I can't help myself."

Nakor stood and helped Kahil to his feet. "What of Fadawah?"

"Mad. His mind was totally gone. I thought to build a weapon, an engine of magic that would create an army of the dead—there were so many of them lying around—and it did that, but it also brought Zaltais out of the pit. I did not expect that. Fadawah could control it, at least for a while, and I could not. I was, I believe the expression is, 'caught between a rock and a hard place.' I was ready to dispose of Fadawah once the Kingdom was defeated and I held all of Yabon, but with Zaltais around, I couldn't quite get to that point."

"You always failed to anticipate consequences, Jorma."

"Kahil, please."

"How do you like being a man this time?"

"It's occasionally useful. But I miss my last body. It was by far the most beautiful." Looking at Nakor, the being who had once been Nakor's wife, the Lady Clovis, and the Emerald Queen said, "You've used that body for a very long time now."

"I like it," said Nakor. "It was the one I was born with. I just change my name every once in awhile." He pointed to the door through which his companions left. "Did you see your daughter?"

"That was Miranda?" said Kahil. "My gods!"

Nakor grinned. "The other was her husband."

"Do I have grandchildren?"

"Not yet." Nakor lost his smile. "You know, you've gone so far down an evil road I barely remember what it was you once were. A vain girl, but no worse than some.

But you have spent far too much time with dark powers. You do not even know what it was you did, do you? You have no idea who really controls your destiny."

"I control my destiny!"

"Oh, you vain woman. You are no more than a pitiful tool of a power far more than you can begin to imagine. He gained your soul so long ago that you can never be saved. You can only go to him for whatever torment he has in store for a failed minion. You know what I have to do?"

"I know what you must try to do," said Kahil, stepping back.

"Your vanity almost brought this world to ruination. Your lust for external youth and beauty caused you to destroy nations. You cannot be allowed to continue."

"So at last you will attempt to kill me? It will take more than a tap to this head to rid this universe of me."

"No, I *will* kill you."

Kahil started to incant a spell, but before he could finish it, Nakor struck him in the face with the butt of his staff. The former Emerald Queen, now in a man's body, staggered backward, his concentration broken and his spell incomplete. Nakor leveled his staff and a burst of white light shone on Kahil. He froze, transfixed, and from his mouth a mournful sound emerged. It grew weaker by the second as the body faded, becoming pale, then translucent, then transparent. When it vanished from view, the sound ceased, and Kahil was absent from the room. Sadly Nakor said, "I should have done that a century ago, but then I didn't know how."

He indulged himself a moment to reflect on everything, then he turned and hurried to overtake the others. Until Zaltais was returned to the pit and it sealed after him, the struggle was not over.

Miranda waved her hand and a brilliant shower of sparks exploded from her palm and sprayed a dozen soldiers hanging back near the gates to the city. As they began to be stung, they turned and ran.

"Not very dangerous," she said, "but dramatic." She looked back to see Tomas struggling with all his considerable strength to hold Zaltais on his shoulder, while Pug could do almost nothing but hang back.

As they cleared the city gates, the building which covered the pit in view, Zaltais overbalanced Tomas and flipped over his shoulder, landing hard upon the ground. The creature thrashed around, and Miranda said, "My spell is failing!"

Suddenly the crimson bands shattered, flung in all directions, the pieces fading from sight. The insectlike creature bounded upright and lashed out with a razor-sharp forearm. Tomas took the blow on his sword and the sound of the clash was steel upon steel.

Bright orange light bathed Zaltais as it pulled back to strike again. "It's casting a spell!" Miranda shouted.

Pug incanted a word of power, which should have given him the ability to sense the monster's magic. Instead he felt a blinding stab of pain in his head and he fell to his knees.

Pug's hands went to his head and tears ran down his face as he struggled to make himself breathe. The images and sensations that flooded his mind were so alien as to cause nothing but pain. The spell he had utilized was designed to sense out the nature of the spell being used, and to counteract it if possible, but even the emanations of the Dread Lord that appeared under Sethanon, and of the Demon Kings, Jakan and Maarg, were comparatively familiar compared to what he was experiencing now. Pug fell to his knees, his eyes squeezed shut and his fists at his temples.

Miranda took a more direct approach and simply tried to burn the creature, sending forth her most powerful spell of flames, a white-hot burst of energy that burned bright enough to blind anyone who looked at the flame.

Zaltais writhed in the center of the flame, his own magic forgotten, a creature trapped in the heart of a star.

Tomas circled the burning creature, and went to where Pug knelt, helping his friend to his feet.

Suddenly the fire vanished as Nakor came hurrying up to them. "Quick! Carry it to the pit!"

The monster was swollen and cooking in its own juices, the carapace cracked in several places. Tomas grabbed one of the forearms and tried dragging it. He made slow progress, but Zaltais was hauled through the large doors of the building and toward the pit.

Then, with a loud crack, the chitinous outer shell broke, and inside the body they could see something writhing. The shell parted and something akin to a giant white worm began to wiggle out.

Miranda said, "I don't have the strength to burn it again."

Nakor said "You don't need to burn it. Get it into the pit!"

Tomas charged the creature as it was halfway out of the smoking insect shell. He bashed it as hard as he could with his shield, and Zaltais was knocked backward, dragging the insect carcass with him, its lower section still embedded in the shell.

The thing shrieked, a sound which cut through the skull like a knife, causing Tomas to falter, but he overcame the sound and smashed the creature again, knocking it back once more, now only a dozen feet from the yawning opening of the pit.

Zaltais frantically snapped his tail, trying to rid himself of the insect corpse. Tomas kicked the thorax section and it spun the creature around, the insect body sliding toward the pit.

Pug wiped his hand across his eyes, his ringing head now clearing, and he uttered a simple spell that threw a punch of air, but one which could crush a man's ribs. The creature was knocked backward and suddenly was overbalancing.

As they watched, arms began to extrude from the worm's upper segment, frantically waving.

Nakor said, "Enough of this!" He ran forward, his staff cocked over his shoulder, and he struck the thing across the upper body as hard as he could.

With a scream that threatened to shatter their ears, Zaltais fell into the pit.

Miranda was knocked to her knees, as was Pug again. Tomas had to use all his willpower to remain upright, and Nakor gripped his staff as if it was the only thing keeping him alive.

Then the sound was gone. Nakor said, "We must seal this pit!"

"How?" asked Pug. "I've never seen anything like this."

"Yes, you have," said Nakor. "You're just not recognizing it!"

Pug took a deep breath and used what little energy he had left to assess the pit. "It's a rift!" he said at last.

"Yes," said Nakor, "but not the sort you know."

"How did you know?" asked Miranda.

"I'll explain it all later," said Nakor, "but you must close it."

A faint breeze stirred, and Miranda said, "Did you feel that?"

"Yes," said Tomas. "And I don't usually feel the wind inside a building."

"There's something trying to come through!" shouted Nakor.

Pug said, "I need help!"

"What do we do?" asked Miranda.

"Give me whatever strength you can!" shouted Pug. He closed his eyes and let his mind enter the rift. He sensed the energies and was again assaulted by an overwhelming sense of alien wrongness. Yet there was a pattern, and as alien as it was, once he apprehended it, he was able to study it, and with study, the structure began to emerge. "I have it!" he said at last.

He let his mind call up the knowledge he had gained as a Great One on Kelewan, as he had studied rifts and their nature. The nature of the rift was that Pug could either use more power to close it than it took to open it, or he could subvert the power used to keep it open. He chose the latter course, as his energy was too depleted to attempt the former. Besides, he felt that even at his best, that choice might prove beyond his powers. He sent a cord of energy that snaked out and engaged the source of the rift.

Suddenly a presence appeared on the other side of the rift. It was massive and powerful beyond anything he had thought possible, and it was nothing but a distillation of hatred and evil so pure it defied human understanding. A part of Pug's mind recoiled and wanted nothing more than to fall to the floor and whimper, as Fadawah had done. But

Pug's mental discipline came to the fore and he held his ground against this horror of the mind.

Whatever it was, it quested. It knew Pug was somewhere close by, but not quite where. Pug felt a sense of urgency rise up inside as he sought to unweave the matrix of power that held open the rift, for he knew that should this being find him, he would be lost forever.

A faint surge of power came to Pug and he knew that Miranda had succeeded in joining her power to his. He felt a sense of reassurance from her when she touched him, and the part of his mind able to perceive her sent forth its thanks.

The questing consciousness on the other side of the rift was becoming more aware of Pug as each second passed. Pug had his own spell ready.

He opened his eyes and for a moment it was if he was seeing two images at once. Before him stood Tomas, sword at the ready, with Miranda and Nakor beside him. Overlaying that image was one of a torn section of space and time, through which a great terror was peering in his direction. More than anything else, Pug was struck by the image of a vast eye peering through a keyhole.

Pug yanked back his own line of power, disrupting the supporting matrix of energy. He sensed a terrible rage from the other side of the rift.

"Get out!" he shouted, and as he turned to run he realized he could barely move. Tomas threw his shield over his back and put his left arm around Pug, nearly picking him up.

They ran from the building as Ryana landed. "I called her," said Tomas. The ground began to shake as they climbed aboard the dragon. As she launched herself into the sky, a terrible crack of thunder came from within the building.

The dragon beat her wings and gained altitude, and Pug turned to watch the scene below. A great wind was being drawn to the building and the building began to shudder and shake. A crack of timber heralded the roof shattering, collapsing into the building.

Miranda said, "Everything's being sucked into the rift!"

Pug said, "I hope not everything."

Nakor said, "It will balance out, but there will be a very big hole in the ground to fill when it's done."

A thunderous rumble sounded, and as Nakor predicted, a huge hole in the ground appeared and the rest of the building fell into it. A giant cloud of dust shot heavenward, and more ground fell into the hole. Then the rumbling stopped.

"It is over?" asked Miranda.

Pug closed his eyes and rested his head upon Tomas's back. "It will never be over," he said.

A ragged boy ducked under the outstretched arms of a guard who shouted, "Hey!"

"I gotta talk ta the Sheriff!" he shouted as he dodged by.

Dash turned to see the youngster scampering up the stairs. He stood on the rampart over the city gates, watching the Keshians deploy in the predawn darkness. "What do you want?" he demanded.

"Trina says to tell you, the South Palace Gate! Now!"

Instantly Dash knew he had overlooked other agents inside the palace. The South Palace Gate was the entrance used by tradesmen making deliveries directly to the palace. It opened on the large marshaling yard used to train Calis's Crimson Eagles; it also provided direct access to the one portion of the palace that was unprotected by walls and gates. Should the Keshians get through that entrance to the city, they would not only be in the city, they would also be in the palace. And most of the city's defenders would be in the wrong place.

Dash shouted to Gustaf, "South Palace Gate!"

Gustaf had a flying company, a company ready to run to any point in the line and reinforce, and they were off as soon as Dash shouted the location.

Turning to an officer nearby, Dash said, "Keep things here under control. Until their agents report the gate open, they'll go through the charade of asking for surrender one more time."

Dash hurried down the stairs and chased after Gustaf and his men. He ran through the streets until he could hear the sound of fighting. "Where is the palace guard?" he demanded.

Gustaf said, "They were ordered up to support the main gate."

"Who gave that order?" asked Dash.

"I thought you did," replied the constable.

"When we find out who gave that order, we'll have found our poisoner."

Dash and his constables raced through the street to the north-most entrance to the palace and found the gate unattended. He motioned for the men to run to the left, around the stables, and into the marshaling yard from the north. At the far end of the marshaling yard he saw a brawl taking place in front of the south gate. He had ridden wagons through that gate when working for Roo Avery what seemed like years before, in a different life, but never before had the marshaling yard seemed so vast.

As he reached a point halfway across the open stretch of ground he saw the struggle was nearly decided. Old men, boys, and a few men of fighting age stood toe-to-toe with armed mercenaries, trained killers who were dispatching them with cold-blooded efficiency.

Standing before the huge bar that kept the gate closed was Trina, a sword in one hand and a dagger in another. A bleeding man at her feet told Dash that he had already paid the price of trying to get by the determined woman.

The mercenaries at the gate were quickly disposing of the thieves, and Dash tried to will himself to be faster. He was twenty yards away when he saw a burly man with a beard strike down a young thief—barely more than a boy—then turn to join his companion facing Trina.

The first man before her struck an overhand blow, which she blocked high, leaving her guard open. The burly man stepped under and drove the point of his sword into her stomach.

"No!" Dash cried as he ran right into the two men without slackening speed. He carried both of them away and down in a heap. He struck out with his sword, killing the bigger man as he lay on the ground, then rolled over to come to his feet facing the first man who had struck at Trina.

The man made a combination attack, feigning a head blow, then turning his wrist to slash at Dash's side. Dash nimbly stepped back, then forward, while the man's sword point was moving past him and, before he could reverse his blade's direction, Dash killed the man with a stabbing blow to the throat.

The constables overwhelmed the attackers at the gate as the thieves began to carry away their wounded. The Keshian agents fought to the last, but eventually they were all killed or disarmed.

Dash looked around, and when he saw everything was under control, he ran over to where Trina lay. The gate was still closed.

He knelt and cradled her in his arms and saw her skin was pallid and clammy. Blood flowed copiously from her stomach and Dash knew her life was draining away. He shouted, "Get a healer!"

A constable ran off while Dash cradled Trina in his arms. He tried to staunch the flow of blood by pressing on the wound, but the pain was almost unbearable to Trina.

She looked up at him and weakly said, "I love you, Sheriff Puppy."

His tears fell unhindered. "You crazy good-for-nothing," he said, "I told you to stay alive!"

He gathered her to him and she moaned, then whispered, "You promised."

Dash was still holding the dead woman when the priest reached the gate. Gustaf put his hands on Dash's shoulders, moved him back, and said, "We have work to do, Sheriff."

Dash looked upward and saw the sky was brightening. He knew circumstances demanded he put aside his personal grief and the numbing sense of loss he felt. Soon the Keshian herald would approach the gate and make his final demand for surrender—for when the Keshian army saw the southern gate wasn't open, they would know their only option was to attack, and they would come.

Twenty-Seven

Intervention

THE HORSES PANTED.

Riders urged them on and prayed their mounts would hold out for one more day. Jimmy had put them on a punishing regimen, from dawn to dusk, with the shortest breaks possible. The horses were all exhibiting the results of the forced march, ribs beginning to show where not so many days before they had been sleek and comfortably fat.

Six horses had come up lame, and those riders had been forced to drop out, walking their animals back to Port Vykor or following after, hoping there would be a Kingdom army waiting when they at last got there. Two animals had been so badly injured they had been put down.

The troop was within minutes of being in sight of Krondor, and Jimmy prayed again that he was wrong in his surmise, and they would find the city peacefully going about its business. He would gladly accept the years of jests and taunts he would endure as a result should that be the case, but he knew in the pit of his stomach he was about to run headlong into a fight.

Dash crested a rise and saw a baggage train before him. Most of the baggage handlers were boys, but a few guards stood ready to defend the Keshian supplies. Dash shouted, ''Don't kill the boys!'' and then pulled his sword. The bag-

461

gage boys scattered, but the Keshian Dog Soldiers guarding the baggage train stood firm, and the battle was on.

Dash raced along the walls as the Keshians began their assault. The Keshian herald had been polite in his contempt, a quality Dash would have found more admirable had he not been in a nearly murderous rage over Trina's death. It had taken all the self-control he could manage to not grab a bow and take the herald out of his saddle when he came for the third time, demanding the surrender of the city.

Patrick was back in his castle, under guard against another attack by agents of Kesh. Dash put aside the sinking feeling in his stomach that, if they should somehow survive the assault on the city, it would be a search of tedious proportions to uncover all the agents of Kesh.

Trumpets sounded and war horns blew, and the Keshian infantry marched forward. In files of ten men, they carried ladders. Dash could hardly believe they'd assault first with scaling ladders, without heavy machines or a turtle to protect the men. Then a hundred bowmen rode into view, and Dash called out, "Get ready to duck!"

A horn sounded and the men with the ladders broke into a run, while the horse archers spurred their mounts forward, between them. The horsemen unleashed a barrage of arrows, and Dash hoped all his men had heard the warning to duck. A clattering of arrows against stones and shields and the absence of more than a few oaths and screams told him most had understood. Then his own bowmen rose up and delivered a withering fire down on those below the wall. Dash crouched down behind a merlon and said, "Pass the word: target those with the ladders. Worry about the archers later."

The soldiers on both sides passed the word, and Krondorian archers jumped up and fired at the ladder-bearers. They ducked as another round of arrows flew at the walls. Dash duck-walked to the rear of the rampart and called down to one of his constables, "Keep the patrols active. They may still be trying to get in through the sewers."

The constable ran off and Dash returned to his place on the wall. A palace guardsman ran over and said, "We found the spy, sir."

"Who was it?"

"Another clerk. Man name of Ammes. He just walked into the squad room and told us you'd ordered every man to the gate."

"Where is he?"

"Dead," said the guardsman. "He was one of those trying to seize the South Palace Gate, and he died during the fighting."

Dash nodded, making a mental note to make sure no palace servant or functionary stayed in place without a thorough investigation. The period when the Prince had resided in Darkmoor and Dash had overseen the transition from Duko's rule to Patrick's return had been too lax. Malar and other agents had easily insinuated themselves into the palace.

Which also meant Kesh had plans for this offensive long before the truce at Darkmoor last year.

Dash kept his rage bottled up, his frustration and anger at Trina's death and the assault on the city. He vowed that should Keshians come over the wall, he would personally kill more of the enemy than any man defending the city.

And should the city endure, he would see that his promise to Trina was not made in vain.

They landed in a clearing a few miles from the city. Pug staggered as he got off the dragon's back and sat down on the grass.

Miranda sat next to her husband and said, "Are you all right?"

Pug said, "My mind is still swimming."

Tomas said, "Where to next?"

"Many places," said Nakor. "And not all of us together." To Tomas he said, "Why don't you have your friend fly you home to your wife? There is still much work to be done, but you can return home knowing you've saved Elvandar and its inhabitants from problems for the near future."

"I would like to hear a few things first," said Tomas.

"Yes," said Miranda. "What was that creature?"

"I have no knowledge of anything like him," said Tomas. "And the memories I inherited from Ashen-Shugar are extensive."

"That's because no Valheru ever encountered anything like Zaltais," said Nakor, sitting on the grass next to Pug. "Mostly because he was not a creature."

"Not a creature?" asked Miranda. "Could you attempt to just explain without the usual convolution?"

Nakor smiled. "Right now you remind me of your mother, the good parts."

"There were good parts?" said Miranda with thinly veiled contempt.

In the most wistful tone anyone had ever heard from him, Nakor said, "Yes, there were, once, a very long time ago."

"What about Zaltais?" asked Pug.

"Fadawah was lured to practicing dark magic by his advisor, Kahil," Nakor said. "I think Kahil has been behind everything that went on in Novindus from the start. He was a dupe, a tool of the Pantathians, who somehow managed a degree of freedom, and he used that to create a position for himself, one where he could manipulate others . . ." He hesitated, then continued, "The same way Jorma became Lady Clovis and controlled the Overlord and Dahakon years ago. Kahil was at Fadawah's side from the start. He avoided destruction and continued to advise and . . . well, I suspect he convinced Fadawah to turn to the very powers that destroyed the Emerald Queen and the Demon King. He served that power we do not speak of, and like most of the Nameless One's minions, he did not even know who he served . . . he was just driven."

"Zaltais?" prodded Miranda. "What did you mean when you said he wasn't a creature?"

"He was not of this reality, more so than the demons or even the dread. He was a thing from the Seventh Circle of Hell."

"But *what* was he?" asked Pug.

"He was a thought, probably a dream."

"A thought?" asked Tomas.

Pug said, "And when I looked into the rift?"

"You saw the mind of a God."

"I don't understand," said Pug.

Nakor patted him on the shoulder. "You will in a few

hundred years. For now, consider that a God slept and as he slept he dreamed, and in that dream he fancied some tiny creature spoke his name and in doing so became his tool. In that dream that tool created havoc and called to him and he sent his Angel of Despair to answer the call. And the Angel served the tool."

"Why couldn't Zaltais be killed?" asked Miranda.

Nakor smiled. "You can't kill a dream, Miranda. Even an evil dream. You can only send it back to where it came from."

Tomas touched his lip. "That dream seemed concrete enough to me."

"Oh," said Nakor, "a God's dream *is* reality."

Pug said, "We should go."

"Where?" asked Miranda. "Back to the island?"

"No," said Nakor. "We should tell the Prince the leadership of the enemy is dead."

"Krondor, then," said Pug.

"One thing, though," said Miranda.

"What?" asked Nakor.

"You mentioned some time ago that the demon Jakan replaced Mother at the head of that army, but you never said anything about what happened to her."

Nakor said, "Your mother is dead."

"Are you certain?" asked Miranda.

Nakor nodded. "Very certain."

Pug stood up, still feeling shaky. Tomas said, "Ryana will bear me back to Elvandar."

Pug embraced his old friend and said, "Again, we say good-bye."

"And we'll meet again," answered Tomas.

"Fare you well, old friend," said Pug.

"And you three as well," said Tomas.

He climbed aboard the dragon's back and she leaped into the sky. Two beats of her wings and she banked off to the west and started on the journey back to Elvandar.

Pug said, "Are you up to getting us all to Krondor?"

Miranda said, "I can manage." She took them both by the hands and closed her eyes, and reality swam around them.

They appeared in the great hall of the Prince's palace in

Krondor as the war horns sounded the call for the reserves to come to the main gate.

Gustaf said, "If you can't slip inside the gate and unlock it—"

"Kick it down," finished Dash.

They heard the rumble as the ram was rolled down the road toward the main gate. The road into the city from the east was a long incline from a series of rolling hills, and the ram was a huge one, fashioned from five trees lashed together by heavy ropes. Horsemen rode on either side with guide ropes, and as they reached the last stretch of road before the gate, they released the ropes and veered off.

The ram picked up speed and the rumbling grew louder as the ram closed to within fifty yards of the gate. As it bore down, Dash reflexively gripped the stones of the wall as he anticipated the impact.

Then someone shoved between Gustaf and Dash and stuck his hand over the wall. A sheet of light extended from the man's hand, and Dash turned to see his great-grandfather standing next to him. "Enough!" Pug shouted, his anger clearly evident on his face as the ram exploded into a thousand flaming splinters.

Whatever the Keshians expected, this display of magic wasn't it. Their attack, timed to coincide with the ram smashing the gate, faltered as men on horseback were suddenly greeted by the sight of a very high wall surmounted by archers instead of an open gate for them to charge through.

They pulled up and milled around in confusion, as the defenders on the wall unleashed a barrage of arrows. Pug shouted, "No!" and with a wave of his hands sent out a curtain of heat that turned the arrows into flaming cinders that fell far short of their mark. Turning to Dash, he said, "I don't see any other officers. Are you in charge here?"

Dash said, "For the moment."

"Then order your men to stop shooting."

Dash did so, and the Keshians retreated to their lines unharmed. Pug said, "Send a herald to the Keshian commander. Tell him I want to meet with the commander of that army in the Prince's palace in one hour's time."

"In the palace?" asked Dash.

"Yes, when he gets here, open the gate and let him in."

"What if he won't come?"

Pug turned his back, motioned to Nakor and Miranda on the rear of the gatehouse, and said, "He'll come, or I'll destroy his army."

"But what do I tell him?" asked Dash.

"Tell him the war is over."

A pale and weak-looking Patrick stood before his throne as General Asham ibin Al-tuk marched into the throne room, flanked by a guard and a servant. He bowed perfunctorily. "I am here, Highness."

Patrick said, "I did not call this meeting."

Pug stepped forward and said, "I did."

"And you are?" asked the General.

"I am called Pug."

The General raised an eyebrow in recognition. "The magician at Stardock."

"The same."

"Why have you summoned me?"

"To tell you to take your army and go home."

The General said, "If you think that display outside the gate will turn my attention—"

A guard ran in and said, "Highness, fighting has erupted!"

The General said, "I am under a flag of truce!"

Patrick asked the guard, "Where is the fighting?"

"Outside the wall! It appears as if cavalry from both the north and south has attacked the Keshians."

Patrick said, "General, those are units not presently under my command. They are obviously riding to relieve Krondor and do not know of the truce. You are free to rejoin your men."

The General bowed and turned to leave, but Pug said, "No!"

"What?" asked both the Prince and the General simultaneously.

Pug said, "This will end now!"

He vanished from sight.

Nakor, who had been standing in the corner near Miranda, said, "For a tired man he manages to get around, doesn't he?"

"Yes, he does," Miranda agreed with a faint smile.

Pug appeared over the heart of the battlefield and saw that baggage wagons were afire at the rear of the Keshian position and that a company of horse was attacking along the coast road from the north, catching the Keshians between two attacking columns.

Pug hovered a hundred feet above the battle and clapped his hands together, and a peal of thunder struck those below, knocking some of the riders directly underneath him out of their saddles.

Men looked up and saw a man floating in the air, and from that man a brilliant light erupted, a golden glow that was as bright as the sun. His voice carried to every man as if he were standing next to them: "This ends now!"

With a wave of his hand he sent a force through the air, a ripple which visibly distorted the air. The wave hit horses and knocked them down, throwing more men to the ground.

Men turned and ran.

Jimmy sat firm on a bucking, frantic horse, trying to bring the animal under control. After two more kicks, the animal set out at a run, and Jimmy let it, turning it and then bringing it to a halt. He turned the animal around and saw more animals running in every direction as Keshians raced back toward their burning wagons.

Then he glanced up to where Pug hung in the air and again came Pug's voice: "This ends now."

Then Pug vanished.

Nakor said, "Well, at least you got them to stop fighting for a while." The three of them sat in an abandoned room in the palace, after the Prince had retired and the Keshian General returned to his army.

"I will get them to stop for good," said Pug.

"Or what?" asked Miranda.

Pug said, "I'm sick of killing. I'm sick of destruction. But more than anything, I'm sick of the mindless stupidity I see on every side of me." Pug thought of the losses to war he had endured, from his childhood friend Roland and Lord Borric to Owen Greylock, a man he had not known well, but one whom he had found himself liking from their winter together at Darkmoor. "Too many good men. And too many innocents. It can't go on. If I have to . . . I don't know, put up a wall between both armies, I'll do it."

Nakor said, "You'll think of something. When the Prince and the General have time to calm down, you can tell them what you want."

"When are you meeting again?" asked Miranda.

"Tomorrow at noon."

"Good," said Nakor. "That gives me time to see if what I think has happened has happened."

"You're being cryptic again," said Miranda.

Nakor smiled. "Come along and see. We'll get something to eat."

He led them out of the room, then out of the palace, past guards who stood an uneasy watch knowing they might have to return to the walls and a terrible fight at a moment's notice.

As they left the palace, they saw horsemen riding into the marshaling yard through the southern gate. At their head Pug saw his other great-grandson and waved.

Jimmy rode over and said, "I saw that display, Pug." He grinned and Pug's heart squeezed slightly when for a second he saw Gamina's smile echoed in it. "You saved a lot of my men's lives. Thank you."

Pug said, "I'm pleased you were among those who benefited."

"Is Dash . . . ?"

"He's inside, alive, and until Patrick regains his strength, in command of the city."

Jimmy laughed. "Somehow I don't think he enjoys that very much."

"Go see him," said Pug. "We're going to Nakor's temple and will be back in the morning. We have a general meeting at noon to end this nonsense."

Jimmy said, "I will be more than pleased to see that. Duko's a marvel, and he's managed to keep the South under control, despite this Keshian adventure, but we're sorely tested along both borders, and I haven't any idea how things go in the North."

"That war is finished, too."

Jimmy said, "I am relieved to hear that, Great-grandfather. I will see you in the morning."

Nakor said, "Let's go. I want to see what's happened."

They hurried through a city cautiously returning to normal activities as people ventured out of their houses. With so few people about, they reached the Temple Quarter of the city quickly.

No one was visible outside the tent, but once they stepped through, they saw a crowd sitting on the floor. In the center of the room the woman Aleta sat on the floor, rather than floating in the air, and the light about her was gone. So was the ill-aspected darkness which had hovered in the air beneath her.

Dominic hurried over and said, "Nakor! I am glad to see you."

"When did this happen?" asked Nakor.

"A few hours ago. One moment she was floating in the air, and the next the blackness below her vanished, as if it had been sucked down through a hole, and she gently floated back to the ground, opened her eyes, and began speaking."

Pug and the others turned their attention to what the woman was saying, and instantly Nakor said, "Her voice, it's different."

Pug had no knowledge of what the young woman had sounded like before, but he knew it could be nothing like what he heard now, for her voice was magical. It was soft, and yet easy to hear if one but took a moment to listen: a musical voice.

"What's she saying?" asked Miranda.

"She's been talking about the nature of good since she awoke," said Dominic. He looked at Nakor. "When you first began this temple, and when you told us what you would do, I was skeptical, but knew we had to try. But what we see before us now is absolute proof the power of Ishap needed to be shared with the Order of Arch-Indar, for there, before us, sits a living Avatar of the Goddess."

Nakor laughed. "Nothing so grand as that. Come." He led them through the seated crowd and came to stand before the young woman. She ignored him and continued talking.

Nakor knelt and looked into her eyes. "Is she repeating herself?" he asked.

Dominic said, "Why, yes, I believe so."

"Has anyone written down what she's said?"

Sho Pi was sitting to one side and said, "I have had two acolytes recording her words, Master Nakor. This is the beginning of her third iteration of the same lesson she taught."

"Good, because I'll bet she's getting hungry and tired." He put his hand on her shoulder and she faltered in her speech.

She blinked and her eyes seemed to change focus, and she looked at Nakor and said, "What?" Her voice was different, what one might expect of a mortal woman of her age, without the magic that had made it soothing and wonderful a moment earlier.

"You've been asleep," said Nakor. "Why don't you get something to eat? We'll talk later."

The girl got up and said, "Oh, I'm stiff. I must have been sitting like that a while."

Nakor said, "A couple of weeks, actually."

"Weeks!" Aleta said. "You can't be serious."

"I'll explain everything to you later. Now go get some food and then a long nap."

After she left, Dominic said, "If she's not an avatar, what is she?"

Nakor grinned. "She is a dream." He looked at Pug and Miranda, and said, "A wonderful dream."

Miranda said, "But Nakor, she's still here. Zaltais is gone."

Nakor nodded. "He was a thing of the mind from that other world, projected into this. Aleta is a normal woman, but something reached across worlds to touch her and used her to hold back that blackness."

"What was that blackness?" asked Dominic.

"A very bad dream. I'll explain over dinner. Let's find something to eat."

Dominic said, "Very well. We have food in the kitchen."

As they were walking, Nakor said, "By the way, we have to change a few things around here."

"What?" asked Dominic.

"To begin with, you must notify the Ishapians you are no longer a member of their order."

"What?"

Nakor put his arm around Dominic's shoulder and said, "You look very young, but I know you're an old man like me, Dominic. Pug told me the story of the time you and he went to the Tsurani homeworld. I know you've seen lots of things.

"Sho Pi over there is a perfect choice to teach the young monks how to be monks, but you are the one who must teach Aleta."

"Teach her what?" asked Dominic.

"How to be High Priestess of the Order of Arch-Indar, of course."

"High Priestess? That girl?"

"*That girl?*" repeated Nakor. "She was an Avatar of the Goddess a moment ago, wasn't she?"

Miranda laughed, and Pug put his arm around her shoulders. It was the first time in a long while he had felt like laughing.

Erik said, "We can only assume Subai got through to the magician. By all reports they simply stopped fighting everywhere about the time all the corpses fell over."

Earl Richard said, "Thank the Gods for that."

"I wish we still had cavalry," Erik said reflectively. "I have a hunch we could get men up to Ylith without much trouble."

"Well, order up a unit on foot and see how far they get."

Erik smiled. "I already have. And I'm sending Akee and his Hadati through the hills toward Yabon."

Richard said, "Do you think we'll ever know what happened, truly?"

Erik shook his head. "Probably not. I've been in battles where I still don't know what happened. We'll probably read more reports on this fight than we want to, and I'll write a few of them myself, but truth to tell, I have no idea what really occurred.

"One minute we were struggling to beat back an army of dead men and crazed killers, and the next the dead men all fell over and the killers were walking around slack-jawed and apparently without minds. I've never heard of a fight going from hopeless to easy in a second before.'' The very tired young Captain said, "But to tell you the truth, I don't really care now that the fighting's stopped."

"You're a remarkable young man, Erik von Darkmoor. I'll mention that in my report to the King."

"Thanks, but there are a lot of men out there deserving of praise more than I." He sighed and looked out the tent door. "And many of them won't be going home."

"What should we do now?" asked Earl Richard.

"Without cavalry, I'm inclined to sit tight until we get word of the situation down in Krondor. But my instinct tells me we need to advance northward as fast as we can. Fadawah may have fled or been killed, but that doesn't mean some other petty captain won't try to grab power and fashion a modest little Kingdom for himself. And as far as we know, Yabon City is still under siege."

Earl Richard said, "I'm tired of sitting around, myself. Give the order to advance."

Erik smiled and stood up. "My lord," he said with a bow. He went outside and found Jadow Shati near the Crimson Eagles' campsite. "Break camp!" he ordered. "And ready to march!"

"You heard the man!" said the former sergeant. "I want every man ready to march in an hour!"

Jadow turned and grinned at his old companion, and Erik found once more he couldn't resist that man's smile; he grinned in return.

Patrick showed every sign of being on the way to a full recovery. His color had returned to normal and he sat firmly upon his throne.

The Keshian General Asham ibin Al-tuk again stood before the throne, looking even less pleased than the last time he had appeared. Now he faced a Kingdom army reinforced by cavalry units from Port Vykor and from the North.

Pug walked in.

Patrick said, "You demanded we be here at noon, Pug. What have you to say to us?"

Pug looked at Patrick, then at the General, and said,

"This war is over. General, you will refresh your soldiers outside one more day, then at first light tomorrow you will return to the South. You will return beyond the original borders south of Land's End. You will carry orders to all Keshian units to cease their attacks on Land's End and you will relay the following message to your Emperor: should Kesh come north again, uninvited, no man crossing the border under arms will survive."

The General stood ashen-faced and shaking with rage, but he nodded.

Patrick beamed. His smile was one of victory. "Dare to linger, Keshian, and my magician will destroy your army where it stands."

Pug turned. "Your magician?" Pug advanced upon the young Prince and walked up the stairs to stand before him. "I am not *your* magician, Patrick. I loved your grandfather and counted him among the greatest men I've known, and I treasured the love of your great-grandfather Borric, who gave me the name conDoin, but you don't own my soul. There are forces loose in the universe so far beyond your petty dreams of power and wealth they are a flood to a drip of water. It is those forces who command my attention. I just refuse to sit idly by any longer and see innocent women and children slaughtered and brave men die because rulers are too foolish to see they have abundance."

Turning to the General, Pug said, "You may also tell your Emperor that should any Kingdom soldier move south uninvited, every man under arms who crosses the border will be destroyed."

"What?" said Patrick standing. "You dare threaten the Kingdom?"

"I make no threats," said Pug. "I am telling you that you will not be permitted any retribution against Kesh. You will both return to your respective sides of the border and act like civilized neighbors."

"You are a Duke of the Kingdom, a member of the royal family by adoption, and a sworn vassal to the crown! If I tell you to destroy that army outside the gate, you will do so!"

Pug's anger rose up and he stared the taller young man in the eyes. "I shall not. No power you possess can compel me to act against my will. If you want those Keshians outside the walls dead, take a sword and go out and try to kill them.''

Patrick's rage erupted. ''You traitor!''

Pug put his hand on Patrick's chest and shoved him back into the throne. Guards throughout the hall put hands on the hilts of swords to protect their Prince. Miranda stepped forward, hand upraised, and said, ''I wouldn't!''

Nakor stood at her side, and held up his staff. ''The boy is all right.''

Pug leaned over, almost nose to nose with Patrick, and said, ''You who have never drawn a sword in a battle more serious than chasing some goblins around in the north call me 'traitor?' *I* have saved your Kingdom, you fool. I did not save it for you anymore than I saved the Empire for that man's''—his finger shot out, pointing at the Keshian General—''master. I did it because of the countless souls that would have been lost had I not.''

Looking first at Patrick then the General, Pug said, ''Take word to your father, and your master, that Stardock is free. Any attempt to force Kingdom or Empire rule on that entity will bring my intervention. They have my word on that and I shall enforce their independence.'' Pug turned and stepped away from the throne. ''I care not who sits on your father's throne, Patrick. You gather together the shards of your broken crown and rebuild your nation. I care not for your titles and rank. I am done with your Kingdom.'' He put his arms out and Miranda and Nakor came to stand on either side. ''I renounce my title as Duke of the Kingdom. I foreswear my oath as subject to the crown. I have larger concerns than your vanities and national agendas. I am here to protect this world, not just one part of it.

''Let it be known that Pug of Crydee is no more. I am now merely the Black Sorcerer. My island is no longer a hospitable place for the uninvited. Anyone sailing within sight of it is at peril, and anyone setting foot upon it without my leave will be destroyed!''

Then with a thunderous crash and a thick cloud of black smoke, he vanished with his companions.

* * *

Dash said, "Great-grandfather certainly twisted Patrick's smalls, didn't he?"

Jimmy said, "I've had more pleasant afternoons."

They had just retired from a council with the Prince. The withdrawal of the Keshian troops was discussed as well as what exactly Patrick would report to his father. It had lasted long past dinner and into the night.

They were walking toward Jimmy's quarters for a quiet moment alone before retiring for the night. "Did you talk to Francie?" asked Dash.

Jimmy said, "No. I saw her a brief second but didn't get a chance to really speak with her."

"She's afraid that once she's married to Patrick you'll just stop talking to her. She doesn't want to lose your friendship."

Jimmy said, "That won't happen. One thing about this war, it taught me what really is important and what just seems important."

Dash said, "I know."

There was a note in his voice Jimmy had never heard before. "What is it?"

Dash said, "Just some people I cared about didn't get through this."

Jimmy stopped. "Someone special to you?"

Dash turned and said, "I don't want to talk about it today. I'll tell you all about it someday, just not today."

Jimmy said, "Very well." He was silent a minute as they continued to walk along the hallways. "I think I learned something myself, and maybe it's important, too."

"What?"

"Francie is . . . someone special. But I think I feel the need for something and she is the person I elected to cast in the role of the person to fulfill that need."

"Grandfather and Grandmother?"

"Yes, what they had. I think that seeing how they felt, especially after seeing how cool Mother and Father always were to each other, it makes me want to have what Grandmother and Grandfather had."

"Few gain that."

They reached the door to Jimmy's room and opened it.

Three people were sitting inside. "Come in and close that door," said Pug.

Jimmy and Dash entered and Dash closed the door.

Pug said, "I could not leave without speaking to you two. You are the last of my line."

Trying to lift the mood, Jimmy said, "Please don't put it that way."

Miranda laughed.

Dash said, "And we do have relatives in the East."

Pug laughed. "There is so much of your grandfather in you two." He looked at Dash. "Upon occasion you look like him when he was a boy." He looked at Jimmy. "And sometimes you look so much like my Gamina it haunts me."

He opened his arms and Jimmy and Dash came and hugged him in turn. "I shall not return to the Kingdom unless it is for a reason far more important than the whims of kings," said Pug. "But you two are my blood, and you and your children will always be welcome on my island."

Dash said, "You have influence with the King. Do you have to make this sort of break?"

Pug said, "I knew King Lyam as a boy in Crydee. I knew Arutha better, but both knew my heart. The King knew me from his father."

Nakor said, "Borric knows me well, and my words might carry some weight, but what Pug is being diplomatic in avoiding is that, short of an unexpected disaster, Patrick will someday be King."

"We are avoiding an argument of momentous proportion later by having it now," said Pug. "The Kingdom is in shambles. Patrick is forced by circumstances to yield to my demands. If this confrontation occurred years from now, how many innocents would die as I enforced my will?"

"And what would that make him?" said Miranda. "Only a different tyrant than those men of whom we just disposed."

Dash said, "You cut yourself off from so much."

Pug said, "I have seen worlds and traveled through time, my boy. I have so much more to see. This Kingdom of the Isles is but one of many places that are now dear to me."

Nakor said, "And if need be, we'll be back."

Dash said, "Well, we have a lot of work to do, and if you want my opinion, you're doing the right thing."

Pug smiled. "Thank you for that."

Jimmy said, "I can't say I agree with Dash, but I know that it is your choice and I wish you well." He smiled at Miranda. "Shall I call you Great-grandmother?"

"Not if you value your life," said Miranda with a smile.

Dash said, "I shall think of you a lot."

Jimmy said, "As shall I."

Pug stood. "Be well," he said, holding out his hands to Nakor and Miranda, and they vanished.

Dash sat down on Jimmy's bed, leaning back against his down pillow. "I think I'm going to sleep for a week."

"Then make it next week, Sheriff," said Jimmy. "We have a lot of work to do in the morning and one hell of a mess to unravel." He glanced over and saw his brother was already asleep. For a moment he considered waking him, then he shrugged, left, and went next door to sleep in Dash's bed.

Twenty-Eight

Division

GATHIS BOWED.

"I am pleased to see you all return and looking well," he said.

Pug, Miranda, and Nakor had just materialized near the fountain that was the centerpiece of the garden of Pug's estate on Sorcerer's Island.

Pug said, "We are equally pleased to see you. How fare things here?"

Gathis smiled his toothy goblinlike grin. "Very well. If you would indulge me, there is something I think you should see before you rest. It should only take a few moments."

Pug nodded and Gathis led him out through the building and across the meadow toward the hidden cave that was the shrine to the lost God of Magic. The cave stood open to view.

"What is this?" asked Pug.

"You observed, I think, Master Pug," said Gathis, "that eventually the appropriate person would find this shrine."

Miranda said, "And that person has arrived?"

"Not as we thought," said Gathis.

Pug entered the cave, with the others behind him, and looked at the statue that had once resembled Macros the

Black. He faltered as he saw his own features upon the statue. "What?"

Miranda stepped around beside her husband and she saw her features upon the statue. "I see myself!"

Nakor said, "Watch a moment."

The face on the statue shifted and they saw the features of Robert d'Lyse. Then they saw the features of other students on the island.

"What does this mean?" asked Miranda.

"It means," said Nakor, "that all of you are servants of magic and that there is no one person who shall be the god's agent on Midkemia. Rather, many people will work on behalf of returning the lost God of Magic to his place in this universe."

Pug studied the statue as other faces appeared, magicians known to him and those he had never met. After a few minutes Pug saw his own face again. Pug said, "Let's return to the house."

As they walked toward the house, Pug said, "Nakor, I didn't see your face upon the statue."

Nakor grinned and shrugged. "I know there is no magic."

Pug laughed. "It is an all or nothing proposition, Nakor. Either everything is magic or nothing is magic."

Nakor shrugged. "I find either proposition equally probable, but aesthetically I prefer the concept that there is no magic. Just power and the ability to utilize it."

Miranda said, "This borders on the type of long debate you two enjoy over wine, and I am very hungry."

Gathis said, "Food and wine wait you in your study, Master Pug."

"Join us," said Pug to his servant.

When they returned to the house, they found a sumptuous table set for them. Miranda took a plate and began piling on fruit and cheeses. Pug took a large flagon of wine and filled goblets.

"Gathis," said Pug, "you are the keeper of that shrine. What is your opinion on what we've seen?"

"It is as Master Nakor has observed: no longer will one individual act as an agent on behalf of the lost God of Magic. Perhaps the powers have learned the error of depending too much on one individual. It says that those who practice the arts will aid the return of magic."

Nakor shrugged. "It means that whatever power seeks to return, the God of Magic has deduced that assigning all that responsibility to one individual is risky. Macros, for all his power, made mistakes."

Pug said, "I appreciate that fact, having already made quite a few myself."

Miranda said, "Now that you are no longer a Duke of the Kingdom, what are your plans?"

"I still have many thousands of Saaur to relocate to the Ethel Du-ath. Eventually I will have to return to Shila and destroy whatever demons may linger there, then be about the business of reseeding enough life on that world so that in a few centuries the Saaur may return." He smiled. "Then there's the matter of the students here. They need to be taught, and learned from as well. And there's the problem of finding and destroying Nalar's agents wherever they may be hiding. Other than that, I think I may take up fishing."

Nakor laughed. "Fishing teaches patience. That's why I never took it up."

"Tens of thousands died during the Riftwar, and more than twice that number during this latest war, this Serpent-war. These catastrophic events must never be allowed to be duplicated again."

"How are we to insure they don't?" asked Miranda.

Pug said, "That I need to think on. And it's something we all need to be involved with. I think I may have some ideas I'll share with you and the others living on this island. The first thing we must be certain of is that there can be no manipulation of those who serve on our behalf. Those are the tactics of our enemy, and as one who was subjected to such manipulation by your father, my love, I find the idea of continuing that practice distasteful. This is why this island must become our bastion, and those who serve here must do so willingly and with as much knowledge as it is safe for them to possess."

"What of Stardock?" asked Miranda.

Pug said, "Stardock was begun with good intentions, but I made too many errors. I thought I would give the students more of a voice in the organization of the Academy, and to be frank, I was a product of the Tsurani Assembly. It's been enough years since then that I think I recognize those errors.

"Stardock will continue and be an asset to us; before I built the community there, magicians were often persecuted by those fearful of their talents. 'Witches' were hunted down and their pitiful woodland huts burned to the ground, or 'wizards' were walled up in caves to die of starvation and thirst, unless they became powerful enough to keep people away through fear, or they had patrons who were noble or rich. At least now those have a haven if they care to make their way to Stardock.

"And we may find recruits to our cause among those who study at Stardock for a time and leave, seeking something else."

"How do we insure we don't make the same mistakes?" asked Miranda.

"There are many things we will do differently; I will be the final authority here. I may seek your wisdom and that of others, but in critical matters I will decide. I erred in thinking that was ignoble and arbitrary at Stardock, and now I know it is the opposite. Without a vision, we become a debating society and a place where habit quickly becomes 'tradition.' Tradition often becomes an excuse for repression, bigotry, or reactionary thinking."

"My Blue Riders will keep them from being too tradition-bound."

"My friend," said Pug, "your Blue Riders will become another tradition. And those who survive the fight of the those traditionalists who are now calling themselves 'The Hand of Korsh' and 'The Wand of Watoom' will become just as fixed in their ways. Even Korsh and Watoom would be appalled to see what their followers have created."

"Maybe I should go back there," offered Nakor, half in jest.

"Maybe not," replied Pug. "Stardock will endure, and there will be times we will be grateful it does."

Looking around the room, Pug said, "We here are embarking on a long fight. There are powers moving through the universe, vast terrible powers that we have only glimpsed. The two great wars we have so far endured are but the opening moves in a game of chess.''

Miranda said, ''What are the Gods on our side doing about all this?''

Nakor said, ''They are helping you.''

''How?'' asked Miranda.

''In ways obvious and subtle,'' said Nakor.

Pug said, ''During the Chaos Wars, the very nature of things changed, and since then the Gods have acted through agents and minions. We are who we are because the gods have chosen us to be their agents.''

''Even Gods need to learn,'' said Nakor. ''Your father's relationship with Sarig was not particularly effective, from the God's point of view, so rather than repeat that mistake, he's elected to try a different tactic.''

Miranda said, ''There seems a great degree of futility in what we attempt.''

''Perhaps,'' offered Nakor, ''but we have seen wonderful things. The creation of the Temple of Arch-Indar is no mean feat. It will be a tiny, inconsequential sect for centuries, and most who encounter it will not think it equal in importance to the long-established worship of Astalon, Dala, Sung, and the other lesser Gods, but the fact that enough purity of the Goddess exists in the universe to serve us in balking Nalar's attempts to again create havoc on our world is a miracle. There may not be another such manifestation for centuries, yet we know one may come.''

''What of you?'' asked Pug. ''What are your plans?''

''My work here is done, for a while,'' said Nakor.

''Where will you go?'' asked Miranda.

''Here and there . . . I will seek out Nalar's minions and send you word should I encounter them. And every so often I will encounter likely candidates for your community and send them to you. And from time to time I will return to eat your food and drink your wine and see what's new and interesting here.''

''You will always be welcome, Nakor.''

Miranda said, ''Who do you serve, Nakor?''

Nakor grinned. ''Myself. All of us. Everything.'' He shrugged. ''I don't know. Perhaps someday I will, but for now I am content to wander, learn things, and help out where I may.''

"Well," said Pug, reaching for another cup of wine, "stay a while longer while I bring about the creation of my new council here, and give me the benefit of your wisdom."

Nakor said, "If you think it wisdom, then you do need my advice."

Miranda laughed.

Trumpets sounded and drums beat as the Prince and his fiancée departed the throne room. After six weeks of relative peace since Pug had ended the war, the crown judged it time to make the formal announcement. Patrick had just finished informing the court that he and Francine would depart at the end of the month to return to Rillanon for the royal wedding. The nobles and influential commoners in the room cheered and waited to disperse until Patrick escorted Francine out of the hall.

Jimmy approached Erik von Darkmoor and said, "Captain, I just wanted to tell you how impressed I am by what I read of your actions in Yabon."

Erik shrugged. "After what Pug, Nakor, and the others did, we had little serious opposition."

"Those forced marches, though, must have been punishing."

"They were," said Erik, "but mostly on our feet, since we had no horses. We had very little problem securing any area we entered, and once we freed prisoners in Ylith and Zun we had enough men to leave behind and act as jailers. By the time we reached LaMut, we were hunting bandits, nothing more. Now that General Nordan has agreed to lead those who want to leave—and a few who don't—back to Novindus, and the rest are being sent down to serve with Duko, things are getting relatively quiet."

Jimmy said, "Still, it was an impressive three weeks."

"I just wish we had more ships," said Erik. "This business of having to do business with the Quegans to get the invaders back across the sea has me feeling itchy each time I see a Quegan ship anchor off of Fishtown."

"Blame your old friend," said Jimmy, pointing at Roo,

who stood with his wife talking to a minor noble.

"Roo always could smell an opportunity. I just wish I knew how he got the Quegans to make the deal. They're usually impossible to deal with."

Jimmy shrugged. "Probably just found something they really wanted and agreed to get it for them; that's usually how you do business."

"I'll leave business to Roo. Being the Captain of the Crimson Eagles is enough for me."

"I'm surprised you didn't accept the promotion," said Jimmy.

"I'm happy where I am. Being Captain of the Prince's Household Guard is a lot more ceremony than real soldiering."

"But it's one step from there to being Swordmaster for a Duke or the Knight-Marshal's position here in Krondor."

Erik smiled. "I'm happy. I like running the Crimson Eagles, and I think the Kingdom needs an army independent of the other nobles. We might have had a different war had we had Kingdom garrisons in Sarth, Ylith, and Zun."

"You may be right, but the Dukes will resist the idea of garrisons in their Duchies they don't control."

"I'll think about that when I return to Krondor," said Erik. "Right now I'm going to Ravensburg and to my wife. It's been months and I wonder if she remembers what I look like."

Jimmy said, "You're not easy to forget, Captain. Few men come as large as you."

Erik laughed and said, "What of you?"

"I am the King's servant. I'll return with Patrick to Rillanon and His Majesty will tell me where I serve next. I suspect I'll be back in Krondor quickly enough. With Rudolfo dead and Brian unable to walk since the poisoning, we'll need a new Duke in Krondor quickly. Duke Carl survived up in Yabon, but between those two Duchies we have enough work to keep a score of nobles occupied for a century.

"I'll probably be given a title, and too few resources for too much work. That's usually the way it works."

Erik smiled and patted Jimmy on the shoulder. "Well do I know that, Jimmy."

Roo and Karli joined them and were warmly greeted by both men. Erik said, "When the Keshians were marching across your estate, how did you avoid being captured like the others in your area?"

Roo laughed. "We were sleeping in an outbuilding while we're rebuilding the estate house. When the cavalry showed up, they went inside the big house, and we snuck off into the woods. I have a tidy little cave set up to lie low in. I stocked it first thing after I returned. Too many armies running around here in the West for my taste."

Erik said, "We're trying to solve that problem, Roo." Karli hid her smile behind her hand.

Roo said, "I haven't seen your brother around, Jimmy."

"Dash is off somewhere. With everyone heading off to the wedding, he's being left behind in charge for a while."

"I'm sure he's distressed at missing the wedding," said Karli.

Jimmy smiled. "Probably not as much as he is at the work to be done putting this city back together again."

Roo said, "I know. Someone broke into the basement at Barret's and took every scrap of food and all the coffee! How can I open a coffeehouse without coffee?"

"I guess you'll have to buy more," said Erik. He playfully squeezed his friend's shoulder. "You always manage to find a way to make a deal, my friend."

Roo smiled. "I have to work a little harder since Jimmy's grandfather is no longer around, but then I'm getting to keep the money I make rather than pay taxes."

Jimmy said, "I could speak to the Prince about that if you'd like."

Roo put up his hands in mock surrender, "No, that's fine. I'll pick my own time to bring up the matter of the crown's debt to the Bitter Sea Company. Let's get the West back in order before we start that long and boring wrangle."

Karli said, "There's your brother, Jimmy. Who's that he's talking to?"

Jimmy turned and saw Dash entering the room deep in conversation with another man. "He's a court functionary, named Talwin. I'm still a bit vague on what he does for Patrick, but I've seen him around over the last few years. He's being named Castle Reeve while everyone else is go-

ing to Rillanon for the wedding. I'm sure he and Dash have
a great deal to discuss.''

"You can't have it both ways, Dash," said Talwin.
"You're either taking care of your duty or you're not."

Dash looked at the head of Royal Intelligence and said,
"Look, we're going to be stuck together for over a month
while the wedding is going on, so why don't we agree to
work together. You take care of the business of the Principality and the castle itself, and I'll take care of the city."

"Because you're unreliable," said Talwin.

Dash's face flushed in anger. "Explain yourself."

"Twice in the last week I know you have arranged to
get minor offenders released without trial."

"They were hungry people!" said Dash, raising his
voice enough that a few lingering members of the court
turned to look. Dash lowered his voice. "We've got enough
trouble dealing with the prisoners we have. I'm not going
to throw a child who stole bread into a cell with murderers." Then he laughed. "And I'm damn well not going to
toss him in with those damned Jikanji cannibals we inherited from Fadawah."

Talwin laughed. "Very well, I'll concede there may be
some sense to your decisions. But since the fighting's
stopped, I've noticed that a great deal of street crime is
returning to Krondor, and you're far less vigilant than before."

"I'm tired," said Dash. Then he said, "Yes, that's exactly it." He smiled. "You just made me see something
important. Thank you."

"For what?"

"For seeing something I've been ignoring for weeks."
He patted Talwin on the arm. "I'll have my resignation on
your desk tomorrow."

"What?"

"I don't want to be Sheriff of Krondor any longer," said
Dash. "Find someone else to do the job for you, Talwin."

He turned and walked across the hall to where his brother
stood with Erik, Roo, and Karli. After he exchanged greetings, he said, "Roo, I could use employment."

Jimmy said "What?"

"I've resigned as Sheriff."

"Why?" Jimmy persisted.

"We'll talk about that later," answered Dash. To Roo he said, "Could you use some help?"

"Someone of your talents, certainly," said Roo. "But the last time I employed you, it ended up costing me a great deal of money."

Dash grinned. "Well, then I was really working for my grandfather. This time I'd be working for myself."

"Meaning?"

"I think I would rather seek my own fortune than continue to trade on my nobility and work for the crown. I think that with the Bitter Sea Company I can find a position from which I can someday start running my own business concerns."

"We can certainly talk about it," said Roo. "Come to Barret's tomorrow and we'll discuss the matter." He took Karli's arm. "Now, if you will excuse us, we need to be on our way home."

They left and Erik promised to drop by on his way to Ravensberg. He turned to Dash and said, "Are you certain about this resignation? The King might insist you stay."

"Not if I resign my offices," said Dash.

Erik said, "I'll leave you two alone to discuss this. I'm off to Ravensburg to see my wife and family."

Jimmy grabbed his younger brother by the arm and steered him to a window, away from the others who lingered after court. "Are you mad? Resign your hereditary offices?"

"I may be mad, big brother, but I'm serious. I will have a resignation on Talwin's desk in the morning for him to pass along to Patrick. Unless the King repeals the Great Freedom, no man can be compelled to hold office against his will. I don't need a title. I can do fine living by my own wits."

Jimmy looked appalled. "What about everything we've done? What about Grandfather and Father? Are their deaths for nothing?"

Dash grew angry. "Don't throw those deaths in my face, Jimmy. They died for what they believed in, and my choosing to go another way doesn't diminish their sacrifice. I am just tired of living their vision of what I should be. *Who* I should be."

Jimmy said, "Why don't you come to Rillanon with me? I'll get Patrick to name another Sheriff in your place. We'll go to the wedding, then we'll take ship to Roldem and visit Mother. A week or two with her and you'll be aching to get back to your criminals."

Dash laughed. "No doubt. No, you go. Kiss Mother and Aunt Magda and the others for me. Tell Mother I'll come to visit someday; I know she'll never set foot on Kingdom soil again."

"She might if I'm crowned King," said Jimmy.

"Maybe for that," agreed Dash, and they both laughed.

Jimmy put his arm around his younger brother's shoulder. "Are you going to be all right?"

"Eventually," said Dash. "Right now I just want to get started on a life of my making. I want to use my wits for something other than getting people killed."

Remembering the wild charge at the Keshians' rear elements, the fighting outside the wall before Pug appeared, Jimmy said, "I can't see much wrong with that. It's just . . ."

"What?"

"It's just that we're our father's sons."

"I know. This isn't easy, but once I made up my mind, I knew it was the right thing. We have duties to each other that are more important than our duties to a flag or a king. Can you honestly say you can work on Patrick's behalf without question?"

Jimmy said, "I would never work for Patrick the man; it's the crown for which I labor."

Dash lightly poked his brother's chest. "And that, dear brother, is the difference between us. I saw common men and women die to protect this city, and what reward is there for them?"

"They get to keep their liberty!" said Jimmy. "You know what Keshian rule would bring to Krondor: slavery, press gangs, children being sold to brothels."

"Are we so noble then?"

"We have problems, certainly, but we have just laws."

Dash said, "I've been administering those laws for a

while now, Jimmy. I'm not so sure sending a ten-year-old boy to the labor gang for stealing food is just.''

"That's just an extreme case," said Jimmy.

"I wish that were so."

Jimmy said, "I have to go. We have been invited to dine with Francine and Patrick. Are you coming?"

"No," said Dash. "I'll send a note with my regrets. I have a lot of things to do before the morning if I'm going to turn my office over to someone else."

Jimmy said, "I wish you'd at least wait until Patrick returns from Rillanon. Maybe by then you'll have changed your mind. It's not too late, you know."

Dash was silent for a while, then he said, "If I do, that will give me more time to get my affairs in order. Very well, I'll wait until the Prince and Princess return from Rillanon and then I'll resign my offices."

Jimmy grinned. "I'll talk you out of it."

"I'm still not coming to supper. I'll see you in the morning before you leave."

They embraced and Dash left the great hall, heading out the main entrance and through the courtyard, toward the New Market Jail.

In the darkest hours of the night, before the sky to the east began to lighten, a single man hid in the shadows near the docks. He kept looking back, as if fearing he was being followed, and at last he ducked into a doorway, waiting to see if anyone was behind him.

Long minutes passed then he stepped out of the door, only to be slammed back against it with a dagger held to his throat. "Going somewhere, Reese?"

The thief's eyes widened. "Sheriff! I wasn't on the dodge, honest. I was just heading back to my hole to sleep the day."

"I need information, and you're going to give it to me," said Dash.

"Sure, whatever you want."

"Who's the new Daymaster now that Trina's dead?"

"If I told you, it would be my life," said Reese.

"If you don't, it will be your life. I don't mean hauling

you to New Market for a trumped-up trial and a hanging, I mean cutting your throat right now.''

''It doesn't matter,'' said Reese. ''There isn't one. There's barely what you'd call the Mockers since the Upright Man and Trina died.''

''Who's the Nightmaster?''

''He died during the war. There's no leadership anymore. Even Mother's ain't safe no more. Someone's setting up a new gang near Fishtown, for boosting goods unloaded off ships. And there's some bashers setting themselves up down near the old docks. Times ain't what they used to be, Dash.''

''Tell me where to find the gangs in Fishtown and down by the docks.''

Reese told him what he knew, then Dash said, ''Here's what you need to know. Things are changing in Krondor and we're going to be the ones making the changes.''

''We?'' asked Reese.

''You and me.''

''I get caught working for the Sheriff, I'm a dead man,'' said Reese.

''Oh, before we're done, you'll wish it was that simple. You're a bright one, Reese—you were smart enough to hook up with Talwin and me and get out of the work gang.''

''Well, I saw my chance and I took it.''

''Who's another really smart lad or lass, someone who works well with the children?''

''Jenny's got a level head and the beggars and pickpockets like her.''

''Good. I want you and Jenny to meet me by the old landing below the north wall reservoir, an hour after sundown tomorrow.'' He let go of the man's shirt and put away his dagger.

''What if I just don't turn up?''

''Then I'll find you and kill you,'' said Dash. ''An hour after sundown. Just the two of you.''

Reese said, ''I'll bring her.'' He ran off into the dark.

Dash looked around to make sure he was unobserved, then went the other way.

* * *

Jimmy rose to depart, and Francine said, "Jimmy, may I have a word with you?"

Jimmy smiled. "Anytime, Francie."

She came over and said, "If we still had a garden here, perhaps we could go for a walk."

"A turn around the marshaling yard?"

She laughed. "That will have to do."

She turned to her father and Patrick, and said, "We won't be long." They went down the long corridor from the Prince's great hall to the balcony overlooking the marshaling yard. The evening air was warm and the air held a hint of blooms.

"When we return, I shall see the garden is restored as soon as possible."

Jimmy said, "That will be nice."

"Are you returning to Krondor in time for Midsummer's Festival?" Francie asked.

"Probably not. I shall sail to Roldem to visit Mother. With Father dead, she'll never return to the Kingdom."

Francine sighed. "They never grew to love one another?"

Jimmy shook his head. "I think at best they enjoyed things about one another. She admired Father's skills as a diplomat; Roldem's a nation of courtiers. He was a very fine dancer, did you know?"

"I remember seeing him at a celebration in the King's court. He cut a very dashing figure. I had a crush on him as a child."

"He was a very fine father," said Jimmy, suddenly missing him a great deal. "He always liked Mother's ability to organize. If there was one guest for dinner or a hundred, she always had everything right by the time the event began. He used to joke that she'd have made a better Duke than he."

"But they never grew close?"

"No," said Jimmy sadly. "I know Mother had lovers, though she was always very discreet about it. I don't know about Father. He always seemed so occupied with whatever Grandfather set him to. He probably was too busy to really care."

"He cared about you and Dash."

Jimmy nodded. "I know he did. He was always generous in his affections with us."

She put her hand on his arm. "I don't know what I'm going to do, Jimmy. I like Patrick well enough; the three of us have always been friends. I used to think I was going to marry you, back when we were children."

He smiled. "I know. I used to find it irritating, then I found it pleasing."

She leaned over and kissed him, lightly but lingeringly. Then she said, "Be my dear friend. I don't know if I'll become like your mother and ignore Patrick, or if I'll turn my life over to raising a future King of Isles. I may take up gardening, and if I decide to have a string of lovers, I'll make you the first one, but most of all, I'm going to need good friends.

"Everyone I know is now trying to be my friend, and I know that what they see is the future Queen of the Isles. You and Dash and a few of our good friends back in Rillanon are all I have."

Jimmy nodded. "I understand, Francie. I'll always be your good friend."

She took his arm in hers and snuggled into his shoulder. "Thank you, Jimmy. Now, let's go back and rejoin the Prince."

Jimmy knew at that point that he also would eventually marry for reasons of state. He said a silent prayer to any God who would listen that the woman fate had in store for him was the match of the one holding onto his arm at this moment. And prayed she would also prove as good a friend as Francine.

Two nights later thieves drifted into Mother's. Many looked around for boltholes, for by general consensus Mother's wasn't safe anymore. Still, a few lookouts hung outside, keeping an eye out for the Prince's men.

Reese stood up on a table and said, "Is everyone here?"

From the back of the room, someone shouted, "Everyone who's coming!"

That brought some guarded chuckles from a few, but no one felt easy enough to really enjoy the weak humor.

Reese said, "We've got new rules."

"Rules!" shouted a large man in a corner. "Whose rules?"

"Mockers' Rules!" shouted a young woman entering from a far door. She was solidly built, and plain of features, but she was known for being one of the smarter thieves in the guild. Her name was Jenny.

"Who says there's a Mockers to make rules for?" asked another man.

"The Upright Man!" shouted Reese. "He says."

"The Upright Man's dead!" said a man from the back of the large room. "Everyone knows that."

From deep within the shadows behind Reese, a deep voice said, "The Upright Man's died before, and always returns."

"Who's that?" said the beefy man in the corner.

"One who knows you, John Tuppin. You run the bashers."

The man looked pale at the dark figure knowing his name.

A thin man in the rear said, "Everyone knows Tuppins. He's too big to miss!"

Others laughed, but a few glanced around, worried expressions on their faces.

From the shadows the voice said, "I know you, too, Rat. You're the best point lookout in the Mockers. I know you all.

"I know every thief, cutpurse, dodger and basher, every toffsman and whore who calls Mother's home. And you know me."

"It's the Upright Man," whispered someone.

"You can claim to be whoever you want," said John Tuppin, "but claiming and being ain't the same. I could claim to be the Bloody Duke of Krondor, but that don't make it so."

From out of the shadows the voice said, "The Fishtown gang was run today."

Suddenly people throughout the room were talking. Reese picked up a large wooden club and slammed it against the wall. "Shut up!"

Silence fell, and the voice from the darkness said, "Tomorrow the Sheriff will run the Old Dock bashers. No one works the streets of Krondor without my permission.''

"If those bashers get run tomorrow," said Tuppin, "I'll believe you're who you say you are.''

"I will too," shouted the man called Rat.

"Pass the word," said the voice. "The Keshian renegades who sell drugs out of the caravansary will be run. The swine who grab kids to sell to the Durban slavers will be run. Anyone not doing business with the Mockers will be run.''

A few in the room cheered.

"Reese is Nightmaster, and Jenny is Daymaster. You have a problem, you bring it to them."

More cheers, then Reese said, "Get out there! Pass the word, the Upright Man is back!''

The thieves dispersed until only three people remained at Mothers.

Dash stepped out of the shadows. "You did well. Tell Tuppin and Rat they did well, too.''

"It's a hard sell, " said Reese. "You're going to have to bust a lot of heads before they get it.''

"I've a couple of months before the Prince returns and installs a new Sheriff," said Dash. "Between now and then we'll get organized.''

The girl said, "I don't get one thing. Why are you taking on this job? You're the son of the Duke of Krondor! You're never going to be as rich on the dodgy path as you could be on the straight. If we get caught, we do time in prison, or the work gang. If you get caught, you get hung for treason. Why are you doing this?''

Dash said, "A promise." Jenny seemed about to ask another question, but Dash cut her off. "You have a lot of work to do and so do I. You need to get someone into the palace and close to Talwin. You need to get him followed, and that won't be easy. We have to find his contacts and identify his agents. He's going to be the worst threat to the Mockers we'll face.''

"I have just the girl," said Jenny. "Young, innocent looking, can wash and sew, and will cut your heart out for a copper piece.''

"I've got a man I can get into the kitchen," said Reese.

"I'll get them inside," said Dash. "Now, go.''

They left and Dash ducked out the back way. He waited, and when he was satisfied no one had seen him depart the thieves' headquarters, he knew that his life would never be truly his own.

He knew he'd earn riches as a merchant, and marry some well-thought-of young woman, one whom he would probably love, and father children. It would be, to outward appearances, a good life. Publicly he would be a man of importance, one worthy of envy. But he also knew he would live in two worlds, and that most of his life would not be his own.

More than his duty to the crown, given to him at birth without his consent by his father and grandfather, this duty to a ragged bunch of thieves and thugs was far more binding upon him, for it was a duty he elected, one chosen as a matter of honor, and he knew he would never fail in that duty short of death.

Dash set out through the sewers that would be a second home to him for the rest of his life.

Epilogue

Pug STOOD.

The students who joined him, Miranda, Nakor, and Gathis looked around the cave curiously. Two torches burned, cutting the gloom.

Pug said, "We come together tonight to ratify a vow each of you has already given to me in private. Others will come to join us over the years, and a few of you will leave, but this group will endure.

"We meet in a conclave, for no one outside this group may know we exist. We must linger in the shadows, hidden from the sight of those who live in the world of light."

Pug looked from face to face, and said, "Each of you will act on behalf of people who will never know you exist, who might even fear you or oppose you if they knew of you, out of ignorance or because they are misled.

"Death will be the reward for many who choose this path."

Pug pointed to the mouth of the cave. "Out there are men who have taken a path that leads into the darkness. Some are allies, others are ignorant of one another; some are unaware of who they truly serve, and others willingly embrace the evil we face. They will all seek to destroy us.

"Some of you will leave us, seeking to find our enemies.

Others will be looking for new students to send here for training. Others will remain here, to teach and organize.

"The school at Villa Beata will continue as it was, and those who find us, without us seeking them, as many of you have done, will be welcomed here as before. Again I repeat, no one outside of this group may know we exist.

"We will deal in dreams and nightmares, in a war few out there can imagine. We are brothers and sisters in this calling, and we must be obedient to the needs of this conclave. No one of us can be above that need. If our lives are the price, so be it."

No one in the room spoke.

Pug said, "We are the Conclave of the Shadows and we oppose the madness of the Nameless One and his agents.

"We have endured the Riftwar and we have survived the Serpentwar. We now prepare for the next struggle, one that few will know of, one that will be fought where few can see. It will be a war in the shadows."

Pug put out his hand and Miranda took it. He nodded to Nakor and Gathis, and led his followers out of the cave, down the path to their home.